September Summer

Virginia Babcock

ALL RIGHTS RESERVED

Cover Art:
Michelle Crocker

http://mlcdesigns4you.weebly.com/

Publisher's Note:

Solstice Publishing - www.solsticepublishing.com

September Summer

Virginia Babcock

Chapter One

The fine Italian restaurant was lit by candlelight from sconces on the walls, chandeliers, and red glass globes on the tables. For a Sunday evening, it was quieter than usual. The exclusive back room was reserved for a private party of the unlucky number of thirteen. If the restaurant had been located in Chicago, an outsider may have viewed it as a mob hideout. The place oozed the same old-style charm and private setting that would seem perfect for a mobster movie. However, it housed a different crowd altogether. Located in a ritzy, private suburb of Washington DC, it catered to a calmer, more secretive clientele with rather odd requirements in a dining establishment. The location was regularly patrolled by unmarked US government cars and the owner, known only as Smith, was notorious for his weekly checks and inspections where he searched the place for spy equipment. This restaurant was selected by the group who reserved the back room for just this reason. They required privacy suitable for the highest ranking members of Congress or the Supreme Court.

They seemed like any other group hosting a celebratory work meeting "off-site" for a change. The nature of their work usually required briefings in a large conference room in their secure headquarters in downtown Washington DC. However, tonight was special. Unlike a normal work party that involved a celebratory dinner on Friday night, this group was celebrating tonight on Sunday in preparation for a big meeting early Monday morning. Only the proprietor, an ex-CIA man, knew the group's agency and affiliations. He'd made the reservation himself for an old buddy of his, the group's boss, who worked for the FBI.

Mitchell Harper and William—Bill—Thomas lounged outside the restaurant in the parking lot against

Bill's old rusted-out yellow Camaro, waiting for the rest of their group to arrive. It was a clear night, with just the hint of a cool breeze ruffling their hair. At 6'3" Mitch was the taller of the two agents; his partner Bill stood at just about six feet. Both agents were handsome, but for different reasons. Mitch was regularly labeled as "tall, dark, and handsome" with brooding dark brown eyes and a somber personality when he was on the job. Bill was graced with bright red hair, the expected clear green eyes of his Irish heritage, outrageous freckles, and a ready wit with a wicked sense of humor.

When called to be the "bad cop/good cop," or "good agent/badass," as they called it, Mitch was usually the quiet menace, while Bill cajoled the criminal into confessing. They were both athletic, as required by their job as field agents for the FBI, and had been track-and-field stars in high school. Bill was lanky, a former cross-country runner with muscles less apparent than his hulking partner who'd excelled at sprints and the javelin. Both agents were crack shots and generally scary as hell when on assignment. Tonight they weren't on duty, and it showed in their relaxed appearance.

They waited for fifteen minutes before the rest of their group arrived. Mitch was grateful to see their boss arrive, and remarked, "Dammit, Bill, do we always have to be so early for everything?"

"Shut up, Mitch. If I didn't get you here early, you'd be ten minutes late and you know it," responded his partner of over ten years. Their crafty supervisor Stanley—Stan—Hammond, "the man," as he was called in the office, arrived exactly on time with his friend Albert Horowitz, another supervisor in their area and a well-loved figure in their department. Behind him, arriving together as usual, were Reva Findstein, the only female in tonight's group, and her partner, Carl Miller. Bill called out to her as she exited the driver's seat of a cherry-red 1973 Chevelle that she only drove on weekends. "Hey Red, where'd you get that rig? It's older than you are."

"Shut it, Mr. Rust, this is my baby. You play nice today or else." Smiling at the usual banter between the agents, Carl opened the restaurant door for her, and the two went inside. A sleek, black, nondescript sedan pulled in next, carrying Mitch and Bill's favorite agent and good friend David "Jonesey" Jones.

Fascinated by his parking lot behavior, the men watched Jonesey drive through the parking lot, scoping it out, then back into a spot that was both protected by the back fence and near the lot's entrances for a quick escape.

"You'd think that guy'd get sick of being so paranoid eventually."

Bill snorted. "Yeah I know, but with him being holed up with those crazy anti-establishment dudes out in Idaho, can you blame him." The two men paused to watch Jonesey scope the lot one more time before getting out of the car. "Did you know the other day he frisked the new security guard?" At Mitch's questioning look he went on. "Yeah, he came in for work and checked in downstairs as usual, but he didn't recognize the dude at the desk. When the guy didn't properly check his badge, Jonesey pretended to be friendly, until the new guard turned back to the desk. Then Jonesey sneaks up behind the guy, grabs him by the scruff of his neck, throws him down to the floor, and proceeds to frisk him for weapons and then checked his identification."

"You're shittin' me," Mitch said, shocked.

"No, man it was great. The security cameras caught the whole thing, and Stan has a great shot on his desk where Jonesey is kneeling on the dude's back as he's checking his wallet. Classic Jonesey."

"No reprimand, I take it," Mitch remarked casually.

"Nope. As usual, Stan made a partial apology to the head of security and then proceeded to lecture him about

FBI security. Then, as he left the meeting, he gave Jonesey a pat on the back, and said 'next time don't do it when the director is in house.'" The two agents chuckled as their friend approached.

Jonesey, the quietest and most deadly agent in the group, stared back at Mitch and Bill as they watched him approach the front door. He didn't look surprised and was clearly not happy to see his two best friends laughing at him, as usual. "One day soon you bums are gonna be caught off guard and I'll have to be the one to save your asses, again."

Bill grinned. "Yeah, good old Jonesey, always good in a pinch."

With an obvious lack of sincerity, Jonesey brightly asked, "Hey ladies, have you seen my boss tonight?"

"Yeah, sister, right there." Mitch hitched a thumb toward the door. Laughing, they entered the building together.

***

The meal was a success. As the agents hunkered down to their entrees, Stan listened to the conversation. "This lasagna is to die for," exclaimed Carl.

"Yeah, thanks Bill, for making the boss take us somewhere great this time," Reva chimed in as she ate her seafood Alfredo with gusto. All the comments about the food were positive, and Stan was glad everyone was relaxed and happy. He stood up at the head of the table, tapping his knife against his wineglass to gather his team's attention.

"Okay, everybody. First, I'd like to thank everyone for taking the time to do a work dinner on your busy Sunday." At the playacting grunts and groans he frowned and paused, gesturing with his hands to quell the byplay. "I know you all had things to do, but I wanted us all to get together before we finish the briefings with the big boss tomorrow. Also, it was Al's idea to have the unofficial celebration before the final meetings, to give us all a chance to relax a bit before we close this one up. You've all been working so hard on this latest assignment. We wanted to show you our personal appreciation and since Al wasn't about to let Jessica cook this time..." The table interrupted as everyone gushed compliments on Al's wife Jessica's famous cooking, but quieted as Stan continued. "She wanted to be here, but we'll be having a small business discussion, for our ears only, after dessert. Before that, eat, enjoy, and be happy for once." Everyone laughed at Stan's little joke; they were not a team known for their all-work, no-play attitude.

Stan switched into full boss-mode. "This assignment has been especially difficult. When Mendoza grabbed that teenager and used her as a hostage, we were all concerned. But, thanks to Reva and Carl, we were able to give that girl back to her mom and dad and still grab the bad guy. My thanks go out to each and every one of you. Thanks to all your hard work, we had a near perfect capture this time." Stan raised his goblet. "Salute!" Beer bottles, water, wine goblets, and a couple of soft drink glasses joined in the congratulatory toast.

Bill spoke up to say, "To a job well done!" More clinking glass sounded.

After those drinks, Jonesey responded, "And no more travel across the country for another month!" Laughter joined the clinks. Everyone knew how much Jonesey hated to fly.

Mitch replied when the din had quieted, "Just because you hate planes, don't complain so much. You didn't have to hide in the dirt for two days just sneaking up on the guy. To green grass and cool showers! Salute!"

Reva spoke next. "To a fantastic team who caught the bad guys without losing anyone this time. Salute!"

Al slowly pushed away from the table, stood, and took his turn to toast. "As the only person here not officially part of the team, per se, I'd just like to say that y'all were amazing this time. I was only involved with the financial parts and a little at the end, and didn't get to witness all the preparation, but y'all handled the takedown with amazing skill and tenacity. I salute your team as one of the best working, well-coordinated, most competent groups in our branch of the agency." Raising his glass to the ceiling he added, "And thanks for sharing this with me and also for a damn fine veal cutlet. Salute!" *Clink, clink, clink* and a few cheers this time. Everybody loved Al and it showed in their faces as he took his seat.

Stan patted his good friend on the shoulder as he stood back up. "Well done, well done! You all need to pat yourselves on the back and enjoy this spread on me. As your boss this is just a small way that I can show my appreciation for you guys. Each and every one of you took to this case with the need to see the guy stopped. You gave me good old-fashioned, honest hard work and good planning. You devised the methods and tasks, planned out every contingency, and followed through excellently. And this time, it all worked. No glitches, false starts, and especially no casualties. We were also able to save the victims, and you all know how rare that is. So celebrate your skills and also celebrate life tonight. Eat up and enjoy the evening." A group chorused, "Salute!" and they all settled down to finish their meal.

Stan enjoyed the remainder of the meal, watching the team converse. He was glad they were all here and able to be together for a good reason for a change. Usually their only bonding happened on assignment in rough conditions. He saw Albert speaking with Reva and thought of his school days when he'd gone through the FBI Academy with Al. As head of the financial office, Al had been moved closer to his office and they now worked as peers. Stan felt a deep sense of satisfaction about his job. He had a team of good people and had the power to decide who could join and facilitate how they would work. So far things were good. They had found a good, even mix.

Stan and his team covered a specialized area assigned to capture terrorists within the US and were considered experts at it. Thankfully things were relatively quiet right now. Mendoza had been another small-time terrorist who'd called a bomb threat into a small high school in Texas. They'd nabbed him and found the bomb and everything was fine for now. Tomorrow's briefings would close this case. With this case now closed, Stan was thinking of all the other ones that were still open.

That thought brought him to tonight's discussion. He glanced around and saw that everyone was finishing up. He saw that Al and Reva had finished their conversation and caught Al's attention between bites. "So Al, did you get to the bottom of the travel database's issues?"

"No, not yet. The IT guys are still looking into it. For now they've shifted the records to your servers while they locate the breach," Al answered.

Stan was worried, but it was good to know Al was taking steps. Someone had hacked into the FBI travel logs. So far they hadn't captured any agent's direct data, but they knew which flights carried agents and it was a worry. "That should be fine. I'll have Denise speak to Alicia tomorrow to make sure our offices can work around that way for now."

"Yeah, lately our secretaries talk to each other more than we do," Al remarked.

"Yes, I know. I thought that if we had adjoining offices, we'd get to talk more." The two laughed.

In a few minutes the meal was completed, and Stan called for a round of spumoni ice cream to finish. With the resulting "oohs" and "ahhs," he knew he'd done the right thing. With this team, ice cream was always a hit, even pistachio flavored. Stan looked to the doorway and caught Smith's eye. At the owner's eyebrow raised in inquiry, he nodded. The proprietor nodded back and the door was closed. Stan clapped his hands and called the meal to a halt. "Okay, lady and gentlemen. The official portion of this meeting is now in session." As people reached for their notebooks, he halted them. "No. No need for notes, I just want you to be aware of this. There will be time for more detail tomorrow. You just need to know now as the scandal has already hit the office—you missed it while you were in Texas."

A knock sounded at the door. Stan went over to open it and received a long, rectangular box. Returning to the table, he opened the box and removed a large screen. When he had everyone's attention, he set up the screen and gestured to a potted plant across the room. A light from a projector shone from above the leaves and illuminated the screen.

Stan stood up. "Okay, everyone. Time for the briefing. Let's take a moment to stand and stretch." He motioned the waiting servers to clear the table.

Once everyone was seated again, Sam began narrating his slide show. "This is Senator Leaver. He serves on a critical Senate committee overseeing some of the US loans to the World Bank. He is currently being blackmailed by this man, Michael Gooding." The screen changed from a portrait of the senator to a black-and-white surveillance photo of a plain-looking dark-haired man. "Gooding is a very dangerous fellow and heretofore has remained under our radar. His style leans more to industrial espionage and smuggling. We don't know why he's taken to blackmailing senators, but you need to be aware of this as immediately after our nine o'clock meeting tomorrow morning, you will be fully briefed on him. He's a member of the ritzy DC social whirl, so I wanted you to all see him, to see if you know him or know of him. We don't yet know how deep his activities go criminally, but preliminary research shows his criminal past is extensive even if he has yet to be caught. And there appears to be something big planned in his future. A Secret Service contact found him nosing around the White House recently, and we just found out he's a bomber. We also just learned that he's masqueraded as an FBI agent in the past and may be attempting to do so again. He's been seen downtown and may attempt to capture your information and persona. So, be wary. Watch yourselves."

Stan looked up to gauge everyone's expressions. He watched closely, looking for negative signs. Reva was stone-faced, staring at Gooding's picture. Bill, Carl, and Jonesey were staring off into space while Mitch's eyebrows were drawn together. They seemed surprised as expected, but no one looked nervous or jumpy.

Stan had purposely surprised them with this information now, both to make them ready for the big meeting tomorrow, and to see if he caught anyone off guard. They didn't know it yet, but there was a security breach in their department. If one of these agents was the breach, he'd find out tonight in this room. Smith, the owner, and his crew were ready for his sign to take someone down. Stan scanned the group again. No one looked at him nervously or fidgeted uncomfortably. Good, it appeared that these agents were innocent. Stan caught Smith's eye and nodded. Smith returned to the kitchen; no takedowns tonight.

Stan made a show of stretching his arms above his head and motioned to the next slide. "The big meeting tomorrow morning is about Gooding. Al and I suspect Gooding is part of a travel records security breach we found on Friday, and we believe he may have made another breach in our personnel records last week."

Stan tried to keep his voice steady as he spoke. Someone had been in his own office and used his group's computers while they were gone to Texas. So far, only these twelve agents had an alibi for the breach. The person who had hacked in not only accessed the building and penetrated secure areas, but knew that these particular agents were gone and used their area to hack into the FBI computers.

He and Al were in charge of watching this group for questionable activity. The other supervisors were watching agents in other compromised areas. Everyone was desperate to find the FBI insider. Stan had seen the threats, the letters, and been shown the plans. Thankfully, this first group checked out—so they could start work to seal the breach.

"Because you were all in Texas when the breach occurred, you are the first team actively assigned to find Gooding. Someone, maybe Gooding—maybe not, is feeding our secure information to an unidentified terrorist who seems bent on attacking the US government at any and all levels, but especially us and the CIA." He motioned for Smith to kill the projection as he finished, "We need to find him and catch him. Now." Stan wondered if the other groups would talk and realize that many teams were having unusual Sunday meetings tonight. He prayed for help and a quick resolution to this leak.

Chapter Two

"If one could see the bare bones of Thornton Michael William Gooding's plan, his purpose would become clear to some of us. But, in actuality it would not appear to those everyday observers who see things from the outside—or in casual observation. We are here to help all our agents try a different tack—to teach you and your agents to look deeper and to know better. We already know that most terrorist organizations are shaped by internal forces as well as external ones, but we need the teams to be educated, to know that some physical objects are also shaped internally. These objects are formed by the forces within. We are reiterating this so that our agents and support staff don't overlook any of Gooding's art pieces and discount them as simply objects of art without an internal purpose."

The speaker, a high-ranking FBI profiler, continued, "Michael Gooding's plan is simply this: to change the focus of common Americans. He thinks that if every day Americans saw the truth inside this nation, not the outside appearance, they would rise up and revolt in some type of patriotic fervor. Initially, we discounted the reports..." At the sounds made by the crowd in the auditorium as they protested such an allegation, the speaker paused reading from his notes and spoke up to calm the listeners. "Please, no interruptions. We all know that budget constraints require a picking and choosing of threats. However, we believed that such a motive as Gooding displayed seemed harmless enough at the time. We did spend allotted resources to investigate him just in case, which has resulted in a reevaluation of the level of threat he represents. We found out that he intends to bomb a major, as yet unknown, US government military or civilian target or targets. We also know now that he is handling his so-called 'Summer

14

Plan' in the same manner that he handles his photography displays and shows."

Stan and Albert's supervisor, Homer Call, who was top supervisor of the FBI's DC Terrorist Neutralization sector, continued to read the paper copy of the analyst's report as he listened to the presentation. He'd already instructed Stan and Albert to begin investigating Michael Gooding in earnest. The FBI's latest intelligence indicated that Gooding had already helped influence two critical bills in the Senate, and current signs indicated that he was moving on to more violent activities for more dangerous clients. Homer glanced up and watched the speaker as he continued the details about Gooding. This analyst, borrowed from one of the more specialized profiling areas, continued to lecture the top brass in a cold and methodical way about how artists think, so they could prepare their teams to capture Gooding.

"Just like a consummate actor, good singer, or wise poet knows, the first focus of an artist who wants to tell a story is their audience. They learn their audience, because they know that you must know to whom you are speaking in order to impact them. We think Gooding has chosen his audience, so to speak, as the American public. He is planning something very big, something very American, and he's planning on doing it on our national holiday—the Fourth of July. We also fear he's planning on doing it in DC, so we need to neutralize him as soon as possible. Also, we see his plan or potential threat occurring when we are most vulnerable, with most of our domestic personnel on vacation, as well as most of the other security agencies and the armed forces granting vacation time as well. Especially critical are the security forces stationed here in the capital. They will already be on high alert, and we think Michael Gooding is counting on the distraction of the holiday to aid his plan." Homer continued taking notes. He had a lot to talk about when he met with Stan and his team at 9:00 a.m.

Chapter Three

Michael Gooding stood high on the widow's walk that was the only remarkable feature of his father's Chesapeake mansion. The moon was full tonight, and a breeze played with his hair. The clear skies invited peaceful meditation, and he contentedly smoked an expensive Cuban cigar as he considered the events of the past few days and ruminated on the events that brought him to this stage in his life.

Looking to the north, he imagined what he would see if he could actually see the buildings of Washington DC through the trees and hills. He thought of his new status as a dual British and American citizen. "Fancy that, me, a son of Scots aristocracy, an American. I am an American now." He wondered how that term, American, remained in effect over the past two centuries. He'd spent too much time in the "other" American nations to not wonder why no one in the current world order had changed the term to apply to all the peoples in the Western Hemisphere. But, then, he thought, Benjamin Franklin coined the term at a critical point in the nation's history, and the term cemented this great flawed nation into one people. None of the other "American" countries had ever used it in the same way. "So the United States remains the only country populated by Americans, and the only country so undeserving of the term."

Last summer, he made it to Chesapeake just in time to see the July 4 fireworks over DC. From atop the colonial house placed on a small rise above the river, he'd stood at the rail watching the July 4 explosions as he'd done each summer for the last ten years. Thinking of the fireworks reminded him of his childhood. As a kid stuck with a never-there father, Gooding had hated the July 4 celebrations when he'd been forced to stay in the US for the summer. However, as an adult he'd learned to appreciate them and never missed them once he'd finally separated his childhood anger at his father from the pure enjoyment he derived from all explosions. In fact the July 4 fireworks in Washington DC amazed him every time. He usually had to make the time to be here, but found it well spent, the time celebrating his favorite holiday.

"It may be too damn hot and muggy in Virginia for any self-respecting Englishman, but I am not an Englishman," he mused. Gooding's Scots grandfather had taught him how *not* to be a self-respecting Englishman when the situation called for it. The summer heat in Virginia stopped bothering him soon enough. He'd complained so much about his father, and about the heat, that after that first summer his grandfather relented and allowed him to stay in the UK with him, taking custody of his only grandson. To the delight of his grandfather, after years of training, at sixteen he'd proved he was more than capable of managing the family empire. That summer he'd so pleased Grandfather that the old man let him leave the UK and the family obligations for a while. He'd escaped to his father in Virginia, pretended a contrite apology for leaving DC, and celebrated his personal independence once his father had fallen for the act. Gooding now enjoyed the Washington DC area lifestyle his ambassador father embodied and encouraged, which was freer than the life of his grandfather, a British aristocrat. That was the summer when he watched the annual fireworks display, and it returned him to his childhood love of fireworks.

On a lark, he'd left his father's posh July 4 party in the city and escaped to see the fireworks from the compacted and dry grass on the National Mall. He'd been just one in a crowd of thousands on that hot night. His spot was a good one, near a tree, just across from the reflecting pool where he had a clear view of the sky. That night he also felt the power and majesty of America in the display, stronger and somehow more pure to him than other patriotic displays he'd witnessed across the world. It made him appreciate something larger than his individual wants and desires. The explosions rejoiced in their purpose, and he was moved by their commemoration of an ideal nation that would accept all comers if they promised to sanction the same ideals. America would take even him. The younger Gooding readily accepted the invitation and from that moment on became an American in his heart, if not in his passport. Years later he made it official once he'd gained enough freedom from his overbearing grandfather. Luckily, his grandfather thought his dual citizenship change in name-only, and approved of the change, as having an American CEO allowed them to vastly increase the Thornton Industries fortunes.

Gooding stubbed out his cigar. The cold air of this December night was nothing like July. He missed the warmth and the excitement in the air. July in Washington DC was different, different from July in Egypt or London or anywhere else he'd been. In the week prior to the holiday, he would watch and see every day American folks show up in the alternatively cracked and planned capitol city. Rather than worry about the political machinations, these people spent their time in the sweltering streets and parks, paying their respects to the great historical monuments and capping the festivities with parades, concerts, and fireworks.

These people fascinated Gooding; they were more than tourists and they differed from the general populace of other cities he'd seen. Other countries would declare a national holiday with feast days and parades. Here in the United States, half the population went shopping, while any feasting happened outside over a fire. These tourists in DC added a secondary purpose through the holiday; they relived history. They carried an odd mix of patriotism and pilgrimage to this city more contrived and designed than most others in the US.

Gooding had spent so much time in Washington DC that he'd built up a clientele for his shady hobbies. When not guiding the family empire, he worked on contracts to "encourage" certain congressmen to vote in particular ways. While pursuing this hobby, he was surprised to see patriotism alive and well in this city of greed, bribery, lobbying, and politics.

On a warm summer night in an earlier July he'd devised the "Summer Plan." This country founded and based on rebellion and revolution had become too complacent and more meddling than its parent country had ever been. Gooding's disgust with the manner in which US foreign and domestic policies changed was tempered by a fascination with the patriotism he'd believed to be extinct.

He thought about the winter of 1776, when the US colonies' congress had no power to tax or any way to reinforce Washington's army. Gooding juxtaposed the congress of that time, which would have died had Washington not gambled everything on the crossing of the Delaware River into Trenton, with the congressional system of today. Washington's gamble turned the tide of the revolution and cemented this idealistic country, while making him a national hero at the same time. What has happened to this nation? Here, masquerading as an artist, he would take dirty pictures of congressmen who were so worried about their reputation, that they would change their politics. He wondered if John Adams or Thomas Payne would have succumbed to a bribery or extortion attempt.

Gooding enjoyed his new life being a mostly shunned, American member of British aristocracy, part Scots/English, and truly relished that small American chunk of himself. This kernel of US citizen in him had blossomed deep inside, into a nugget of what he termed Americanism.

The business arrangements he fulfilled for various organizations in and around Washington DC were just that, contractual arrangements. Gooding cared little for the outcome of the usual "contracts" he fulfilled; he focused on just meeting the terms. He used his legal training in this nontraditional career very well. Besides, what did he care about some dam or power plant's congressional funding in Nevada being blocked by a reluctant legislator. He didn't care about the oil and chemical companies that needed a polluted river situation hushed. If he didn't do the job, someone else would, and he was very good at what he did.

He'd put the same intensity into his work at becoming a US citizen. He noticed in his studies that the people voting seemed to have little say in their government once their elected officials reached office and sometimes not even before. He saw this at home in Britain and was used to the idea, but the inconsistencies between the system and the reality of how things really worked in the great "democracy" of the USA aggravated him. He hated the hypocrisy and how most of the congressmen in his acquaintance didn't care about their voters unless there was another motivator like an election year or a lobby encouraging them to do so.

He'd studied all the histories of the countries he'd visited on his grandfather's orders. Gooding had also absorbed as much US history as his studies at university allowed. He knew well and remembered the ideals of the American Revolution and wondered where they went in this thoroughly modern nation. Of course those ideals were believed to be outdated and extinct by most, and it was too bad that Washington DC no longer showed its "Americanism" very well, except around July 4. At that time, what seemed to be dead ashes flared up in sparks and explosions of patriotism. Gooding noticed people on the street and in grocery stores, just going about their business but acting happier as they bought fireworks and barbecue makings and enjoyed the summer holiday with real zest. He especially enjoyed the displayed flags that popped up, seemingly overnight.

Gooding thought of the people, and they reminded him of his father. His father only ever cared about his work and social position. He'd never cared about his wife or his son, caring only to find a way into the elite by marrying the only child of Thornton Industries. That sole summer Gooding spent with his father as a child was the last time he lived with his father. At the time, Gooding was still a kid trying to find his place in the world. He quickly learned that his place wasn't with his father, in DC, or in the United States at all. At the time, he was unhappy and depressed and wondered if there was a place for him anywhere. His father met him at the airport, then abandoned him to a private school that took in the other diplomats' offspring. Worse, he couldn't handle the heat and was teased by the other kids about the heat rashes that afflicted him daily. He was happy to leave the US after that year, because his grandfather treated him as the heir even though he always demanded something from him.

In America he didn't know how to act, being removed from the culture he knew back in the UK. On his birthday, his grandfather had flown out to DC to greet him. He had pleaded with the old man to take him back to Scotland. Gooding shuddered at the memory; he'd cried and sobbed like a baby—one of the few times he'd lost control in front of his grandfather. His grandfather seized the opportunity to keep him and was delighted when Mr. Gooding gladly relinquished the care of his only son, though he worked to ensure his grandson never lost control like that again. Back in Scotland, Gooding vowed to never return to the United States and opted to stay on his family's estate with his grandfather. That is, when he wasn't with his, to quote his grandfather, "marrying and divorcing," "carrying on and defaming the family name," "she'll be the death of me one day," flighty, irresponsible mother whenever she had a maternal moment.

During his breaks from school, his grandfather did all he could to show Gooding that he belonged to and owed his life and duty to his maternal bloodlines. Thornton Michael Gooding would be the one to make up for his mother's shortfalls and restore the dynasty as his grandfather had restored the family fortunes. His very Scots grandfather also liked to drag him all over the world to educate him in other cultures, world events, and the family empire. At seventeen, when Gooding decided he wasn't much of an aristocrat either, he began his side career of odd jobs, consisting of tasks considered criminal in most Western cultures. His grandfather didn't even check on him. He left Gooding to his spare time with no restrictions because he excelled at the business and made millions despite his young age. Gooding spent all his time furiously pursuing his varied interests.

In his mid-twenties on one of his smuggling expeditions, Gooding ran afoul of his Colombian partners, at the time, and found he needed to hide out for a few months. His American, ex-army bigwig, now ambassador-diplomat father was in London, so Gooding hid out at his father's Chesapeake mansion for a while. He rather liked the idea of being an expatriate Englishman living in the States, especially with the ease he found in his smuggling and other operations, and his father didn't care whether he stayed in the mansion or not.

He spent the next year laying low and letting some of his odd jobs fade into memory. He resurrected his old Hasselblad camera from his student years (having spent some time at university taking dirty pictures of coeds) and revived his old talent for the lens. He enjoyed photography so much that whether handling the family shipping line, real estate, or one of hundreds of other ventures, Michael took time to use his cameras. He especially adored photographing the human form, or what polite society refers to as "nude," for both the beauty he saw in the human form as well as the shock value his pictures inspired in most galleried audiences.

He recovered his other interests eventually, the Colombians having been blown up after Gooding tired of running from them and used his other favorite hobby—explosives. He acquired a ruthless, yet impeccable, reputation for success in all his ventures. Gooding had perfected his usual exit strategy of "ask nicely once" and "remove the issue second." His Colombian ex-partners would not have let him go, having decided to be mortally offended at his actions toward one of the daughters of the group. However, their compound was dispatched with little fuss and a satisfying big boom. Gooding was free of them and remained free of undesirable relationships from that moment on. In that venture, Gooding had also lived by the statement of, "The enemy of my enemy is my friend," and was only too happy to turn his ex-partners' cartel over to their rival.

Gooding found other associates and honed down his life until he only had close ties with his trusted crew, crucial business managers across the world, a few mistresses spread out in convenient locations, and his cantankerous grandfather. Periodically he still had to "check-in" with the old man, who required personal visits as part of the terms of his use of family funds. Unlike his father and mother, his grandfather more or less approved of Michael Gooding the man, who seemed to be as good at making money as himself. This helped Gooding develop a natural rapport with his grandfather that bordered on familial affection partly based on common genetics coupled with shared approval. Meanwhile, his mother's serial relationships and his father's cold behavior helped broaden his distance from his parents. Over time, Gooding successfully cultivated this distance between them, and now rarely saw his parents at all. It was a mutually beneficial arrangement.

Gooding considered his cigar stub. Manuel, one of his crew, had smuggled a case of them to him from his mother's home in Cuba as part of a regular arrangement. They were delightful and the well-earned fruits of his labor. He thought of his success over the last few years. He could now take time, in weeks and months, away from the business. He had the time now for the Summer Plan. His latest deal with Chile would make his grandfather millions in the shipment of fresh fruit to California.

Gooding thought of all he'd done for his grandfather. He improved the family's commerce, delving into sometimes shady but lucrative deals, only picking up the hobby of blackmailing congressmen when he was in DC and bored. Lately, though, he was disgusted by the latest bout of greedy bastards in DC.

"If another snot-nosed baby of a congressmen comes crying to me again, I will hurt him. These pampered pets of the power brokers can't even fathom their role in this country." He crushed the cigar stub angrily. "How can they make such a mockery of this nation? They have no concept of what they could do." He would follow through with the plan. He would hurt them where it hurt the most—their voters.

Chapter Four

"Mitch, that latest idea of Homer's is never gonna work. I mean, how are you going to get an operative anywhere near Gooding? The guy knows about all of our agents in the Northern Hemisphere. Not that there's that many. We need to come up with a better plan." Bill flipped his cigarette butt off into the grass as he and Mitch sat next to a lake that had square, cement sides on a sunny but cool Washington DC day.

"Bill, don't you think I'm aware of the problem?" Mitch shook his head. Bill, according to his badge, William J. Thomas—his middle name was Jar after his great-uncle—was on one. Whenever he got off assignment, he was worse than antsy. Mitch's grandpa used to describe Bill as, "Itchy as a two-dollar whore in a churchy town." Bill got up again. He stomped over to the phone booth, then stomped back toward his partner. He strode over to the concrete embankment and jumped up to stand on the curbed, cement edge.

When he landed, he looked almost contemplative for the fifteen seconds he stayed there. Mitch watched him throw his hands out and jump off. As Bill slid on his buttocks onto the bench next to him, Mitch remarked, "You know, we could use anybody to entice Gooding. Anybody could do this. But by using one of the thousands of federal employees we could at least compensate them without alerting Gooding to new blood on the payroll." Mitch lowered his voice and tried to calm himself.

Bill rolled his eyes and countered, "Not one who has ever been to DC on a government travel voucher, and you know it."

They sat in silence for a while. While Bill looked like any FBI agent portrayed in the movies (except for his red hair), Mitch knew he himself was hard to place as an agent. He had black hair, but he wore a mustache and/or beard most of the time, especially in winter—a habit he'd learned from his grandfather and the winters they shared in rural Montana. He was heavily built and tall. His boss' secretary, Denise, was always asking him to put on a pair of jeans with suspenders and a flannel shirt; she liked to call him lumberjack. Bill, too, loved to tease him about it, especially using "tall timber" jokes. Sometimes he would even sing the Monty Python song about lumberjacks on boring overnight plane and car rides.

Mitch took it all in stride. His black eyes usually hid his thoughts, while Bill's green ones flashed their annoyance when he was stirred up, as he was gifted with a rather tempestuous nature.

Bill lit another cigarette and smoked with Mitch in companionable silence. Mitch watched Bill's half-inch long ash fall off into the turf. Bill finally broke the silence and sent him a curious glance. "What do you mean, you think any federal employee could work? You aren't thinking of going down to Center Street and grabbing Mrs. Dawson, the post-mistress, are you?"

Mitch started to laugh. "Bill, you are clueless as usual, but you've got the gist of the idea. We know that Gooding can sniff out an agent at fifty paces and he knows everyone on the FBI's payroll. But we just need someone to be in the gallery when the boys break in, not an agent, just eyes and ears. In reality, they only need to be a warm body to hold the wire or be the witness. Besides, we might get lucky and get someone who would treat this like their patriotic duty and do what we say. Federal workers do take the oath of office. We just need someone who's not a civilian. It'd be too hard to fly them around or pay them on the government's dollar without alerting Gooding."

Bill pursed his lips, looking pensive, but otherwise remained silent.

"Remember what Homer told us,"—Mitch dropped his voice to a gravelly shudder, imitating Homer— "'Dammit, you get somebody that that bastard hasn't slept with or gotten our files of, and you get them in his gallery by the Fourth, or else! I don't care if it's the damn cleaning lady.'"

"Mitch, you're letting the big boss snow you in this. We need a damn agent, not some baitfish who'd probably shoot us in error, maybe get killed no matter what we do, and ultimately let Gooding get away."

Mitch lapsed back into silence while he contemplated their latest assignment. Beside him, Bill was equally quiet. Homer, their supervisor and Stan's boss, had been red in the face, with veins popping out at his temples as he'd finished his orders: "I want someone who we have enough information on, that we can track, and who has a high level of respect for this country. I know that there are no agents in the agency that Gooding doesn't know something about, so I want you to find someone in another agency. For all that FBI versus CIA bullshit, we all work for Uncle Sam, and we all took the oath of office, even that cigar-smoking jackass from Arkansas." Bill and Mitch enjoyed Homer's hatred of the Legislative Branch of the US government, and both men had smiled as Homer had continued: "With the exception of those bastards in Congress, lots of other federal workers I know have enough integrity to do this job. Also, we should try to find somebody outside of DC, to keep away from Gooding's crew. I am tired of Gooding's flunkies tailing my agents wherever they go—get enough bodies out of here so he'll have to split his forces, and maybe we can force him to run low on resources chasing agents across the country."

Once Stan decided who would go where, he'd called in the profilers assigned to the case, who briefed Bill and Mitch on the type of person to find. Homer really wanted bait for a trap for Gooding, a beautiful, female, non-agent who could speak intelligently about Gooding's art. All the data showed that Gooding could spot an FBI agent from miles away, even the deep-cover ones. Maybe they could catch Gooding using his only known weakness—beautiful women.

Chapter Five

As required by his grandfather, Gooding had been forced to expand the Ivy League university education of his teens to include culture. Having no desire for music and no inclination to hone his natural talent for drama in school, he found an eye for the visual arts, especially photography. Rather than playing a concert or performing a play, his grandfather accepted art exhibitions as proof of a modern classical education and upbringing. Gooding's photography garnered him yet another successful enterprise, which he easily maintained in DC, being close enough to New York to keep in touch with the American art world.

Gooding watched the culture creators in New York target Americans to make money. He saw them fawn and pander to this audience, divide them into demographics and local markets, and create the American way of life. He saw how many people used this audience for their own personal profit.

Who did Bill Clinton or Michael Jordan or Bill Gates really want to reach with their messages? And not only powerful men desired an image, but women, too, strove to reach the American audience—look at Oprah and Madonna and Hilary Clinton and others (although it seemed to Gooding that Madonna had forsaken America for the UK).

The Summer Plan came into being on a summer night under the stars and sparks of a July 4 night as Gooding smoked his cigar and stared at a dollar bill. Under God, the all-seeing-eye, the pyramid on the back of a dollar bill, shows its eighteenth-century heritage in symbolism. Gooding noticed not the eye on the pinnacle, but the foundation blocks supporting it.

He had seen the Great Pyramid at Giza. The first time, he'd stared at it for hours and days. What do most of us see? A great monument. Each time Gooding saw the Great Pyramid, he saw it much the same as anyone, but focused on the bits of crumbling limestone that still capped the pyramid. He saw in his mind's eye the golden cap. He pictured how it must have looked clad in dazzling white limestone that gradually disappeared into nearby Egyptian buildings for years. Just as the inner tombs of the pharaohs forfeit their costly gold, the outside of their tombs forfeit their rich dressing.

The shining image of the pyramids first impressed Gooding at sixteen. He had endured a winter trip to Giza with his archaeologically obsessed grandfather, after his grandfather kicked out his self-indulgent mother. One day, bored to tears, he sat on a wall outside the pyramid compound, contemplating the cruel fates at play in his life. Though he was glad to be away from his mother and out of DC, Gooding missed the freedom he'd had in America. At least in DC, he could be free; the Americans seemed so much looser than their British counterparts.

The pyramid beckoned him. Its scale fascinated him. Why bother worrying about cramped tunnels and bare tombs, when the pyramids' massive sizes proclaim their might? It made Gooding question the Pharaohs' true motives. So engrossed in these thoughts was he that he sat on the wall and stared at the huge pyramid for hours. As he sat, Gooding meditated on the pyramid's effect on Western Civilization. The all-seeing-eye supposedly symbolized God, but Gooding saw below him the excavated workers' cities. The all-seeing-eye was supported by millions of rocks, carried on thousands of backs.

Years later in DC, Gooding took this remembrance of Giza as a sign. He had been brought to the feet of the Great Pyramid for a reason, just like he had been put in DC for a reason. He'd always been fascinated by American money. It felt so different than his homeland's currency. Instead of Royals or the truly important people, the Yanks put buildings and past presidents on their bills. Instead of different sizes for the different denominations, the United States uses bills that are all the same size and color. But still he'd been fascinated by their currency; he enjoyed its seeming simplicity. He often thought that it was done purposely so that a poor American could feel as important with a wad of one dollar bills as his counterpart did with his wad of hundreds. He was fascinated by the pyramids in the same way. They seemed so simple, but still no one had uncovered all their secrets.

Whenever Gooding thought about his Summer Plan, he'd take out the single dollar bill he kept in his wallet. He'd contemplate the pyramid on its back. The US Congress and the White House show up on other bills, but the dollar, the most commonly traded US currency, shows the pyramid. In his youth, he'd realized the significance of the pyramid being on the dollar. It was a sign. He hadn't been sent to Egypt to escape his mother, but to learn, to plan, to realize. He studied his souvenir dollar closely. The great eye symbolized the eye of God, he knew, In God We Trust and all that, and he enjoyed how the capstone showing the eye was separated, floating out of reach of the thirteen courses of stone representing the thirteen original colonies. The capstone limestone separated the tip of the Great Pyramid from the lowly base in a similar way.

The teenaged Gooding had also stared at a dollar, the wheels in his head turning. He noted that the US powers knew when they created the seal shown on the dollar, that the pyramid representing the United States needed a firm foundation, a base. To legitimize themselves, they used the Founding Fathers and gave them extra significance by imprinting MDCCLXXVI (1776) on the base. The representation of the base itself interested Gooding.

That the base was clearly seen was unexpected, as it should have been buried by the stone layers above it. It appeared even stronger and thicker than the courses above it and not split by joints. The pyramid created by the Founding Fathers had to have a solid base. A young Gooding had glanced at the looming pyramid before him. He knew it, too, had a solid base under all that debris and litter around it. He also knew its base was the entire plateau he sat on. It lay silently under his feet, beneath the hut where his grandfather kept his foreman under them all.

His head too full of significant thoughts to bear to sit idly, the teenaged Gooding had finally slid off the mud brick wall and headed out into the bright night. His landing dislodged rock from the base of the wall and sent it skidding down the path. He looked around him and thought of geology. Man had forced those blocks out of the earth and into the pyramid. Earth wanted them back. Man had anticipated the earth's want and started building the pyramid on a base of solid sandstone. Gooding especially appreciated how man had thwarted the earth with its own skin. He stared at the rock, which now rested in a crack at the base of another wall.   Cracks... The cracks caught his imagination. If the base underneath the pyramid were destabilized or even cracked, thousands of years of solidarity would be compromised. The whole thing would come tumbling down, along with the other pyramids on the plain.

His gaze was drawn anew upward to the limestone capstone. People focused on that capstone as a symbol of the glory of the pyramid, completely forgetting the millions of sandstones supporting it as well as the smoothed sandstone base below. They focused on the tip. But without the tip, the pyramid would still stand. Like a mountaintop blown off a volcano, the caldera would remain. The base was the key to its strength.

Remove the base, however, and the entire pyramid would collapse, including the glorious top. Looking about him, he imagined the devastation that would be caused by the pyramid's collapse. Enormous blocks would cover miles of desert, millions of tons of tourist cash gone. He imagined the chaos it would cause. Gooding found that he liked the idea. All things diminish into chaos eventually. He noticed the hovels and huts and mass of squirming humanity surrounding him and the Great Pyramid; he felt it a just reward for the arrogance of man. "Some people need to become reacquainted with chaos," he'd said aloud, then had hummed his way into the bright and dark Egyptian night.

Gooding was no longer a lanky teenager, but a strong man in his prime. He'd spent the remainder of his teenage years doing every job in his grandfather's shipping company. Tussling with the dock workers who didn't think the boss' grandson should get off easy built his muscles, while hanging around with his grandfather's best men sharpened his wits. Branching off into his own hobbies helped him test himself, and he'd made many mistakes, but had more successes. His underworld activities sharpened his instincts and filled in those times when he'd felt bored in his rich man's life. Gooding now considered himself in his prime, and fully ready to start working on the Summer Plan. He'd returned to DC just in time to catch the fireworks while he worked to clear out his DC headquarters.

These current fireworks reminded Gooding of the fireworks during the night he'd thought up his Summer Plan. In his mind, the last fanfare lit up the summer night sky over DC, making the waters of the bay glow red, but he didn't see the cold marshy waters of the Chesapeake. Gooding reached the kitchen level of his father's mansion and grabbed the phone. "It's time. I'll call Mortimer. He'll get Manuel ready before I leave for New York."

Chapter Six

The gallery was crowded with hundreds of people milling around large collages of photographs that showed amazingly realistic map-like scenes. From some angles the images looked like life-size cutouts of quaint, neighborhood yards. Once you were close enough to pick out the details, tiny objects like bushes or domestic animals appeared with minute detail. The quality of the photographs was amazing. Each collage measured between twelve and twenty feet long and about ten feet high—the size of a small wall mural, but the clarity of the photographs showed no blurriness even when viewed from a distance of six inches. The collages also revealed an entirely different combined image when seen from a distance—usually a decorative object or an interesting geometric shape. Only a closer inspection would reveal the seemingly seamless joints in the pictures. The unpredictability of his art and its visual appeal made Gooding's exhibits sell-out shows on a regular basis.

Excitement filled the gallery. Because of its modern design and its designed function to display large art installations, it was one of the few galleries in the district capable of displaying Gooding's massive photographs. The layout of the walls allowed Gooding to not only set off his large collages with complimentary, smaller, three-dimensional collages that looked more like sculpture, but gave way to a circular open area where he displayed his rarely seen "11th Image." It, too, was a collage, but of massive proportions. At forty feet by fifteen feet, just the reassembly of the wooden backdrop took hours to complete and required absolute precision.

Another smile brightened Gooding's eyes as he thought of yesterday's rush to get things ready and remembered the quote he'd given to the art director for this exposition's brochure: "People think that the assembly of these pieces is overly complicated. It isn't. With planning and care, each piece is numbered and organized to allow for quick assembly and storage. Just like the London Bridge, we can put them up anywhere." He still smiled at the joke he'd made about the bridge put out in Arizona, even if the Yanks wouldn't appreciate it. He loved how Americans blew off the fact that the owner of the London Bridge had meant to buy the Tower Bridge in London, not realizing the prettier bridge was not in fact the London Bridge of the children's song. Gooding, like most of his British friends, smiled each time he thought of the older folks crossing that bridge out in America's desert because someone didn't ask enough questions before putting the money down.

Gooding was as excited as the gallery crowd. The "11th Image" was the key to his Summer Plan. Tonight he'd be unveiling it for the first time for the FBI. He wondered if they'd get the satire built into the collages or even conceive that he'd laid out all his clues for them in one place. He figured they'd be clueless like his typical audience who would just revel in the clever play on images from tiny to enormous, but all important.

The last, 11th Image, the largest one, made a giant graphic of a NASA space shuttle purposely scaled in a larger size to make the viewer sense their own insignificance. That you could see each individual tile on the shuttle's belly was just part of the plan. Gooding smiled as he thought of the write-ups in the local paper: *Michael Gooding clearly loves the USA. He lives in Washington DC and loves to show off this nation's best qualities in his capturing of our national icons.*

He chuckled. "If they only knew."

Gooding began to wander the exhibit, watching the people and slipping through the crowd, confident that his disguise, consisting of large-rimmed glasses, a fake beard, contacts, a different hairstyle, and a dowdy suit would keep him from being recognized. *It amazes me how people miss obvious clues with only a little distraction*, he thought, smiling. *People really are like cattle. They can be herded so easily.*

***

Jonesey was in a foul temper. Just because he wasn't working on any current cases, he was volunteered to hurriedly catch Gooding's exposition while the other agents were getting their assignments. "After last week's dinner, they all get to go gallivanting across the nation 'off the grid' to find bait for Gooding while I have to get on a plane on a voucher that will clearly show in the FBI computers and go to New York," Jonesey muttered to himself.

"I hate my job sometimes. Next time, Mitch is gonna have to do the ground work. They made him team leader, so he should be the one figuring out the damn plan. Not me. Why I always get stuck with the first reconnaissance, by myself, with no plan, I'll never know. It's not bad enough that I get to miss dinner, taking the commuter flight today. But then I have to get here in time to catch Gooding's big speech and be back here at the crack of dawn to get the photos for the team—all on record for Gooding's leak. I hate Mondays." This morning had dawned too early for Jonesey, but he was not lazy. After calling Stan to verify the objectives for the day and getting Reva's status, he headed out to the gallery. He grabbed a program from the kiosk as he paid the hundred-dollar donation to a local children's hospital that served as an entry fee to tonight's lecture and entered the exposition.

"Man that thing is huge! How the hell did he not make obvious pixels on something that size?" Jonesey wondered. All his years of gallery-hopping with his wife Amy, girlfriend at the time, had made Stan think that he should be the one to scope out Gooding's photographs and art exhibits. Jonesey had never seen such large photographs with such good detail. Most of the time, the images lost quality in direct proportion to how much they were enlarged. "Man, blowing the things up this large, he must have had a massive camera and a huge computer." Jonesey knew that Gooding could not have physically captured enough data for these images to remain in focus with traditional photography. He filed that thought away for the preliminary reports. *No way traditional film could chemically catch this much detail. Stan figured he must have a lot of sophisticated computer equipment, but this proves it. The guy's gone digital.*

"Give some damn megalomaniac a camera and let some dumb-ass politicians think it's cool to have one of his pictures and now I have to wander a stuffy, uncomfortable museum with a herd of cattle to try to make some sense of some dumb 'installations.' What a way to call an empty room with a chair and some posters slapped up." Jonesey could be heard muttering nearly under his breath as he wandered around the museum. He wished Amy were here with him at the expo. However, the top brass—specifically Homer, who was not above using female wiles to catch criminals, but hated it when his agents were similarly distracted—decided it would be safer for Jonesey to go alone until they had more data on Gooding.

He pictured his wife sitting in their DC hotel room, bored to death, and smiled. She still loved museums and would have been ecstatic to see Gooding's art. If she were with him, at least the museum wouldn't be so tedious. The fact that he knew what an installation was got him the job. Mitch and Bill just laughed at him when he'd complained about this task. Bill had nudged Mitch and said, "See, that artsy wife of his has got him trained and he knows how to walk through a museum, unlike us high school dropouts."

Jonesey settled into the assignment at hand. While he and Amy dated, he'd been dragged to plenty of museums and they had found a common fascination by the political undertones of much that was "art." Some of the neo-classicist paintings from France during the revolution had captured his attention while on a date one day. Amy had helped him research the painter's politics along with the owner's requirements and the placement of the painting. In this way Jonesey had found a way to enjoy the art his wife thrived on. He went through Gooding's entire exhibit, documenting it. Since cameras were strictly forbidden in the museum, he sketched the layout and design of the exhibit in a notebook, while his spy-style camera pen relayed digital images and video to a tiny hard drive in his pocket, and on to the computer geeks waiting in the FBI van.

"This is too obvious," Jonesey remarked in a quiet whisper. The agents in the van picked up his radio transmission through the tiny microphone on his jacket. "There is no apparent pattern here, but there are ten photograph collages in the exhibit. They all look slightly different, but all have some satellite photographs in them. Then we go into another room for number eleven, the space shuttle." Jonesey shrugged. It wasn't his job to interpret, only to capture. Silently he went through the rest of Gooding's New York exhibition.

Soon enough he was through the exhibit. Reva, a fellow FBI agent in Stan's team, was waiting for him outside the museum. Reva and her partner Carl were in New York tracking down bait candidates, and were giving Jonesey some light support this morning. She grabbed his arm at the door and together they pantomimed a loving couple walking the streets of New York. They took a taxi to a nearby restaurant, where Reva sat at the table, ordering their lunch as Jonesey walked past her to the restrooms in the rear. There, he quickly put on a ball cap and hooded sweatshirt, left the restaurant through the back door, and made his way down the alley. Reaching the side street, he quickly walked away from the restaurant and hailed a cab.

Reva sat for a minute, then walked out the restaurant's front door and zig-zagged her way back to where Carl was waiting in their car.

The New Jersey hotel room was dark and cold. Jonesey really hated the heating systems that some hotels used. He could tell the heat pump was doing all it could to keep the room above freezing, but sixty degrees wasn't satisfactory. It was too cold to stay here. Leaving his computer in its bag, he hefted it on his left shoulder as he grabbed his overnight bag with his right hand. He was supposed to check out in the morning, but felt a creepy bad vibe about staying here. Making a snap decision, he decided he would leave for Washington in a few hours. He left the key on the dresser and exited the hotel from the side entrance. Taking the parking garage elevator to his car, he dialed Mitch's work desk. No answer. *Better not leave a message there in case Stan has him in a meeting,* Jonesey thought as he reached his car. A quick scan of the parking lot verified the coast was clear, and Jonesey headed south to his wife and the crew.

***

The next day, Stan demanded a preliminary report. A disheveled-looking Jonesey grabbed Mitch, as the senior agent, and briefed both him and Stan. "Right now the experts are going over the data I gathered at the Met. So far we know this much: There are clearly ten maps in the exhibit. Some have classified images from top secret military satellites. It is clear Gooding has access to more than the FBI's information. One of the images was traced to a CIA satellite and the second collage in the exhibit shows a picture of a specific type of Navy helicopter that has been modified for top secret SEAL missions. Other collages show a submarine and a US Naval Destroyer. Each collage is different, has a different character, and the vehicles like the submarine and ship are treated differently. It appears that Gooding has ten targets, all tied to US government agencies like ourselves, the CIA, and the military with specific targets in the Army, Navy, Air Force, Marines, and the Coast Guard from what we can tell. If this is the case, Gooding is not even trying to mask his intent. It's like he's laying it all out for us to see, like an outline, but I can't figure out his purpose. And that big, final collage just stumps me. I get that he might be targeting NASA too, but the space shuttle is just weird or out of place with the other pieces. The analysts tell me they'll need time to analyze the photographs to make sense of them. I have no idea why the smaller collages seem to be military in nature, while the last one is of a space shuttle."

Mitch shook his head, "Jeez, that guy is playing us."

Jonesey nodded his agreement.

"Well, give me the preliminaries to look over, and then gather the rest of the team for a briefing in one hour," Stan instructed.

As the door closed to Stan's office, Jonesey and Mitch headed to Mitch's desk, knowing that the Gooding operation had begun in earnest. Jonesey grabbed his cordless electric razor from his duffel on Mitch's desk and began working on his beard. "Hey, man, that's it for me. From here I am off to get Amy and head back to Idaho on a commercial flight under personal tickets. Holler if you guys need someone bird-dogged in Denver or Phoenix."

Mitch tucked a portfolio into Jonesey's bag as he remarked, "Will do. I figure me and Bill will have the Rockies' candidates covered, but we'll keep you posted."

Jonesey smiled. "At least neither of us have the California herd." Mitch smiled, and Jonesey knew he shared the joke. So far Homer had identified fifteen bait candidates in California, but they were spread from Sacramento to San Diego, and none of the group was looking forward to driving all the way to California, then up and down the state in just four days. Most groups of agents were interviewing one or two candidates in a much smaller area.

Chapter Seven

"Damn, it's cold today," Jenny Johnson complained to her fourteen-year-old nephew Calvin as she sat on the scratchy hay bale in the barn. She watched him as he preened and posed in his dark blue Wrangler jeans and new FFA jacket. She smiled over the bright yellow lettering on the back of the navy blue corduroy jacket proclaiming his name and office in the local high school chapter of the club. He was so excited with his election to be the treasurer in the club. As a freshman in high school, Calvin was Jenny's oldest nephew and the favorite grandkid in the family. He was having the time of his life socializing with his friends and showing off to all the girls at school.

As she watched him take her father's lariat and practice his cattle roping techniques, she thought about how fast he was growing up. *He's grown up so much. He must be almost six feet tall by now.* She smiled as she saw the rope's loop sail past the plastic cow's head to land on the ground. *He's only wearing Wranglers to fit in with the cowboys as school. I'll bet he threw a fit when his mom tried to buy him Levis at Christmas.* Jenny thought of her older sister and felt a pang. At thirty-five, her sister already had a kid in high school. In five years, she could conceivably be a grandmother. *Why does twenty-five feel so old?* Jenny wondered. As one of the younger children in her family, she was singled out in family discussions, not because of birth order, or her age, but because she was the only single sibling still eligible for razzing about getting married. All of her brothers and sisters were out of the house, with only her eldest sister Fran unmarried. Fran was an exception at forty; she'd been too independent and no one expected *her* to marry at this late date. As she watched her next oldest sister's pride and joy practice his cowboy techniques on this cold, sunny, wintry day, Jenny felt a sense of failure about her life.

Jenny was the only child in the family to still live at home and had been trying for the last three years to fix her life. She completed one year of college directly after high school on an art scholarship she'd won with her fantastic photography, but had tired of the party lifestyle at Utah State University in Logan, Utah. That lifestyle helped her grades slide a little and lost her the scholarship. Out of money and disillusioned, at nineteen Jenny quit school to work full time. One year of teaching little kids at a local daycare taught her that she needed to take her life in a new direction—daycare wages just didn't cut it.

So she quit that job and at twenty years old moved to Jackson Hole, Wyoming to live and work in that beautiful tourist town, figuring she could still take beautiful photographs in her spare time. Only six months living with four other girls in a tiny rented house and working two jobs cleaning rooms in two different hotels for a living convinced her to move back to Utah. At twenty-one, Jenny packed her old Jeep Cherokee with all her possessions and made the three-hour drive home to her parents. She got a job at a local grocery store and went back to school, switching colleges to go to Weber State University in Ogden, Utah. Soon after, she had secured a job at the Internal Revenue Service's local service center. *Three failed life choices in three years.*

Now three years later, finally, she had a good job, with good pay and benefits. She had found it pleasant living with her mom and dad as the only egg left in the nest. She and her parents had found a good rhythm to their combined home life. Jenny helped around the house and was around, but stayed out of the way of her parents' normal schedule. She worked the afternoon, or swing, shift, going to school in the morning each day before work and coming home late at night. She'd felt comfortable in her routine, but had lately wondered if maybe this routine was really a rut. Jenny waved goodbye to Calvin's mom as her sister pulled out of their parents' driveway. She thought about ruts. Grandpa Johnson had always said that a rut was really a grave with no ends. Jenny wondered if there was something wrong with her. Sure, she'd accomplished a lot in the last three years, but she still lived with her parents. She wasn't married or even dating. In the past four years, the ladies in her local church group had hounded Jenny off and on about her single state, and the years of comments had eroded her confidence in her plan for her life. *Then again*, she thought, *why do we Mormons have to be so fixated on marriage? It's not as if I am a lesser person just because I'm not married. I'm still a person.*

Calvin tripped just then and interrupted Jenny's internal pity party. "No. Wait. Here, I'll help you." She reached over and took the rope from her nephew's hand. Jenny stretched and sighted the hay bale with the practice calf's head stuck on one end. Straightening her stance she gathered the loops in her hands, prepared her arms, and began to swing the rope. A few circles and she threw. The loop landed neatly over the horns to rest quietly on the plastic cow's forehead. "There, like that."

Calvin's jaw dropped. "Man. I knew you were voted the FFA Sweetheart in high school, but wow! When Grandma told me to ask you for help I figured she was lying to me and just wanted me out of the house."

Jenny winced. She'd had no idea that her mom still had the old scrapbooks with the newspaper clippings and pictures of her roping a fake calf in the high school gym as part of the Sweetheart obstacle course, or that she'd shown them to Calvin. She remembered the competition her senior year, but had put it out of her mind until today. As a high school senior she'd competed in front of the whole school in the timed competition for the sweetheart title. In the obstacle course she'd milked a cow, shown a decorated cake she'd made, saddled a horse, and roped a dummy calf to prove that she was a woman worthy of the FFA title.

She shivered. *I could have wrestled down a live calf and roped it off, too. I am so glad that was not part of the show.* Her grandpa's cows were long gone, the land being sold when he'd died, but she could still remember watching and later helping her mom and uncles rope the calves for branding in the spring when Grandpa would move the herd from the home ranch to the summer range in the mountains above Brigham City, Utah. Jenny used to rope things as an excuse to go outside or to take a break from her schoolwork. It also helped give her privacy. Roping was the only activity she had to do alone; all the other family activities in her household growing up required a sibling or two. Her mother sighed over such a masculine pastime, but her dad supported her. He thought Jenny's roping was as valuable as his sons pitching baseballs at a target painted on the barn—both activities kept the kids out of the house and taught them good hand-eye coordination. Jenny didn't get to rope very much anymore. Yet another sign that her life had changed and she was a different person now.

Chapter Eight

At the Chesapeake mansion music came blaring out of the basement-level French doors at the back of the house, brashly echoing off the gently flowing waters. It was near sunset and no one could be seen moving in or around the house except a groundskeeper trimming the bushes along the drive on the far side of the house.

The back lawn flowed gradually down to the marshy riverbank, giving the house a peaceful air. A foolish soul noticing the priceless antiques and art in the house might be tempted to sneak into the house via the open French door, thinking that the loud music would mask any sounds of their presence. The two gray-black, hulking wolfhounds lolling just outside the door usually handled that issue. Gooding liked to catch salty, marshy breezes in the evenings, and having an extreme dislike for interlopers, had brought the dogs home from his grandfather's estate in Scotland. With relatively few deer left around his grandfather's castle, the dogs needed some new sport, and trespassers and burglars were more fun to hunt anyway. The last time an incident occurred, the police, alerted by the hidden silent alarm, had to transport the wounded would-be burglars to the hospital before they could be arrested. Gooding did have use for the police in some aspects of his life. They made disposing of small problems fairly simple.

Gooding was home just now, hence the new groundskeeper working outside. It had not been a good day. Having just returned from a week in New York, he'd taken a violent dislike to the overgrown state of the yard. He'd fired his last groundskeeper this morning after finding that, while being happy to take the monthly maintenance stipends, that person was not willing to actually keep the grounds. Vexed by this behavior, Gooding almost "fired" him literally. He'd been able to check his rage, but only just barely. Some days he could almost wish that the days of feudalism were back. Had he been laird or even a nineteenth-century plantation owner, he could have whipped the man to death for insubordination.

Gooding had come home to Virginia to locate his housekeeper. Someone had been feeding the FBI information, and he'd ruled out any other sources. After firing the groundskeeper, Gooding accessed his secret security system that supported the main, visible system. He had crushed the paper coffee cup in his hand as he watched the monitor show the elderly lady picking the lock on his office filing cabinet, then taking pictures of documents with a small camera.

His palms itched to hold a whip, but he consoled himself with the actions he had taken. He'd let the groundskeeper go, knowing that the "gift" left in the departing van would not explode until he triggered the timer. The housekeeper was unconscious in the hall at the top of the house. The injection he'd given her would metabolize after death, making it look like she'd collapsed of a heart attack. He'd loved to have whipped both staff to death instead. Meanwhile, he contacted his assistant, Mortimer, who found a new gardener quickly and immediately sent him over. Gooding liked the looks of this new fellow. Well-seasoned and efficient in his response, he began trimming the hedges nearest the house first. His professionalism soothed Gooding's nerves after a long day. Gooding was satisfied that all would now be well, especially knowing that Mortimer knew this fellow and counted him as a friend and vouched for him. He was grateful for good help and smiled at the old adage as he thought it. The guy could also truthfully report that everything looked fine at the house when he arrived. He also had a hefty stipend to guarantee that he'd tell anyone asking that the housekeeper had hired him and directed his work. When this was over, there would be no proof that Gooding had been in Virginia, let alone in this house today.

"Good help is truly hard to find these days, but worth all the money," he mused aloud. His studio awaited and he descended to the basement level of the mansion, then one floor down to the cellars. His dogs, bored in the still evening air, came up to him and begged for a treat, but retreated smartly when he barked back at them. Gooding shut the French doors after them.

He entered the large room that stored his favorite down-time passions. He glanced at the monitors and saw the dogs were in the back yard over by the gardener. "Good. I'll have Mortimer get the groundsman to retrieve them later," he remarked as he set the alarm system to lockdown. Now, no one could enter or leave the house without the key codes—not even the dogs. This large house, or his US domain, as he liked to think, stored all his US art and a photography lab—all below ground level behind sturdy concrete walls. He also had a small workshop in the back, behind the old plantation owner's hidden wine cellar, accessed via a fake wall in the basement. There he stored his bomb making supplies when not on his ship.

Gooding deposited the detonator for the device he left in the old groundskeeper's van on the worktop and surveyed the shelves. Luckily, he had set up his materials amongst the rest of the shop items in here. Only bomb-squad professionals would differentiate this space from any backyard mechanic's space. There was even an old cellar door that connected to the garage from here. Gooding took a moment to consider the furnishings and art on the walls in the rest of the house as he rotated his neck and shoulders and tried to relax. He'd left the music going and it was booming through the downstairs. He could slightly hear it through the floor above his head. *I am tired of this. I am tired of his art. I am tired of Dad's crappy taste in this house.* It was time for another bomb. He set the detonator for the van to explode in twenty minutes. The signal confirmed the bomb timer was started. He left the detonator on a shelf in a box of old car radios.

Gooding started systematically gathering bits of other electronics and papers from the desk and placed them in his duffel or briefcase as he thought about New York. The exposition had gone well, so well in fact, that the FBI agents staring at his installations and collages had not noticed the bomb shaped like a sculpture he'd stashed there for emergencies. The agents were too busy trying to document all the images and scanning the crowd for him or any accomplices. They also were harried by the crowds as they tried to notice if any one of the presenters in the last exhibit looked funny. He'd spotted that Jones fellow taking notes, and had planted the bomb to take him out if necessary. Luckily enough, the FBI agents were following the plan. Dutifully they documented everything, which should prime them to accept his "hints" and figure out the pattern, but not yet. He didn't want any FBI agent figuring out the Summer Plan before he was ready. Gooding sighed as he tucked the last detonator into the pack. "Unless I can get back to within a block of the museum, that expo bomb will just have to wait. I wonder if they'll find it when they disassemble the show."

Sometimes he was tempted to lay it all on the table just to see if the agents could figure it out. This need he had felt illogical. Was his life was too calm these days? Did he want to be caught? For an instant, Gooding felt these inner questions fully. He was always willing to ensure that he understood his own motives as clearly as possible. Did he just want to "spice things up," or was he really trying to warn innocent bystanders? Either way, he decided, soon he would open his Summer Plan with a few personal "fireworks" before he presented the full plan to the US. It was in this exposition for all to see. Not just a few bombs, but a larger statement to encourage the larger population to evaluate their nation. The United States was meant to be great. Too bad that most of the people in it did not encourage its greatness. Gooding looked around the space one last time and checked off his mental list verbally. "Components packed. Documents secured. Housekeeper neutralized. Dogs out. Old groundskeeper off the property. New grounds guy away from the structure. Hidden door secured; they may find it or not, either way we're clear here."

He reached up to open a false-fronted brick access panel above eye level. Feeling for a slot with his fingers, Gooding placed his index finger over the fingerprint scanner he felt. A beep sounded and the rear wall of the workshop slid open twelve inches revealing a dark, dirty, stone-walled tunnel. "Thank heavens that somebody here worked on the underground railroad. Time to go. Good luck, dogs." Gooding shouldered his cases and disappeared into the tunnel. The door closed automatically behind him.

Chapter Nine

At 2:00 a.m. on a silent morning, Mortimer called Gooding with his report, right on time. Picking up the report on D. Jones, FBI agent, Gooding discovered that, sure enough, the FBI agents missed the plan. They didn't understand the visual language Gooding had used. They saw his images of the dollar bill and George Washington, but didn't understand their significance. His intentions had been met. The FBI would not know too much too soon. He had plans for them. That Dave Jones fellow, who spent his time following skinheads in Idaho, was an odd choice to follow a suspected terrorist through the galleries of New York. Gooding didn't want to blow him up, as the mess would certainly alert the FBI of their security breach, but he'd learned that Jones was an expert at spotting things that most agents missed.

Even Alicia had warned him about Jones. She'd always been wary of him, having known that Jones was the only agent in her office that suspected *everyone* of something. She thought he was absolutely paranoid, but in a scary, suspicious, controlled way. Even worse, he could charm the socks off anyone when he wanted to. He liked to lull people into a false sense of security, then he'd let loose on them. Jones was known to have made one of the white supremacists he'd apprehended scream for another agent when they'd arrived at headquarters. The man was scared out of his wits by Jones' behavior, and no one was ever able to get the details of what Jones had done. When pressed, Jones simply refused to elaborate, only stating that, "That cell is no longer a problem." Alicia heard the agents retell the story with awe and heard one group whisper, "No bodies or buildings or trace of them were ever found." No official sanctions or personnel actions were taken against Jones. Gooding recognized in this particular FBI agent a shared trait; here was another man who solved problems permanently and irrevocably. Gooding wasn't worried. "Now that he's back in Idaho, I'll shelve Jones until he pops back on the East Coast."

As a footnote to the report, Mortimer wrote, *Somehow, Jones appears bored by the exhibit, and had not noticed the plot. He appears to relate to the exhibits just like the other gallery patrons—as just art pieces.* Many other visitors had found Gooding's companion photographs and art pieces in the exhibit desirable, and those additional sales would finish paying for his Summer Plan. It was good that the plan could pay for itself. It kept the paper trail from his other legitimate enterprises clean and would help him fade back into his "normal" life. As Gooding had negotiated the terms of his art sales with the gallery, he'd watched Jones leave the place earlier than usual and very unobtrusively fiddle with his earpiece as he left. He saw him embrace a dark-haired lady when he reached the curb and hail a taxi. All these were clear signs that the agent was off the assignment. Later, Alicia confirmed that Jones reported that there was no obvious suspicious activity at the show. Things were in the clear. He had the money, the plan, and soon it would be time to put it all into motion.

Gooding decided the name "Summer Plan" not only applied to his favorite time of year in America, but also to the eternal summer that the American culture lived in. Intentionally he aimed his spotlight at those fun-loving capitalists of America who strove to live in an eternal summer, never caring about the rest a long winter could provide or the hard work that used to be done in spring and fall.

Lately he'd seen too many good, supposedly hardworking US citizens believe the rich freedom and playtime of summer should last forever. Gooding had started thinking about the "summertime" attitude that infected the United States when he'd had a dream about the nuclear winter that had threatened his parents' generation. He'd grown up with a healthy respect for a possible nuclear holocaust, and being somewhat caring about the earth, had decided that, while a nuclear winter would destroy too much life, a nice autumn of hardship may be just what his target needed. His plan would create a nice frost to finally end the endless days of youth, fading innocence, and false summer.

Especially irritating was the attitude of the Americans around him. How could they seem so oblivious to the fact that their callous attitudes toward the earth and the other countries in the world adversely affected themselves. The most obvious example for him was their addiction to fossil fuels and the way the entire nation polluted the world. Soon enough these summertime people would find themselves in an overheated, desert, summer-only world once their pollutants had finished melting the ice caps.

He'd watched the busy citizens of New York City walk right past him and decided at that moment that he really missed the lower class citizens that seemed to be hidden by this society's idea of the ideal American life. That day when he'd left the New York gallery for the docks instead of the airport as expected, he began the Summer Plan. His ride on his grandfather's yacht back to Virginia took him out of "known whereabouts." With the final US exposition over, it was time for the FBI to lose track of him. From shipside, he dialed the home number for the Chesapeake house on his cellphone, typing in a special code connected to the security system. A few keystrokes later and things were all ready. He could start the countdown at any time.

Chapter Ten

Jonesey, Bill, and Mitch studied the file on Gooding. It showed how Gooding was a well-known photographer in the higher circles of the Washington DC elite. There was a thumbnail print of a photograph marked "subject A." Here was a classic example of Gooding's latest gimmick. DC underground sources confided that Gooding was known to influence legislators for a price. He hid his blackmail pictures operation within his "nude photo of your partner" scheme. Recently Gooding began taking life-size photographic portraits of Washington mucky mucks, alone or with their significant others in their "evening wear." This evening wear was optional and didn't usually involve sequins but did show a lot of skin. The final result was a life-size, framed print suitable for display. Smaller copies could be delivered in any other desired format or electronically. Gooding's latest work involved putting congressmen in pink flannel pajamas for luck, and he hit it big when one of the younger congressmen's girls really wanted to get her man something "nice" for Christmas. Gooding put her in a black teddy and took her picture on a blue rug that mimicked the one in the oval office. That picture was rumored to be infamous in that congressman's game room, hidden in a secret compartment behind the paneling. It started a craze. Power players would do one for their spouse or a girl/boy-friend or both.

"Woo-hoo. That is quite a shot," remarked Jonesey as he showed the latest snapshot to Mitch, appearing a bit jet-lagged from the quick flight back to DC.

"Yeah, too bad it's not illegal to take erotic pictures," Mitch muttered. He was itching to lay hands on Gooding.

The file gave background information on how Gooding had come to the FBI's attention, and filled in his activities up to the Summer Plan. Gooding would use his portrait scheme in whatever way necessary. Sometimes, he would threaten to share the commissioned photo with interested parties, while others he'd use the portrait session to get access to confidential information. One of Mitch's cousins was a congressional aide for a representative from New York; she had been at the party when that particular congressman's wife had found the portrait in her hubby's "hobby room." Since then, a lot more hobby rooms had locks, and a lot more ladies had "taken it off" for Gooding.

Gooding also seemed to have scruples in this scheme. Many of the legislators interviewed actually refused to help the FBI. When they'd paid up, Gooding had returned all copies of the photos as promised and never contacted them again. He was unlike all other blackmailers—he'd contact them once, then truly consider the transaction complete when the demand was met. Some even stated they'd continued to see or work with Gooding after the blackmail. Both sides treated it like water under the bridge.

Bill laughed as Mitch read the file and related a dirty rumor from the Secret Service guys that Clinton had done one of Gooding's pictures in the buff. It was said that when Hilary received it in her mail, that she smiled, and later removed the groin area with a White House letter opener, then stuck the scrap of paper onto the president's desk. The kicker, according to the White House guy, was that the paper was pinioned to the desk in a rather *prominent* way, and the letter opener had to be pulled out of the wood with a pair of pliers. That was just a rumor told like a dirty joke around the office. They knew there was no substance to it; they were the FBI—they'd checked.

Mitch ignored the nasty joke, thinking about how some of the female employees in his office would have been offended by the off-color humor. While Stan was away, he was in charge of the lesser important administrative duties, and he hated dealing with office politics, especially since his department was trying to recruit more females for their undercover work.

"Did they find out if Leaver changed his vote yesterday?" Bill asked. The official meeting would start in about twenty minutes, and they had time to kill.

"Yup. Just like Jonesey figured he would after this hit the mail," Mitch responded as he held up another photograph. This one was of a very pregnant, very lovely Chinese woman who they knew worked for the Chinese Ambassador. She wore a yellow baby-doll dress. Her senator was not pictured, but they knew that his WASP wife had *not* been pleased to receive this picture on top of some grainy surveillance photos last week. Mitch, Bill, and Jonesey had only heard the latter part of the senator's stubborn discussion with their supervisor last night—as he stomped out of the office. The senator had been most uncooperative, having found a way to spirit his girl out of town and striking a rather lucrative bargain with his wife and the Chinese. He'd responded to Gooding and had escaped an outright scandal. His vote was already changed officially, as requested, so he was not willing to further jeopardize his career by "'fessing up." In his relief over securing a satisfactory arrangement with all parties, the senator also was not smart enough to wonder why in the world the FBI cared about a little sex scandal anyway.

"Hey did you know that Reva and Carl located one of their bait candidates here in DC? They found the girl's mom in Manhattan and learned she's down here as a congressional aide. They were waiting for her in the congressional cafeteria when they spotted Gooding leaving the coffee counter. He made them as agents at the same time and slipped away. By the time they made it out to the street, Gooding was gone and the senator he was meeting had pocketed the negatives and split," Bill remarked conversationally.

"Yeah, the Secret Service guys saw him but didn't recognize him through the disguise. The only reason Reva and Carl ID'd him was because Gooding was wearing the same disguise in New York at the exposition," Mitch replied.

Jonesey nodded. "Yeah, the word among the 'scared few' is that Gooding has actually been good on his word. The parties get their negatives back and never hear another word from him."

"It makes you wonder what's in it for Gooding," Mitch speculated. "He gets the results, and is done? You'd think he'd milk a little blackmail money out of the deal."

"Nope," Bill said. "He sticks to the letter of the contract, fulfills it, and then moves on. It's like he's a professional about it. So much so, that he's been in high demand lately. That's why he's been so busy, and also why we can't catch him keeping any set schedule. He goes all over the greater DC area doing his pictures."

Gooding's antics used to be relatively harmless. He used to make "art" as social and personal commentary on somebody or something. Mitch had actually seen one of Gooding's newer creations in an acquaintance's den. Gooding had taken a picture of Dwight Eisenhower and placed it on a lovely lady's torso. His friend said that the lady happened to be Miss March for December 1998. Gooding had been no more than a colorful DC character until now. The agents were worried. Mitch had seen the photos of the New York exposition. The collages meant something. The first collage in Gooding's art exhibit featured a US Coast Guard ship. Stan had informed Homer of their findings so far, and they could only hope that the Coast Guard authorities had taken the warning seriously.

Chapter Eleven

The sun shining off the cerulean-blue water shimmered in Mortimer's eyes as he maneuvered the yacht closer to the sandbar near the closest Key at hand. Working for Gooding had its perks. The Florida Keys were beautiful this time of year, and the warm weather was a welcome change from New York in winter.

Dropping the anchor, he waited patiently for the divers to surface. The targeted buoy was just a few feet away, and the water was clear enough that he could see the shapes of their dark bodies against the sand below as they worked.

After a few moments, the divers rose to the surface. Gooding flipped up his goggles as he grasped the ladder at the back of the watercraft. He turned back to George, the other diver assisting him. "Do you need a hand?"

"No, I have it, sir," was the response from George as he hefted a black box out of the water to land behind Gooding on the deck.

When everyone was aboard, Mortimer gently steered the craft right up to the buoy. George reached out and held the buoy steady as Gooding finished installing a black box just under the warning light's housing. A few adjustments later and the buoy was completely fitted with its new light and signal box. A few checks with the transmitter and George signaled the "all's good" sign to his boss. Gooding nodded and set his toolbox down, then proceeded to change into some dry clothes. Mortimer steered the craft a small distance from the buoy, where a rubber life raft was anchored in the sandbar. George stripped out of his wetsuit and put on the ragged shirt and shorts Mortimer handed him. Gooding brought over a water bottle and two sandwiches in a bag, along with a radio and the transmitter.

"Stick to the plan. Manuel will be back for you late tonight after the moon sets. Check the gear in the raft and make sure your breather and the tank are still there. Any last minute questions?" Gooding addressed George who responded, "No, sir. I should have everything under control. I will give the signal once I have checked everything."

Gooding shook his hand. "You're a good man, George. I am glad we were able to pick you and Manuel out of the sea all those years ago."

With a small salute, George grabbed the waterproof bag with the gear and stepped off the boat and into the water. He soon surfaced and easily swam the short distance to the raft. From their vantage point on the yacht, Mortimer and Gooding observed George heave himself into the raft, stow his bag, and check the hidden gear. He turned back to them and gave the "thumbs up" sign. Gooding returned it, and Mortimer turned back to the steering wheel of the craft, started the engines, and sped off into the sunshine.

"George was certainly a good choice for the job, boss," Mortimer remarked conversationally.

"Yes, I agree. He and Manuel have really been assets to our organization. Fate stepped in to bring us together that night Grandfather's yacht spied them in the waters off Cuba." Gooding looked at Mortimer, who was a quiet, supportive assistant. Reliable and careful, but not too serious, Mortimer was a perfect apprentice for him. Things were going very well. Settling down in the seat next to Mortimer, Gooding made himself comfortable for the two-hour journey to Miami and prepared to call the US Coast Guard.

Chapter Twelve

A few hours later, the Coast Guard vessels radio chirped. "Sir, we just received a report from a pleasure boater who spotted a refugee raft just south of here."

"Did they rescue any survivors?" the coast guard captain asked the ensign.

"No, sir, the person wanted no part of it. Something about how it's our job to retrieve the riff-raff from Cuba and send them back, sir."

The weathered captain pinched the bridge of his nose and closed his eyes. Heaven deliver him from selfish snobs whose yachts clogged the waters off Florida. "Did the Good Samaritan give us a location, Richards?"

"Yes, sir, and the chopper buzzed the raft, reporting one occupant; appears to be a male, who seemed strong, sir. The chopper's awaiting your orders."

The captain looked away from the ensign standing before him and stared out the bridge's windows, scanning the sea and sky around the ship. It was getting near dusk, but they were pretty close to the raft's location themselves. The swells were increasing; the chopper would have an increasingly difficult task if they attempted an air-rescue. The captain answered the ensign, having made his decision. "We'll intercept the raft ourselves, Richards. Send the orders, have the chopper stand down and report back to base."

"Aye, sir. Our expected ETA will be nineteen hundred hours, sir."

The captain nodded, then addressed the mate. "I'll be below, and will return at eighteen hundred hours."

***

George lay back in the raft, using the shade from the side wall to shield his eyes from the sun. It felt good to lay here and drift, letting the waves tug and pull on the raft.

Steering the small raft far enough up current from the buoy to lend an appearance of a drifter, who'd found the buoy through luck, had taken only a few minutes. Since then, letting himself drift back on the current while Gooding called in his location had been pure pleasure. When the raft had drifted back close enough to the buoy that George could close the final distance using the oars, he'd jettisoned the small engine into the deeper water just off the bar. He reached the sandbar easily and attached himself to the buoy. The sun shone on a deep angle from the west, turning the clouds that had been white and fluffy a rosy pink, and the swells were not as large as predicted by the weather reports. It was time to sit and wait to be rescued.

This raft was just a bit more stable than the rowboat he and Manuel had stolen off a beach in Cuba as teens. Since then, they had both become much better sailors and working one of Gooding's freighters was hard work, but rewarding in its own way.

George listened with half an ear to the two tiny waterproof radios in the raft as he daydreamed. On one he would receive reports from Gooding periodically, while he listened to the Coast Guard ship's communications coming from the other. He had about a half hour more to wait for them to arrive. Using a bit of rope meant to look like a survivor's only hope, he'd tied the raft to the buoy and ditched the anchor and line that had held the raft in place, which sunk into the depths. The only thing keeping him from drifting away was the new chain anchoring the buoy to its current spot.

The breathing apparatus Gooding had hidden on the raft was on a cord around George's neck with the mouthpiece hanging under his shirt. He wore the small, support-only oxygen tanks on his back, also under his clothes, where they were strapped over the waterproof pack that held his gear and the transmitters that were needed for the buoy and to send the signal to Manuel and the crew on

Gooding's black yacht, the Maryann, that would retrieve him.

Gooding named his sleek, charcoal-gray painted yacht Maryann after his grandfather's mistress as a joke. She was the yacht he took on his clandestine trips, while he reserved the traditional white monster of luxury yacht his grandfather christened Goliath for showing off to family and clients. They had used the white boat to doctor the buoy and drop off George. Then Gooding and Mortimer returned it to Miami, partly to continue their role as millionaires who'd spotted another refugee and dutifully called in a report to the Coast Guard. They would leave her in her berth, taking the helicopter from there to the freighter, while Manuel and George and the Maryann would rendezvous with Gooding and the freighter in Galveston.

The other transmitter let George know that the Coast Guard had picked up the Goliath's position on radar and sonar. However, they'd honored what they thought was a concerned citizen's request to remain anonymous and did not contact Gooding after his report.

Manuel had radioed too. He was waiting on a desert Key about an hour's drifting from here. They would pick him up as soon as it was dark, and by morning would be waiting safe off Texas for Gooding and the freighter.

For a minute George dozed. It had been an early morning and a long day. He awoke suddenly. It took him a moment to figure out where he was. A buzzing sound in his ear caught his attention. Gooding's radio had gone to static. That connection was cut. Turning up the Coast Guard radio, he learned they were very near. Carefully taking the Gooding radio, he opened a plastic, zipper-closing bag that held a big rock. He dropped the radio in the bag, partially sealing it closed, and carefully levered his torso into an upright position. He looked to the north and spotted the Coast Guard ship coming at him. They were about a half mile away, but he knew they could see him with their binoculars. Frantically he sat up and began waving his arms like a desperate castaway. The Coast Guard ship shone a signal light at him in the falling darkness. Good, they spotted him. He feigned an exhausted wave and fell back into the raft.

George worked quickly to hold the zipper bag with the radio under the water in the puddle that had formed in the bottom of the raft. When it was full, he finished sealing the bag and sat up again, watching the Coast Guard ship. The swells began to rise. He waited and counted. Every seventh swell was larger and the dip would take the Coast Guard ship momentarily out of sight. On the last dip, George threw the plastic bag over the side, where the rock and water sent it sinking. He then waited to be rescued.

***

"Sir, we've spotted the raft," Richards responded to the captain who'd just arrived on the bridge.

"Report, ensign."

"Sir, it appears that the man has tied himself to a buoy on one of the sandbars off the key."

"Good, that's held him in one position. How are conditions?"

"A little choppy, sir, but we're on the seaward, deeper edge of the sandbar, so we should be able to maneuver fairly close." Using the buoy's anchor location, they triangulated their distance from the dangerous sandbar. "Sir, we can get within fifty yards of the raft."

"Very good, ensign, take us that close and signal the rescue craft to be ready for deployment in ten minutes." The captain raised his binoculars and surveyed the raft. "This one looks to be in good shape—have you notified the medical team to get in position?"

"Yes, sir, they are on standby."

"Good. Let's do this."

***

George calmly watched the Coast Guard ship approach. He remembered the other Coast Guard ship from years ago. He and Manuel had been exhausted and dehydrated from their journey north. They had run out of water, and the wave that had nearly capsized them had taken their oars. They were desperate. He remembered the loudspeaker voice, shining the bright spotlight on them and telling them to turn back, that there was no place for them in the United States. They received no rescue that day. Had Gooding and his grandfather not found them two days later, they would not have survived. The pain and anger was mostly gone now, but George was glad that Gooding had allowed him the honor of the first Summer Plan bomb, and the bonus from this job would really help him and Maria with the baby.

The Coast Guard ship never knew what hit them. As they neared the raft, the captain watched the castaway stand on his knees to watch them hit the sandbar. The impact stuck them fast in the muck. None of the crew had time to react. The two sailors readying to deploy the rescue craft, along with a handful of others, were thrown off the deck of the ship and into the water. Those who remained able, watched with the captain while the person they were supposed to be rescuing dove out of his raft and began to swim away. They lost him in the swells and the darkening night and as the captain ordered a status report, a few watched the buoy drift the remaining few feet closer to them. It appeared to be propelling itself to them. When it came under the edge of the hull, a few sailors spotted a motorized propeller attached to its base. As they reported this to the captain, the buoy emitted a red light and began to make a high-pitched squealing noise. This and the remaining sequence of events were pieced together by the few sailors in the water who survived the explosion.

The buoy started to list to one side as a rocket that turned out to be a firework shot out of its bell housing. As able eyes looked skyward, the red, white, and blue firework exploded above them and the buoy blew up, taking half of the hull with it. The explosion compromised the engine compartment, and the resulting secondary explosions blasted the ship into a fiery hulk.

Since the debris landed all around the shallow sandbar, most of it, including some crew members' remains, was recovered. The investigation revealed that the buoy had been set free from its original anchorage point and repositioned in the two days before the rescue attempt. Its position, like many other buoys', had been verified by GPS, but the satellites only checked it every month or so. The last check had been forty-eight hours before, but it had shown the buoy to be in the correct location.

The Coast Guard and FBI officials were still trying to determine the type of explosive used. They only knew that there was quite a lot and that it appeared to be military grade—stronger than anything used in civilian applications.

The Coast Guard had not only ignored the FBI warning but also treated this like a freak attack with no justification or explanation—until Gooding sent a little letter to his friend Alicia's boss, Albert, at the FBI.

"Mr. Horowitz, please." The courier gave the name of the recipient of the package to the guard at the front desk of the FBI building.

"I'll sign for the package. Just leave it here." The security guard motioned the courier closer. Once the invoice was signed, the courier left and the security guard called his supervisor.

The letter was immediately hand-carried to Stan, who reviewed all of Albert's mail since Al's secretary Alicia was suspected to be Gooding's accomplice in the security breach. Stan put the team on high alert. They had to hurry to keep this quiet and avoid a nationwide panic. The letter indicated that Gooding would soon publish his plan in every large newspaper in the country. "At least now the other agencies will believe me." Stan sighed.

Chapter Thirteen

Gooding's skills with computers turned out to be the clue that helped the FBI learn what he was really up to when using his art as a cover. He would finish the nude pictures in a studio on the Chesapeake Bay, but besides the traditional negatives, he made digital copies on site, the day of the shoot, and showed them to the customer for their perusal. Many times the images were downloaded directly from Gooding's laptop to the resident computer. Gooding often offered to save them directly to his host's hard drive for an additional fee to provide the instant gratification that seemed requisite to his clients, who hated waiting for the printed, life-size version.

Of course Gooding needed a quiet spot to hook up his laptop, and wasn't it easier to just hook up his laptop to their personal system? This prompted many an unsuspecting Washington insider to let Gooding into their personal offices.

The most recent surveillance tapes caught Gooding removing a hard drive from a senator's computer. The senator didn't notice until the next day, and by then Gooding had slipped away. That was just before New Year's. Frustratingly for the FBI agents trying to discover more about his activities, soon after that incident Gooding stopped doing public photographs, citing "personal reasons." Which upset many folks who had wanted Valentine's Day pictures.

Initially, the FBI was only interested in what data Gooding took away, not realizing that he left special codes and viruses behind him. At the same time, Stan's staff continued to work the breach of security issue and attempted to figure out what information was lost. Stan's team figured Gooding had gone inactive for a time until some different high-powered senators and representatives started changing their politics. All of a sudden more legislators started having various changes of heart, while others in Washington declared bankruptcy after their bank accounts were drained by checks made out to "cash."

When Mr. Greenspan started receiving interesting mail just before Groundhog Day, the FBI was called back in to reinvigorate the Gooding blackmail investigation that had gone cold. By then, it was too late. On February first, a tragic house fire consumed the artist studio loft Gooding had leased for months in a seedy part of Washington DC. Then a bomb exploded in a source's car. When the FBI had investigated Gooding's whereabouts, they found that he'd been doing a private portrait, which gave him a perfect alibi for both the fire and the car bomb. It appeared that Gooding was cleaning house and preparing to leave town.

FBI agents then rushed to another house, where the latest portrait sitting had been scheduled, to see if they could bring Gooding in. However, they were too late. It appeared that the customer had apparently refused to cooperate with Gooding somehow, as he was found dead with a plastic bag around his head and Zip© disk nailed through the bag to his skull. The Zip© disk held quite a few interesting pictures. Most of which showed the customer with his boyfriend—to the horror of his new widow and constituents. This congressman, too, had begun to change his politics, but the investigation found documentation showing that the week before, he'd reverted to his old "conservative" ways—at least on the Hill.

Finally, just before Valentine's Day, the last known and documented Gooding photograph was delivered to an unexpected recipient. Rather than a top political figure or influential lobbyist, this non-commissioned portrait was delivered to one of those government workers who happen to live near Washington because they work there. Stan's counterpart and FBI budget chief, Albert Horowitz, became the winner, receiving Gooding's first direct threat to the FBI related to the Summer Plan.

In typical Michael Gooding fashion, this last photographic stunt was a double whammy. The eight-foot photograph, which appeared to have been taken in Mr. Albert Horowitz's office, was a rather informal scene, a double portrait of Albert's stunning blonde secretary Alicia Birmingham and a tall African American man who looked a lot like Albert. The man wore a suit identical to one of Albert's along with a hat very similar to Albert's best Fedora. The man was looking down with the hat pulled low over his face, obscuring his identity. Alicia, on the other hand, was clearly identified. She was looking straight at the camera, fully nude, showing a distinctive pattern of moles down her torso. The man's hands were protecting Alicia's naked breasts from view. The wedding ring on the man's hand would have made this a charming anniversary gift, but for the fact that it appeared to be Mr. Horowitz's ring, office, and his wife Jessica who received the picture as it was delivered to the Horowitz's home. Their daughter, thinking that her dad had prepared a surprise for her mom, directed the deliveryman straight up to her parents' bedroom. Albert had been shaving as his wife ripped the pink paper down the front to reveal the photograph.

The gift included a note from Gooding, saying that his hands were right at that moment on those particular Birmingham attributes, and that she wasn't at the doctor's office. Albert had grabbed the note as it fluttered to the floor next to the picture. He had called out to his wife as she left their bedroom to get her suitcase from the hall closet. Before she could stomp back in from the hall to tell him what he could do with himself, her husband ran out to her, told her to give him twenty-four hours to explain, then had hurried out of the house and started the car. By the time she reached the open door, her black Buick was speeding out of the cul-de-sac. He'd taken her car, knowing that his wife wouldn't leave him if she had to take his truck, and was gone.

When Albert reached FBI headquarters and his office with two security guys in tow, Alicia and the infamous photographer had disappeared. Not that Albert knew it at the time. Instead of heading directly into Albert's closed office, they stopped at the desk just inside the first door. There on the desk was Alicia Birmingham's computer as always, but its computer "tower" was in a different place. It was on the left side of the monitor when it usually sat on the right. Her calendar was open to Monday, February 12. On the top of the page was a note: *Dr. Gooding, 2:00 p.m.*

"Damn, she didn't even hide his name," Albert exclaimed.

Though the FBI task force had suspected Alicia was the leak, they had not yet removed her from the office in the hopes that they could follow her to Gooding. Albert clenched his fists. "I knew I shouldn't have let her take today off." Alicia had stated she had an afternoon appointment to have her annual physical. With her husband gone on a business trip to Orlando, he couldn't pick her up to take her across town, so she requested extra time off to get her car out of parking to get to her doctor. Afterward, she said she was going do some surprise Valentine's Day shopping for her husband and wouldn't be back.

The FBI security officers began taking notes as Albert prattled, "She was to leave the office at eight this morning. I wasn't planning on getting to the office until late, because I have a six o'clock meeting this evening. I came early, as soon as Jessica received the package. Y'all saw that she was already gone when we arrived." They checked the rest of the office. No one had seen Alicia leave early. The other staff verified she had been there early and had remarked that she was finishing inputting last week's payroll accounts into the computer, but no one had seen her since 7:30 a.m. or saw her leave. None of the agents had tailed her, because she knew them all, and made sure they knew that she knew they were following her.

After the staff was questioned, the picture became clear. No one had noticed her carrying a larger-than-usual case. No, no one had seen her go down to the subway entrance instead of going to her car. Because of the time frames, the budget office had to meet. They started the day early, with many shifts starting at 6:00 a.m. By 8:00 a.m. when Albert was getting the delivery and Alicia left, it was early break/breakfast peak and the "regular" start to the day. Everyone had been hurrying to go to a meeting or grab a bite to eat. No one would have noticed Alicia turn left instead of right; only the surveillance cameras noticed. Besides, who got back on the subway before closing time?

Also, it didn't help that any guys they interviewed didn't notice her hands or where she was headed. They were too busy looking at Alicia's fantastic assets. The morning surveillance tapes showed that Alicia came to work via the subway entrance, which would explain why they had been unable to find or track her car coming in or leaving the parking garage.

By the time her car was located after being impounded from where it had been abandoned and her frantic husband was located after he'd called the office looking for her, three more days had passed. Her husband had suspected Alicia was having an affair and they had planned to be apart for a few days. He'd truly been on a business trip, but in Atlanta, and when he'd arrived home for a Valentine's Day reunion with his wife, he found an empty house and three FBI agents waiting for him.

It took the computer technicians four days to track down just how much information had been taken from Alicia's terminal and what files had been accessed and, they inferred, copied. Although they had tightened the security measures on the task force's computers and limited

Alicia's access to the internal network and servers, she'd gotten past all their barriers. A lot of the physical memory on her computer was gone, and they had to go through the office's network to find out what else she had accessed along with what other hardware and information was missing. Technicians carried various pieces of computer equipment out the door as one of them quipped, "Just as it's damn hard to drive on the Internet without a search engine, it's damn hard to search out what's been posted there without a hard drive." It was only later, when one of these technicians noticed his own laptop begin to e-mail secure files to an unknown server through the FBI's network, that they found some of Gooding's malicious code.

***

Bill and Mitch had been called in as part of the internal investigation. As their offices had worked together often in their various assignments, both of them both knew Albert pretty well. Also, Albert and Stan had come through the FBI academy together and remained fast friends. In fact, Stan's work group, including Bill and Mitch, had been to Albert's Christmas party and were usually coddled by Jessica when they were over at their house. When they arrived at Albert's office, they feared the worst and got it. By now they had been tracking Gooding for weeks, but never expected that their investigation would take them back home. Both agents watched Albert pacing his office in a circular path around them. "Damn it! Why didn't we pull her out the minute we suspected her? Dammit. We knew she was working with Gooding. Why did I let them convince me to let them 'wait and see'? We should have just nabbed her then, grabbed her husband too, and threw both of them into the basement until Gooding popped up somewhere else."

Bill and Mitch prepared to wait for Al to calm down. Stan tasked them with getting him home, and while there, doing what they could to mollify Jessica as they secured Gooding's photograph. Stan suspected it had been doctored, but they couldn't continue the investigation until certain folks had calmed down. Mitch motioned to Bill and they both sat down as they kept watch on Albert. It was clear he was still running high.

Bill looked at Mitch. "Do you think that Stan or the IT guys were ever going to tell us that they thought Alicia was the breach?"

Mitch shook his head. "I don't know what to think. I know Stan was sure the leak was internal, but I had kept hoping it was external, a hacker, or something. It's too bad we lost the gamble. I bet with Gooding's help, Alicia got it all."

Bill smiled crookedly. "At least this puts the rest of our missions to go hunting bait on hold."

Mitch smiled back. "Yeah, at this rate, I figure we'll end up in a firefight with Gooding long before we can set up or trigger a trap for him."

Chapter Fourteen

Gooding entered the kitchen and poured a full glass of the nearest top-shelf alcohol at hand. The bottle happened to be some fine English brandy and pictured a man in a riding jacket and his hound, all finely dressed and labeled, so very proper and well, Western.

Gooding decided he disliked Western thought and ideals today, especially the idea of the richest landowner type knowing how best to run the world just because he owned enough of it. He didn't want to run the world, just his small part of it. Then again, the last time he was here, he'd dreamed of being that landowner and dealing with a misbehaving servant in a very old-fashioned way. However, seeing the street kids in Jamaica had really affected him this time. He somehow spotted the street kids, the ones without parents—the ones typified and immortalized by Dickens, in every place he went. These ones had darker skin than the ones he spotted in DC or London or Glasgow, but they were also barefoot and wearing ragged shorts in deference to the warm weather. It must be the time change affecting him. He'd only arrived back in Virginia this morning. He usually didn't ruminate over his life or feel so maudlin or sentimental. His head throbbed; maybe it was just the long ride overtiring him.

He'd seen the agents watching the house from down the road and sighed. "I'll have to use the tunnels then, but I have time." Gooding calculated it would take them fifteen minutes to get the clearance to secure a warrant and another ten or so to make it to the house. Having just left Jamaica after dropping off George and Manuel in their new home, Gooding had spent the ride back to Virginia thinking about the different societies he'd experienced. He continued these thoughts as he did a quick run-through to ensure his earlier preparations to "clean" the mansion remained intact.

George had been reluctant to participate in the Summer Plan ever since he'd found that the local girl he'd kept tucked away in Kingston was expecting their first child. The imminent birth of his first son was causing him to question some of his priorities. Gooding didn't mind that. If only his parents had let the birth of a child affect their lives. Gooding did not like his employees getting distracted or questioning what they were doing. It made folks inattentive and sloppy. So, Gooding always granted his employees and associates a "pass" option—if anyone wanted to opt out of participating in a job or contract for any reason, they received the option of passing on the job. No explanation necessary; no questions asked, but they could only opt out once every two years. Most of his people were made of sterner character. Options were rarely taken, and when they were it was a sign that someone was done with the life and ready to move on.

It had appeared that George was going to use his pass on the Summer Plan, until Gooding gave him the option of doing the Coast Guard/raft explosion. George and Manuel, having received the US citizenship as adults on Gooding's sponsorship, were finally able to enjoy the pros and cons of being an American. Surprisingly, Gooding was going to miss George. Of all of the people he'd met in his life so far, George was the closest to being a friend, and a true friend at that.

The brothers had fascinated Gooding from the first. He knew them very well, having spent most of his teen years with them. From this long association he'd also found that George, unlike his brother Manuel, had never quite forgiven that first Coast Guard ship for not rescuing them. Their father had been a revolutionary in Cuba and wanted nothing more for his sons than for them to make it to America if they couldn't live in a better Cuba. Their patriotism in the face of their rocky journey to citizenship amazed Gooding. They'd kept it strong within themselves even in the face of the imperfect nation they'd adopted. George was also truly a "George," not Jorgé, as his father had named him after George Washington; he'd never changed it to the Spanish pronunciation, and never would, his patriotism was so strong.

However, Manuel was more intellectual, like his father. He had understood why the Coast Guard couldn't pick them up that day and had let it go. George was always more emotional, like their mother. He understood the why, could even accept it in his mind, but in his heart he didn't understand how the ship could have left them to die like that.

The pink stucco house George and Maria lived in, and shared with Manuel when he was in Jamaica, was cool and inviting. Gooding, Mortimer, and the rest of the crew had been warmly welcomed by Maria and had rested in safety after their journey from Galveston. The freighter would take Gooding and the remaining crew to the North Sea once it left the Gulf Coast. Gooding figured they had two days to hide their trail from the US authorities. Keeping the freighter in Galveston would help with their cover, since it made it appear that the crew of that ship was *not* running away from anything.

Meanwhile, Maria was delighted to have George home for a while and was happily being domestic around them. Until she and Manuel had got in a heated argument about the religion of the baby. The argument started with Manuel asking Maria about the child's baptism. As a staunch Catholic, Manuel was debating on sneaking their mother out of Cuba to witness her first grandchild's initiation into the church. Maria, a polyglot mixture of Jamaica's culture, was against the baby being Catholic. The argument shifted between them to between George and Manuel when George saw his wife getting upset and began defending her position to his brother. But the two could reach no agreement. Mortimer and Gooding had taken the shouting as their cue to depart and signaled the crew. They left the brothers to their argument, which would probably never be resolved.

Gooding and Mortimer had ferried the crew back to the freighter on the Maryann. Manuel and George had done their part of the Summer Plan. Although he denied it, this would probably be George's last act as an employee of Gooding. He would probably retire, and this loss tempered Gooding's triumph over the explosion. As a first movement in the Summer Plan, the Coast Guard ship had been a masterful stroke. The US sailors were only doing their job, trying to help someone, but they paid the first price for their loyalty to their government. An ironic event, but well-tailored to the manifesto Gooding had whipped up.

Gooding sipped the brandy and thought again of his earlier wish to whip his ex-groundskeeper. From the poverty of the Caribbean islands, his thoughts turned to Haiti and Jamaica and about the Maroons that had helped populate those islands. He thought about Castro and Manuel and George's father and the life he desired for his sons. He thought about how his Scots ancestors forced their peasant-crofters to abandon Scotland for America.

He wondered if he should consider himself an icon, one who was "enlightened." Was he truly one who abhorred the idea of Western thought, and for that matter, Eastern thought as well? But even the question he asked himself was flawed. He disliked any grouping of abstract ideas into neat little bundles—bundles based on hypocritical societal beliefs and mores. What he felt earlier was the honest need to punish someone who'd earned it, which was to him, a just act. It was not an action felt by himself as a landowner. His reluctance to act on the thought had nothing to do with the idea that physical punishment was believed to have been required in the "slaveocracy" of the American past. Even if this house had once belonged to a wealthy plantation owner, Gooding did not identify with the master of the house. What others saw as violence in his life and work, was his way of ensuring proper conduct in his associates. However, he'd only been stopped from inflicting bodily harm on that gardener by the probable consequences he would suffer if anyone else saw him beat that man to death.

So where did this apparent fear of reprisal come from? He didn't care about what others thought; he disregarded the mythical "they" of the Western Civilization. Who cared what "they" thought, and why "they" said this or did that. So he'd decided that he would do something about the gardener after all. Especially since he knew he could escape any dragnet "they" set to try and catch him.

Spring had begun; it was time for the Summer Plan to usher in the call of an Indian summer that would create a craving for the cool autumn. Despite his rational restraint, he was still upset over the groundskeeper. Angrily he rampaged through his studio, thinking that if they were already damaged before the fire, then they would be totally destroyed when the house blew. "My Eastern friends have the right idea," he said to himself. He pictured the marketplaces of his youth where thieves lost their hands or worse when caught. His anger ignited, surprising him. It had been a long day. "Now, before I'm fully ready, I have to burn this place before I can get the art out."

His thoughts of justice warred with the ones his mother or his father, and especially his grandfather, attempted to instill in him as a young man. They, his family, always worried about what others would say, especially when the "they" changed. For his mother, it was her tight social group, while his father had to impress the powers that be, whether in Washington or London, and his grandfather had to please the people he felt responsible for, his employees and those descended from his clan's crofters, the little people as they were called in America. What should have been his serfs had he been Russian. His grandfather felt guilty that he was privileged and they were not.

Not Thornton Michael William Gooding. He had had to make his own way. Having earned his current prosperity, he had done justice to his aristocratic upbringing and would now help the people for his own reasons and edification. It may not be his birthright as the Scottish castle would be once his grandfather passed, but it would be as a choice, made almost as one of them, but not an equal. More like George Washington vs. the common soldiers under his command.

No more actions tonight; Gooding was tired. The brandy had not relaxed him as he hoped, but he felt a surge of energy he could put to good use. At once, his long trip, his grand Summer Plan, the possible lack of adequate help…it all got to him, suddenly increasing his furor. His rage tonight was a palpable thing, but without adequate outlet. However, Gooding was not ready to lose his temper. He may be maudlin and tired after the last few weeks, but he was still in control. Yes, the housekeeper's body made the upstairs reek, but fire would take care of that and make it harder for the FBI to figure out when she died. Mortimer had done well to ensure folks could swear they'd seen the housekeeper in the interim. With his friend, the new groundskeeper, Mortimer had secured the dogs and removed them to a safe location weeks ago.

Gooding grabbed his laptop and briefcase. He went past the French doors in the basement and walked down to and through his studio one last time. Taking the key from around his neck, he unlocked the heavy door nearly hidden at the back of the trashed studio. He was glad he'd trashed it. The debris would make it harder for the investigators to get to the workshop and tunnels. He'd miss this place after all. Usually he could staunch his rages through a stressful business transaction or a risky deal or with a female companion with specially chosen attributes. Tonight he had no outlet and no time to vent with the agents coming any minute and Mortimer down in Georgia to secure the last of his supplies. He had no way to cause a diversion other than the bomb he'd kept here for emergencies. He'd always meant to set this bomb, but was glad he'd waited until the best possible moment. If he couldn't trash the entire house to vent his anger, at least he could finally enjoy a satisfying explosion after months of planning.

He shoved the heavy oaken door to the workshop open. Gooding paused at the entrance, meditating on his options—wasting a precious minute of time. He stared at his stack of "not for sale" photographs, the ones he kept to help keep others quiet and well behaved along with the special ones that were banned in every public gallery "for adult content." He resigned them to their fate. He would find something else to occupy himself when he got settled again. He moved past the incriminating art and headed to the darkened end of the room. He reached up to a control panel hidden next to the nineteenth-century beam above his head and keyed in the override to the bomb code he'd called in the last time he left here.

A security camera video monitor on the wall showed the agents pulling into the drive. Gooding shut himself in behind the steel vault door that backed the oaken one. Calmly he set the timer on the last bomb that would come from this workshop. He would miss this house and its memories, but from now on the sea would be his home as he worked. He automatically triggered the final steel door to the tunnels and let the coolness of the stone corridor calm him.

He would continue the Summer Plan and attack the corrupt tip of the US government as planned. Those evil people who cared little for the ones they served—their great bureaucracy would fall. Gooding would accomplish its failure by attacking its foundations. The cogs and gears of the system, the soldiers and workers who made the great bureaucracy propagate. He would begin with the next little bombs. He'd set the timer for five minutes. His office computer upstairs began to tick with the countdown. The agents were probably breaking in the front door right now. Two minutes down and he was at the end of the tunnel. He hit the remote in his pocket that brought the ceiling down in the workroom, collapsing it. As he quickly navigated the path down to the waiting yacht at the secret marina, he thought, *The Coast Guard ship was just the opening pitch. Let the games begin!* The agents clearing the first few rooms saw the countdown ticking down on the computer but had no time to react before the blast.

Chapter Fifteen

The FBI team scaling the wreckage of the Chesapeake mansion eventually found the remains of some nasty bomb making equipment. It took time to separate the bomb components from all the other components and wreckage. Some pieces appeared similar to the bomb that had killed Gooding's ex-groundskeeper when it blew his van. At the time they had learned that Gooding had fired the groundskeeper, and figured the van bomb was payback for something. It wasn't until they'd found human remains in the wreckage that they saw how evil Gooding's plans had been. Gooding left no loose ends. It seemed clear that no one who'd ever worked for Gooding in DC would survive this latest round of bombs. The mansion body had been burned down to charred bones, but Stan hoped a forensic anthropologist could help determine cause of death. The dental records proved this body was Gooding's housekeeper, and some speculated he'd used the bomb to kill her, while others believed she'd been killed first and the bomb was set to destroy evidence of Gooding's bomb making.

Mitch and Bill stood outside the SWAT van serving as the mobile FBI HQ at Gooding's mansion site, relaying pertinent information to Stan. As they worked, Mitch remained worried about Albert's personal life. Albert had driven his wife's Buick to work again today. They now knew Gooding had doctored the picture but were told that Albert had not yet had time to explain this to Jessica. Bill remarked, "I sure hope they can get someone over to explain to Jessica soon. Albert can't keep up this pace with both work and the home front burning down around him."

Mitch nodded. But that was just one worry. Everyone was really worried about Albert's office documents, especially the travel vouchers. IT was still surveying the damage, but it was clear that Gooding had tapped into all the FBI personnel records, and Alicia had spent a great deal of time copying the travel records, which included names, dates, carriers, and places. No one knew how much damage Gooding could inflict using this information, but all reports hinted at horrific possibilities.

Albert—and thanks to some inner-office politics, Alicia—had been in the process of revamping the FBI's travel receipts. Some people high up were upset at agents flying first class when they were put on planes in emergency situations—as if they were senators. For the past fourteen months, all travel requests, even emergency ones, had to be cleared through Albert's office. Politics demanded that the flight requests be reasonable and not place an undue burden on taxpayers and Albert was nominated to be head bean counter.

The final expenditure studies had just been completed for the Fiscal Year report in October, which meant the resolution scheme was scheduled to start in March. This left Alicia's computer chock-full of all of the agent's travel plans for the last three years and the next nine months. Those busybodies higher up had also insisted the CIA be checked as well, so copies of much of the CIA's travel log data also were on Alicia's computer. From this data Gooding could have and probably had hacked his way into all the FBI/CIA personnel records. He had agents' real names, home addresses, and travel history.

Albert had sent an e-mail just the week before to tell Stan's office that the finalized travel vouchers for all of the FBI agents traveling in the next two months had just been input by Mrs. Birmingham on that very computer. The study was completed, so that they should have no problem getting their travel expenses approved for the "bait run." To everyone's horror, Gooding now probably knew that Mitch and Bill, along with every agent in their department, was flying to New York in two months to complete some mandatory training exercises slotted for a compound the Northern Woods of New York state. He also had hundreds of other FBI and CIA agents' travel requirements for sure.

Bill held up the phone so Mitch could hear Stan. "At least we had a bit of luck. I am so relieved that the higher ups balked at using civilians as bait, and we put off our plans to go get the bait candidates again. Gooding may think he knows who is flying out next month, but we know we're staying near to home." Leave it to Stan to see something positive in everything.

As the afternoon wore on, the agents returned to DC to check in with Stan and Albert. Mitch left Bill in the central office going over Alicia's desk and went in to talk to Albert. He found him rubbing his shiny, black scalp as the technicians showed him the holes in his computers where the hard drives used to be. Albert was muttering quietly, "Shit, shit, shit, damn," over and over while his free hand twisted the gold band on his finger continuously. Word in the grape vine said that if Albert didn't fix the mess by two hours ago, his head would be first on the block. Mitch knew that Albert didn't care about his job or reputation as much as he worried about the agents he'd jeopardized; he always referred to all of the agents as "kids." Mitch also knew that although the agents' safety was his first concern, Albert would soon be really concerned about his wife. Jessica's patience only lasted a day or two when her car was gone. Thankfully, Jonesey had been sent to the house to explain to Jessica how good Gooding was at altering photographs. He hoped that Jessica wasn't too angry by now; it didn't look like the bigwigs were going to let Albert go home tonight.

"Thirty years. I've been with the Agency thirty shittin' years. I knew better. I know better to trust any damn secretary, especially a looker," Albert vented.

Mitch shooed the technicians out and closed the office door. "Al, tell me you have an idea of what they got.

84

We've got to know how bad it is." For the first time in years, Mitch was rattled. He needed to hear it firsthand from Albert. Maybe what Bill and Stan had told him was exaggerated. He knew that was a false hope, but Mitch persisted. Talking it out would help Al.

"Mitch, I know the IT guys are saying they can't be sure how much stuff had been taken, but a few minutes ago, Randy came in real hush-hush. You know the computer guy, Randy, the Agency's head computer geek? Well, Randy says that all the files on the network, even the secure ones, have been accessed without authorization, and most have been copied and sent out. I'm betting Gooding got it all."

"Like I thought. Holy Hell." Mitch sat down with a whoosh as his head hit his hands and his elbows hit his knees. For the first time, the enormity of this really bad day hit him. He breathed for a while, then raised his head to say, "Has Gooding made any demands yet?"

Just then, Bill entered and quietly closed the door. "Did Randy get you guys?" At the affirmative nods, Bill too sat, seeming just as heavily overwhelmed by the threat facing them. Stan came in a few minutes later. No demands from Gooding, nothing; the trail was not only cold, but gone.

Six days later they found a lead. This chilly but sunny day had dawned unlike most February days. The office workers of DC were just arriving at work when the news hit the FBI office where Mitch and Stan were having coffee. Gooding had sent the US both a card and a late gift for Valentine's Day. He'd even been solicitous enough to make copies for his favorite people.

At 6:01 a.m. EST that morning, Mr. Birmingham, who had just been released from FBI custody, while Alicia was still wanted for questioning, was blown up along with the lovely, nineteenth-century home that he and his wife had bought only last year.

The police knew the exact time of death because he was on the phone with a 911 operator when the bomb blew. Having been awoken by a Trans-Atlantic phone call at 5:55 a.m., he had called 911 in hopes that the bomb squad could help. It was too late by then. Alicia had planned a special Valentine for him that he'd ruined by getting arrested and not getting into his house. Gooding made it up six days later with a phone call and a picture with the card he'd sent with the bomb. Out in the mailbox in front of the burned-out foundation that had been the Birmingham residence, a small FedEx box held a snapshot of Gooding and Alicia holding hands and smiling on a bridge in what appeared to be Amsterdam. Gooding was holding up the February 12 edition of the New York Times for reference.

While the agents were photographing the picture, the envelope started beeping and a small smoke bomb went off, burning everyone's eyes within twenty feet. No one knew what agent he'd used, but when the smoke cleared, the photograph had disintegrated, while the film in the FBI cameras was eaten up by some acidic quality of the gas. However, the phone guys were luckily able to track the phone call to Gooding's possible location in Iceland.

Chapter Sixteen

David S. Jones, aka Jonesey, was a native Idahoan from Boise who had been lucky enough to snag a permanent assignment out of the FBI Denver office. The lucky part wasn't the location itself since Denver was still a long plane ride from DC. Nor was it the work; he dealt with internal terrorists and nut cases living in the woods. The luckiness was for Jonesey as a person. He'd been born out West. He loved it. He never could get comfortable in DC. There were no mountains. You couldn't see the lay of the land for the trees. The whole time he'd trained back East, he'd been wishing he was in the West.

When his boss Stan at the FBI headquarters had asked him where the specialists in "forest" warfare should be headquartered, Jonesey had told him out West somewhere. They'd gone over possible locations like Portland, Oregon and Boise, Idaho. Denver was way down on the list because it was too crowded—too large a population center. But when they compared all the logistics, Denver became the logical choice. Because it was on the Washington DC side of the Rocky Mountains, but still a Western city, it was more easily accessible to more of the country, and had a more cosmopolitan atmosphere than other Rocky Mountain cities. Once Jonesey had outlined what the FBI office would need in order to watch the deep-woods factions on the West who threatened the United States, Denver was chosen to be the base for those operations. Stan then assigned Jonesey to be the head of "tree hugger" operations there. Having been a counselor at a Boy Scouts of America camp for most of his teens, and having always thrilled at the adventure of surviving anywhere with little supplies or support, Jonesey had spent most of his summers since acting like a mountain man, and as such was well skilled in outdoor survival.

He had been born in Eastern Idaho, so he was well versed with the Western ideals of individualism and grew up skeptical about Washington's ability to listen to and take care of the smaller-populated and under-represented Western states. Duly, he was grateful to escape the East forever and enjoyed his post in Denver, even if he was rarely in the office.

Jonesey was no stranger to grass-roots movements trying to get Washington's attention. Every four years, he watched his father follow the presidential election, especially, on CNN and C-SPAN. He listened to his father and grandfather's political conversations and heard them escalate as they would rail about how none of those high-and-mighty candidates would set foot in Idaho. During election years these conversations usually ended in family brawls.

Jonesey also grew up around plenty of patriots who felt under represented and forgotten by their nation's leaders. His grandfather's brother was one of the most bitter. In the '50s, his uncle and his grandfather had gone to Russia with a group of Idahoan farmers to meet with some heads of the Russian Agriculture department to talk farming, especially potatoes.

The trip was exciting for his great-uncle and grandfather, who'd been able to talk dirt with Russian farmers just like themselves. They'd made friends both with some of the movers and shakers in the US agricultural lobby, as well as with their Russian counterparts. They helped shape US policy at that time. Since then, his great-uncle felt disenfranchised. When he would come and visit his brother, the two old men would argue for hours about how to fix the USA. The biggest bone of contention between them was his great-uncle's belief that the strength of the agricultural lobby had slipped. The original family farm was still making money and luckily still in Jones family hands, but they'd all watched prices fall over the past few years while costs continued to rise.

Jonesey knew that his family wasn't the only unhappy family in the United States. All sorts of special interest groups felt shafted, but Jonesey identified the most with the Western ideals of his family. He also hated the fact that the Western states, while having more land, just didn't have enough people or large enough populations to get their voices heard.

After majoring in political science in college, intending to go into politics to make a stand for his kind of life, Jonesey had left the university feeling as if he could make a difference. He became disgusted and disenchanted after visiting Washington DC and trying his hand as a congressional aide.

Jonesey didn't last very long in the political world. After his first session as an aide, he left Washington DC and spent two months in an old family cabin high in the mountains near the Frank Church River of No Return Wilderness, living with only the barest of necessities. He emerged jaded, but willing to try again. At twenty-four, the older edge of the FBI's age limit for applicants, David Jones joined the FBI.

He remained in top physical condition while in DC and passed the FBI physicals with ease, graduating near the top of his class at the Academy. Soon his special skills and understanding of US Western life made him a specialist in cases involving militant groups in the West. Only ATF officers worrying about gun-running knew more about how to handle some of the groups than Jonesey.

Years before, he'd been assigned to Stan's team to give some specialized training to his crew. He met Mitch and Bill and they formed a tight kinship. Thereafter, he could be found with Mitch and Bill whenever their respective teams were in the same area. Jonesey was assigned as team leader for his task force. Therefore, he was denied the opportunity to have a partner, and sometimes he missed collaborating with someone, so he often caught up to Mitch and/or Bill when he needed to discuss a tricky issue.

His first big assignment was watching a white supremacist group outside of Coer D'Alene, Idaho. Afterward Jonesey had earned some extra time off. He used it to spend Christmas with his family in Rexburg, Idaho. After the Christmas Day dinner, his mom called him into the kitchen and casually remarked, "David, I saw Amy Coolidge at the grocery store a couple of days ago. She's graduated from the Art Institute in Chicago and is staying here for a few months before she moves out to San Francisco. She asked about you." Mrs. Jones had looked at her oldest, and only still-single son, with the worry of a mother whose son works for the FBI and who'd been known to escape to the middle of nowhere for months.

He had black circles under his eyes and looked ragged and shaggy. He hadn't shaved for a month or more. David, well aware of where he stood on the "get me some grandkids *now*" list his mother had, felt annoyance creep through him. As if it wasn't enough that he had to babysit a bunch of bored, out of work rednecks playing KKK games with their guns in the forest, his mom would set up a date for him during his only week off. He knew he should have headed out to the canyon after he'd dropped off the Christmas gifts.

"What did you tell Amy, Mom?" Jonesey asked his mother, fearing that he already knew the answer.

"I just told her you that you'd be here this week and that she should come over tonight for pie," his mother answered innocently, shrugging as she turned to face him from doing the dishes. "You two were such an item in high school, and since you're both still single, I figured you could catch up some." Knowing that he was too respectful to argue with her, Mrs. Jones shared a meaningful look with him, dried her hands, and left her son to steam in the kitchen.

As plotted by their parents, he and Amy had got back together. After more than ten years, neither one of them were the kids they'd been at eighteen. Their adult selves got along much better and soon it was clear that they could be good together. Jonesey was still the only guy in their neighborhood who could talk about art intelligently, and Amy was independent enough to be fine holding down the home fort while Jonesey was up in the mountains for weeks.

They married and Jonesey took his bride back to DC after the wedding to live while he worked at FBI headquarters for a while as he closed some of his old case files. He was thinking that he'd served his best time in the field, not at a desk. Neither he or Amy were happy in DC. So when Stan asked him to go back to Denver, this time in another area as a special agent team leader, Jonesey jumped at the chance. He and Amy moved back West with their three little girls. This post would allow him a great geographic freedom. His assigned area was the entire Intermountain West, from Mexico to Montana. He just reported to Denver occasionally, and would work from whatever office he was nearest to.

From there Jonesey took care of assignments all over the Western United States. Until recently, he'd been specializing on watching "internal terrorists"—those US citizens who were not so happy with the United States—like the Oklahoma City Bomber and worse, in various groups and singly throughout the West. In places like Montana, Western Wyoming, Northern and Central Idaho, there were plenty of people angry at the status quo in the United States. Mitch and Bill had seen him haunted by the Oklahoma City bombing and were among those who spent time praying that Jonesey wouldn't have to experience another scene like that.

This winter he'd spent months in DC, designing and updating the training courses for the new recruits assigned to tackle "backwoods USA" groups. He shuddered any time he thought about the deep-woods assignments where he'd worked with ATF agents in the pine forests outside Coeur D'Alene, Idaho. He was still grateful he'd made it out of the last standoff alive; and to think that it was started when some guy abandoned his teenage kids in their cabin in the woods. He still thought about their terrorized faces when they'd finally let the officers into the house. The situation had escalated when one trigger-happy rookie had fired at the cabin, causing the fourteen-year-old sister to blow his arm off with a rifle. That had been last summer. He was tired of people, especially his fellow FBI agents, just winging it when they were out in the field. He'd been vocal enough that Stan had got wind of his attitude and commandeered his presence at headquarters to "fix the training, then, dammit."

That's how Jonesey had ended up in DC at the time of the New York exposition. Although Stan and Albert were relieved, Jonesey himself was not pleased that he was already at hand when Stan needed someone with the background to check out the remains of Gooding's New York exhibition. He hated art. He was one of their few agents who'd not been jeopardized by the computer hijacking, since he'd been on sabbatical for a few weeks, and had been so deep undercover for the last summer, that there had been no paper trail for his last targets to sniff out. Amy had received his payroll in her maiden name. Luckily he was left out of Stan's plan to use the bait search (when it resumed) to give all the agents a break from the tension. Stan confided to Jonesey, "I want you to be out West to support any of those teams that hit a snag. Otherwise, I want everyone to get out of DC for a few days and use the travel to get some perspective." Jonesey knew what Stan meant. Constant worry over an investigation burned folks out. Everyone needed time to rest, try to relax, and enjoy the things that made life worth living.

Chapter Seventeen

Mitch and Bill were zipping west down I-80. Bill had said he hated crossing Texas, so they had chosen a more northern route to get from DC to Utah. They would have to climb the Rockies, and being March, late winter storms were a worry. Albert gave them his navy Chevrolet Suburban for the trip. After all, there was no way Albert would be let out of the director's sight for the duration of this mission, or the next six months at least. So he wouldn't need his SUV for those long weekend fishing trips he adored. Besides, as it was a personal vehicle, it was not listed in the FBI's databases. The computer guys were still finding more data that was lost in the information breach.

When the FBI travel funds were finally approved, including those for the bait search, all of the agents were informed that they would have to drive their own vehicles for now, especially to the retreat in New York, since there was not time to find a backup plan for the transportation to the retreat. Stan really liked the idea; it made for a random schedule that should stymie Gooding's tracking methods and protect the agents. They would be compensated for their mileage, etc., but Albert wasn't sure how quickly. Some of the agents were in a pickle trying to get to work with unexpected vehicle issues.

For instance, a vehicle was one thing Mitch lacked. He had left his old truck with his grandfather in Montana and mostly used public transportation since he'd moved to DC. Usually he and Bill had an agency vehicle for most of their work travels. Bill did have a car, but the idea of driving his old, rear-wheel-drive Camaro in the snow, especially Rocky Mountain winter snow, made Mitch and Bill both weak in the knees. Thankfully, Albert offered to let them take his Suburban. As Albert's personal fishing vehicle, it didn't have government tags, had four-wheel drive, and it wasn't Bill's '82 Camaro or a public bus. Just the idea of riding in the Camaro for three thousand miles made Mitch's posterior ache. Around the office, the rusted-out yellow Camaro was also a big joke. All the ATF guys liked to tease Bill by asking him if he was going undercover as a drug dealer, then they'd laugh and say that "good" pimps and dealers drive 'Vettes if they go for Chevys, or Escalades if they're into Caddys. Bill just ignored them; he'd gotten the car as a teenager and rebuilt the engine and transmission himself. He just wasn't any good at bodywork and the interior clearly showed its twenty years of hard use.

Mitch, having grown up on a cattle ranch, a long way out of the nearest town, appreciated that Albert's Suburban had GM's Vortech 350 cubic engine, so it could really go fast if it wasn't towing a boat and still be able to pass a gas station. Ironically, Bill's Camaro had a big 350 cubic engine too, which made it a real screamer. A clearly disappointed Bill (he was very vocal about the fact that he hated doing the driving with Mitch, who loved to give driving advice whenever he was a passenger) accepted the keys to the Suburban from Albert as Mitch razzed him. "At least with you driving that big truck we'll be able to see the trees on the ride out instead of a green or brown blur we see when you take your Z28 out, you speed demon." Bill elbowed Mitch in response as they headed down to the parking garage.

A few minutes later, they stopped by Bill's condo to get his gear, then proceeded to Mitch's apartment for his. An hour later, the two were headed west.

It had been a long, three-day journey. Mitch and Bill had taken turns driving and planning as they made the trip. Finally, they had reached the Rocky Mountains and had just passed Cheyenne, Wyoming, aiming for I-84 and Evanston, the last big town on their way to Ogden, Utah.

Mitch adjusted the heater and thought about the last two weeks. Bill's expression had been priceless when they had been introduced to the Treasury officers from the IRS' national headquarters last week. The identities of most of the available government agents in the FBI and CIA needed for this mission against Gooding had been compromised; therefore, the security task force needed a non-agent—but still someone who acted like, talked like, was trained like, and capable like an agent—to do the job. Homer had been only half serious when he'd suggested that *any* federal worker could do it. Bill and Mitch's first assignment had been to try to find a DC mole who could get close enough to Gooding so the government could get evidence on him, enough to put him away. After days of searching, they found no one closer than a CIA operative in Israel. Then they'd found that more computers had been sabotaged than originally estimated.

The CIA's personnel office/time card office's computers, including some servers, had flat disappeared. This meant that the CIA's people were in worse shape than FBI personnel, because everybody paid through the CIA was affected by the breach. Their entire payroll information was gone or missing and potentially in "bad" hands.

At this news, Homer called a brainstorming session with all the crew to come up with some serious options. He and Bill had got talking about the Secret Service. They had the firepower and the training, and didn't have a military mindset. Bill had mentioned that Congress was really serious about its money, because the Secret Service was part of the Treasury Department.

"Holy shit," Bill had said. Bill also had a buddy that was a special officer under the Treasury Dept. He had trained at the same place in Georgia where they trained Secret Service personnel, but he was a Treasury officer. His job was connected with the IRS. He used to joke that he was just a collection agent with a badge and a gun.

However, Treasury officers also were the watchdogs of IRS personnel themselves. Bill had to explain to Homer about how Treasury officers watched IRS personnel. Homer had been curious about why that required a gun.

Mitch answered, "Have you ever opened the IRS' mail?"

"No," Homer replied.

"Well, what would you be tempted to do if you opened some envelope that only contained a check for a hundred grand and a note listing somebody's Social Security number?" Mitch smiled and continued, "Congress is real careful with their money. Of course they set watch dogs over it. The IRS is *very* careful and ensures they have the most dependable personnel."

That conversation had faded from memory until the CIA mess was discovered. All the department heads agreed that no active, stealthy agent from *any* agency could be used to fight Gooding face to face. Besides, Gooding had also stolen the CIA pictures of all their agents from those personnel files. The damage report worsened every day when yet another computer's data or another hard drive would turn up missing.

Mitch remembered the Treasury officers the night Homer had met with his FBI crew. Later, after the meeting, Homer had said, "Now, here is an untapped outlet for serious government workers." Apparently, his niece had been working for the IRS service center in Philadelphia for years, and she had talked about the close scrutiny the IRS was under ever since the Roth hearings in 1998. IRS workers were picked to be careful with private, personal information, and show great integrity when working with tax dollars. Homer said that his niece was now required to attend special training meetings where IRS workers were shown the consequences for stealing or taking advantage of personal information. Federal jail time, fines, mandatory replacement, and the knowledge that whoever they trespass against could sue them were effective deterrents to unlawful dealing. Homer also said that the IRS agents who padlocked people's houses were much, much stricter when it came to IRS employees. His niece had been nearly written-up for simply requesting an extension to file her personal taxes. To Mitch's way of thinking, strictness like that must lead to basically honest employees. Homer agreed, and had wasted no time in announcing, "That's it! We'll find an IRS agent!"

He got on the horn, and two days later met with some lovely people from the Treasury Department. The commissioner, the head of the IRS, had contacted all of the directors of all ten of the IRS service centers in the nation, and struck gold. Not only did many of the centers have employees that were qualified for the task, but some had employees actually traveling to Great Britain this summer. The latest intelligence showed that Gooding was going back to the United Kingdom now that the US agencies were earnestly looking for him. His exposition was slotted for showings across England and Scotland, and the British authorities reported that Gooding had not canceled his UK tour.

Mitch and Bill had sat in on several meetings where Stan and Homer had finalized the list of mole or bait candidates. They added the IRS personnel to the pre-existing list, which was ordered by geographic area and then age. The task force support staff released steam by organizing a pool on the winning mole. Stan had seen the stats, and though folks were worried that he'd disapprove, he just laughed. Currently the smart money was split between a New York socialite who moonlighted in the national gallery and a South Carolina Navy brat who worked summers at a forest service reserve.

The FBI was playing catch up. Gooding had disappeared from the US, but was keeping up with his European art tour. The FBI hoped to quietly follow

Gooding on this tour. The plan called for the mole to frequent each affected gallery and strive to be near Gooding at all times. That way, the government could have eyes in the gallery to watch Gooding, and hopefully allow them to catch him. If Gooding became attracted to the mole and sought her out, even better.

Gooding was scheduled to chair a photography symposium in Edinburgh at the end of June. He had been traveling back and forth to England and Scotland for the past eight months in preparation. Optimists hoped in addition to throw the mole and Gooding together during various social events happening at the same time. The task force had to tread carefully and work with the countries they entered as they went. The CIA was most helpful with the international issues. Before the FBI information breach, a CIA agent in London had spotted Gooding acting suspicious, and reported that Gooding had been shipping huge crates to an unknown location in Western Scotland. Before the agent could finalize his report, his plane crashed into the North Sea off of Aberdeen in January in a "mysterious accident."

The only lead was the gallery. Mitch smiled at the irony of this plan. Stan had complained bitterly over the fact that even though the US had initially approached the British asking them to treat Gooding as a criminal and help them catch him, the UK refused. The Brits did concede that they would not interfere if the US could capture Gooding—after all, he was no longer *just* a British citizen. Then the UK gallery and its affiliates refused to drop the exhibit, officially stating that they believed a man was innocent until proven guilty. Homer and Stan were vocal in their belief that any publicity generated by using the media to pursue Gooding would only benefit the museums by boosting their visitation. So the task force had no choice but to pursue a covert operation. They worried over the body count. No one wanted to involve any more innocent bystanders than was strictly necessary, and Gooding had shown little reluctance for killing people who got in his way.

There was strong motivation to catch Gooding as soon as possible. Every analysis of Gooding's Americana art, like that of his New York show, pointed to something big for July 4. Mitch was horrified at the idea that Gooding was planning his biggest explosion for July 4 in DC. At that busy time, keeping the capitol city secure would be an organizational and security nightmare. Stan was working the team as hard as he could, but there was a feeling of impotence. For now they were trying to talk to the New Orleans Police Department to get tips on how that organization handled crowd-control during Mardi Gras, but had hit a dead end when they couldn't disclose why they wanted the information. While Mitch and the rest of the team, under Stan's careful direction, tried to find a way to get Gooding, he kept killing CIA officers and FBI agents in between bombings on US military installations, and more galleries continued the trend of refusing to cancel Gooding's shows.

They could only watch as Gooding spent the bulk of his known time in one of the three main galleries he preferred in Europe. The surveillance teams reported they also believed Gooding visited many of his favorite places in disguise since he had fallen off their radar.

The US was desperate to catch him before July. To do that, the heads of the agencies decided that somebody needed to hang around the gallery and be looking for Gooding. The CIA and British group monitoring the galleries would report that Gooding would just "pop up" seemingly from nowhere, and disappear as readily. Still, no more agents could get to the UK easily. Gooding had proven that he could pick off anyone already there—or trying to get there—with fatal results. They could not afford any more casualties. FBI and CIA agents were already in place in many galleries, setting up a cover that could last for weeks so they could be on the lookout for Gooding. More than once a high-ranking official would remark, "If only those FBI agents had grabbed him on Capitol Hill that day," and sigh.

Gooding capitalized on the hysteria and warned the agents to "be careful" in various ways. He enjoyed letting them know he knew they were after him in earnest, but that he wasn't going to make it easy, and that he'd continue keeping his big profile now and then. The profilers warned everyone within hearing that the signs showed Gooding was enjoying himself and would consider any agent near him an adversary or worse, a target.

On March 1, Gooding had left an off-assignment FBI agent's left hand at the US Embassy in London, with a map taped to his wrist. The agent's body and that of his Irish girlfriend were found later at an outlying farm west of London. Their bodies were thrown in a ditch on a path just beyond the red-and-white tape that kept visitors from entering and bringing "mad cow" germs back on their shoes.

Gooding had left a photographic print of a picture he'd taken of the murdered agent while on assignment two weeks before, on the agent's chest. A smuggler had been shot through the heart in an earlier raid, and the photo was nailed to the same spot on the agent's chest. A note saying, *I don't always need a computer,* was nailed to the girlfriend's forehead. Ironically, Gooding was spotted on the French Riviera the next day.

All normal operations were appropriately canceled as emergency protocols were created and followed. Alicia had been spotted in London and, later that day, the reporting CIA field officer's car was blown up. British authorities were asked to do the remaining reconnaissance while the CIA/FBI leaders determined how to continue.

The initial mole list was scrapped. Things were getting too dicey. The profilers refined the criteria for the mole. Through another massive personnel search, other federal agencies, even including the IRS at Homer's special request, had tracked down all of the US government employees going to Britain in June and July, and found a few hopeful subjects. An Air Force secretary from Atlanta was taking her family to see Princess Diana's grave and memorial from June 15 through July 6. In Newark, New Jersey a retired Army surgeon and his wife were taking their second honeymoon in Aberdeen where she was born. An Oakland, California Social Security accountant was going to Ireland to visit his grandmother. The list went on and on. Then two possible candidates were found at the last minute. First, an ex-Army officer from Phoenix who'd served in 'Nam with Homer's brother, called Homer to tell him that he and his wife were planning a European tour on June 15 through August 2, starting in London. Homer moved his friend to the top of a tiny pile. An ex-sniper would be an excellent choice for the mole. Especially as this sniper was a grandpa and looked old, but was still in fine physical shape. Then a fax came in from the IRS commissioner. He'd heard from the IRS director in Utah. An employee from the Ogden, Utah IRS service center had requested a month-long leave of absence to stay in England and Scotland for college as part of a studying abroad trip.

Mitch and Bill would still get their trip out West, but most of the other task force agents were moved to follow Gooding.

***

Homer fiddled with the stack of files on his desk. He and Stan had pored over the profilers' lists of qualities the mole should have. Ideally they needed a seasoned agent for the job, but Gooding had proven again and again that he could ferret out an FBI or CIA agent easily, so they had seriously considered using a greenhorn—a female, if possible. The profilers believed that if they could find the right female they'd have a better chance of getting to Gooding. He had a habit of changing his ladies every few months and even used some of them in his schemes. They just had to find the right mix of attributes. Alluring, but intelligent. They could use a femme fatale, but every so often, a naïve girl would grab Gooding's attention.

He enjoyed females of all types and ages. From all reports, he hadn't gone after an "innocent" girl in a while. Homer could picture his best profiler's words as he explained their directive about Gooding: "He seems to have a need to redeem himself by associating with some of these younger women. At times it seems he is looking for some ideal, some woman who's the exact opposite of his mother." Homer felt chilled thinking about it. He hated to see even his most experienced agents in such a dangerous position, and here they were contemplating using a civilian, not even a recruit, to be the bait for such a cold-blooded killer.

This single file disturbed him. Stan didn't like the idea either, but the profilers picked her as number one. Homer's hands found the faxed image of the college student from Utah; the Utah DMV sent her driver's license picture. She was an art major nearly ready to graduate, but finishing her bachelor's degree coursework by earning a minor in English at a local state university. Her school's English Department was going on a "MacBeth" tour studying Shakespeare, including English and Scottish history and she would be in the UK from June 1 through July 3.

She hadn't been on the first candidate list, because the IRS commissioner had not been aware of her itinerary. In addition, when the commissioner had first answered Homer's request, he had not considered any female employees due to a communication problem. *I'll be glad when our network is secure again and I can use the normal, sensitive channels to communicate,* Homer thought. He'd had other agencies disbelieve the request when it was sent in abnormal ways. He'd instructed Stan to e-mail the IRS commissioner personally in an unsecured e-mail in an effort to bypass Gooding's spy software in the FBI and CIA systems. Because the two were friends, the commissioner had called Stan to make sure he'd correctly interpreted the slightly coded request and finally forwarded a list of female possibilities.

Homer thought about the communication error. The commissioner figured they would need a male to be an FBI agent. He'd told Stan he'd just made an automatic decision without knowing all the facts. Homer thought of his own years of training that enabled him to think past his first snap judgments, but also taught him how to make balanced decisions quickly. He thought of the other reason his profilers wanted a female mole. Gooding was a renowned male-chauvinist. He would probably underestimate a female mole. But that didn't mean Homer had to like the idea of sacrificing some girl to capture a monster. *No wonder the princess is always saved by the knight before the dragon can eat her,* Homer mused, thinking about the psyche of the culture that had shaped both he and Gooding.

The student's itinerary shocked Homer; unlike the other candidates, this college trip had been scheduled for the exact same weeks as the photography symposium highlighting Gooding's latest works, and would be visiting many of the same cities. She seemed to meet the ideal qualifications that their research had required. Ideally, they needed a youngish woman to captivate Gooding and keep him on the radar. Until this file, Homer had been trying to figure out how they could groom a twenty-two-year-old army surgeon candidate into a vulnerable target for Gooding's affection. They were having trouble. He had hoped that she would have not yet acquired the manner of an Army sergeant, but had been disappointed to find her to be the daughter of a general with a brusque manner that spoke volumes about her capabilities. Her best qualification so far was the fact that her daddy had raised her with weapons from a tot. She had the necessary firepower and skills to protect herself in a volatile situation. Most of the other candidates interviewed so far were current or ex-military and acted too "military" for the task force's purposes.

This Utah student gave Homer some hope. He wondered what "art" she majored in. He scanned the dossier and saw no details about her emphasis. "I wonder if this is a sign?" he considered. "No one else is going at exactly the time we need them to. We should have the travel issue solved by then, but just in case, it would be nice to have a plausible cover for our mole."

He continued mulling over this new development. It was probably too much to ask for a photography major who knew her way around a 9mm pistol. However, they were running out of time and needed to pick someone. Stan had started training a couple of the other candidates anyway, just in case. They needed someone who would be innocuous and who could understandably linger in any museums. And, until they figured out the travel problem, the person had to have an already planned trip across the Atlantic and appear to have no government involvement, while having an understanding of the situation. Retirees, students, agents' family members; any of these should work out fine as his mole if they could find the right qualities.

Homer shuffled the file until he found the other picture of the student. It was smaller, but more recent, taken from her IRS identity badge. He compared her face with the head shot of the Army surgeon. Thankfully both girls were lookers, but he'd have to meet them to make the final decision. He'd much rather have the surgeon on the job. Gooding might sniff her military tendencies, but she could probably take him down in a clench.

Setting both files aside, Homer stood up from his desk. Staring out his office window, he could see the gray skies of this wintry day as he prayed for a miracle or two.

He also liked the idea of using a student for their mole, especially a female student. Profiling had shown that Gooding had a real weakness for pretty girls if they were intelligent and vulnerable in certain ways. He just wished he could turn one of his die-hard FBI agents into an alluring student. A male mole could work, but he'd have to be attractive to Gooding as a potential accomplice or protégé.

Homer finally felt a breath of hope after weeks of worry. Due to the limited number of possible candidates, and to limit suspicion, the final search for moles involved only ten agents in five sets who were dispatched across the country to interview the candidates. They would bring likely candidates back to DC for preparation and send the finalists to Atlanta for training at the Secret Service compound. So far they had about seventy-five candidates in total on the list, with only twelve females in the group. Only eight of those women fit the profile. Currently, the student was the single female who met the most criteria for their mole. He would keep Carl and Reva working with the Army surgeon. There was still hope for her if she wasn't too hardened. Also, Reva was their best female fighter and had hit it off with the surgeon. He had watched the two spar and take down the male FBI agents in practice. Mitch and Bill were setting off to Utah to track down the student who, hopefully—with God's grace—could be trained to spar with a killer and not die in the process. He wished them luck.

Chapter Eighteen

Mitch and Bill had been on the road for three days straight now. Mitch was grateful to leave his paperwork and heavy caseloads behind, but driving across country really wore him out. Bill too, was a bit grumpy after being stuck in a car for the better part of the last two days.

They had interviewed about fifteen people so far on their way. A day here or there or a few hours would be spent finding the address and talking to the folks who may or may not be good candidates to help them capture Gooding. After Memphis and St. Louis, they had detoured down to Texas—something Bill clearly hadn't been thrilled about—and paused in Amarillo to interview a retired postal worker grandma who was going to Glasgow in July and had ended up staying at her house for dinner and stayed the night. That had been their last home-cooked meal in days. However, that nice lady had a heart condition, which exempted her from the list. And, although she would be unnoticed watching Gooding in the museum, she would not be able to capture his interest and keep him where they could find him.

They beat a blizzard into Evanston and had the luck of being one of the last vehicles allowed on the road to Evanston before the freeway closed. Across Wyoming, when Bill had pointed out the snow gates on the roads, Mitch had explained how they were used to close down the freeway when the nearest town was miles away. Bill said that Western Wyoming had to be okay. After all, it had Yellowstone and Jackson Hole, but he added that these snowy expanses of nothing you had to pass through on the way were hard for him to take.

"You can tell you grew up down south, Bill," Mitch said as they pulled into the last motel with a vacancy sign. Bill had about died when they had seen the first snowpack on the freeway. He'd remarked, "I have never seen freeway traffic go thirty miles an hour on the freeway." He expressed shock by weather that would have shut down DC or his hometown in Georgia. He complained bitterly about how the vehicles had to push their way through deep snow drifts caused by what Mitch called ground blizzards when not sliding on the icy snowpack.

Bill had really hated driving past Cheyenne in a blizzard and had spent the last couple of hours watching the semis pass the 'Burb like it was standing still. Mitch had watched him grip the armrests so tightly each time that his knuckles turned white. As the latest tractor-trailer sped by, Bill breathed a sigh of relief. "I'll sure be glad when we've got the mole chosen and off to training in Atlanta, so we can head south to Phoenix to meet Jonesey and get through the preliminary meetings. I need eighty degree weather, man." He shivered and looked horrified as another semi passed them. "I don't understand the need to go that fast in the snow to keep from getting squished by a big rig."

Mitch just shook his head. "Bill, look at all those wheels. Now imagine how much weight is in those trailers. Then look at the chains on the tires. Those trucks have massive weight on good traction, like spikes on mountain climbers' boots," Mitch had patiently explained in another attempt to calm Bill. However, at that moment, the tires hit an icy patch of snow. Mitch concentrated for a moment on controlling the skid and was able to pull out of it by "driving into it." Once the Suburban was back in control, he glanced at Bill and shook his head. "Geez, Bill, didn't you take any physics classes?"

Bill threw Mitch a dirty look in answer and pertly mocked, "Excuse you, smart ass, but if you say 'surface area' or discuss Newton's laws with me one more time, I'll deck you." After a moment Bill took a deep breath and looked slightly calmer. Mitch laughed, then held his silence as they continued on to Utah.

They started to slide again. Mitch engaged the 4x4 lever, and the subtle tail shifting of the back tires was steadied instantly. "I hope Albert's four-wheel drive is in good shape. Going seventy miles an hour in four-High can be hard on an improperly maintained transfer case," he said.

Bill had turned green and sounded a little panicked as he asked, "Mitch, are you going seventy in this storm?"

Mitch only smiled meanly as Bill shut his eyes. That had been ten hours ago. He was glad for the 'Burb, but also glad to have a hotel room up ahead, soon hopefully, and very glad to have brought a winter coat and boots. Initially, he'd balked when they had gone shopping for winter wear in Kansas. "'Eddie Bauer' is what snobs have written on their too expensive turtlenecks and Fords. I am just a poor southern boy," Bill had muttered as they left the register. But now, as they trudged in their thermal underwear, flannel shirts, and goose-down parkas from the freezing parking lot of the motel in Evanston, Wyoming up to their room just past the lobby, Bill looked to be grateful for the gear. Mitch hid a smile as they entered the slightly-less-than-room-temperature room.

The next morning, Mitch breathed in the cool, crisp air as he and Bill crunched through the icy parking lot of the motel; there were no cars in the lot, just pickups and SUVs. In DC, there were few trucks or SUVs—there usually was nowhere to park them and no money for their gas. But here in Wyoming, most all the vehicles were SUVs or trucks and Albert's "fishing-only," weekend warrior vehicle fit right in. Mitch took another deep breath. They were now in Evanston, a whole hundred miles away from their most important prospect. In Ogden, Utah, just across the state line, they should be able to find her at work or at school. Tomorrow, they would find the student, and find out whether she was the key to Homer's plan...and learn how much work would have to be done in the next three months.

Chapter Nineteen

It took five phone calls and a federal security guard plus the Ogden IRS center's director to get them in the gate. Homer had contacted the national commissioner of the IRS himself in DC to authorize their temporary badges to get access through the gate, then into the building. Stan had made the initial arrangements for their visit from DC and everything appeared to be fine, until they called to confirm their appointment and found that there was a mix-up in the itinerary. The IRS office didn't expect them until next week. Mitch had complained about the delay and wondered at the need to meet the student at her place of work, until Bill reminded him of just how easy it was to get into the FBI headquarters and that they could not be sure of the student's whereabouts without wasting valuable time. They knew from her work history that she had a good attendance record at work. So they waited, patiently, happily, the additional thirty minutes it took to get them access to the building. Their temporary identification badges were only good for three days, and had a "temp" sign where usually a picture of the individual owner of the badge should be.

Finally, they were escorted through a narrow gateway into the building. It was now 10:00 a.m. Time to get moving. It was just past breakfast, and as soon as they interviewed the student, they could call Homer with the "yeah" or "nay" he was waiting for and be on the way to Fort Douglas in Salt Lake City by lunchtime. They had one last interview in Utah before they could head for the final bait meetings in Phoenix. The commanding officer of the largest Army reserve unit in Utah was waiting for them. He was the last of their possible moles and a good candidate if he could be a little less "military" in person. Over the phone, he had struck Stan as an Army general, and *not* someone who could appear innocuous in an art gallery. This CO was taking his daughter to Liverpool to study abroad in June. With the family planning on traveling through England for a few weeks before heading back to the States, their itinerary was perfect to mesh with Gooding's expositions.

Mitch stood in the wood paneled hallway of the IRS building, plotting the rest of their day. If they could get the student in the interview room now and make the final decision for Homer ASAP, then they could get to Salt Lake by lunch and be on the road to Phoenix right after dinner. Bill was just down the hall, looking at the pictures of the IRS directors, when a professionally dressed lady approached them, flanked by another woman.

"What do you mean, we can't see her until four this afternoon?" Mitch tried to not blast at the director. The director only smiled at him and sweetly said, "You are aware that Ms. Johnson works swing shift, aren't you?" Mitch felt sheepish as Bill stepped in to explain their misunderstanding of the schedule change and to apologize for any "ungentlemanly" behavior. "I'm sorry, it's been a long trip."

She smiled again, obviously no stranger to deadlines herself, and clarified the situation. Ms. Johnson, in order to facilitate her school schedule, worked the night or "swing" shift. The director was very gracious and helped them understand the situation and gave them the student's supervisor's phone number and showed them to the area where Ms. Jenny Johnson worked.

Only afterward, in a conversation with Stan, did Mitch and Bill learn what happened. They learned that the IRS director had fully cooperated with the FBI and had forwarded the details to DC, but the itinerary had not been properly forwarded to Stan before they left. He'd only found the memo when they had called him from Ogden and couldn't get access to the center. The original memo gave today's date, but the date had been changed when the student's boss learned that she had today off. They were supposed to have rescheduled the meeting for next week.

As they walked through the service center, the two hardened FBI agents were amazed at the scale of the place. They were used to government buildings, but neither had consciously thought of the IRS in the same way as any government agency. Also, neither had considered that folks actually worked for the IRS. Maintenance workers passed by them in the halls on bizarre motorized vehicles carrying boxes of paper—tax returns, from all appearances—and went speeding down the corridors. Each intersection of a walkway was marked by huge mirrored globes anchored to the ceilings. As the next wheeled employee came to the intersection, Mitch could see why the globe was needed. He watched the fellow driving the yellow machine slow down slightly, scan the oncoming traffic in four directions, then zip on through the intersection. They came to rooms inaccessible to normal employees for security purposes. They saw huge areas where employees were typing at what seemed to be million-miles-per-hour rates at rows of computer terminals. Then, past huge rooms that housed the central computers, they saw a room filled by rows and rows of gray-colored cubicles. "I haven't seen a computer that big since Buck Rogers," Bill quipped as they entered the student's work zone.

Twenty minutes later a clearly vexed Bill and exasperated Mitch stomped back to the 'Burb. Even Ms. Johnson's supervisor worked swing shift. They'd left a note on the supervisor's desk, left a few voice mails, and stomped out of the building.

They had six hours to kill before Jenny's shift started, and would likely be staying the night in Ogden. The director politely and calmly directed them to a nice hotel just down the street, which had one of the best restaurants in the area. Mitch and Bill taxied back out the gates, parked at the hotel, and had the best T-bone steak in the West for lunch. Mitch sat carving steak into juicy morsels as Bill flirted with the hostess until she brought them huge ice-cold mugs of root beer. Mitch shook his head; Bill loved root beer, even in forty degree weather. As the pretty hostess brought them the icy mugs, she explained, "Jeremiah was this huge grizzly bear that was shot just up this street, up the canyon. You may have seen his skull on display at the Smithsonian in DC. It was so huge that the State of Utah had it on display at the Capital in Salt Lake and then sent it back East. Which explains why you're sitting in 'Jeremiah's Restaurant,'" she finished, looking at them expectantly. Bill smiled and handed her his credit card with a twenty dollar bill on top. "That's for you, sweetie."

As she walked to the register, Mitch's sarcasm was thick. "Always charming the ladies."

To kill time at lunch, they digested as they went over their files at the table. The student was still Homer's star candidate, but they needed to rule out the other possibilities. They *had* to catch Gooding with this scheme. They needed to interview more candidates to get enough data for Homer to be able to match with Gooding's profile and make a decision. Six more "moles" were on their list. The other agents had similar files. Mitch, as team leader, had been nominated to go after the star, the student. Both he and Bill were aware that Stan had also given them this assignment as a sort of break. As if a cross-country trip could be a break. "We should check with Jonesey and see how his Denver Bunch is doing with their nine candidates," Bill commented as they worked and ate.

Mitch nodded before returning his attention to the file in front of him. Ms. Johnson didn't live in Ogden. Jennifer—Jenny—Johnson commuted about an hour to get to work, and her university wasn't as keen on sharing her school schedule as her employer was.

Yesterday they'd pulled her employment records from their file to find her home address. The city she lived in wasn't on any of their maps, so they decided that must mean she lived only fifteen to twenty miles from her job, thinking that she must live in some suburb to Ogden, a result of their thoughts of Eastern commuting. Mitch revised his thinking as they left Wyoming. She didn't live in any suburb to any largish town. In fact she lived in an entirely different county in the middle of nowhere in Northern Utah. Somewhere no more densely populated than South Western Wyoming where they'd stayed the night before. Bill was visibly shocked, but Mitch took it in stride, having grown up in his own sparsely populated corner of Montana.

Mitch and Bill tapped their good friends from Jonesey's team in Denver to help them locate the student's hometown, then located it on a satellite map. Her parents' house was fifteen miles from the nearest town, in the middle of huge fields, and fifty miles from her job. There were roads near her place, but it was far enough out of their way that they decided to wait for her at work. They'd nearly revised that plan when they bought a local map of just Utah and laughed when they saw her commute, which was a straight forty-mile stretch of I-15; freeway all the way. Since they had not been allowed access to her school schedule yet, they had even started north to try to locate her. Staring down the empty freeway in front of them, Bill asked Mitch, "When's the last time you averaged seventy-five miles per hour on your commute and made it fifty miles in about forty-five minutes, *daily*? Wow, man, I would love to drive this drive every day instead of the run into DC Al does." Bill shook his head. "That's what I get for not shifting my brain into agent mode. I should have remembered that not all things work the same out here."

Mitch smiled. "You've been in DC too long. You need more field time. As for myself, I feel right at home. At my grandpa's in Montana, we were twenty miles from the nearest store, and you'd have to go fifty miles to find a movie theater or a McDonald's." He shook his head and added, "And, we counted on it only taking an hour to get that far. It'd take at least two hours to go the same distance back home in DC."

Earlier, before lunch, Bill had commented, "Hey, we could go up there. It's only fifty miles, and even with the snow, it should only take a couple of hours and it would help us get to the Ft. Douglas meeting today."

Mitch shot him down at the time. "I am in *no* mood to traipse across the boonies where she lives to find her house, when she could be at school right now."

Bill seemed to brighten up immediately. "Then—"

Mitch cut him off, knowing his partner so well that he interpreted the coming thought before Bill could say it. "*No*, we are not going to 'hang out on campus,' scoping for her so you can check out the local wildlife."

Bill just grinned wider. "Okay, we'll hit the school tomorrow if we can't catch her at work, but on the way, I need to get some warmer socks and more underwear."

Mitch continued griping. "I should have known that motel in Evanston wouldn't have a washer and dryer, and this hotel's laundromat has a frozen pipe and is out of commission. I told you to get more stuff in Kansas."

"How do you know about the Laundromat here?" Bill asked, neatly sidestepping the criticism.

"Because while you were flirting with that cute redhead checking in behind us, I listened to the clerk as the hostess was finding us a table," Mitch replied.

Now, having decided to explore Ogden while waiting for Jenny Johnson to show up at work, Mitch pulled out of the hotel's lot and headed for the freeway entrance. He was still miffed that the IRS director had not been more forthcoming about their target. Of course, they had broken protocol in their hurry to track her down, but the IRS officials wouldn't even allow them to call her boss at home personally or guarantee that the director would call the student or her boss into work early. Mitch relaxed a bit, watching Bill get comfortable in the passenger seat as they headed north.

It was Bill's fault that they were actually going on this fool's errand to kill some time this afternoon. Bill had been chatting with their petite, brunette waitress at lunch about how they had a few hours to kill, and needed some winter gear, could she recommend anything? "I heard you talking about heading north," she'd stated. "If you are going north on I-15, you can stop at Smith and Edward's. It's kind of an institution around here." She'd been speaking to Bill, but had continued to make calf-eyes at Mitch as she continued, "Great clothing selection, especially winter gear and Western styles, and just about anything else. They started out by selling Army surplus, but expanded so they now sell a little bit of everything from guns and hunting supplies to Dutch ovens and hardware," she'd gushed, then smiled again at Mitch, but glanced absently at Bill in an attempt at politeness.

In her pause Bill had smirked, trying to keep her attention, and unsubtly cleared his throat. "Well, thanks, ma'am. We might just do that."

Blushing, she'd told him quickly how to get there, then turned from Bill back to Mitch with a smile and batted her eyelashes at him. To which Mitch flashed her his own best smile and replied, "Thanks, can we get the check?" Bill wasn't the only one who could capture a lady's interest.

Bill kept wiggling and twitching in the passenger seat of the Suburban. It appeared that he was trying to get his feet as close as he could to the firewall under the dash to the heater vent there. Mitch knew that Bill was a dang good agent. In fact, Bill's antics were comforting to Mitch. Bill only let loose and became irresponsible when he relaxed. Besides, the "ladies man" technique Bill used actually helped on most investigations. Mitch was usually amazed by what Bill could gather from females when he turned on the charm. The behavior with the waitress today was a good sign. If Bill could relax now, then they both would be in good shape come June when they would be deployed to the UK. Mitch took a breath and tried to become un-vexed. He decided as he sped down the freeway, that he was enjoying the sunny, if cold, day and the empty freeway. If he tried, he could enjoy this particular mellow mood he was experiencing. Maybe, if he enjoyed the next couple of hours, he'd be calm enough by this afternoon to properly assess the student. For now, he glanced over, watching Bill continuing to squirm and commented, "Feet cold, good buddy?"

Bill smirked. "Haha, funny boy, just keep driving. I am going to buy me as many warm socks as I can find."

Frowning, Mitch tried to picture Jenny Johnson from her pictures and what she'd be like based on what they knew. He had little faith in the college kid the profilers were determined to choose for a mole. Homer had even expressed hope that she would be a photographer so she would really catch Gooding's interest. On the plus side, she wasn't too young. At twenty-five, she was young enough to be attractive to Gooding, but hopefully old enough to handle the situation. It still seemed like too extreme a risk. Gooding was known to be a cold-blooded killer when the mood struck him. The idea of putting an untrained, inadequately prepared female in his path was chilling. Stan had called earlier with some updates to Gooding's profile. Apparently the profilers believed even Gooding was aware of that part of himself. He preferred older females, just because they were more mature and had more experience to handle his decisive ways. Alicia was a prime example. Mitch shied at the idea of using any female for this job. He preferred the idea of using the ex-Army father. It wasn't that he was being sexist against the idea of a female mole; he knew some killer lady FBI agents, take Reva for example, but they were trained. This student would have to become a passable FBI trainee/recruit, if not agent, in just eighty-two days.

After many discussions as partners, they had decided to trust Homer's judgment and not discount the student. "After all, he *is* the big boss and our pensions depend on making the man happy. So we better do what he wants in this instance," Bill had said at the end of their last big conversation about the student. Mitch thought about the possibilities as he diligently tried to stick to Homer's mandate.

Bill was one of the few people who could make Mitch unwind and loosen up. Mitch and Bill both knew this. It was one of the reasons that Stan had made them partners. Mitch could handle Bill's craziness, and Bill kept Mitch from becoming too uptight to function. The steak was settling pleasantly as they drove. Things were okay. They would interview the student today. For now, Mitch's thoughts left FBI agent mode and he returned to being a guy with cold feet in the middle of a Rocky Mountain winter.

His thoughts turned to the waitress at the restaurant earlier. It had taken Mitch a few minutes to extricate himself after Bill sauntered out of the restaurant, having tried to make it clear to the waitress that Bill, not him, was the one she should "eye." Bill had wandered over the icy patches and piles of snow, casually picking his teeth with the complimentary toothpick as he folded the hostess' number into his own wallet.

Mitch knew something was up when he saw Bill flip through his wallet and wave a little slip of paper. "The waitress knew that the hostess had called dibs on me," he remarked.

Mitch, still shocked at Bill's ability to charm females asked, "That's what, five phone numbers for five meals since Kentucky?" Bill's crooked smile answered silently.

After ten minutes of freeway driving, they exited under the store's huge billboard. Smith & Edward's Discount Store was something new to the agents again. Mitch was reminded of a flea market married with a hardware store and living in an armory, but most of it was indoors in a huge, flat building that had odd ends, turns, bends, aisles, and even some nooks and crannies. From the outside it was easy enough to tell the place had grown over the years, and expanded one extension or add-on at a time. Bill filled a basket with socks, then found some heavy leather boots on clearance and happily trotted to the back of the store for some ammo for them both as Mitch loaded up on wool socks, more underwear, and some new ski gloves. After checkout, they showed their purchases to a nice security guard who checked their receipt on the way out. In typical Northern Utah fashion, the day that started shockingly bright started to darken. In the partly cloudy sky, a cool sun now shone down though sparse snowflakes on the icy patches and dirty snow left over from the plowings of last night's storm. White salt stained the pavement around them, turning the black-and-gray asphalt white, and the freezing breeze hurried them into the shelter of the SUV.

"Well that took care of a hundred bucks and almost as many minutes," muttered Mitch, but his smart-aleck smile belied his sarcasm. Bill just laughed and returned to lacing his brand new, ultra-weatherproofed, three-times-padded, luxury model work boots while squished in the front seat of the Suburban.

"I can never find a good, down home, mom-and-pop place to find necessities like work boots in DC." Bill arched his back and again stretched his now "guaranteed to stay warm," tootsies as far forward as the firewall of the Suburban would allow and sighed happily. The extra adrenaline in his system was infectious as he ordered Mitch, "Hey man, turn off the heater, let's see what the AC can do!"

Mitch just shook his head—as usual—at Bill's antics. Hell, they both deserved to let off some steam. Heaven only knew what kind of fun or hardships they'd be enduring while on this mission until Gooding was caught.

A slow but relaxing forty-five-minute crawl through the ice and some old snowfall and a few new flakes coming down on the old highway back to Ogden accomplished the wasting of the final hour before 4:00 p.m., when the unsuspecting student would *finally* report to work. With luck, they could get the chick interviewed and either signed on or scared to death (and consequently eliminated) in plenty of time to get to Salt Lake City tonight for their late dinner date with Jonesey and the Denver Bunch before they continued the last leg of their journey to Phoenix.

Chapter Twenty

Jonesey was the first agent Stan called to research Gooding's expositions, but he was still really needed at his home office in Denver, especially now that Gooding had skipped the country. There were still hotheads out in the woods to deal with. So, Jonesey and his "Denver Bunch" were in Salt Lake City for a hush-hush meeting with various government and civil experts from all over the Western United States to brief them about Gooding before they had to return to Denver to finish their regular case assignments. Stan would still tap Jonesey for his thoughts on Gooding. It was a sign of how much Stan counted on Jonesey's killer instincts on important investigations.

Other FBI agents from Washington, Oregon, Arizona, and New Mexico were also attending the briefings to learn their part in the Gooding mission once Jonesey finished presenting the initial reports to the leaders. These other agents had all arrived in Salt Lake. This series of meetings would help the final team get into place for the June rendezvous with Gooding. The list of names was mighty impressive for those in the know. Meanwhile, Jonesey had taken the opportunity to bring his wife Amy and their kids to stay with her grandma in Utah, while he was in Salt Lake. After the Salt Lake conferences, the groups would split and the new Gooding task force members would follow Mitch and Bill to Phoenix.

"That's one good thing about this guy—he's made it clear that he's going to do something big on July Fourth. We just don't know exactly what or how big," Jonesey had told Amy, so she could understand a little about why he was wanted by the big bosses in DC and why he wanted her and their kids to stay in Utah for the summer while he was busy assisting on this assignment in addition to his regular tasks.

Unlike Jonesey, whose input was needed to help the bigwigs prepare the outline for the general meeting, Mitch and Bill would take part in the briefings later if they could, and only after they had secured their mole. They were rushing to leave Ogden and get to Salt Lake City tonight. They would be taking the remaining members of the Denver Bunch with them to interview the ex-Army guy in Salt Lake tomorrow. Then Mitch and Bill with the Denver Bunch would head to Phoenix, their final destination before returning to Washington. Jonesey was leaving Utah tomorrow morning and heading back to Idaho. He'd only grudgingly agreed to a dinner date with all the agents tonight because he had not been able to meet with Mitch and Bill since Gooding's New York exposition. However, both parties insisted that they meet now so Mitch could make good on the bet they'd made and feed Jonesey a snazzy seafood feast before they were called to their separate assignments.

Jonesey felt sure that Homer would pick the Utah student as the mole, while Mitch was just as sure that she was wouldn't suit their purposes. Hence the friendly inner-office wager. If the student was chosen, then Mitch would buy a seafood feast for the guys. If not, than Jonesey would by them the best steak dinner in the Rockies.

When Mitch related this information to Stan, Bill commented—loud enough for Stan to hear, "What a crock. Mitch, you know you owe Jonesey a lobster dinner after the Jessica mess!" Mitch ignored him as Bill finished with, "Good old Jonesey, picking a state to meet you for dinner where no one eats seafood easily or cheaply. Buddy, you are gonna pay!" This earned them both a lecture about the seriousness of the situation. Stan called everyone together and the bet was canceled officially, while everyone agreed to meet for dinner in Salt Lake anyway, if only to celebrate Jonesey's successful review of the New York exposition. Without that mission, they would still have little clue about of Gooding's intentions. Jonesey's successful recon that trip was still the task force's only success in the Gooding nightmare.

***

As they neared the IRS location in Ogden, Mitch noted the time—3:30 p.m. They should just make it back to the IRS service center in time to meet the student and get ready for dinner. The delay was tiresome, but they would soon be back on schedule.

They arrived back at the IRS building in Ogden at 3:45 p.m., just at shift change. "Boy, when these folks want out, they mean it!" said Bill as Mitch impatiently thumped on the steering wheel as they waited behind four other vehicles turning into the north gate for an opening in the line of cars leaving the south gates just up the street. Heedless of the slushy muck on the roads, cars were swooping out both gates as fast as possible—meaning as fast as they could without garnishing a federal speeding ticket—prepared especially for those who dared to forget that even the parking lot was federal property.

Across the lot, Mitch, who'd been scanning the vehicles, looking for Jenny's, noticed a couple of full-size pickup trucks near the door closest to the student's area. One was tan and the other golden with a rust-colored mid-body stripe. All the tag info for their particular student said was: *light brown, half ton, GM truck, license plate: TRUCKY.*

"Can't miss that plate. How in the heck did they miss the huge rust stripe? Light brown, my ass." Bill always did give the best color-commentary; he was a vehicle fanatic and was most particular on how vehicles were described officially, even if his own vehicle was more rust colored than yellow.

Mitch was well aware of this tendency and ribbed Bill a bit. "So, is it General Motors K one fifty or K two fifty tan?"

"There's no GM term K one fifty…" Bill started to answer, than spouted, "Oh, just shut up. Let's go," and hopped out of the SUV.

"Shit," Mitch muttered as he opened his door. He had just noticed the skiff of snow across the hood of the vehicle in question; it had been here for some time. They had driven through more than a few flurries on their way up north. "She must have got here early. I wonder how much time we wasted shopping."

Bill, not appearing the least bit repentant, replied, "At least you were right about trying to find her at home or at school with no idea of her schedule. I wonder if they called her after all?" At the dirty look from Mitch, Bill shrugged. "Hey, if you hadn't have gone to that Smith and Edward's place, I wouldn't have these snazzy boots, and you would be hearing me bitch about cold feet like you were all the way up here." Bill slammed the passenger door as he headed up to the gates where their temporary badges awaited.

The IRS director was even more gracious now than she had been that morning when she greeted them coming in, but she saluted them on her way out—her day was over. Mitch and Bill, as FBI agents, were now "officially" escorted by the night-shift security officer who was, surprisingly, wearing a black Megadeth T-shirt and jeans—plain clothes, apparently—down a long hallway past the dozens of desks that were now occupied by folks listening to headphones on their personal music players, then past carts filled with paper, and a cool, shady cafeteria to what a tacked-up sign proclaimed as "The Hall of Cubies."

"I bet Stan called the director to smooth our way after our conversation this morning," Mitch quietly remarked to Bill, who smiled in response.

"That director sure smiles a lot for someone who runs a huge IRS office. Who ever thought taxes garnered a happy disposition," Bill mused as he half turned back to smile at a little blonde gal in passing. Of course, she smiled back just like the White House interns or congressional aides Bill usually flirted with while on assignment, but kept walking. The security guy led them a different way than earlier, beyond most of the cubicles to an un-walled desk, behind the supervisor's—near the back wall of another cubicle-filled area.

Bill was checking out yet another lovely blonde filing documents two rows over as Mitch happened to notice a nice set of female legs, the longest he'd seen in a long time. They were encased in what appeared to be Levi's 501s (jeans he fondly remembered from his Montana days as a hot-blooded teenager), stalking back and forth behind a desk just over to his right. His first rational thought was, *Damn, I hope that's not the supervisor I requested be woke up this morning.* His second rational thought arrived as he noticed that the desk was turned away from them, and the person was stalking in front of, not behind, it. His last thought prompted a male, appreciative grin and a thankful prayer to heaven for putting him back out West where cowgirls still wore tight jeans.

She turned at that moment and he saw her face and recognized her as the student from the picture taken from her IRS ID badge. *Double damn, her hair is the same golden-brown color as her truck.* The thought shot through his brain. Being out West, eating steak for dinner, thinking of his grandfather and the home ranch must have kicked in something deep. It had been a long time since he'd been around sweet "western" women. The sleek political DC gals he'd dated lately had never tweaked his libido as this female was after only few moments of simply watching her. The male animal inside him was frantically cataloging her beguiling traits. Mitch had not expected to be attracted to their mole candidate. Hurriedly he squelched his raging hormones and put on his best "agent" face, forcing himself to remember that he was an adult male on a mission, not a teenager at some dance.

The golden-brown hair in question had been bundled in a thick braid that was currently swinging wildly as its owner paced. Mitch wished for a moment that he hadn't noticed the wispy, curly tendrils escaping that braid just at the pulse point of that lovely neck and nearly hidden temples, as he fought to get his hormones controlled. He remembered the description in her file: *subject is of medium to tall height, 5'7", blue eyes, and brown hair.* For once Mitch could appreciate Bill's obsession with proper color descriptions; "golden brown" was the better term, as this angry angel in tight jeans was no brunette. Absently he wondered what had pissed her off.

As Mitch squelched his ungentlemanly thoughts, he turned back to Bill, just in time to see him shift into his typical female-charmer persona once again—his natural reaction to a pretty female. Bill moved his attention from the retreating blonde who was finishing her filing to the pacer. Bill was just as quick as Mitch in deciding that here was their quarry, the student, Ms. Jenny Johnson herself, and had probably noticed her legs faster than Mitch had. Bill adored a good pair of "stems."

Bill, unlike Mitch, let his admiration show as the figure whipped back to face them and stopped, poised for a confrontation, her pink lips pursed and stress lines visible between her finely arched golden eyebrows. Bill began his usual assault in his typical, charming way. "Why, Miz Johnson, if you ain't the prettiest assignment I've ever seen!"

Mitch grimaced as he felt compelled to intervene. The security guard interrupted and said, "Miss Johnson, these gentlemen need to speak with you. If you will just follow me into the conference room." He gestured for Mitch and Bill to stand back as he escorted Jenny into a nearby room.

Noticing that her name badge verified their guess as to her identity, Bill and Mitch followed behind Jenny and the officer. The three sat as the security officer left them, closing the door. Mitch cleared his throat and faced the student—Jenny. "Miss Johnson, I must apologize for our lack of manners, it's been a long day. This is Agent Thomas, and I am Agent Harper. We just need a few moments of your time."

Her short reply cut him off and caught him off guard. "Can I see some identification, please?"

Conveniently, their security escort had disappeared into the background, and her supervisor was nowhere in sight. She stood up expectantly, straight-faced and ready to leave, as Bill recovered quickly and swept aside his jacket to reveal his leather-cased badge. Her eyebrow lifted as she noticed the holster he'd also conveniently revealed. He handed her his badge and reached out to Mitch for his. She remained no-nonsense as she actually compared his features to the picture on his badge, then did the same to Mitch. She looked shocked for a moment as she met Mitch's eyes. Her manner then warmed a little as she seemed to realize how curt she'd been. Mitch enjoyed watching her blush explode as the realization struck her. "Gosh, I'm sorry to be so rude. I just got through speaking to the director after my boss called me at home and asked me to come to work early." A second sentence seemed to burst out unexpectedly. "I also didn't figure FBI agents wore jeans."

Her stammering continued as she tried to regain her composure. "I have an art project due tomorrow, and I was up most of the night working on it, so I'd only been in bed for a couple of hours when she called, and she *never* calls me at home unless it's an emergency. I had today off and so I was sure there was some emergency. *Am* I in some sort of trouble?" Her question nearly flew by as she belted out her statements in a continuous rush.

Mitch caught it, as he was enjoying watching her fine features and lovely lips for just a moment, and was quick with his reassurance, as was Bill. "*No*. No, miss. Everything's fine, we just have an assignment…"

Mitch cut in. "An opportunity for you." He gently grabbed her arm and motioned to a water pitcher he'd spotted earlier on the table. "Here, have a drink while we talk."

Chapter Twenty-one

From the moment they all sat at the table, Mitch and Bill turned their personas into agent-mode, and became the most strictly businesslike people Ms. Jenny Johnson had probably ever met.

Mitch was shocked by her behavior. Once she quit stammering, she settled down and was able to listen to all their questions and provided her answers in a quick, intelligent manner. Bill did the talking while Mitch made notes on her reactions and information. She possessed all the qualities Homer's profilers had requested, all right. To himself, Mitch thought as he jotted his notes, *Wow, I'd forgotten how fine-tuned Homer's instincts are.*

After their interview, Bill and Mitch left Jenny to do her work as they followed the head of security back to the director's office.

Stan had worked out the general paperwork for the moles' reassignment to the secret task force; he'd even made a setup backstory for Jenny in advance. It waited while they determined if Jenny was a viable candidate before finishing the forms. After speaking to her boss and Jenny herself, she seemed to be a perfect mole-in-making. Mitch switched his terminology for the bait into the mole. His heart shied away from thinking of Jenny as bait for Gooding.

The security officer left them at the IRS director's office when the interview was over. The assistant director called them in. They sat down and finished the paperwork that made up the details of reassigning a federal employee to a different agency for a time.

Clearly intelligent, slightly sassy, and mature enough to know when to hold her peace, also known for her passion for the arts and good photographic eye, Jenny not only could act the student, she *was* a full-time student and had withstood the long interview well.

Bill pointed out afterward that, because she was going on an English trip as an art major, as her minor was English, she could separate from her school group to see "artsy" sights during her free time—neatly giving her a plausible excuse to slip away from the civilians she'd be going to England and Scotland with. Bill and Mitch agreed; it was best to have as few liabilities as possible in an operation; and untrained, uninformed civilians were definitely a liability.

Ten minutes later, Mitch waited outside the IRS campus' security door as Bill surrendered his temporary badge to the head of security who'd appeared out of nowhere the instant they had exited the director's office. *The guy may look like he's going to a rock concert, but he knows his job*, Mitch thought. He stood in the foyer, watching the heavy steel-and-glass doors reluctantly open to let Bill out of the IRS building. They waved to the guard, who saluted back, then they headed out into the brisk dusk. "Dinner time. Do ya feel like another steak?" asked Bill as he zipped his parka and headed for the 'Burb.

Mitch smiled. "Nope, time for Jonesey. Tonight, lobster for me, steak for you, and fuel tomorrow before we go to Phoenix. Let's go." They found the 'Burb, with four inches of fresh snow covering it, and flipped a coin to see who got to drive to Salt Lake City. Mitch won, again, which meant that Bill got to fulfill the navigator's duty of clearing the snow off the Suburban while Mitch got the engine warming up. He jumped into the driver's seat to start the heater. As he reached over to adjust the temperature, he glanced up and saw Ms. Jenny Johnson heading out of the building. He watched her walk past to her own rig nearby and, for the first time in years, he was glad for his job.

Mitch sat in the driver's seat of the blue 'Burb as he waited patiently for Bill to finish cleaning off the accumulated snow. He watched Jenny and enjoyed the picture she made as she stretched to reach all the way across the hood of her truck to clear a swath of snow, then shift to attack the frozen drops on her windshield. Her winter parka rode up just right. He'd seen her shiver and get in the cab, then saw her forehead drop to the top of her steering wheel for the minutes it took her truck to warm up.

Just when he'd decided to get out and comfort her, she'd put the truck in gear and headed out.

He watched her go, not caring that Bill seemed to be more interested in watching him watch her than to clear snow. Jenny didn't wipe her eyes or anything, but he'd seen how she'd seemed broken-down as she left the building. They'd been apprised of her art major/ English minor status of course as part of her qualifications as a possible mole. Hell, that's why they were there, but he'd not considered what scheduling it took to work full time and go to school full time and sleep sometimes, before now.

Bill got in the SUV, and Mitch glanced over and caught the assessing look his partner leveled on him. Shaking his head to indicate that he was not discussing Ms. Johnson, he picked up his cell phone. He punched a few numbers and dialed Stan for their report. A few quick calculations had shown them that Ms. Jenny Johnson met 98% of their requirements. Now Stan and Homer and everyone else would know that Homer had been right to push to interview her. However, formalities still had to be observed. All their other interviews would still be performed on the slim chance that there was a better candidate out there. Stan also was considering having a couple of moles, just in case. As far as they could tell, Jenny's only problems were her occasional self-doubt and lack of experience, both of which caused her to falter in certain circumstances. In her favor, she was a bone-deep fighter. A little pushing really got her temper to flare, and she could definitely hold her own in stressful situations. Still, they'd have to work on her and they only had scant weeks before their time was up.

Chapter Twenty-two

Jenny sat in her truck, its heater finally sending hot air full blast past her cheeks and onto her lower legs, but she hardly felt it. The phrase "bone chilled," popped into her thoughts. She'd been running her engine for five minutes now without moving. Having only been parked here at work for a few hours, her truck had heated up quickly. "Good thing I'm made of money and can afford the gas," she muttered sarcastically, thinking of the fifteen miles per gallon she managed in her truck on a good day, but unable to force herself to leave the relative safety of the parking lot just yet. She felt drained, but hopeful that she'd get some clarity on the drama earlier today. She had a telephone appointment with the agents' supervisor tomorrow afternoon after her art test. She hoped this Stan could make sense of what the FBI needed her for.

Earlier today she'd rushed down to work after her supervisor had called her at 1:00 p.m. Jenny needed to come to work ASAP! Normally a forty-five-minute drive on a sunny day without speeding, today her commute had been an hour-and-a-half ordeal in Utah's famous snow. The drive culminated with some dude attempting to cut her off, then trying to tailgate her to death when she'd gunned her engine in an irresponsible reaction of trying to outrun him on the freeway in a snowstorm. She'd barely got into the parking lot when she dropped her badge with its keycard out her truck window at the gate and held up traffic trying to enter the parking lot behind her. Of course, she had had to get out of her truck to retrieve her badge from the slushy muck, because her truck was too wide to allow her door to open without smacking the side post. So she'd had to back up a few feet and still had to get all of the way out of her truck to get her now soggy badge from the curbside. Then, badge in hand, she was finally able use it to get through the gate. She ignored the dirty looks from the coworkers parked behind her; apparently, she wasn't the only one running late for work.

When she finally made it into the building, she sat down at her desk and began to work. She had planned on working from 4:00 p.m. to only 9:00 p.m. tonight instead of ending her shift at 12:30 a.m. as usual, since she couldn't concentrate on her work caseload while worrying about her test tomorrow and the weaving project that was due.

Jenny had only managed to log into the computer system when her boss came to her desk. She was informed that they had called her into work early to meet with the director and some agents from the FBI. And, as soon as they were ready, she needed to report to upper management. In the meantime it was okay for her to work. Jenny had prayed her boss would clarify her situation so she could start working or at least know when she was supposed to meet with the agents. *FBI agents?* Jenny thought. *Why ever do I need to talk to them for?* This news worried her enough that when her boss left, she'd headed outside and taken a moment, deeply breathing cold air. When she got back inside, her boss came over again and asked her to come to her desk for another quick meeting in a few minutes. At the time she'd been grateful for the information. A quick meeting, then she could get some work done so she could leave to get her school work finished.

Dutifully, she went to her boss' desk and was grateful for the momentary reprieve, as her boss was nowhere in sight. Then Jenny saw the head of IRS security approaching. With him were two scary-looking IRS special agent types. Jenny faltered. They showed her their badges. Rippling anxiety dropped through her body. The only US government agents she was familiar with were the super scary IRS agents of the Treasury Inspector General for Tax Administration—TIGTA, the US Treasury's office in charge of overseeing misconduct in the Internal Revenue Service, including any misconduct of IRS personnel, but these were two IRS special agents. Similar to TIGTA, but not TIGTA—IRS. She had no experience with the FBI, except for what she saw on TV, but she knew some TIGTA and a few IRS special agents and they intimidated her with their no-nonsense attitudes and scary personas.

Her boss had arrived shortly and took her directly to the IRS director's office for a meeting, the IRS security officer and the IRS special agents following. In her experience at the IRS, meetings with upper management were rarely good, and the higher ranked the employee hosting the meeting, the uglier the experience for the lowly employee. Jenny had never felt so lowly. Besides, she couldn't think of any reason why the big boss would need to talk to her. If TIGTA was in on it too, she was in real trouble. As for her boss, the look on her face could melt the ice in the parking lot. Whatever was happening was causing her boss a whole handful of headaches, apparently.

Once in the director's office a single TIGTA officer joined them and Jenny was asked a lot of questions about her upcoming school trip. *Am I not going to be allowed to go?* In confusion she answered as best she could. She had already cleared the time off with her boss. Since she only needed nine more credits to graduate, if she took six credits over the summer on this trip, then she would be nearly done. *Done!* with her degree. Next fall she could take a last light class load to make up for all those heavy credits heretofore. Her trip would also give her a month-long break from work and she could rack up the six credits without weeks in the classroom. It was all planned and she'd thought everything was okay. Now, after the quizzing about her final school-bang, she was excused to go back to work and okayed to leave early, as planned.

Why on earth did the director or TIGTA care about her school trip? Jenny had had no idea. Shaken by the interview, absolute terror engulfed her. First the call at home, then the meeting with the director and the upcoming FBI interview—it was too much. *I won't survive this day.*

She'd no sooner got back to her desk and logged onto the computer again when her boss had called her desk phone and told her the FBI agents were coming, and to report at her desk again in ten minutes. Again, Jenny showed up and no boss. This time, she couldn't stop her upset. She was still reeling from the conversations with the IRS agents earlier. In the director's office she'd been seated across from the director with her boss and the security officer on one hand and the two IRS agents on the other with the TIGTA officer behind them. In her mind, she could still see the "special agent" insignia on the IRS agents' badges. One of them, the man, had noticed the look of horror in her eyes. Jenny imagined she had had that deer-in-the-headlight scared look of an innocent person who's being arrested for something they didn't do, when she'd halted in front of them. Jenny knew her pause had prompted them to draw out their identification badges. They were really nice in reality. Just some details, they said. They told her it had to do with the FBI's request for some help from them. Nothing to do with her personally, but the director just needed to clarify some details before she could meet with the FBI agents. Then she received all the questions about her upcoming trip and her work schedule. Her boss and the security officer had simply sat there. Jenny faced the director, remembered again how personable she was, and felt grateful that she was the one posing the questions.

She remembered how she was caught pacing in front of her boss' desk by the security officer, but this time with two guys in casual clothes. These two, who also were two of the most handsome men she'd ever seen, turned out to be the FBI agents and as a pair were a study in contrast. The taller, broader one was dark and brooding; while the other one, still tall, was redheaded with a ready wit and really green eyes. Charmers, both, and supremely businesslike in the interview, even though they wore jeans.

When it was over, on her way out, the two IRS special agents had caught up to her again. At the time she'd thought hysterically, *I just spent hours talking with the FBI; these two agents shouldn't even bother me.* Thankfully, they just needed her input so they could finish their report. Apparently, any officer of the law's entry into the IRS building was documented. She was fine. What a relief. They also wanted to be sure that her answer to the FBI was yes. *Was* she willing to go on a work detail with the FBI? They gave her their cards and told her that she was an IRS employee first and foremost, and in light of her lack of "agent" experience, she only needed to call them if she had a problem, or a question, anytime, anywhere if she needed help.

She still didn't know what to think about that offer. Two hours before, she'd urgently needed to know what was really going on. *Now, I know what's going on.* The knowledge didn't comfort her. *I'd thought I'd done something wrong in my job, but instead, people are dead or in danger, and I get to help...somehow, someway, and I have no idea how.*

The horrors of the day got to her. Deciding that she was in no shape to work after all, Jenny waved to her boss, turned around, and logged off her computer. She was done working tonight.

As she clocked out of work, her brain, overloaded at that moment, proved that she *must* be crazy, because, in the midst of this workday, the other reality of life and her school load hit her with the force of a broadside, and even more horrible thoughts surrounded her.

"Shit, how on this great green earth am I going to get my weaving project done in time? My hands are shaking, and they have the steering wheel to hold on to.

Besides, if I don't warm up soon, there's no way I am going to be able to make my feet work the pedals on my loom. Shit, shit, shit..." Jenny continued muttering to herself as she angled her truck out of the gated lot and up the road to the university for a—now early—start to a long night of weaving.

Chapter Twenty-three

Jonesey grabbed the phone in his hotel room and heard, "Jonesey, this is Stan. Where are Bill and Mitch right now?"

Jonesey answered, "Don't know, boss.

"I can't reach them on their cell phones, but I think they may still be in the meeting with their latest mole. I am leaving in a few minutes to catch a chartered flight to New York to speak to the supervisor there about Gooding's collages. He left one here and we need to go over it."

"Okay. Sounds good. We're meeting at eight tonight for dinner. Do I need to call them before? Is it urgent?"

"No. Just pass it on when you see them. Mitch asked me to keep him posted and I wanted to call him before I left. I'll have more details at the briefings day after tomorrow when I arrive in Phoenix."

"Shoot, boss."

"Tell Mitch that we don't know where Gooding is. We thought the picture in Amsterdam may be accurate, but it's a fake, as feared. We traced the call that came to the Birminghams' the morning of the mailbox bomb to a number Gooding's used, but it was routed through four university switchboards and then we lost it in South Africa. We think he's in the Atlantic somewhere, but we have no idea where. Could be he's on a ship somehow. We haven't yet found all his corporate connections or found out how he made it out of New York. That's part of what Homer and I will be researching tomorrow. Sorry, I'm rambling. Just tell them to keep to the plan of traveling incognito. Gooding's people set off two more bombs today. One blew up a marine transport plane that was carrying two of our own to Germany, and the other blew up a CIA car at a hotel just outside the Amsterdam location. Thankfully, both bombs were small for Gooding, and we didn't lose any civilians this time. I'm not worried about you guys out there. There seems to be no activity outside of the East Coast, so you should be fine, even though we think Gooding may have stopped in Texas."

"Okay. Thanks. I'll let them know. Can I share this with the others?"

"Only those on the mole search. We are curtailing the other agents' activities starting tomorrow and they'll get their orders from the director himself."

"Okay then, boss. Anything else?"

"No, just keep to the task and I'll see you in forty-eight hours."

***

Alicia shrugged off her new designer handbag, leaving it on the bed, and flung her long, blonde hair over her shoulder, sending a sultry look in his direction. Gooding followed her into their suite, unimpressed by her pouting lips. The French chalet was quiet and isolated, especially chosen for its discreet and private atmosphere. "Why couldn't we stay on the Riviera?" Alicia asked, attempting a pout. "I miss the ocean."

Gooding hid his growing impatience as he answered. "Because we need to give Mortimer a few more days to prepare for our entry into England, as well as keep under the FBI's radar. You don't want to have to stay in a tiny, awful London hotel, do you? My grandfather's flat has just been renovated and Mortimer needs to make sure the work is complete."

She sighed a little too theatrically. "Oh fine. I suppose there's a nightlife here at this resort, isn't there?"

Gooding was really tired of Alicia's habits, but humored her as she had not yet finished her part in his plan. "Yes. In fact, the formal dining room will be opened promptly at seven and there's dancing after that. You can wear the new gown I bought you in Paris." Alicia's eyes glowed at this news. She looked even happier than when he'd let her play with some of his explosives and took the time to explain some of the technical workings to her.

A rapping came at the door. While Alicia went into the bathroom to freshen up, Gooding went to answer the knock. In French the porter offered them a light snack and some local wine. Answering him likewise in French, Gooding graciously thanked him and accepted the wine. He went outside to the room's veranda to watch the sunset fall across the vineyards and fields as he waited for Alicia.

His phone rang. *Just in time*, Gooding thought as he answered Mortimer. "Yes?"

"Sir, I have completed the assignment. London is ready as planned. I also checked on the Yanks' records. They believed the Amsterdam photo as planned and we caught two CIA agents on the Dutch run." Mortimer's voice came through loud and clear over the international connection.

"Any survivors?"

"No, sir, the usual result. It will be some time before they're found and the US authorities realize you slipped their grasp again."

"Good. And the package?"

"Waiting in the flat as requested. When you're ready I will help Alicia open it."

"Well done. What about transportation?"

"The car is on its way now. We should arrive at the chalet by eleven tomorrow morning."

"Good. We'll be ready and waiting. Until tomorrow."

As Gooding ended the call, Alicia came out to the veranda in a silk dressing gown that highlighted her toned skin. "Are you ready to go to England tomorrow, my dear?" he asked her.

"Oh finally! I've so wanted to see your homeland," she gushed.

Swallowing a sigh, Gooding smiled and handed her a goblet. "To the Summer Plan."

"Yes, to the plan, and to a lovely time in France. Thank you for showing me so much," Alicia said, for once seeming genuinely moved by how her life had improved. "You are so good to me. I will have to make it up to you somehow."

Unfazed by her gratitude, but appreciative of how the soft sunlight flattered her looks, Gooding smiled. "Just keep to the plan and you will, my dear. You will."

Chapter Twenty-four

Now that Mitch and Bill had approached Jenny with the proposal and cleared the red-tape requirements of having the IRS release her on temporary work assignment to the FBI/CIA task force, he and Bill could get a good night's rest, then head out to connect with the Denver Bunch and their last three mole contacts. Even though their latest tasks were going well, Mitch knew there was going to be no good night's rest for Jenny. She was on her way to Weber State University to finish her midterm weaving project.

Mitch was thoughtful as he drove himself and Bill down the freeway from Ogden to Salt Lake City. He needed to be available tomorrow afternoon during the phone interview between Stan and Jenny. The schedule was tight. Mentally he calculated how he and Bill would get through dinner tonight and check with another mole candidate tomorrow morning before leaving Utah. Also, tomorrow Jenny would attend classes all day, then would be at work by 4:00 p.m. and off work at 1:00 a.m.

He chuckled, remembering a particularly tense moment earlier that afternoon. He fondly remembered Jenny's scathing comment that she snapped at him, "...as if my *weaving* was the only thing due tomorrow. Thank heavens I got my sculpture finished tonight, and my eight-page paper is due Monday!" It was so rare for any female to rail at him. Usually his dark demeanor and tall, bulky frame was very intimidating to most women, but not this one.

Jenny had finished with (what was a typical reaction for her, per her supervisor) sarcasm by commenting, "At least I got that book read for Modern British Lit. James Joyce is *so* easy to understand—I am sure I'll just whiz through the test now; *not!*" in a weird imitation of a 1980's valley girl phrase.

When their interview was over, she'd apologized for making her comments. However, Mitch had been bemused to see her be pleasant to her boss, even in her agitated state. Jenny even hugged her as she left work, saying, "I'll bring you a latte from Grounds for Coffee on the way home." Mitch also knew that Jenny's supervisor had been talking to the IRS service center director, and had been delayed meeting them this afternoon, because of that meeting. They learned about the IRS special agents on their way out of the building. That was intriguing. Mitch knew Bill's friend in the Secret Service. He knew that guy could be lethal. Those two IRS special agents had the same serious, yet quiet look about them. He would definitely have Stan and Homer reevaluate their thinking about using a civilian as a mole. Those IRS agents looked like they could be handy in a fight.

Mitch also found out that Jenny's coworkers knew something was afoot. They had passed by the interview room and Jenny's desk now and again, sending anxious looks at Jenny and affectionately clucking over her when the meeting was over. A bunch of them had been outside the building in a small park-like area, smoking cigarettes. They called to Jenny as she exited. In the snow, five ladies came around Jenny and they all stood talking to her. The hardened FBI agents were shocked by Jenny's coworkers. They showed great concern to her. Mitch and Bill had watched the women pat and hug Jenny before she was released to go to her truck. Such affection between coworkers surprised him. Bill had even remarked, "I am going to have to go over Ms. Johnson's personnel file in a little more detail. I've never seen our office gals act like that."

Mitch had replied, "I have, but only when no one 'official' is around. I agree with you. I'll call Stan tomorrow and ask him to get some details for Homer as well. Maybe we need to find some female companionship for Jenny during the training."

Judging by Jenny's reaction to the service center director, no little IRS employee had casual contact with the director. Mitch remembered the last time his supervisor's chief had talked to him. He cringed in sympathy for Jenny and her boss. No wonder her coworkers were worried about her. They knew which office she was in, and half of them had seen the IRS special agents and her boss leave it. He liked the fact that Jenny's work group was close knit, though. Hug your boss. Bring her coffee, what an idea. They had watched the news that something was up with Jenny spread quickly through the group inside. Jenny went through even more mother-hen moments on her way past her cubicle and out the door before reaching the other friends outside. He didn't envy the boss who'd have to get this group moving after their shocking day where one of their own had been called into the director. He wondered if they would be informed that Jenny had received a dangerous assignment, especially when no one would know the hows, or whys, and hopefully not the whos—the FBI.

As the two agents continued down the freeway to go pick up Jonesey, Mitch's cell phone rang. He motioned to Bill. "It's Jonesey."

"Hey, man. 'Bout time you answered. Stan called and we need to talk. When will you be here?" Jonesey asked.

Mitch answered as he tried to juggle the phone and keep his hands on the steering wheel. "We're just leaving now. What's happened?"

"Oh nothing much. He just wanted to bring you up to speed, but you were too busy scoping the hot student."

"Shut it, buddy. Who says she's hot. What's the news?"

"No news, really. It's no biggie. Just the latest on Gooding. I'll tell you all about it when you get here. It can wait. I just wanted to check your location for an ETA. As for how I know she's hot, Bill called me while you were on the pot."

Mitch sighed and looked over at Bill, who'd heard Jonesey and grinned. "Fine. We'll talk when we see you in a half hour."

"Okay, bye."

By 5:00 a.m., after the night's dinner, a long discussion, and some very uncomfortable hotel beds, the navy blue Suburban stopped at the nearest gas station from the hotel in Salt Lake City. The groggy Denver Bunch, chauffeured by Mitch and Bill, filled up with fuel, both high-octane and high-caffeine, before they headed south to Arizona with one mid-morning stop planned for the interview of the last and least likely mole candidate in Utah.

Chapter Twenty-five

Albert had almost fallen asleep quickly tonight for the first time in days. He had been able to convince Jessica to not leave him immediately, at least, but only barely. They had a long and strong marriage, but lately she'd been increasingly vocal about the fact that she was getting tired of the Agency's hold on her husband. Bless Jonesey for taking the time to explain the situation to her. Thankfully, Jonesey had still been in DC the morning of the portrait delivery. And, since he was Jessica's favorite of all the "boys," meaning the agents that adopted Albert as a pseudo father figure, she was willing to listen to his explanation as to why her husband would be practically living at the office for a while.

Really, it was amazing he could sleep at all with things as they were. Too bad the phone had to ring at that minute. "Wait a damn minute!" Albert sat straight up in bed. "The phone rang!" The security detail had rerouted all his calls to headquarters for a while to protect the family in case Gooding made Albert's involvement in the attacks even more personal. *They must have reopened the line in the night,* he thought as he tried to answer it. Albert fumbled, but succeeded in getting the guest room's extension into his hands and up to his ear. Just as he did, Jessica burst in from the hall with the cordless phone in her hand. Albert paused, listening to the office in one ear and his wife in the other. "It's your office. They called to let you know, well, that a Navy transport down in Baltimore harbor was bombed." Albert froze and the handset dropped from his boneless hand. Through a fog he could just hear Sal, his second-in-command, through the phone, trying to get Jessica off the extension.

"Al, Al, are you there? Jessica, I need to speak to Al. Put him back on…"

He heard Jessica in stereo, in person and through the phone as her voice caught, "Al, it was the one your boys were on."

Jessica knew those FBI boys; she and Albert regularly had agents over for dinner. Jessica hated to see the newest agents going without good, home-cooked meals. In fact, many of the field agents also got to know Albert through their payroll problems, and remembered him if they had other problems at work. Albert's house was nearly an unofficial after work club for his crew and those in need. In tears, she flung the cordless phone in her hands at Albert as Sal repeated the news.

Albert frowned. The boats were already in the water, and slipping a few men on board with the soldiers should have been easy. He dressed one-handed with the phone back to his ear as Sal relayed more messages. Gooding had been busy once he'd blown up his Chesapeake mansion. He'd delivered two messages to the FBI just this morning. One to the FBI headquarters in Washington DC and another to the FBI field office in Boston. Boston received a present from Gooding in the form of an airplane ticket stuffed into a plastic submarine that floated in a Ziploc© bag full of brownish-tinted liquid.

Adding more horror to this day, Albert received yet another stressful call once he arrived at the office. This one was about the plastic bag. Normally as the team's head accountant, he wouldn't be involved directly with any active investigations. But the airplane ticket, a phony printed-up version, was registered to an FBI agent that had been newly called back to home base after Alicia had compromised the travel vouchers. Boston needed Albert to check the itinerary on the ticket, to see if it was valid or not.

Not only was the information about the FBI agent's destination and identity accurate, but the trip was scheduled after they had found that the computer was compromised and implemented the first set of advanced security measures. Stan came into the office just as Albert agonized into the phone, "But we used pseudonyms and fake identities. The reservations were made through a travel agent, for Pete's sake, how could he have gotten it? No. Dammit, my office is not compromised again. I didn't even officially authorize that trip. In fact, we aren't doing any travel vouchers for now. This went through the CIA's system. They called me after you people called them. I didn't even know about it, how could Gooding have found out? How could I still be leaking to Gooding? Alicia's gone, dammit, and you know damn well the rest of us are practically quarantined!"

Albert shook his head and hung up the phone and noticed Stan standing there. "I am tired of speaking to yet another director of another office's bigwig. This all is way beyond my authority. Sure, I messed up by not spotting Alicia's duplicity quickly enough, but I am fixing it. Rather than castigating me every time something goes wrong, why don't they just throw me in jail? I could use the rest."

Stan pulled out a chair and stated in a calm tone, "Because we need you. You know that Gooding didn't attack you as Albert, but as Alicia's boss and a threat. He has no idea how valuable you are to us. He's using the money and travel vouchers to track our agents. He knows too well that the bean counters show the way to the agents." Stan paused. "Now what about the package, can we see it?" he asked Albert.

"Hell if I know. Those boys in Boston only called me to see if I was mole-ing for Gooding. I hope they catch on real quick that I'm a big dupe in this game and go after the real leads." Albert's tone was bitter and filled with self-contempt. He'd heard the doubt and patronizing contempt in the Boston agent's voice. They were thinking he was part of this mess. That really ticked him off. He wasn't sure if he could take any more scrutiny if it came in that fashion.

"If it helps, the Boston agents are bringing it down to have it analyzed for more clues. You know they wouldn't do that if they doubted our office," Stan remarked.

"Oh yeah. Do you know any more details about what Gooding sent them? They didn't feel like telling me anything else about it as they waited to see if I'd spill the details proving I am a patsy in this. Even though puzzling over something solvable like how to capture a madman maybe can make me feel better about my life." The sarcasm was thick.

Stan sighed. "Well the ticket was folded up and placed inside a toy replica of a US Ohio class submarine, and then the sub was put in a gallon-sized Ziploc® bag filled with Earl Grey tea."

"Oh a subtle Boston Tea Party allusion," Albert quipped.

"Uh-huh," Stan agreed.

Albert froze. "Did you say an Ohio class submarine?"

"Yes, why?"

Albert didn't answer Stan's question as his mind clicked details into place. "First his military transport. What if Gooding found out about Jessica's other idea…" Albert's thoughts ceased as his body went into action and he ordered Stan, "Get your boys on the phone. We have got to stop that submarine."

"What sub, Al?"

Albert ignored Stan's second question as he quickly yelled out to the next room to the guys working on the mainframe. "Hey, Carl, have you seen James today?"

"He went to your house to watch Jessica," was the reply.

"Get him back here now, and call the director, *now!*" Albert ordered. Carl immediately did as asked and left the room. Albert caught a glimpse of himself in the mirrored surface of the clock mounted on the wall. He looked worse than ever. His face had gone chalky and sweat was visible on his brow and upper lip.

"What's going on, Al?"

Al shifted his attention to Stan. "Well, see, when I told the director of the Eastern seaboard that I didn't know about the reservations, I lied." He gulped and tried to slow down his breathing. "I don't know where the leak is. I don't know how high up it goes or who's involved, so I called my buddies at the CIA travel section to have them try to get a reservation through for me, so that I could track it, to see if anyone undesirable spots it. But, to protect the agents we're trying to get to the UK, I called an old Navy buddy who arranged for one set of agents to get to England on one of their transport ships and another few to France on an Ohio class submarine." Albert had thought that by making the reservations himself, they'd be safe. *Gooding should have expected us to move the travel reservations out of this office after the leak.*

Stan's thoughts echoed Albert's, "Oh no," finally seeming to understand Albert's upset. The office swung into motion.

In his first "message" to the FBI, Gooding had verified that he was aiming for some action in the UK before celebrating July 4 in DC. So, Stan and Homer had decided to smuggle what agents they could into the UK as soon as possible in an effort to stop Gooding before he could return to the United States. They'd called on Albert's craftiness to do it, figuring his personal contacts would be safe from any residual Gooding leaks. Albert had smuggled two FBI teams aboard a Navy transport headed for England from a New York harbor, and Gooding's crew had blown up the ship early this morning, using a portable missile launcher from a yacht.

Now other agents were in danger. At the last minute, Albert had arranged for another pair of agents to leave Boston on a Navy submarine based on a suggestion from Jessica. The Boston office had faxed the report to Stan, who handed it to Albert to read.

"Late last night, before final boarding, one of the submariners had a medical emergency and had to be removed from the ship due to a suspicious accident. An investigation revealed that the submariner had been inspecting things per his assignment in the engine room, when he found an access door ajar. As he investigated the door, he triggered a trap, and a sharp blade swung out and sliced off his hand at the wrist." Albert continued to read the unpolished report taken from one of the field agent's notes. "His mate heard the action and rushed to his aid. The crew was able to administer medical assistance and got the hand on ice for possible reattachment. The MPs secured the device and note (attached) for examination. They removed them to base as the mate was being transported to the hospital for surgery. Unfortunately, the MPs didn't find the wire, which had connected the trap to the bomb down-ship. The triggering of the trap started the countdown. One hour later, the bomb exploded, causing a chain reaction of secondary explosions and blowing the submarine apart just as it headed out to sea, but didn't compromise the reactor, which the navy was working to retrieve. There were some survivors, but not the FBI agents. They had been below deck, staying out of the way of the ship's activities."

Albert could read no more, so Stan finished the explanation. "Gooding had cleverly hid the device in an area only routinely checked during the embarking activities. He wanted the crew to be on board before the bomb went off. By timing it that way he's proven that he wanted the bodies found and for survivors."

Albert took a deep breath and nodded. "He must have had help with the sabotage of the Navy submarine."

"Obviously, but the Navy cops are understandably not sharing information with us willingly," Stan answered.

"They refused to surrender Gooding's letter to us at first, but anger over losing some of their own folks compelled them to spread the story and they decided to pool their resources with our investigation. They've dropped it in our laps for now. Like the Coast Guard, they didn't believe us."

Albert paused, thinking about the uncomfortable truth. The Navy didn't know who to trust, either. The fact that Gooding had gone out of his way to leave survivors caused them to doubt their own crews.

Stan spoke quietly, echoing Albert's worry. "Even now, the submarine's crew, including the wounded, are in lockdown as the MPs go through their files and the wreckage. On your behalf, I took the liberty of asking Sal to head down to Boston."

Forty-five minutes later, Homer, Albert, Stan, and the other DC FBI chiefs were deep in conference at headquarters. Something had to be done about the transport issues. Gooding's note made it clear that he had broken into more computers than initially thought. He'd obviously hacked into the requests to the Navy. He'd found the FBI agents by their names and SSNs, even many of their code names and pseudonyms. Carl and the IT guys were right. They had to find out how deep Gooding had dug into the databases and fast. It was possible that Gooding had bugged supposedly secure phone and fax lines in addition to hacking into computers.

Transportation was now going to be an even bigger problem. In a few days, the East Coast region FBI's big winter training retreat was scheduled in Upstate New York. The FBI agents desperately needed to get this training to prepare for Gooding. It also would provide them with some critical downtime. So far, all Albert's tricks had not succeeded in moving anyone anywhere successfully. Homer and Stan were frantic. Did they keep instructing all the agents to drive private vehicles and carpool? The consensus agreed. Homer made the decision. "No one's private information has been used against us yet, only governmental. Let's reimburse those who can drive as planned and find all the open civilian government credit cards we have for gas, for now." Albert knew that even that may not stop Gooding. If he could find the agents' SSNs and other personal information, then even the use of personal vehicles posed a security risk. And the use of more government credit cards would leave a huge paper trail. However, nobody wanted to increase the secretaries' bank trips for cash and the current hand-written records. Albert's staff was already working overtime to keep hand-written ledgers and using old 1960's typewriters resurrected from some government surplus warehouse. At least they had not connected the photocopiers onto the computer network. File boxes were stacking up everywhere.

Chapter Twenty-six

Jonesey had his wife Amy meet Jenny Johnson for lunch in a quiet downtown Ogden restaurant to deliver Jenny her FBI packet "starter kit," he'd prepared. The two women had forged a friendship when he had introduced them the week before. Due to the security breaches, he felt uncomfortable being around his wife and family, or Jenny, fearing he could be endangering them. So, in the time before she traveled to Atlanta for the full training, he gave Jenny a loose itinerary and a list of things to "bone up" on to prepare for her mission. Jonesey had promised Amy would deliver the packet once he was able to get it to her through his network of friends between Utah, Denver, and DC. Amy had told him that over soup and sandwiches she and Jenny had discussed kids, neighbors, life, and the FBI, and Jenny had confessed that she liked Jonesey, because he reminded her of her older brothers.

Homer and the profilers had dutifully gone through all the pre-mole interviews, and had agreed with Mitch and Bill's assessment that Jenny would be the only candidate to meet Homer's expectations. After so many agents' deaths, it was formally decided that the only mole that could reach Gooding was an innocent civilian. The FBI and CIA task force had no luck getting an agent anywhere near him. All their intelligence came from nontraditional sources. Therefore, both the FBI and CIA would find candidates and provide intense but minimal training in preparation of catching Gooding. However, because Gooding had no problem with collateral damage, the task force ultimately decided not to prepare any other moles. Though Albert worried about throwing all their eggs into one basket, Jenny was the only mole they would use. Albert didn't know that Stan and the CIA chief's back up plan was for a CIA sniper to simply take Gooding out if Jenny failed.

After the phone interview with Stan, Jenny was informed of her selection and forthcoming official, temporary reassignment to the FBI. She was told only to prepare to travel East sometime in the spring and to follow the information given to her by the local team leader, Jonesey, in the meantime.

Jonesey and Amy met with Jenny soon after the final decision and they formed a loose training plan for Jenny to accomplish over the next few weeks. Jenny began socializing with Amy and would often visit her in the temporary home in Salt Lake City. Sharing her anxieties with an FBI wife seemed to reassure Jenny and enable her to let go of her worries about the FBI and focus on her IRS job and school until they called.

Amy and Jenny's favorite activity was practicing at the local gun range. Jenny had been around guns all her life and was competent with her Dad's old colt revolver and great-grandpa's Winchester rifle, but she'd never fired a Glock or semi-automatic gun before. Jonesey had evaluated her on the first trip to the range, sighed, handed her his Glock, and proceeded to train her in FBI firing techniques. When Jenny wasn't doing her schoolwork, developing prints in her darkroom, or working at her IRS job, she was at the gun range.

Chapter Twenty-seven

Winter in New York was something to see, especially deep in the woods, far away from obvious civilization. The old forest full of hardwoods was not the pine forests of Mitch's childhood in Montana, but the trees shared the same spirit of the woods. The crisp air and sparkling whiteness were the same as the impressions of his memories. He breathed deeply and the non-agent part of him prayed for the safety of his friends and fellow agents in this tense time.

Mitch and Bill had arrived early for the training retreat. Along with Carl and Reva, they were the first to arrive at the FBI's campground deep in the woods north of Albany. They had come in separate vehicles, Carl and Reva coming east from Chicago, and Bill and Mitch traveling from Portland, Maine. Both sets of agents had borrowed a vehicle from someone they knew, but who was not related to them, in an effort to keep their whereabouts from Gooding as they followed his trail.

One of Alicia Birmingham's credit cards had been charged to a car rental outfit in Portland, while one of Gooding's business accounts had been accessed out of a Chicago vocational school's computer lab. Both were found to be red herrings. Both incidents had been traced to a stranger who'd done something for Gooding or his crew. The Chicago student had picked up Alicia after her car was ditched and delivered her to the train station and received the credit card as payment. The Portland car dealer had been told he was helping a friend of a friend while he happened to be in DC. He'd carried Gooding's camera equipment through the airport to the gate. That's how Gooding had shipped it through the airports. The car dealer was a foot shorter and fifty pounds heavier than Gooding, so his carrying a set of camera equipment, while it got him noticed by security and checked, did not stop him from getting to Amsterdam as planned to visit his family. He carried the equipment to the gate and checked the bulk of it there. He left the claim tags with the carry-on case in overhead bin number twenty-five. Unluckily for the FBI, the car dealer's seat was in first class; he never saw anyone get into the bin after him.

Although Gooding may have had an active accomplice on the plane, Mitch believed he had gotten to Amsterdam on that flight, but they couldn't prove it. Gooding's presence in Europe had yet to be verified. One of Albert's connections had claimed to see him in Copenhagen, but it wasn't known where Gooding went after he left for Finland from Denmark.

Then they'd found out the man believed to be Gooding was a decoy, one of Gooding's employees pretending to be the boss. Gooding hadn't been in Scandinavia at all.

Mitch surveyed the scene below them. The FBI's "camp" was situated near a river with a large clubhouse/lodge and small cabins clustered around a large clearing. It also included an obstacle course on the high bluffs above the falls north of the main camp and an old bridge that led into the woods along an old logging trail. He could see Bill and Carl down by the main lodge, which served as a reception area, headquarters, and held the cafeteria and recreation room. Three members of the janitorial staff along with the site coordinator stood staring into an open pipe to the left of the camp, by the latrines, verifying whether the septic leak last fall had been fixed. Although winter still held the woods in its cold grip, it was a clear day. A light snowfall was expected later, but the forecast was clear for the next week's activities.

Reva came up behind Mitch with her binoculars. They had found nothing suspicious. In fact, as it was Friday night, they were planning on heading into town for a good dinner before their four-day stint watching the camp while the site coordinator and his team obtained the supplies necessary to enable 150 people to stay in an isolated environment for ten days and until the actual troops arrived on Monday. Bill glanced upward and signaled to them by issuing a sharp whistle. All clear down there. Mitch pulled his hood up and headed down to the clearing past the obstacle fence with Reva.

Bright and early Monday morning, the senior agents and supervisors began arriving. Many came in carpools in all-terrain vehicles. The parking lot was soon half full. Mitch, Bill, Reva, and Carl stood on the porch, watching the site coordinator direct the filling of the parking lot. "Good thing the bosses go home on Wednesday so that us peons can have somewhere to park on Thursday," Reva remarked on her way indoors to retrieve her binoculars. She and Mitch were heading out to re-inspect the groves surrounding the old logging trails on the far side of the bridge. The bridge played an integral role in the best team-building training exercise during the winter trainings held here each year. It seemed to leap across the deep gorge cut by the falls northeast of camp and led to the old forestry trails beyond.

Like other government jobs which sometimes have few perks when compared to private sector jobs, old recruits would take a certain sadistic pleasure watching the "newbies," as the brand-new agent recruits were called, try to hold on to the frozen girders of the bridge as the wind tried to blow them away. Freezing wind blowing on all four sides was hell to endure, but it was always a true pleasure to watch when the partakers needed to vent a little frustration. The exercise had become an unofficial initiation of sorts.

The bridge was also the other security problem at the camp, besides the single entry road, as it linked the camp to the great wilderness beyond. The camp was the last civilized stop on the road, so both entryways needed watching. Beyond the compound the trees took over. No one really knew how many old trails or hidden ways existed beyond the visible. The camp claimed only the bridge as part of its territory; the rest of the woods and trails beyond were left to regress back to a pristine state.

Usually there was not enough traffic to hide anyone's passing, but there had been enough fresh snow in the last couple of weeks to obliterate any old tracks. The snowfall coupled with the winds that could be generated through the ravine usually kept the bridge in hazardous, icy conditions and blew away any tracks.

Reva had expressed concerned that someone could have concealed themselves deep in the trees on the far side of the bridge. There had been an old logger's shack a mile or so beyond, and they needed to make sure it was empty. "Gives us old-timers a chance to keep on our toes," Bill had muttered as they got ready. Mitch nodded, but otherwise remained silent. Funny, before Gooding's bombings, no one had really worried about a surprise attack way out here.

Reva entered the grove first. Of the security team agents, Reva was by far the best marksman. Because the bosses had already populated the camp with FBI agents, Carl and Bill had decided to join her and Mitch on their reconnaissance for a change of pace from the oppressive atmosphere created by packing a lot of bored, worried people into one place. After four days and nights of relaxing peace and quiet, the typical squabbles caused by too many bosses in one place had also been wearing on all their nerves. The leaders had begun arguing about the team assignments for this retreat again. These four friends, having been outvoted by the big bosses, had volunteered for the security detail to get a break from the bickering.

Mitch set off into the trees on the right. Bill was in the woods on the front-left. Reva stayed at the head of the trail. Carl stood on Reva's left side, waiting with her as they presented a pretty image of two wintertime hikers. They headed down the trail, Reva with her hands in her pockets, her gun ready just in case, while Carl walked briskly by her side.

Mitch reached the shack first. As he approached the side of the cabin, Bill came out of the trees to the rear of the cabin, directly behind the rear steps. There was no indication that anyone had been there in years. The snow around the southern side of the shack by Mitch had been blown into drifts away from the building, leaving skeletons of crusty ice behind, frozen in delicate arcs; any footprints through it would have been preserved in compressed ice, much like fossils. Mitch soon found the northern side's snow to be just as bad for hiding tracks. The cool wind had pulverized the snow there into a scratchy powder and drifted it against the walls of the cabin. Anyone passing there would have caused serious interruptions in the snow. Carl and Reva hung back in the woods as Mitch went around back to check the back door.

Nothing happened. At his signal, Bill shifted to the side, melted back into the treeline, and waved Carl and Reva closer. As Reva approached the front door, Carl came up directly behind her and shifted his coat for easier access to his own gun, while somehow managing to look nonchalant. The shack was so dilapidated that Mitch could see Reva and Carl through a crack in the rear door and the window that looked out to the front porch. From what he could see, the shack was deserted. In fact, he could see where snow dusted a section of rubble covering where a quarter of the roof had fallen in, down through to the floor.

Reva played the part of a sweetheart dragging her beau through the snow, by almost prancing up the porch steps with Carl in tow. After carefully opening the door and entering, she and Carl stood near the huge hole where the roof caved in. The rear door seemed stuck, so Mitch moved forward to un-wedge the door. It opened inward and fell back onto the floor, then right through it. Reva gasped and jumped backward. Carl grunted as Reva nearly knocked him into the hole. A thorough inspection confirmed that the shack was deserted. Carl presented a pretty picture as he carefully toed his way back to the hole in the floor. Mitch stood on the end of a plank and inspected the area where the rear door fell. Carl shone a pocket light below the floor while Reva inspected the ceiling joists with her own flashlight. Nothing moved in either place.

After a few moments, the team heard Bill lightly whistle—their signal. They followed an old game trail in the trees, reaching the bridge and going across stealthily. As Mitch and Bill followed Carl and Reva across, Mitch remarked, "Here we slink across, when anyone can see us without half trying."

Carl heard him and said, "Next time, take the lower trail across the 'new' back bridge upriver."

Reva chimed in, "Yeah, they installed it last year to help hikers get down to the trail that follows the river."

Thursday, the official activity day after three days of preparation, dawned late and cloudy, but the overcast sky gave testament to the lack of cold wind blowing. The newbies were heading out on the bridge, blindfolded, after lunch.

Mitch and Bill watched the new recruits from the porch. The senior agents would be heading into the woods for the stalking exercise at 2:00 p.m., hiding and waiting. Meanwhile, all fifty newbies had reached the middle of the span. Each was separated by a few feet from all others and encouraged to determine what was happening around them.

A cool wind swept around them. The group of fifty was separated into teams of ten, with a two-man team of experienced agents assigned to each of them. The security detail didn't exempt anyone from this duty, but Reva and Carl needed time off for their assignment later that day, so

Mitch and Bill volunteered to take the first group across the rickety bridge.

The bridge exercise was an object lesson, only on a real-life scale. The trainees had been cooped up in classrooms with detailed pictures, old blueprints, maps, and sketches of the bridge and training compound. They were instructed to treat these documents as if they were compiling a case file, for an attack on this bridge. They were even given samples of the type of wood used in the bridge, which had been aged like the bridge, so they could determine its aspects and any special characteristics.

The newbies were not told that they would be going over the bridge blindfolded and without their winter coats. Once they started across the bridge, the trainees were stopped at various points on the bridge and required to answer specific questions. They were allowed some exploration of the bridge, but had to remain blind. Their task was purposely made harder by the lack of sight and little protection from the cold in order to sharpen and quicken their skills.

Although this was the second time Bill and Mitch had been asked to lead a team across the bridge, Mitch felt the special significance of this time. *This* batch of trainees would be their help on the Gooding task force. This bunch would have to learn the job in a third of the time. Because their names were not on Albert's files yet, they were the few agents still available for active duty who had a chance to make it through Gooding's nets.

When scaling the bridge, Bill and Mitch usually took a few minutes before the exercise to help focus their own goals. They needed to know what to look for in their trainees, and this year Mitch took the time to relax a bit before they started. "We need to focus on calm, clearheaded logic today."

"I think you're right," Bill answered. "Let's do the wind test and the speed test, get them thinking." In agreement, they led their ten to the bridge.

They asked the trainees about the wind velocity and how many vehicles could make it across the bridge. They watched as the trainees felt the wood beneath their hands, on the rails, the sidebars, and even the floor of the bridge. Mitch watched Reva's cousin Jordan crawl along on all fours, testing the actual gap between the crossbeams.

While Mitch observed, Bill made constant notations on his clipboard. Senior teams of agents were used as observers here, as the bridge leaders had to communicate silently to each other in order to not tip off the recruits. Mitch made some positive gestures toward one of the female recruits who stood in the middle of the bridge. She had located the middle by going back and forth across the bridge until she felt the curve change. When she had located the apex of the bridge's gentle curve, she licked a finger and held it up above her head, then lay down and held the moistened digit below her to determine if the gusty winds were faster or slower above or below the bridge. He smiled at how serious most of the newbies took this exercise.

At the end of the exercise and before the trainees were allowed to examine the bridge with all their senses, they would be asked to formulate a plan for how a team of agents could disable the bridge undetected. As Mitch watched the same female recruit, he thought of the plan he and Bill had concocted as new recruits. They had found that the wind, while fiercer beneath the bridge, was blocked by the undergirding of the side rails. In their plan, three agents could cross underneath the bridge by using mountain climbing equipment. They could hang upside down and plant explosives every few feet, but still make it safely to the other side. The girders could also block them from sight of any observers. The trainees formulated their plans in the classroom, and after the "lights out" exercise they would reexamine their ideas and determine if their plan could work.

This batch of trainees was doing a great job. A whistle sounded in the air above them. "Time's up!" Carl called over the loudspeaker. Mitch and Bill corralled the newbies back into the center of the bridge in preparation for their blindfolds to be removed. As a sort of payment for the hard work of scrambling over an old bridge blindfolded, newbies were afforded a spectacular view from the center of the bridge for just a moment before they were removed from the bridge. Somehow, by not staring down the face of the gorge until you were in the midst of it, the sight was particularly moving, especially the southern view down from the mountains to the valley. Then, they would be mercifully allowed back into the lodge to warm up as they geared up for the final review of the bridge.

Mitch particularly enjoyed watching the newbies' reactions to the gorge for the first time. He and Bill both smiled over the "oohs" and "aahs." They overheard one recruit remark that his math calculations may not work since his figures were based on projected measurements, not actual ones. The recruit's team agreed to re-run the figures once they got back inside.

Mitch had just turned away from the gorge toward the trainees to gather them up to return to the lodge, when he heard a loud chopping noise behind him. There, coming up the gorge, appeared to be a helicopter.

Bill frowned. "Funny, this is supposed to be restricted air space."

Mitch wondered for a moment; then, the back of his neck tingled. All of a sudden, he felt his fingers and toes also start to tingle in anticipation of danger. He screamed, "Bill, bad news! Get the kids off the bridge *now*!"

Bill sprang into action. Shouts rang in the air as the chopper came closer. "Rip those masks off, get the hell of the bridge now. Either side!" Both Bill and Mitch were yelling as they rushed the trainees off of the bridge. They ended up going for the far side of the bridge, where the trees provided more cover.

***

From her position in the trees behind the buildings, Reva could see the helicopter now, and radioed Carl to get all personnel into the safety of the trees. She could see a missile launcher and some large caliber guns on the underbelly of the flying machine and knew the buildings would be no refuge. "Scatter into the woods!" she screamed into her radio.

***

How did the bridge get so long? Mitch thought to himself as he hustled the last couple of recruits to the end. Bill had grabbed a couple of kids and herded them off into the woods upstream, but the gal they had been watching had tripped and stumbled on one of the planks. Mitch and Jordan had stopped to help her. Each taking one of her arms, they half carried her across the bridge. Bill had secured all the trainees in the deep underbrush along this edge's side of the ravine. Mitch and Jordan helped the brunette off the bridge just as the helicopter shot its first missile.

The bridge exploded in red ball of fire where huge beams of wood splintered in an instant. The fireball blew Mitch and the two recruits ten feet in the air to land in the snowy packed dirt just past the end of the bridge.

Mitch thankfully landed on a softer dirt patch and was able to recover quickly. He turned back toward the chopper for a moment. He saw the brunette—Angela— crawling into the bushes in front of them toward Bill, who was rushing out to get her. He looked down the hill past his feet and saw Jordan a few feet away. While Mitch's brain was struggling to make his body move over to help Jordan, he saw the helicopter circle around and fly back down the gorge. A second missile struck the other side of the bridge. The last remaining trusses plunged downward in fiery arcs.

Before he was able to move, Mitch saw Jordan regain his senses and try to rise. Jordan got up on all fours and shook his head. He scrambled toward Mitch. From what Mitch could see he was having trouble with his right leg. Mitch pushed himself upright and, looking back behind himself, spotted a rocky outcrop which would provide excellent cover for them. He turned back to Jordan and jerked his head in the direction of the rocks and started toward him. Jordan nodded his head to acknowledge the plan and continued his uphill journey.

Too soon the helicopter doubled back yet again. It flew over the compound, raining bullets through the courtyard in a sweeping circle, shattering glass but causing little human damage since few agents were still in the open—until it reached the trees. Mitch knew that Bill had scurried all his newbies into the cover in the woods on the far side of the gorge, while Reva and Carl had got most of the other agents evacuated into the forest on the compound side, but some figures could be seen near the fringes of the trees. Mitch's heart began to pound. The snow gave them no cover and the deciduous tree branches concealed very little. The chopper shot rounds into the trees as it turned. Evergreen needles, whole tree branches, and snow flew through the air in the aftermath. For just a second Mitch saw Carl dart out, grab a wounded man, and drag him back into the woods.

He finally reached Jordan, and saw that his leg had been broken below the knee. Half hoisting him onto his back, he picked him up and carried him up to the rocky outcrop. Before they could get there, the nearest rock of the outcrop shattered into thousands of flying shards as the helicopter's missile struck it. Jordan and Mitch were blown backward toward the cliff. Mitch felt the impact and instinctively held on to Jordan as they struck the ground.

He lay there dazed for a moment, trying to get his bearings. The helicopter circled back, apparently to view the carnage they caused. After swinging over the compound and sending their last missile into the camp's powerhouse, it came back toward this side of the gorge.

Bill was close enough to Mitch and Jordan to offer some cover. The chopper came straight at them. Mitch watched as Bill raised his pistol, clearly aiming for the pilot. Shots from the copter's guns sprayed dirt and snow all around him, but his aim was true. In an instant the copter jerked and swayed and its rounds went wild. Bill had got the pilot. The copter was close enough now, that Mitch saw the copilot force the helicopter back in control and turn it back down the gorge and out of sight. Bill kept firing until his clip was empty, and something that looked like gas started streaming out of the body of the chopper. He shouldered his pistol and rushed down to Mitch.

Mitch struggled to rise to his knees. He still had hold of Jordan, but things were bad. They lay on a snow bank only three feet from the edge of the cliff. Jordan had a large wound in his side from a piece of shrapnel when the rock exploded. Blood was everywhere, seeping out from beneath him. Mitch felt Jordan's neck. His pulse was beating erratically, frantically trying to get blood flowing through his body. As he changed positions, trying to get below Jordan on the slope, he felt the snow give way beneath them. The shifting caused him to lose his balance. Mitch ended up on his chest in the snow as it slid down. He struggled, trying to stop sliding down the slope. Thankfully, with his left hand he was able to grab a rock jutting up, and still hold on to Jordan with his right arm. They held this position for a moment, then Mitch felt Jordan go slack. He couldn't get enough breath to talk Jordan into keeping consciousness, but a minute later it didn't matter.

Another slide started below him, and Mitch felt Jordan drop from under his arm. Jordan became a dead weight as the snow and ice sheet they had landed on slipped off the cliff. Mitch tried to hold on to him, but lost grip, and Jordan fell into the gorge.

Mitch was able to grab the rock with his now free hand as the snow under him disappeared. He found himself dangling from a wet, snowy rock 500 feet above the rapids below. Through excruciating pain, he felt tears come into his eyes. His right arm burned. He almost wanted to let go, but knew he couldn't. He didn't want to die. He didn't know how he could face Reva, or want to see how many others had been killed, but he couldn't die. Somehow, he was able to get a good breath and pull himself upward. He reached the edge of the slope and was pausing at that point to gather the strength to haul himself over the edge when his grip broke and he landed on his chest square on the rock he'd held on to. Tremors started his arms shaking. Feeling rubbery, he was about to give up when he felt someone grab his upper arms. He lifted his head to see Bill.

"Dammit, I almost got here in time, but no rope, dammit. But thank God I had my gun." Bill was talking to himself as he yanked Mitch up with one mighty pull. Mitch catapulted against Bill's chest and they fell back on the snow among the branch and rock fragments. "Good to see you safe, now get the hell off me. My arm must be busted." Bill's statement cleared Mitch's head. He found the strength to roll sideways. They lay there for a moment, cherishing breath. That's how the brunette trainee, Angela, and Reva found them a half hour later.

***

Upstream, at the new footbridge installed on the back side of the compound last year, help arrived. These were the "mucky-mucks," or bigwig trainers, who liked to use binoculars to spy on the trainees' progress on the main bridge below them. Once Reva and Carl had started moving the wounded and others into the main building, she had set out across this footbridge to find Bill and Mitch's group. She'd found Angela and eight of the other trainees huddled near the path to the upper bridge. She checked them all and found some cuts and bruises, sprains, and a couple gunshot wounds.

Radioing Carl to have someone meet them here, she asked after Mitch, Bill, and her cousin Jordan. Angela was the only one who'd seen Mitch after the bridge fell, but they all had seen Bill head back to the bridge. Reva radioed the commander, who'd got the compound's backup generator going and had been contacting headquarters to tell them of their status and to find out the whereabouts of the chopper. Through her handset, Reva heard the commander answer that the chopper was gone. Satellite and local radar stations were tracking it, and they'd heard the chopper radio that they were leaking fuel. Headquarters had local law enforcement and teams flying into the area to start the search for the helicopter and crew. "They'll catch them. Do your best to take care of your people," crackled out of the radio.

"Well, we have our orders. Angela, stay with this crew. You seem to be holding up better than some of them. I have to go find the boys." Reva shifted her gear and headed down the slope to the main bridge site.

"I'm coming with you. Mitch and Jordan saved my life." Angela's tone and jaw were set.

Reva nodded and they headed downhill together. They reached Bill shortly. Carl's voice crackled on the radio to say that agents said they saw somebody fell off the ravine into the gorge. "Get somebody down there now," was heard as Bill reached over to Reva's radio and switched it off. Their eyes met and Reva understood that it was Jordan who fell. They nodded in an unspoken agreement that they all would use the next few minutes as "quiet time" before heading back to the camp.

Bill told Reva about Jordan as Mitch laid there, eyes tightly shut. Angela wrapped Bill's bleeding forearm in a scrap of her T-shirt while he and Reva conversed. Mitch had refused help for a moment. He appeared lost in despair, and clearly he wanted to stay that way for a while. Reva bowed her head and cried for a moment as she began grieving for her dear cousin. Tears ran unchecked down Angela's cheeks as she helped Bill to his feet. Bill lightly hugged her and released her. He pulled Reva up with his good arm and let her cry on his shoulder for a moment. When she had contained herself, Reva took Angela and left Bill and Mitch to come as they may. She knew as they knew, that she, Angela, and both Mitch and Bill needed some time to compose themselves before making the report.

***

Bill walked to the edge of the cliff, reached into his pocket, pulled out a handful of bullets and calmly and systematically refilled his gun clip. Mitch continued to sit quietly on the broken rock behind him, silent as he stared at the bloody snow trail that led off the cliff. Then he moved his arm and felt the pain shoot up to his shoulder. The pain focused him—overriding the part of him that wanted to get up and kick the rest of the snow off, to hide the fact that someone died here. He knew his training. He forced himself to focus and breathe, waiting for the photographer to get here to start the case file, and viciously bit back the urge to get up and kick snow over the bloody track.

All too soon another agent arrived to document the scene. In the sporadic flashes from the camera, Mitch allowed Bill to awkwardly help him to his feet, one-armed. Some of the blood in the snow was his own. He had a large gash in the front of his thigh, but the blood had started to congeal and it appeared to be only a flesh wound, though it hurt like a mother. He also tried not feel the leftover pulling aches in his arms from hanging off the cliff. Bill seemed to be faring much better, and he kept a steadying arm around Mitch's waist as they made their way up to the upper bridge and back into camp. Carl's voice came over the senior team's frequency on Bill's radio as soon as he switched it back on. The wind was messing with the radio transmission; they couldn't hear Stan's part of the conversation, just Carl's. He said, "Yeah, we found him in the water. ... Just through the ice. ... Our own 'copters are coming. ... They'll take him into town. No, I'll go to Reva..."

Then static took over.

Chapter Twenty-eight

As he lay back in the padded leather seat, Gooding drank a deep swallow of the cool, bracing whiskey. His plane was usually well stocked with any satisfying alcoholic beverage a jet-setter would desire, but it had been a long week. He had settled Alicia in London and left her in the care of his driver and pocketbook while he headed north to Scotland to check in with Grandfather. The old man continued to pressure him to knock off the art galleries and go back to the freight line. *At least the trip was not entirely wasted. I was able to check on the equipment at the castle. And it would take even Alicia years to spend all my money,* Gooding thought. He needed to relax and calm down his excitement. So far every explosion had worked perfectly. Manuel had sent Mortimer the documentation from the buoy's explosion and it was excellent. George had captured a few priceless images before swimming away. Soon he'd have the "winter in New York" pictures from Manuel on his visit the FBI's compound. *It was a piece of genius, planting Manuel in the ambulance crew called in to work on the survivors,* Gooding thought. After New York, they were back to the Summer Plan bomb list—next on tap, an army training exercise in Iceland. *Doing the army bomb in Iceland will enable Manuel to get to the UK that much faster. It's just too bad we just don't have the time to nix a full army deployment flight from Ft. Hood, Texas. Those big cargo planes carry a lot of fuel, and I was looking forward to doing just the right size bomb that would blow a huge hole in the plane, but allow a tank to land on someone's house.* Gooding smiled.

He quietly sipped his drink again and decided he didn't want it. Alcohol always depressed him after a high. He hoped the FBI enjoyed the parting "thank you" he'd sent them. He only had a few Mob connections left, and by giving them one of his old helicopters, they'd felt required to pay him back some way. Besides, his old Mob buddy liked to hunt in the woods near the FBI compound and knew right where it was. He smiled. That was the best attack so far. Getting the FBI on their home turf and he was nowhere in sight. He would celebrate this victory well. As soon as he arrived back in London, he would take some time to savor the memory, using the footage he had so far. Mortimer had captured it from the video camera with its satellite connection hidden in the helicopter. He may even share some of the fun with Alicia.

Gooding poked around in the fridge, looking for something salty, and pushed garishly colored bottles out of his way. Alicia had stocked the plane last, so besides the one bottle of aged Scotch whiskey he'd stocked himself, no upscale vodka or bourbon as was preferred by his grandfather had made its way into the fridge. This time the Thornton Industries private jet was stocked with sickly sweet drinks like Kahlua and wine coolers. Gooding smiled. His mother, with her high-class sensibilities, would faint in horror at these contents. She believed that a real lady drank liqueurs, or secretly snuck from the required stock of all the classic items found in a fine "gentlemen's" liquor cabinet. She preferred her father's vodka, brandy, whiskey, etc., over what she termed "cheap drink."

That fine mother of his would also refer to Alicia as a cheap American tramp. Gooding smiled again as he found the caviar and brie and amended the thought. *Mother actually may even call her a slut or whore, if she were angry and drunk enough to forget propriety.* Maybe he should try to have them meet each other after sufficiently lubricating things. It was always fun when his mother met one of his women. He'd do it at one of Grandfather's assemblies. It would be most enjoyable to watch Grandfather see Mother make a fool of herself. Looking absently out the window of the plane, he relaxed as he contemplated a family reunion in an effort to decide how to properly enjoy himself in London after months of being away. *I didn't even get to settle in before he called me away this time. I will need to make up for lost time.*

***

A few minutes later, Mortimer came back into the private cabin from the crew cabin just behind the cockpit. Anxiously peering at his employer's face, Mortimer paused for a moment, checking to make sure Gooding was awake. He had only seen someone wake up Mr. Gooding before he was ready once. He'd had the unappetizing task of disposing of the body afterward. He turned to go back the way he came after deciding that Gooding was asleep. Before he'd taken a step, he heard, "What is it?"

Gooding's question startled him, but Mortimer had learned years ago to show no surprise, fear, or shock around Gooding—any weakness annoyed him. Mortimer turned back and addressed his boss. "Hans just radioed in. Manuel made it to the freighter, and they are on their way to Aberdeen. The Iceland attack was successful."

"Good. Tell him well done and call in celebratory provisions for Manuel and the crew upon arrival," Gooding replied.

Mortimer hid his relief at his boss' good mood as he responded, "Yes, sir. Do you want me to obtain the New York and Iceland photographs when you return to Scotland or when we arrive in London?"

Gooding paused a moment and answered, "They can wait on the ship with the rest."

"Yes, sir." Mortimer returned to the crew cabin with his orders, leaving Gooding to enjoy the remainder of the flight. He was glad that—for today, at least—his orders did not include removing a female companion from Gooding's life. He was tired; it had been a long day, and disposing of another body would just be too much.

***

Yet another successful attack, Gooding thought, pleased at the idea. The plan was in full motion. Had he not had to babysit Alicia to keep her out of FBI hands, he would have joined his crew on their attack of the Army's winter training in Iceland. He could just see his men docking in the bay, claiming a need for emergency repairs. He personally chose the boat that would secret them to the shore and could picture their equipment as they met his officer in town. Motorized scooters and night-vision goggles would have been waiting for them. They would creep to the barracks and place the powerful explosives Gooding had crafted just for the insulated hot water heating system. It would be a good way to get the US' attention in full. Each part of that massive government would begin to feel its members' pain.

Gooding took a bite of the caviar and spit it out with distaste. "Damn that woman," he spat. "The bitch can't even choose good caviar." He sighed as he threw the mess away. At least his mother dealt in quality provisions. Gooding thought about the women in his life. He would have to be more discerning with the next female, he decided. Not that he chose women by their class or even just their looks. He did prefer a woman with ambition and brains, but not one that was too smart if they were going to help him with a project. He preferred them to have a good understanding of their purpose in his life without overreaching. He didn't like women who poked around in his affairs too much.

Thinking of curious women brought an image of Alicia to mind. Once she learned that Gooding was willing to use her husband as one of his targets, she was overcome with excitement and the rush of knowing that someone's life was in her hands. The excitement went to her head and she had become a bit too opinionated about the Summer Plan.

Gooding was glad that he'd left Alicia in Washington while he'd finished unveiling his exhibit. He would probably have lost his temper and removed her from his life permanently had she had one of her illogical temper fits in New York. Once and only once, he'd encountered her at one of the glittering Washington parties. Of course, she'd arrived with her husband, and Gooding had pretended to meet her there. His chief purpose in being seen in public with her was to cause the gossips to blather on about them possibly having an affair. The women at the party were so busy watching how he and Alicia would maneuver behind her husband's back that they didn't notice Gooding slipping off now and then. Alicia's loose reputation was well known and served as an excellent cover. Since then, more than once, he'd snuck into someone's home office, capturing vital information when the rest of the partygoers thought he and Alicia were locked away in some corner bedroom instead.

He unveiled his first "Plus 1" photograph at that first party, commissioned by the host, and it caused a great commotion. It was his first nude and so entertained the gentlemen at the party that the men disappeared into the study for hours. They perused it in a parody of those war-time parties when the bigwigs in Washington would get together and discuss world politics in a back room while their wives socialized out front. With the nosy wives and clueless husbands occupied, Gooding and Mortimer copied then deleted that senator's hard drive while supposedly installing the other, public portrait of the wife in the formal parlor that mimicked the private portrait in the study.

This particular senator was connected to one of the mucky-mucks in the CIA. He had been taking his work home, not trusting the security of his office or the actions of his interns. He still didn't know what had happened to his computer and hadn't reported the breach, fearing the consequences.

A smile appeared on Gooding's face again. He'd personally tipped off the CIA—anonymously, of course. That senator had had a hard time explaining how he had not only obtained the data, but how it came to be loaded on his personal computer in an unsecured location. He'd screamed about how Gooding must have done it. Of course the senator's private "Gooding" picture was shared with the media during the public outcry. For some reason, the DC elite had stood up for Gooding and were convinced the senator was lying. "The divorce will be his final repayment for tattling to the authorities on me," Gooding mused as he settled down into his seat. His reputation remained intact. Even if it wouldn't be for a long while, when he went back to Washington, his niche would be waiting for him. People still clamored for their own portraits, believing that Gooding was just taking a break from portraits for a while he pursued a European art tour. Satisfied, he let himself nap.

Chapter Twenty-nine

In the wintry cool aftermath of the attack, the main dining room of the FBI's New York training compound was crowded. There weren't enough medical personnel to go around, so small groups of healthy agents clustered at each table around those who were wounded. The worst cases were gathered in the back past the kitchen in the smaller, officer's dining room where beds had been brought in, and where Bill led Mitch, saying he figured Mitch qualified as one of the "bad ones."

Mitch obediently hopped up on a stool where Angela came over and handed him a stack of bandages, tape, and alcohol to hold.

"What are you doing back here?" Bill asked the recruit.

"I am a trained EMT—used to be a paramedic on our volunteer fire department's ambulance," she answered, her voice clear and steady. "Hands are short and even mine are needed."

Bill smiled, commenting, "Very well, I approve," in his snobbiest tone.

Angela half smiled in reply. "Reva told me you're a medical hand yourself. Have fun stitching," announced Angela as she handed scissors and a suture kit to Bill and left.

Bill looked at Mitch, who looked back. "You're not touching me with a needle."

"I sure as hell hope not, you'd look like Frankenstein with my stitches," he answered. "Let's see how bad it is." Bill gestured to Mitch's bloody pant leg. "I'll need to cut your pants off, but I really hate to in this cold weather. I don't know how bad the damage is."

"Fine, it's not as if Levis are hard to find," Mitch replied stubbornly.

Bill struggled with the scissors with his wounded left arm, but succeeded in getting to Mitch's leg. The scissors revealed a shallow but wide gash across the top of Mitch's left thigh. "Hell, it's not even five inches long, but it's gaping open. Stitches would hold it together."

Mitch was adamant. "Clean it, pull it closed, butterfly it, and then wrap it tightly. I'll use the sutures to sew my pants back together."

"Fine, but when we get to the hospital, I'm going to have the doctor put you under so it can be put together properly."

Mitch was unconcerned by Bill's dire threat. "Then, while you're at it, put yourself under so the doc can cast that arm."

Reva had splinted Bill's lower arm when they'd got to the lodge; she'd also shot a local into it to kill the pain for a bit. Their medical supplies were rudimentary but effective. Reva had stayed outside until the last wounded trainee was brought in. She had stayed with those who needed to be carried to the compound—watching over them. On one of his trips across the ravine, Carl had brought her a medical kit when he'd collected Angela and the six healthier newbies. She had busily attended the gunshot wounds on the two worst fallen. Her kit included socks for splinting. Mitch shook his head as Bill paused to hold up a blue-and-gray striped tube sock. "Raiding our bunks now, Reevs?"

She had simply shook her head as she methodically cut finger holes out of the toe of the sock, responding, "I knew your socks were clean, Bill. Some of your fellow agents need laundry training."

All personnel were corralled to the main building as it was built of stone and could withstand another attack better than the wooden outbuildings. The commander and Carl had organized small groups to go to the other buildings to retrieve gear and bedding for the night. As senior agents, Mitch and Bill were needed out front to help "calm the troops." Mitch stood and tested his leg experimentally. "Almost sound, though I can't very well flap out there," he remarked in reference to his jeans, which were slashed from ankle to hip.

"Hey, at least I stopped cutting before everyone could tell if you're a tightie whitey or boxer boy," Bill retorted. He wiggled his fingers and felt the dull ache up to his elbow.

Mitch's eyes narrowed. "Good thing you're right handed. Hate to see your love life suffer, buddy."

Bill shoved him back onto the stool. "Hand me the tape!" he ordered Mitch.

One roll of medical tape later and Mitch's pant leg didn't flap as he and Bill headed into the cafeteria just in time to hear Carl ask Reva, "Did you notice the type of 'copter."

"Yup, just like the one in collage number two," Reva replied.

Carl added, "Sure looks like somebody's been shopping at the Air force's testing grounds."

Chapter Thirty

Rain poured down the windows of the visitor's sitting room. It was a very cool April day in Georgia at the FBI's summer compound. The public space was actually made to feel quite private. The FBI agents who entered the compound were assigned to the dormitories, while their superiors and other important folks, not really visitors, received accommodations in the restored plantation house across the lawns. The kind of "visitors" this room was planned for were actually quite rare for the secret Georgia training complex. Only necessary personnel, new trainees, and top government officials were allowed access to most of the facility, while this room was designed for a hazy, middle-group of people. The room was designed to hold the visitors who came in only a semi-official capacity, the ones who needed to see *some*, but not *all* of the operations, or the ones necessary to operations but no senator or general or their family. Mitch imagined that government auditors, GS-13s, and college students were usually about the only visitors encased here.

He stared out the floor-to-ceiling windows ahead of him. The cold rain made rivulets accentuated by hazy condensation down the lower halves of the glass panes. Across the lawns, through the mists rising from the ground, he could just see the converted living spaces created in what used to be the old carriage house and barns of the plantation. It felt significant to him that where he sat used to be part of the old slave quarters. This room would have dwarfed one of those cabins, but its sparse furnishings felt akin to those shacks. It wasn't just for visitors, but for the others. Cynically, Mitch thought of the people the FBI designers considered almost second-class citizens that this room was designed for, who purportedly didn't exist in the land of the free.

Mitch's self-analysis of his thoughts echoed what he knew Bill would say, were he here instead of teaching the Glock Carrying For Beginners, or Don't Shoot Your Ass Off 101, class. He knew Bill would say that these cynical, depressing thoughts in his mind were step one in what Bill called the "never touch the shit" way that he thought Mitch handled his life. To Bill, it was Mitch's way of ignoring, hiding, and/or masking the deeper emotions he was feeling. Bill sure seemed to think that he was especially good at reading people. Mitch would not admit any truth to that just now.

The New York incident six weeks ago continued to haunt him. They were able to tie it to one of Gooding's photographs—the one that didn't clearly stand for a branch of the US government like the others. The only other collage/photograph that fit the same type was the Coast Guard one, the messy, bloody, gory one. Right now, they were no further in their attempts to decipher the remaining nine images. The lack of understanding did nothing to alleviate the stress that plagued Mitch. He felt keenly the loss from the last few days of speaking to widows, orphans, and parents of new and senior agents who'd died in the attack at the training center. Homer had halted the deciphering for a week or so to give his staff time to rest. He'd sent most of Mitch's team down to Georgia early to rest before the special training sessions in preparation for confronting Gooding started. Seven FBI personnel had died. Most of them had been caught in the hail of bullets from the chopper on its last pass where it sprayed the edges of the woods around the compound. Homer was livid. He vowed to not lose any more agents.

The survivors had been dispersed across the nation to recover as well as they could before the next training phase here in Georgia. Mitch and Bill would have normally stayed in the background as assisters in the classes— putting out fires, answering the quiet questions, and noting which of the trainees needed a nudge or two. However, the new recruits were comforted by the senior agents' continuing to fight. Especially Bill. They looked to him for guidance.

Bill's active personality, fire-red hair, and his effective actions had set him apart during the New York incident. No one else had returned fire on the chopper. The trainees worshiped him like a hero and listened gravely whenever he addressed them. With Mitch and Carl keeping in the background, these new "kids" had dealt with, remembered, and were comforted by Bill. Reva, too, was in another of the beginner's classes. She was helping the female recruits in their Agent Roles classes. The trainees respected her as well. She'd patched them up and held firm when another would have cracked. Mitch was almost encouraged by upper management's handling of their grief. Talking with Bill and Reva not only comforted the walking wounded, but showed the newbies how their senior counterparts handled grief. It was not ignored, nor was it forgotten, but survived. Bill and Reva were marked by sorrow too, but were holding up through humor, honesty, moments of clarity, and moments of passionate anger when all the injustices of the world could be railed against. They let off steam in brief bursts, while keeping smart-aleck comments near to help soften the realities that all the agents were facing. Even some Secret Service recruits and CIA agents were mixed into the beginners' classes. After the Coast Guard ship, Navy transport, and submarine incidents, somebody high up had decided to cross-train agents with similar job sets to help prepare the entire combined task force to get Gooding. It also seemed politically correct to combine the groups, since Gooding had no problem attacking any of them regardless of their affiliations.

Mitch knew that their connection with others in other agencies was helping inter-agency cooperation, and worked constantly to focus everyone on the big picture—

Gooding had to be stopped. He was the first of his kind to try killing government agents on a national level regardless of their agency, be it civil or military. Nobody in any of the US government's security agencies wanted his tactics to succeed or news of them spreading to other enemies of the state. However, they had trouble cooperating as usual, until Stan and Homer of the FBI were appointed to be in charge of the task force. Both Stan and Homer possessed a strong sense of fair play and they quickly acted to keep things even among all personnel. It didn't hurt either that both had served honorably in the military in their youth.

Mitch thought of Jonesey's panic attack in Denver. When he'd found one of Gooding's business cards in one of the watched group's meetings, Jonesey was horrified at Gooding's tactics and worried that the white-supremacist types would pick up Gooding's ideas and use them in their own way. He'd gotten hold of himself quickly and had been able to remove the card before anyone took note, but he had gone to pieces for an afternoon. All Mitch knew was that Stan had called Amy, who'd flown to Denver to be with him for a few days. According to Stan, Jonesey now had a good dose of perspective and things were better. Stan had quipped, "A Pink Floyd moment, you know a 'momentary lapse of reason.'" Jonesey was a die-hard Pink Floyd fan and had been obsessively listening to that album in the aftermath. It seemed like everyone could have a bad day lately.

Mitch's stomach trembled at the thought of other wackos using Gooding's tricks. That thought brought the gruesome images in his mind back to life. He thought of the black-haired kid he saw blown up when the powerhouse at the New York compound blew and, of course, Reva's cousin Jordan who fell down the ravine. He still had a hard time watching Bill function with his broken arm, and the pain from his own wound rubbed him raw. He may have never experienced a "war" before, but what they were fighting felt like war to him. He wondered whether he should try to think like Stan and consider Jonesey having a tiny meltdown as a good thing.

Then there was their main mole. That student, Jenny Johnson, had done something to the team. This training phase in Georgia was her first FBI assignment. Amy delivered the last papers to Jenny, and so Jenny knew she was to fly to Atlanta on an IRS government travel card in the next week. She had been and continued to speak to Stan as required on a weekly basis and he was checking her mental progress. For never wanting a career in any type of law enforcement, she was taking to the background and legal training well. Homer measured her progress and had determined that a "correspondence course" type of training covering the basics would suffice for what they needed her to do. Even so, everyone had expected her arrival next week to cause a stir. She was their only mole; their only hope it seemed. Most were sure that she'd require special coddling and would distract everybody due to her unique position on the team. Then she'd surprised everyone. Rather than meekly taking a plane as directed, she'd taken the initiative. Jenny and Amy had visited, as seemed their habit, and Amy had let news slip about the New York attack. Jenny freaked out. She'd called Stan as soon as she had settled down and requested special permission to start now, early. She'd arrived two days ago, a day after the senior agents, and she and Reva appeared to really hit it off from their first meeting. Somehow, Jenny got along with all the senior team members and exerted such a calming influence that she was now right in the thick of things like she'd worked with these people for years not days. It seemed that most of the folks flat out liked her.

Stan was downright proud of her, and had mentioned more than once that he was very pleased by her performance. Jenny had been successful enough in her physical performance that she'd been placed into the beginners CIA training group for this session. She didn't act like an orphan around anyone and was full of competent decisions and actions. Because she didn't have a definite place, she fit in everywhere. Bill said she was an innate agent, born that way. Well, Mitch was not so sure. How could someone have been born to be calm in stressful situations? It was eerie. It was like Jenny was better because things were so tense right now; like she performed at her best when things were at their worst. Of course, Homer also adored her and made a special trip down yesterday just to meet her. There was even talk of her staying on with the team after the Gooding mission if Jenny performed well during real action.

I can just see Stan moving her to DC where she can be some sort of special liaison for him and Homer. Mitch grunted and angrily focused on the rain outside. He did not want to think nice things about Jenny Johnson. He didn't want to think of her at all. He was the team leader now. She was a member of his team, and he should be proud of her ability to be a team player, but he couldn't. His feelings were confusing. It wasn't that he thought Jenny was being fake; in fact, she was very aware of her position as an outsider and seemed to instinctively know when to stay out of tense issues. She removed herself when the team needed her gone without anyone asking her to leave. He certainly wasn't threatened by her and it sure wasn't her big, beautiful blue eyes that got to him. "It damn well isn't," he said to himself as his thoughts turned back to the horrors of this mission. "I will get Gooding. I will. And he will pay." One day, when he'd let himself think about it, it would bother him that it took thoughts of Gooding to banish thoughts of Jenny from his skull.

Chapter Thirty-one

Jenny sat by Reva at the end of the last class of the day. Reva had asked Jenny to stick nearby as soon as class was over for protection from the cloying green recruits who followed her all around the compound. Reva had had a hell of a day and needed a break at lunchtime. Reva watched the last newbie exit the classroom.

"It's good to have the day over isn't it?"

Reva nodded and stretched her neck muscles. "Yeah. I feel like I've put in twelve hours already."

Jenny stood up. "Are you up for some gourmet cafeteria food?"

Reva smiled. They had a running joke about the food around here. Reva mostly ate in the cafeteria because there were no kosher restaurants in town. She set her tray down next to Jenny and felt herself relax as Jenny chatted about different things in her quiet, restful way. One of the CIA gals sat nearby and asked Jenny, "So how do you keep positive about things through the constant briefings?"

Jenny seemed to consider the question for a moment, then said, "I have been thinking...I feel almost like we're in a wet spring, and right now, we're between big thunderstorms—like there's another tornado coming. I can't stop the clouds rolling in, but I can enjoy the sunshine while it lasts. Like today. I have always wanted to learn Tai Chi, and when Reva showed us the Tai Chi moves, I focused on learning them. I deliberately put Gooding out of my head and concentrated on feeling the wood floor in the gym under my bare feet."

Reva smiled. Some might say that Jenny was a talker, but she always went somewhere when she talked, like she was full of stories. As she listened, Reva wondered about what Jenny said, and marveled. *She gave us all a concrete relaxation technique right there. If you can't calm your mind, use your body to focus on something concrete instead. I am so glad Jenny does the talking. The trainees find comfort by being near me, but Jenny holds their attention when I need a break. Bless her.*

Reva knew her own strain was beginning to show, and the same went for her partner Carl. Carl was down here too and did what he could to help the new recruits adjust and stay with them after New York. Reva was glad he could be with them. He was her best friend as well as partner. She sighed. *I wonder if we can keep Jenny on long term. I am tired of being the only senior female officer with the training classes right now.* Although only about one-tenth of the trainees were women, all of those trainees seemed to feel more comfortable with Reva than her male counterparts.

Reva knew Jenny sympathized. They'd spoken about what it meant to be both female and FBI. Surprisingly, Jenny was a bit of a feminist. She drove Bill crazy when she'd refuse to let him open her doors. When he'd razzed her about not letting him be a gentleman, she'd fired right back, "That's a damn lie. You're no gentleman. I'd let you open my door, if you'd open doors for all females, which you don't. Be a gentleman and I'll treat you like one."

Thinking about Jenny and Bill made Reva think about Jenny and Mitch. Stuff was brewing there. Reva knew Jenny well enough now to tell that being around Mitch lately overwhelmed her with some unexpected chemistry. Reva could see that Jenny dealt well with all the male agents, including Mitch, and she could work with them as a pair just fine, but while it seemed like Bill was into Jenny, Jenny was into Mitch, *big time.*

In fact, I know Jenny is purposely helping me, and that that is helping her by allowing her to avoid being with Mitch. Reva looked across the cafeteria where Carl was sitting by Mitch and Bill. He winked at her. Carl had seen it too. They'd discussed it this morning on their morning run when Carl asked her, "Did you see Mitch checking out Miss Jenny this morning. It's like the guy hasn't seen a cute butt ever." Reva made a mental note to update Stan. She was sure Bill was only flirting with Jenny to goad Mitch, while Mitch was in denial about his attraction to Jenny. Reva worried that Stan may have to step in. Mitch sometimes listened to Bill or Jonesey, but he always listened to Stan.

Then there was Jenny. Even though she was holding up exceptionally well, the better she got at training, the more stressed she seemed. Reva believed it was using up a lot of Jenny's natural resilience to deal with Mitch in their "undeclared" state. *Maybe Carl is right. Maybe Mitch and Jenny need to declare themselves and get it out in the open before we get to the UK. This tiptoeing around each other is wearing them both thin.* Reva missed Jonesey's wife Amy. Amy knew Jenny better than anyone here, and she also knew Mitch. Also, Amy could probably work with Jonesey to maneuver to the two into admitting something was up.

Reva knew why Jenny hung around her. She knew that Jenny considered her a grounded person who "radiated confidence and good vibes." Reva smiled. *Maybe Jenny's right. We need a grounded group of positive female companionship.* Reva considered the assignment. It could probably use a more female-oriented focus. It was for Jenny, after all, not Mitch or Bill.

***

Jenny focused on her meal, but kept an eye on Reva as she thought about her work group back home in Utah. Because Utah was such an economically depressed and male-dominated state, many of the good jobs were given to men. The IRS service center in Ogden was one of the bigger employers in northern Utah and because it was government controlled, the service was required to follow equal opportunity employment guidelines. Because of this, a significant portion of its workforce was made up of women. Jenny's own work group of fifteen people consisted of three males and twelve females. The "boys" were typical of the service center's workforce. All three were in their late forties or early fifties and were retired military. Many retired military folks in the area liked working at the service center because their time in military service counted toward their non-military government service for retirement. Their military or veteran status also gave them an advantage during the hiring season. The "boys" were always a fun addition to any work conversations. Especially in her work group on the night or "swing" shift, considering how lax standards were in the middle of the night. The farting contests (until they were thankfully stopped by their boss) were a bit much for all the females, but most of the time the guys were pretty respectful—again thanks to their military background. Jenny thought of them and almost wished they were here and not her. She still couldn't believe that the FBI figured she was the one for their job.

Jenny considered Reva's attitude today. Today Reva had pulled her hair up under a ball cap and faced Jenny with her back toward the cafeteria. Her reddish hair full of riotous curls usually stood out, so Jenny had braided it for her earlier that morning. The braid (until it fell out in the gym), ball cap, and the ATF coat borrowed from one of Carl's buddies helped Reva hide out for a moment.

Jenny leaned forward to see if she could see Reva's expression.

Reva wolfed down her food, which was typical. Reva was an energetic person and always moved her arms and hands in time with her speech. She seemed to prefer standing to sitting and was the first to move when the group was going somewhere. Jenny could sympathize; ever since she'd started the rigorous CIA/FBI physical training routine, she'd developed a ravenous appetite. "Oh damn. Never mind," Jenny said as she looked up. She pushed her half-full tray away. She'd hoped to avoid Mitch today. *Damn, I hope he doesn't come over this way. He puts me off my chow.* Jenny sighed and pretended to focus on her plate, while she waited for Reva to finish so they could take off.

***

Reva looked up when she saw Jenny push her tray out, signaling her meal was over. Jenny was looking down with that wrinkle between her eyelids. "Oh great," Reva muttered as she turned to look over her shoulder where Mitch and Bill were sitting by Carl. *Yup. Mitch is staring at Jenny.* She caught Carl's attention, then Bill's. Carl shook his head and Bill winked. *Damn them. Oh well. Guess lunch's over.* Reva turned back to her plate and grabbed a last bite of steamed veggies. She was sure glad Bill would be done with his teaching assignments after his final class just after lunch so he could help Mitch full-time. From now on, he was tasked to float and go where needed. *He can keep Mitch from boiling over while I work on Jenny. At least she'll listen to me and Carl. I don't need this today. I really don't.* Reva tried once again to swallow the lump in her throat that had grown larger all morning. She said a silent prayer in gratitude for Carl's support and now Jenny's. She looked up and saw Jenny smile. *Good, that means that Jenny is ready to fight, and not in a pity party. That, I can work with.* Looking at Jenny, Reva thought of the pin-ups carried by WWII fighter pilots; soldiers needed to remember what they were fighting for—Jenny typified that, but she was still just a civilian. Reva smiled back as strongly as possible, then closed her eyes and began her fifteen-second relaxation exercise and geared up for the cafeteria exit. She thought about Mitch and Jenny for just a second. *Too bad Mitch hasn't decided he likes Jenny yet; she could heal him and give him a positive outlet for his emotions. It's a good thing Bill can handle Mitch for now, because when Mitch wakes up and recognizes her worth, Ms. Jenny will have her hands full.* Reva looked over to Carl just in time to see he and Bill follow Mitch to the discard counter. They dumped their trays, then headed out. Reva sighed in relief and went back to eating. *Maybe I can make it through an entire lunch without having Jenny or Mitch having a confrontation.*

Chapter Thirty-two

Jenny watched Reva's face soften into a wide smile, then relax into her "de-stressing" pose. Now Jenny could relax. All she had to do was keep others away for the rest of the afternoon so Reva could recharge. Funny, with her work group, when they needed to get over something, they all talked it out. Reva wasn't like that; she talked only a little, just the details—almost as a report. Then she seemed to need silent comfort, the presence of a friend nearby, a warm breeze, privacy. Jenny didn't know quite how to share quiet comfort very well, being a horrible chatterer, but hoped her presence was enough. *Even better, there goes Carl with Bill herding Mitch outta here.* Jenny pulled her tray back and went back to eating lunch, keeping time with Reva, glad that she could focus on Reva instead of worrying about talking to Mitch.

***

Bill angled down the hall from the bigwigs' offices. He'd made a quick check-in talk with Stan to make sure things were going okay so far. It seemed that the group was progressing as planned. Thankfully, all reports showed Gooding either didn't know about the compound or that he was ignoring them. Never one to worry about things that could happen, Bill put Gooding out of his mind. Now, he needed to track down Mr. Mitchell before his last class in a half hour. Mitch's state of mind a much bigger concern. If he didn't get back in control, Stan was going to send him to Montana until August. It would kill Mitch to be taken off the task force, but better he go crazy at home, than lose it in the UK and destroy the operation. At least Mitch ate lunch today. He was averaging two meals a day, having either lunch or breakfast, then a working dinner with Stan each evening.

Bill located Mitch in the visitors' waiting room. Bill knew Mitch preferred hiding here since everyone else liked the rec. room just down from the cafeteria. Mitch sat, head in hands, on the visitors' couch facing the wall of windows. "The psych's gonna love seeing you like this, Mitch," Bill announced, referring to the FBI's psychotherapist who'd dragged Mitch into therapy, trying to get him to "open up" about everything since New York. When Mitch refused to look up, Bill knew a little shock therapy was in order. No more kid gloves. *Hell, how many times do I have to play rough with this guy to get his attention?* Bill thought to himself, then smiled a wicked smile. *Let the games begin.*

***

Twenty minutes later, Bill and Mitch reentered the cafeteria. Jenny looked up immediately; she felt a jolt anytime Mitch was near or in the same room. The jolts had become more frequent, but she just worked harder to function normally and ignore them, refusing to consider that Mitch may be purposely seeking her out. However, this time he'd been staring at her and had kept looking at her when she'd made eye contact. She held eye contact with him (somehow) as he made a beeline over to her and Reva, dragging Bill with him. Carl intersected with them partway and the tableau soon reached the table. Carl, as big of a smart ass as Bill usually was, clasped Reva's neck and began to squeeze it tighter and tighter to test her. Reva, as practiced as always, sighed and said, deadpan, "Keep going, mister, and there won't be any more baby Millers to drive me crazy."

Carl looked down to the knife near his thigh as Bill pointed out, "Damn, Carl, she's getting faster. She had that knife ready down there before you even spoke this time." They all laughed as these "boys" sat down. Bill sat the closest, right next to Jenny and smiled as she reached across him to retrieve her now mostly empty tray.

"Would you care for some roast beast and kittens?" she asked, making fun of the cafeteria fare.

Carl, having appropriated Reva's German chocolate cheesecake, retorted, "At least you get meat. Reevs only leaves me stale cheese and cherries dipped in mud." They laughed as Mitch continued to stand behind Reva and stare down Jenny.

Bill cleared his throat. "So, Harper, are you going to sit, or what?"

"Nope. I need to speak with Miss Jenny here," he said, turning toward her. "Jenny, can I see you in the hall for a few minutes?"

Jenny quickly peeked at Reva, who winked at her. *Okay. Be cheerful, but professional, you can do this,* she told herself in her mind. "Sure thing. Let me drop off my tray."

"Oh I got it," interrupted Bill as he slid her tray back in front of him. "You guys go chat. Miller is finishing his cheesecake, and I need to chat with Reevs." He waved his hand in the air to shoo them out the door.

Jenny somehow found it easy to stand up and walk behind Bill to the other side of the table. When she neared Mitch, he turned and she followed him out into the hall—a typical habit lately. He rarely walked next to her, but led off expecting her to follow him. Jenny sighed and followed. *Geez I wish this guy understood a bit more about treating women as equals.* Jenny had no idea that Mitch couldn't make himself walk by her side—that the last time he'd done so, he'd freaked out when he realized he'd nearly grabbed her hand to hold hands with her as they'd walked. Mitch continued to where the hall turned a corner. In the L at the corner, he stopped by a small sitting area and turned back to her. As Jenny looked up to him, Mitch breathed deeply through his nose, then spoke. "Miss Jenny, you are important to this operation. As our bait for Gooding, you are the most crucial trainee here in Georgia. As team leader, I also am important to the task force and technically the lead FBI agent around here. This tiptoeing around each other stops, now." Mitch looked at her and forced her to look him in the eye.

Jenny didn't know what to say, so she stayed quiet, but complied by holding eye contact.

Mitch continued, "We picked you, because you had the right itinerary and the right qualities per the profilers. We must build on your qualities so that you can survive this mission. Therefore, I am not 'a man' to you. I am the *team leader*. When I serve on your protection team during maneuvers, I am not 'that guy,' but your 'right flank.' If I give an order, you obey it, immediately. If I observe you, I observe a trainee, a recruit, a team member, not a woman."

Mitch reached over and grabbed Jenny's right hand in his to emphasize his point, his voice lowering. "If I touch you it is *not* as a man touches a woman, but as one person touches another, one human to another, one team member to another." He held her hand firmly and looked her in the eye. While keeping her hand in his, he reached into his pocket and handed her a few three-by-five notecards. "Here's your itinerary for tomorrow. From here on, we are just two agents working together on whatever assignment comes our way. I'll hold up my end. And you need to do your part. Understood?" Jenny nodded. "Good," Mitch said, then dropped her hand, patted her on the shoulder, and walked away.

Jenny stood for a minute, chagrined. She was a stellar IRS employee and an outstanding college student. Few people had to correct her and she rarely got lectured, even from her parents or siblings. She held still, trying not to cry. *You deserved that. It's no big deal. This is a job; treat it like a job. Your supervisor was just giving you a much-deserved route correction. You can take it. You're a big girl.* Jenny breathed in and, horrified, felt tears. She sniffed and grabbed a tissue from a handy box on the nearest end table. Noisily she blew her nose and tried Reva's emergency relaxation technique number three. Jenny closed her eyes and pushed her fingertips together so that each finger on one hand was pressed hard into the corresponding fingers of her other hand. She pressed as hard as she could, to the point of pain, then relaxed the pressure until the fingers were just firmly touching. She waited until she could feel the pulse in each finger, so that eventually she only felt the pulse, and could no longer tell whether the pulse was coming from the right hand or left hand finger. When she felt the pulse in her pinkie fingertips, she felt better. Tonight, in the privacy of her dorm room, she'd analyze the conversation with Mitch. In the meantime, she needed to go find Reva and the bunch. Even if Mitch was with them, it was time to be mature about this task force. A new Jenny found Bill, Reva, and Carl much as she'd left them. They smiled back at her. She sat down. Things had been bad, but when you have good friends, company, and food—somehow everything feels better.

Chapter Thirty-three

Early the next morning found the Georgia compound quiet and a little foggy. After yesterday's classes and briefing, the trainees were scheduled for some physical activity. Stan had spoken to Albert earlier and found his friend and colleague was having a hard time picking up the pieces. Albert had been moved into a separate bedroom by Jessica after too many late nights and too many early morning phone calls. And, having the higher-ups going all over his office and picking into their computers and systems had thrown the finance office into turmoil. Albert confessed that what got him through the day was running around the park like the other office workers. He spent an hour jogging at lunchtime, and it helped him clear out the extra adrenaline and get back to work.

Stan was grateful for whatever helped Albert get through the day; he felt deep in his gut that Gooding had attacked Albert personally because of his professional position. He felt that Gooding had chosen both Alicia and Albert, because he knew that, one: Albert had the data and, two: Albert's office was his biggest threat on the computer front. Albert's planning was legendary; his skills for preparation and anticipation were well documented. They were the reason he was the head of the finance office. Without someone who really understood the true costs of things, the bureau would have run out of money a long time ago. He was also the best the FBI had for finding cash flow drains. Since his appointment to his current post, no misappropriation-of-funds incidents had occurred in the office.

More importantly, Stan needed Albert to keep figuring out ways around Gooding's plans. Albert had also flipped the FBI's investigations from some of Gooding's drug trafficking buddies to Gooding himself. Having spotted some irregularities in the details of a congressional aide's finances, Albert identified a trail that went through the drug lords to Gooding. The aide was being investigated when they found he got into the mess to protect his boss and that the congressman, while denying everything on the surface, was being paid off by Gooding to change a key vote. From documents retrieved from Alicia's files, he knew that Gooding had wanted Albert's dismissal as part of his plan. By keeping Albert around, Stan hoped to throw a wrench into Gooding's great plan, while secretly hoping that Gooding hadn't realized Albert's significance in the investigation.

After watching the FBI doctor check Albert's blood pressure and determine the physical activity of the running had done Albert great good physically and mentally, Stan vowed to work the stresses out of his team by really "working" them out. That's why they were debriefed down here in Georgia at the training grounds. This conventional plantation had originally contained acres and acres of cotton and tobacco, which were now acres and acres of obstacle courses, trails, and other facilities. Stan decided that he was going to make the team too worn out to worry for a while, as he built up their reflexes. He would help them focus on what they could do by getting them moving and doing. Besides, after the NY incident, every supervisor and team led below Stan's authority had been lax on the workouts. Stan had seen entire gym-fulls of people break down into prayer circles when they were supposed to be running laps, and it wasn't helping them hone their skills, especially skills they'd need to catch Gooding. They would use good physical condition to improve the mental condition. At least everyone would be tired enough to sleep at night.

Bill and Carl stood by Stan on the observation deck at the "finish line" at the end of the main mountain trail obstacle course. Carl and Bill were congratulating themselves on their wise choice and good fortune in landing the time-keeping job. Stan elbowed between them and told them to be on their best behavior. "Carl, you keep track of the female trainees as well as the non-FBI personnel, while you, Bill, keep track of the male, FBI runners. That should divide the troops evenly for you," he stated in his usual matter-of-fact way.

Bill and Carl continued to grin at each other as Stan handed them clipboards with a checklist of each group's names and the stopwatches. "How come Carl gets to watch the girls?" Bill whined with a smile as Carl set up shop on the other end of the tower.

Stan just smiled at him and replied, "He chose to help me late last night when the CIA guys got here when someone else, who will remain nameless, felt it was more important to get pizza for the midnight poker club."

"But we saved you your own pie, Stan!"

"No good, William. The last thing I need is the lady recruits around here yelling at me for your poor, wolfish behavior." Stan clapped Bill's shoulder, smiling at him to let him know he was only teasing, and waved to Carl. Then he walked off to the tower on his way to the control desk to monitor the entire race from the cool, air-conditioned comfort of the security sector of the building.

***

The cool mists were back today. Everyone was to start this segment of their training exercises by focusing on the physical. Jenny was excited to try her hand at the firearms training—to see how well her practice with Jonesey's Glock had served her, as well as the "duck and toss" class, where Reva would show the ladies some dirty tricks in hand-to-hand combat, but right now she was tired, cold, and ornery. She'd been up all night with the ladies poker gathering. The boys refused to share their poker night with any females, so she and Reva had decided to fight fire with fire, so to speak. They'd had a great time,

202

commandeering the carriage house's kitchen and grilling steaks to go with their poker game. The boys got pizza, which happened to be cold—thanks to Millie, one of the CIA gals, who waylaid the delivery boy and detained him for twenty minutes. They were all tired and a bit bleak-eyed, but it felt good to have a girls' night after the manly stuff they had to do all day.

Thinking of manly stuff, Jenny tucked her new knife into the holster in the side of her hiking boot. Her dad had spoken to Stan long and hard when he'd found out about Jenny's assignment and, being an ex-Marine, had found her his old hunting knife and showed her how to use it. Jenny felt a bit silly, but both Mitch and Bill had spent most of the long drive from the airport to the compound lecturing her on safety last week. Having heard about the New York attack second-hand, Jenny was taking no chances.

***

Mitch had left Bill at breakfast. He needed to get warmed up and used to the day. As Carl and Bill were the only senior agents lucky enough to get tower duty, he and the other seniors were to run with the trainees, gauge their progress, skills, weaknesses, etc. He was looking forward to the run, actually. The ground was muddy, but years of runners had made a respectable trail through the pines. And although the plantation was near the mountains, this run would be on the lower trail, which had just a few rolling hills as it skirted the base of the mountain, with only a couple of steep segments. The morning air was crisp and cool and Mitch always enjoyed running when it was cold—a legacy of his early morning, before school practices and warm-ups for his track days back in Montana.

As he started toward the trail, he spotted Reva, Jenny, and Millie warming up. Jenny and Millie, having the least seniority of the other trainees, had said they wanted to run the trail once to make sure there were no surprises.

Later that morning, in shifts of twenty people, the trainees would be watched and timed to check their endurance and woodland skills. Mitch overheard the girls talking as he approached.

"I don't know how they are going to test our 'woodland' skills on a groomed trail?" Millie was saying.

"Who cares, it's a beautiful morning for a run," answered Jenny.

Reva remarked, "Just wait till you see the crevasse, girls, then we'll know what you're really made of."

Mitch entered the conversation by saying, "Are you ladies truly planning on running this three-mile, mountainous course twice today?" He'd heard the commotion in the gym this morning as the other trainees gave these girls, or women, Mitch mentally corrected himself, a hard time, which was becoming a regular scene since they arrived.

Right now, all the available workout areas in the compound were full of anxious recruits and newbies working off their tension and warming up for the run later in the day by doing traditional and non-traditional exercises. Tempers had been flaring up, so Mitch agreed with Stan's decision to divide the training classes into physical and non-physical activities to help everyone vent in a more productive fashion.

Reva looked hard at Mitch and frowned. Mitch understood her not-so-subtle hint to change the subject. Unbeknownst to Millie and Jenny, the other trainees were barred from entering the course until Mitch and Reva gave it their clearance.

Chapter Thirty-four

Ever since the New York training ground was attacked, security had been heightened at all FBI training facilities. The plantation was no different. However, the Georgia woods were a security nightmare as bad as the New York forest had been. But no matter the devastation caused by the helicopter attack in NY, the Agency learned from it in the manner that all humans learned from hindsight.

Secret, special ops troops outfitted with night vision and other snazzy gear had been installed in the woods for weeks now. At first, they just patrolled the areas, looking for suspicious activity. Then, on Sunday night, coinciding with the arrival of the trainees, the full-time troops moved into strategic locations along the trail and outposts. Mitch and Reva were assigned to do a walk-through this morning to communicate directly with the special ops and to give those troops a taste of what the run would entail later that day.

Stan had decided to allow Jenny and Millie their experimental run for a few reasons: They were alienated from the rest of the trainees, Jenny, because she was a civilian, and Millie, because she was the only CIA female detailed to the combined team, assigned specially because of her unspecified but "special" talents per her dossier. The old rivalry between CIA and FBI was alive and well. Millie was a green recruit, and this would be her first field assignment. Stan believed that the CIA team had allowed her to train with the FBI only so that they could spy on the FBI's training program. Then, having watched Millie, he soon learned that she wasn't very good at intelligence work yet, but was a whiz at undercover communications. The CIA needed her there in the field for the mission to use her skills and because she was their only communications specialist not in Gooding's stolen database data.

Bill had stopped a particularly bad incident involving the female recruits in the gym and he was angry over it. He'd had to personally override the group leader in charge of the group and it took physical methods to split up the two people causing the scene. The incident made Stan recognize the special needs of these particular females. Because no one in the group would give the full details to him, he left the team alone, but charged their leader to better handle the issue. Mitch flat out refused to elaborate to Stan, only letting him know that it did involve CIA personnel, that Jenny had stepped in to help before Bill arrived, and that Bill pulled her out of it after he'd stopped the fight. Stan could see that things were a bit strained between Bill and a couple of the CIA operatives and that Bill now sat next to Millie at mealtimes. He filled in the missing pieces of the story. He knew Jenny and Millie were friends, and that Millie often spent her recreation time with Jenny and Reva. He'd just bet the CIA guys had played rough with Millie. Stan asked Mitch if he needed to speak to the CIA team leader, and Mitch had adamantly told him not to, saying, "Please don't, sir. It's under control for now and will go away soon." No explanation was given, but Mitch was a good team leader. Stan would trust him to watch the gym more carefully for now.

Regardless of the tension, Stan was determined to help the ladies become fully qualified for the Gooding task force, regardless of their "non-traditional" status. His task was complicated by the fact that Jenny and Millie were both too attractive for their own good. Though they were lovely like Reva, unlike Reva, they did not know how to establish professional boundaries as Reva had years ago; some of the male agents were making nuisances of themselves. Stan was having a hard time keeping some of the rowdier males in check due to the high intensity of this mission. However, since the security upgrades, many of the training schedules had been shuffled, opening the way for some manipulation of the teams' tasks. Also, due to the shuffling, someone miscalculated the number of women trainees in this session and booked twenty-five recruits for a facility that could only accommodate twenty females. As three of the women were seasoned agents, Reva included, the women's gymnasium was filled with the twenty other more seasoned, FBI, female agents in training—leaving Jenny and Millie out of the lineup. Stan seized this double opportunity to provide specialized assistance to his group of twenty female newbies and get Jenny and Millie up to speed in a separate, more intense and personal group.

So Stan sent them to go with Reva, which kept them out of the crowded main gyms where the males' testosterone levels could get out of hand. He also tasked Mitch to help Reva as needed. As planned, isolating them from the rest of the female recruits also helped the two, ten-women, regular training groups bond better—by making even numbers of fully FBI committed women. Because Reva and Mitch knew the training trail completely, their job would be to watch and focus on the search for things that would halt or slow down the trainees. Therefore, these two, as the most inexperienced runners who needed the most supervision and would be most likely to find any pitfalls (he hoped not literally), could be assisted by the two best trainers. To Stan's analytical mind, he was sending Jenny and Millie with Reva and Mitch on the exploratory run as a "control group" to test his "work 'em hard" theory.

***

The air crisply burned Mitch's throat as he breathed deeply. He correctly interpreted Reva's look and made a great show of rolling his neck and stretching his muscles, hoping Jenny and Millie would think he was only there to test his running skills on the course. He mentally got back to his business and refocused on the run.

"Are you gals ready for a good morning run?" Reva asked Millie and Jenny. At their affirmative nods, Reva turned toward the hill and jogged into the woods with Millie and Jenny at her heels.

Mitch waited a heartbeat or two, then followed after tugging his black pants down over his white socks. Too bad neither Jenny nor Millie had noticed or remarked on his entirely black attire and become suspicious. He was worried that maybe their training hadn't sunk in. Jenny and Millie's pale heather-gray FBI sweatshirts stood out in the dark and gloomy woods, where he intended to blend into the gloom better by wearing black. In a couple of hours the woods would be warm enough to make infrared detection of body heat tricky, and he didn't intend to make it easy for his special ops buddies to find him just by sight.

Mitch thought gratefully of Jonesey and the tricks he'd been taught. Jonesey was the one who pioneered the woodsman tactics the special ops guys used. He learned first-hand from monitoring all those weird meetings in the great pine forests in Northern Idaho, Washington, and Montana.

**

Reva was pleased with the security measures she'd noticed thus far. The special ops guys had made themselves quietly known at key points and gave her signs that things were going well. The girls were keeping up well besides. They made smooth progress on the first half of the trail, which wound toward the top of the next hill. The crevasse bisected the trail nearly in half, and was located just below the summit of this particular hill where a mountain stream cut a path down to the river. Normally, Reva enjoyed this gap but now shuddered to think of it. It was eerily similar to the ravine in New York where the logging bridge was destroyed, although it was on a smaller scale. This crevasse was narrower and not as long but deeper and rockier, with the creek running at the bottom of it. What really should concern her here were the ropes and net—she refocused on her agenda to work on these girls.

Where the trail ended at the crevasse just below the edge of the gap, there was a large net similar to what trapeze artists used, because the only way across the crevasse here, was Tarzan-style swinging on ropes. She and Carl had been obsessively coming here to check the ropes and nets all week. Just yesterday morning, early, she and he had dived off the ravine, wearing mountain hiking survival harnesses, to check the net. It worked beautifully, and didn't appear to have been tampered with. After climbing out of the net (there were rope ladders on both sides, cleverly hidden from above) both she and Carl had then swung across the gorge a few times to ensure the ropes were sound. No tampering was found, which was good, because all personnel were vulnerable here regardless of their skill set.

An entire team of special ops guys were assigned to secure the crevasse and equipment, and today there were special divers and rescue crews by the creek below the crevasse to help any of the runners. So, hopefully, even if the net or ropes were compromised, no one would be seriously hurt. Thankfully the creek was deep right here, with no rocks near. One could safely dive into the creek from the top of the gorge if they were careful.

Reva casually waved to the commander of the special ops who stood neatly concealed just across the gorge from her as she waited patiently for Jenny and Millie to arrive. This half of the trail was a gentle uphill climb until the last hundred yards to the gorge, where the trail climbed the steep slope to the outcrop carved up by the creek. Reva felt good; this was going to be a successful run.

Chapter Thirty-five

With a joystick, Stan toggled the view on the video monitors in the compound's security hub between the crevasse cameras where Reva and the girls had just appeared, and the outpost below the outcrop where Mitch had left the trail to go over some last-minute instructions with the special ops commander there. After Stan watched Mitch head back to the trail after speaking to the outpost coordinator, he watched Millie and Jenny balk at the ropes at the gorge.

***

"We have to swing across?" Millie sounded horrified. Jenny stood there looking bleakly at the gap. Reva, well accustomed to the foibles of newbies, calmed them down.

"See this log buried in the dirt. It's the jump off point. That's why the ropes are looped here." Reva indicated the log ten feet back from the gentle slope that led down to the drop-off.

"Do you want to watch me or try it yourselves?"

Jenny and Millie looked at each other. Each took a deep breath but remained silent, not willing to volunteer at the moment. Before Reva could nudge one or both of them into action, and as Mitch quietly snuck up behind them, Jenny said, "Well, Millie, you said we should try running the course without the others watching us and making fun of our ineptness. We should try this rope jump now without an audience." Turning to Reva, she asked, "Did I see a net down there?" Reva nodded.

Jenny moved forward to the log, but before she had gathered enough courage to grab a rope for herself, Reva and Millie looked past her and stepped back as Millie yelled, "Watch out!" The impact knocked the wind out of Jenny as a large black shape grabbed her by the waist and she flew into the air. It was clear to Reva that Jenny recognized Mitch somehow, maybe by feel, scent, or his "*Gotcha!*" as she screamed in frustration and fright, "Mitch, damn it, put me down!" as they flew into space. Reva watched in amusement while Millie looked on in fright as Mitch gripped Jenny tightly as he held on to the rope and swung out over the gap in a high-flying arc.

It happened so fast.

Just when Reva and Millie thought Mitch and Jenny would land on the other side, Mitch shifted his weight, leaned back, and pushed his feet against the tree ahead of them, the one growing closest to the gorge, and swung them backward back the way they came. "Okay, down you go!" Mitch announced when they were again over the middle of the gap as he let go of the rope, allowing them to fall into space.

Millie's scream mingled with Jenny's as Mitch and Jenny fell the eighty feet down to the net. Reva clapped her hands, then was joined by six other sets of hands clapping as the special ops guys came out of hiding to watch the fun. They made an appreciative audience standing above the net.

Shouts of "Way to go Mitch!" echoed up the gap from the divers below. Reva ventured up to the edge of the gap and watched Jenny vigorously trying to get up out of the net.

Jenny looked pissed off, embarrassed, and ready to kill. Her shout made that clear. "I am going to kill you, asshole. You scared my heart out of my body, you big fat jerk!" Reva could see Mitch was having a great time teasing Jenny by jiggling the net just so, making it hard for her to keep her balance.

"You're too serious, Jenny. You need to loosen up," he shot back.

Reva overheard one of the special ops guys remark, "That one must be fantastically fun to tease, with her violent temper and all that passion. Listen to her rant."

Reva, along with Millie and the six special ops guys, were enthralled with the show going on below them. The whole FBI group had heard about Mitch's supposed case on the "student" and those who hadn't seen any fireworks in action had been dying to see if the rumors were valid. The commander signaled to Reva and said, "Guess Bill was right about these two." The special ops guy added, "Mitch caught up to you guys just when you guys stopped to discuss crossing the crevasse. Apparently Jenny was temptation he couldn't resist." Everyone atop the trail laughed. They watched Mitch tease Jenny. He alternated between just standing in the middle of the net and jumping lightly each time Jenny tried to get a foothold on the ladders which were positioned about two feet above where the net was tethered. Jenny turned back and glared at him as she impatiently pushed her bangs out of her eyes.

"Dammit, you asshole, knock it off!" she yelled at him and continued, "Mitchell Harper, you're a dead man when I get my gun!"

Mitch smiled. "You're sure pretty when you're angry. And yeah right, you couldn't hit the broad side of a barn with that relic your dad gave you. You should use your knife instead," Mitch called back to her.

Reva smiled and laughed. "Yup. Okay, Millie, time to go across. It'll be a while before they get back up here." As Jenny huffed and climbed up the ladders across the way, Reva helped Millie get a good grip on the rope. Now that Jenny and Mitch were both on a ladder and climbing up. They would wait a minute for the net to calm down before crossing.

Reva looked over and checked with the special ops guy to see if he knew if Jenny and Mitch were clear of the net and on the ladders in case she or Millie had to ditch. At his nod she gave Millie permission to go. "Now, notice right across there's an open space. Don't be afraid to just drop down there, the ground's soft, padded with soft leaves and grass." Millie nodded, looking too nervous to speak. She clutched the rope tightly and backed up to the log jump-off. Reva gave a final admonition. "Don't let the rope fall back to the center of the ravine, or you'll have to retrieve it. Just when your feet touch the grass, stop yourself and pull the rope up to the tree next to the clearing."

Millie nodded, jumped lightly backward, and sailed across the gap, touching down a moment later. She turned back and Reva smiled in her direction. She was bundling the rope as directed as Reva landed a moment later.

"Hold the ropes for just a second." Reva turned and yelled back across the crevasse, "'K Charley, throw me the weights." Millie stood patiently, her cheeks flushed, as one of the shadowy soldiers reappeared across the way and chucked a gray-colored weight across to Reva, who caught it like a football across her abdomen. "Okay, send the next one," she called as she dropped the first weight on the grass next to her.

Charley dutifully sailed the next one and stood waiting as he called back, "Ready when you are."

Reva came back up to Millie and proceeded to tie each of the weights to the two ropes. She turned and sent the weighted ropes back across to Charley, who looped them with the others.

"Fascinating," Millie said as Charley melted back into the forest. "I never expected that."

Reva answered her with a smile and continued, "See, you need to expect the unexpected. Welcome to the FBI, even if we FBI guys aren't near as good at surprises as you CIA creatures." They both laughed.

They waited for a minute to see if Jenny would appear on this side or the far side of the gorge. Reva stretched her back and looked at her watch. "An hour and fifteen minutes over rough terrain to do this half of the trail, you guys aren't half bad."

Millie looked at her and asked, "Now what?"

Reva gestured over to the innocent looking, but lethal, gap. "Now, we wait for our wounded sister so we can continue on our journey."

Reva pulled a hidden, tiny radio transmitter out of her pocket and said into it, "Hey, Bill, can you stop the clock while we wait for our circus performers?" Reva heard some crackling static before Bill replied in the affirmative. "Thanks, you're a doll," she said. "Dinner's on me—you won the bet. Signing off." Reva tucked the little unit back into her pocket and made eye contact with Millie.

"What was that about?" asked Millie.

Reva turned Millie to the left and showed her the camera posted there. "That's the only obvious posting of our eye in the sky. Wave, honey, you're on FBI TV." Millie and Reva both started laughing again.

"Did Bill record the moment so that we can prove our story?"

Reva laughed. "You are quick, girl. Mitch has been so cocky and lecturing some of the new recruits about *professionalism* to the point that Bill has been dying to get some blackmail material on him to calm him down. He knows that Jenny has Mitch's number and he's been hoping for some fireworks." Turing back to her with an assessing gleam in her eyes, Reva asked, "Sure you don't want to trade sides and be an FBI'er like us?"

Millie just smiled and said, "Foreign travel all the time, darling."

Just then, Jenny's head appeared at the completed-journey side of the ravine. She clawed her way to her feet and came stomping up to Millie and Reva, fury emanating from her in waves. Mitch soon followed, but at a more sedate pace. As he came up to them, he paused a few feet away from the ladies and appeared to be waiting for them to precede him. Reva checked Jenny for any hurts and glanced back to Mitch, wanting to say something to him, but Jenny cut her off with a glare as she sliced her arm through the air in a snappy gesture, dismissing him. Mitch, who'd been slowly approaching them, halted as Jenny turned and glared at him, her arms crossed across her chest.

"You're not following us back. I've had enough of your kind of fun today," Jenny spat at him. Mitch, nonplussed, just stared back at her, still grinning. Squaring his shoulders, he folded his own arms across his chest and began to stare her down.

Both Reva and Millie's eyebrows rose at this. "Can we be more child-like here?" Reva muttered under her breath. Millie elbowed her as they watched Mitch and Jenny silently tussle.

Millie nudged Reva again. "She's getting madder, isn't she." Jenny broke eye contact with Mitch and looked around, as if she only just realized she had an audience. She glanced at Millie and Reva and a couple of the special ops guys as well. Nostrils flaring, she glared harder at Mitch. A movement behind Mitch caught Reva's attention, and she saw one of special ops guys move across the way. She then noticed how close Mitch was to the drop-off. Reva followed Jenny's line of sight and knew what she was thinking. She pulled Millie back a pace, then two. Jenny turned back to Mitch and advanced on him. Reva remarked, "He's just watching her, not moving. Dummy. Think with your head not with your balls, mister." When Jenny stood nose-to-nose and toe-to-toe with Mitch and before he could speak, she reached up on tiptoe and kissed him full on the mouth. Mitch's arms moved up from his sides and Jenny moved closer. The audience watched as the kiss deepened. As Mitch moved to grab Jenny, she quickly pulled back with her body and pushed forward with her arms. Just like that, she shoved him away from her. Mitch fell into space, neatly into the crevasse. Jenny had shoved Mitch off the edge and back into the net.

***

Stan shook his head and sighed as he continued to watch the monitors and listen to the others snicker and joke around him. *Heck, there'll be an office pool next thing you know,* he thought to himself. He'd heard over the radio Bill and Reva discuss their bet. He watched as Reva, Millie, and Jenny navigated the downhill half of the trek to the end of the trail on one screen. On another screen he saw what used to be one of his best agents lying in the middle of the safety net, smiling ear to ear as the special ops dudes melted back in the forest. *This day is just getting longer and longer.*

An hour or so later, Stan watched the end of the first day's run.

Millie and Jenny reached the tower first. Reva hung back, double-checking the cameras on the end of the course. There were fewer trees near the end of the course due to the plantation's fields, which were still clear for cultivation, and the cameras scoped a wider area. Bill and Carl had just come down the tower ladder as she arrived. Bill hugged Jenny. "Great work, my gal."

Carl added, "About time somebody showed that bear who's boss."

Jenny's anger cooled instantly. "You guys saw that?" she asked, horrified to think that there were more witnesses to her morning's activities.

Millie nodded, laughing. "Didn't you see the huge camera by the gorge?"

Bill, in his typical honest fashion, acquainted Jenny with the truth. "Saw, shared with Stan, recorded." He consulted Carl with a look. "And broadcast over the closed circuit TV, if I'm not mistaken." Carl nodded agreement.

Everyone but Jenny stood there and laughed as "Shit, shit, shit, shit...," Jenny's favorite cuss word, spilled out in an endless stream.

Reva, honest herself, and kindhearted, decided to stop the laughter and took over her charges. "Come on, Jenny, Millie, into the training rooms. You have to get your score entered into the computer."

Millie looked confused. "What do you mean our score?"

Reva turned them away from Carl and Bill and steered them back to the compound as she answered, "There's no point of making you guys run the course again as you made it in just over two hours, which is a respectable time around here. You guys passed the test with flying colors."

"That's why you had Bill stop the clock while we waited for Jenny!" Millie exclaimed, clearly remembering Reva's quick conversation on the radio.

Reva smiled. "Yup."

Millie hugged Jenny. "We don't have to do it again!"

Jenny, clearly relieved and starting to recover her moxie, stated, "At least I won't have to repeat my high wire act live in front of the other trainees," and sagged against Millie.

Millie answered, "Great, I need a break, too. Let's go have breakfast."

Both girls were shocked when Reva confided, "I guess I shouldn't tell you that Stan asked Bill and Mitch to come up with a diversion for the task force. I guess you were it, Jenny."

Jenny responded, "Yeah, the one time he can nix acting professionally." Her tone mimicked Mitch's lecture voice perfectly.

Stan watched the two women head up the drive after laughing with Reva. He saw how Reva held back and waited a moment until Carl and Bill joined her. The three agents looked at each other and smiled in agreement, then they turned and looked directly at the camera and waved to him. The group broke up, Bill and Carl heading back to the trail to finish checking the course, while Reva followed the girls back inside. They all needed a break, and breakfast too.

Chapter Thirty-six

Mitch was fidgety and edgy today. He wasn't sure he could handle meeting Jenny alone, just the two of them, for a last-minute meeting after the spring training session. The trainees had finished six weeks of intense preparations, and he and Jenny had done well keeping it professional. Most of the FBI senior and junior agents had left to get back to their other regular assignments, readying for the long deployment this summer. Bill had gone on to Denver to make sure Jonesey had enough information to get his team together for the imminent trip across the Atlantic. Reva and Carl had already left to join the British team in London. Millie, being judged too green to handle the mission, was staying in Georgia to do some special training for her reassignment in the CIA to the Washington DC team gathering data. If needed, they could use her as a double for Jenny, but that was still to be decided. Jenny had flown back and forth to Utah in order to keep up with her schoolwork, including to take her spring semester finals and to finish her final art projects.

They knew with certainty that Gooding was now in the UK. The CIA specialists had tracked one of Gooding's helpers in the Ukraine getting supplies for more bombs. They also knew that Gooding had gone to Amsterdam to pick up that equipment and helper, even though the initial Amsterdam photo was faked. British agents were watching Gooding and his family estate in Scotland. Unfortunately, neither they, nor the US agencies, had enough hard evidence to seize Gooding yet. Of course, Mitch thought sardonically, the CIA could just go in there and assassinate him, but the higher-ups felt that due to Gooding's connections to the British monarchy, such an action would create an "incident." Therefore, they had to stick to legal channels to stop the bastard, at least for now. And because of Gooding's dual citizenship and that the FBI had most of the case compiled due to most of his activities being planned from the United States, the US would keep jurisdiction, at least for now. *Who would have thought the guy is a cousin to Queen Elizabeth II. Of course, half the rich folks in England share that distinction,* Mitch thought to himself. A perverse part of him was glad for the required restraint. Although he wasn't so naive to think that the US government never killed anyone to bypass legal channels, he felt some small comfort that even the massive US government didn't have a wholesale license to kill those they considered enemies of the state without a lot of proof. His loyalty to the United States was founded on his belief in what the Founding Fathers wanted—a state where the people were ensured their freedom and rights to strive for a better life. Like many people who worked for the government, Mitch chose to stick with the government to fulfill a patriotic need within him to make the United States a better place, rather than focus on the purely monetary fulfillment of working in the private sector.

Such thoughts momentarily distracted Mitch from those "other" thoughts that had been driving him crazy lately. Surprisingly, since meeting Ms. Jenny Johnson, he was often bothered by thoughts other than chasing and capturing Gooding, or the horrible events he'd endured in the past five months because of Gooding. Instead, he found himself meditating in much of his free time—about a lithe feminine form and long, dark blonde/brown hair. Before he could stop the errant thought, it ran through his mind. *Levis on long-legged girls should be outlawed.* Mitch closed his eyes and counted to ten, trying to calm himself.

Jenny, damn her, would slip into his thoughts in quieter moments and would, he was sure of it, eventually drive him crazy. If it wasn't her inexperienced yet usually successful actions, or other attempts at becoming an FBI field agent, then it was her quirky humor at the most inappropriate times that caused him more stress than he could easily handle. Worse, he'd been named the team leader for this operation, so not only would he be directly responsible for her, he was responsible for the rest of the agents as well and couldn't afford to jeopardize anyone by getting distracted. He'd been team lead before, and had worked with Reva, Carl, and even Jonesey in operations before. He knew that they, being well-seasoned agents, could operate well during the pressure of an operation. Jenny was the only civilian going to the UK that would remain in direct contact with any of the teams. The other moles would perform in peripheral tasks that should keep them well out of danger while still helpful. They had been taught to do their jobs independently and would be remotely monitored with the goal of keeping them and, as a consequence, Gooding, unaware of their significance to the investigation.

Also, although he'd have liked to not be in charge of the only civilian team member (especially because the civilian in question happened to be Jenny), no one else, not anyone in charge of the CIA or military teams, or the UK agents, could or would take the time to nurture her. Because the FBI team was in charge of the mole action as a whole, and because they had more agents at risk due to Gooding's capture of all of their computer information along with Alicia's involvement, earned them the privilege of handling Jenny too.

Because the UK and CIA teams had more experience in international issues, the FBI team was limited to just the Gooding capture and chase, if any, portion of the operation. After all, the FBI's jurisdiction covered US interests at home, not abroad. A grouping of top CIA and British agents would be in ultimate control of the operation now that Gooding had landed on British soil.

Mitch was grateful that his team, while small, did have the complete support of the others, and would handle

Gooding directly, because their goal was not to kill but to capture him. That type of thing was more the FBI's specialty, and Mitch, having ten years as an agent under his belt, knew the type of work, had handled teams in similar situations (though in the United States), and knew this job was well within his limits, so, he could focus on nabbing Gooding. He would do so on behalf of those killed by Gooding. Reva's cousin Jordan's face flashed in his mind for an instant, only to be replaced by Jenny's image as she came skipping down the steps in front of him.

Everyone had made excellent progress in their preparation for the hunt to get Gooding, especially the greenest members of the team, Millie and Jenny. Millie, having been singled out by the CIA part of the team as a possible counterpart or replacement for Jenny, was doing well. They would keep her on as a secondary agent, focusing on her excellent communications skills for now and keeping her in the States for a time, since Jenny was doing so well.

The task force members had met in various locations in the US, including Jonesey's Denver training campus, and the FBI headquarters in DC. They were back in Georgia for this last-minute coordination meeting. Now, everyone, having been evaluated and assigned to specific jobs in the task force, had only a few weeks to make their preparations for the rendezvous in England.

Meanwhile, Gooding's attacks had continued. To the best of their knowledge, Gooding had remained in England and Scotland while these attacks occurred, which caused Stan, Albert, and the other supervisors incredible consternation. No one knew for sure if Gooding was slipping back and forth across the Atlantic, causing the attacks by remote, or had a huge network of underlings doing his dirty work.

Chapter Thirty-seven

Jenny looked fantastic. She had been delayed reporting to Atlanta for her second session of training due to her spring finals. Her hair was down today. Mitch just loved watching the way the wavy curls floated around her shoulders and back. Unlike the rest of the agents, she looked happy today. Apparently she'd had a good time back home. Stan had congratulated her on her good scores in her classes this semester, which could be the reason she seemed so glad at this stressful time.

Watching her come toward him, Mitch wondered if she'd be willing to date him after this was all over. He'd never met anyone like her, intelligent, funny and, of course, lovely, but she seemed to fit him. When he needed something good to think about, she often spontaneously flung a joke at him out of nowhere, like she was tuned into his moods. She was also the only person besides his own mother and Bill who ever teased him. She knew just how to push his buttons, and most importantly to Mitch, she was kindhearted about it. She teased to make someone smile, not to deride them.

"Hey, Mitch, are you ready to take me out for my steak dinner to celebrate my good grades? I hear you like to buy for Jonesey too." Jenny smiled as she stood before him.

Mitch, curious to know why she thought he should feed her, questioned, "Why do I have to take you out for a steak dinner? Why aren't you going to dinner with the rest of them?"

Jenny sent him a teasing glance. "Well, I was going to, and although Stan promised to buy me a steak dinner because of my grades and my high score on the firing range, Reva said that they'd banished you from the group tonight on account of your orneriness, so I decided to find you and give you an opportunity to do something nice for someone else and leave them to their own dinner."

After that long explanation, Mitch frowned, confused. "That's not what happened. I told them as team leader, they needed to take a night to themselves to unwind before we go over the orders tomorrow."

Jenny, looking entirely too innocent, rebutted, "So why did Bill say he was glad you were growling by yourself over your dead meat tonight?"

The whole team liked to refer to Mitch as a bear due to what Reva called his "fuzziness" when he wore a beard and his overbearing, ornery attitude. Mitch's countenance darkened in response. He hated being referred to as the bear. It caused him to scowl and growl more, which only served to heighten the similarity between him and a grouchy, woke-up-from-his-winter-hibernation, grizzly bear.

Jenny laughed. "See, there you go, the bear scowling at me. In a minute you're going to be growling that you're a vegetarian. They're all going out for seafood, and since I hate fish, I figured you, being a land lubber like myself, would be willing to scare me up some barbecue or a steak." When Mitch growled, "Why me?" Jenny answered, "Because you look like you need some raw meat, you ornery one. Besides, I figure that since no one else wants to go with you, and you get mean and nasty when you're hungry, and it's now dinner time, with no evening meetings scheduled for us for the first time in weeks, and since the last time I was in Georgia you threw me off a cliff, you owe me dinner, dammit." Jenny, in her typical fashion, grabbed his arm and began to drag him away from the compound toward the parking lot. "I'm doing my Christian duty by helping you be a better person, so be a gentleman and take this lady out to dinner."

Mitch, always one to enjoy Jenny's often bossy way of doing things, even if she talked too much, decided to let go of his temper and, enjoying her grasp of the situation and of his arm, dutifully let her drag him to Al's Suburban. He lost a bit of his playfulness when she finished, "Actually, since you fed Jonesey over a bet that was not very flattering toward me, I believe you owe me the same consideration, Mr. Harper." Embarrassed to think that Jenny had heard about the bet where Jonesey was sure Jenny would be Homer's choice for mole because she was the sexiest candidate and Mitch bet otherwise, Mitch felt his face heat, and Jenny laughed.

Jenny was right when she chastised him for his grouchiness; Mitch had been unbearable the last few days. They'd hit a dead spot in their planning for the next months. Gooding's last attack had occurred a month ago, and there was no new information. Everyone was tired of going over the data again and again. Their plans were set and no one could find a way to strengthen them. Arguments were rehashed, discarded, and reinvigorated. Mitch wasn't the only one who was tired of the futility surrounding them. Gooding was across an ocean, and arguing in the middle of the woods wasn't helping them catch him. Besides, there were plenty of terrorists running crackpot schemes here. Someone had snapped in the last meeting, "It's not like the FBI needs the work."

Mitch's temper was not improved by his belated realization that he was well and truly fixated on Ms. Jenny Johnson. Bill had stopped razzing him about it, and had even been serious when he'd admitted that it was no fun to tease a dead man. Mitch knew he meant that Mitch was a goner. Reva had never teased him, but had pulled him aside a week ago and told him frankly, that as the team leader, he needed to be an example and get his feelings back in control. Reva was right. A little entertainment for the crew was one thing, like that incident at the crevasse, but they were professionals on a mission. He should not get personal with one of his team members, especially a subordinate.

Hell, I even apologized to Jenny after the rope thing. She said she understood that it was a planned bit of comic relief for the task force, and accepted it was a one-time thing. Maybe I wasn't as professional with Jenny after that. I must be slipping.

Reva's conversation had helped Mitch know he needed to handle his attraction for Jenny in a more professional manner, but having never experienced the feelings he felt for her before this strongly, he was at a loss as to how to change his behavior. That lack of inspiration was really the cause of his bad attitude. He hated problems he couldn't solve. He was a fixer and couldn't fix this. His attitude bordered on surly, and he'd attempted to curb the behavior—unsuccessfully. His team was angry with him, but couldn't show it, and nobody could spare any time for the contention between themselves this close to their deployment to the UK. Thankfully, Reva and Bill were doing what they could to smooth ruffled feathers. It was them, Bill and Reva, who had talked about letting the team take a night for themselves out of Mitch's influence, and had initiated the discussion about the dinner. *Funny, they don't want any team leaders with them, but it's okay for Stan and Jonesey to go,* Mitch had thought to himself, half hurt by the team's wish to be free of him for a night. Then he recovered. Stan and Jonesey were focused on their objective and were, as usual, competent, strong leaders. They deserved to go along for the last night of relative freedom.

As they reached the car, Jenny patted his shoulder as if to reassure him as she left him by the driver's door of the 'Burb and crossed in front of the truck to wait patiently by the passenger door. Mitch pulled the keys from his pocket and unlocked the doors. As they each settled in and buckled up, he felt the joy at the thought of enjoying a nice dinner, just the two of them, wash over him—fulfilling a fantasy he'd had since that afternoon in March when he'd first seen her. It helped him forget to worry about the rest of the team. Too late, he thought, *I should have opened the door for her.* Another thought countered it. *Yeah, how professional that would have been.*

"So does this count as a date, Miss Jenny?" he asked as they pulled out of the spot.

Clearly nonplussed at his attempt to tease her, Jenny shook her head. "Nope. That would be inappropriate as you are technically my supervisor for the moment. Consider this two coworkers sharing a meal before a big meeting." She smiled at him. Mitch laughed and felt deliciously happy for a split second as they left the compound.

***

The restaurant was clean and tidy with a welcoming atmosphere. Jenny was glad for all her teasing that the prices were reasonable. She had no intention of actually letting Mitch pay for her steak dinner; in the process of dragging him out to dinner, she tried to remember that she had to pay for her next semester before she left for England.

The walls of the dining room were painted a deep rich red above the dark paneling on the walls. Green plants were generously scattered about, and candles lit the tables, while antique brass chandeliers added a romantic twist to the atmosphere. Not that she and Mitch needed a romantic atmosphere. The chemistry between them had been building steadily as they got to know each other through the arduous required training before the final mission. Jenny smiled at Mitch across the table as she sipped the cool ice water in her glass. The meal had been pleasant. Mitch was an excellent conversationalist when he was able to let go of his responsibilities. The steak itself was divine, juicy, tender, and cooked exactly the way Jenny preferred it, slightly rare in the center, but warm, and well done on the outside. Its flavor required no steak sauce, and the mixed greens salad with a delightful, spicy, house vinaigrette served to improve her mood and tinged their conversation with her satisfied sounds. She'd forgive the mediocre backed potato. *Not everyone can get fresh Idaho potatoes,* she thought.

Over dinner, Mitch had opened up to her about his past. Having practically grown up on his grandfather's cattle ranch in Montana, he was no stranger to a good steak, and partway through the meal, Jenny revealed her own vast knowledge of beef and a rural lifestyle. Her own maternal grandfather had raised beef cattle, and as long as she could remember, her extended family was known to keep whole beeves in their freezer. Mitch sat quietly and listened to Jenny reminisce about Sunday afternoons at Grandma's. Her hilarious stories seemed to strike a chord between them, because Mitch then shared a few of his own.

In this fashion, Mitch's tension evaporated and Jenny relaxed, leaving her school and work worries far behind as she geared up for her task this summer.

By the end of dinner, both were stuffed and well satisfied. Mitch leaned back from the table with a hearty grunt. "That was fantastic. I'm as stuffed as a Thanksgiving turkey."

Jenny smiled and showed Mitch that a full stomach was one of the few states capable of rendering her silent and thoughtful.

"What, nothing more to say?" he inquired.

She roused herself from her pleasant, restful feelings to reply, "Nope, sorry, all the blood's rushed to my stomach, making me contented and sleepy."

The waiter soon came with the check, activating Jenny. She reached to snatch the bill, but Mitch, displaying his well-honed reactions, grabbed it off the table and held it out of her reach. "Hey, you agreed I'd be paying tonight," he taunted her. Subconsciously, Jenny's independent nature asserted itself. She had to maintain some control over this dinner in order to keep her equilibrium intact around Mitch.

She made a grab for the check. "I was just kidding you. I came fully prepared to pay for my dinner."

Mitch, looking delighted at having turned the tables on her for once, shot back, "Nope, honey, the man pays, and besides, you Mormon gal, without "drinks" or beer, this particular tab is tiny compared to when me and the boys go out for steaks." Jenny reached across the table and tried again to grab the check. Mitch just moved it behind his back. "Hey, sister, do I need to make a scene?"

"Well, at least let me pay the tip!" Jenny exclaimed.

"Nope. Man pays for all, man drives, man opens doors, and man pulls out your chair." His tone ended the argument.

Jenny recognized that Mitch was going be stubborn about this, so she gave in, almost gracefully. "Fine, man, but remember that woman has burned her bra, and will find a way to get back at man for his constant repression."

Mitch just smiled as he slipped a bill from his wallet into the folded carrier and tried very hard *not* to think of Jenny in or out of a bra. "Before you crucify me on the altar of feminist attitude, please understand that I am trying to pay you homage, and honor you as a fellow warrior in the battle we are preparing to undertake."

Jenny, unmoved by Mitch's flowery comment and sensing the unique smell of bullshit, just shook her finger at him. "Pretty words won't work on me, mister. An honorable victor would not torment the loser with flowery bullshit." Mitch just laughed and handed the waiter the folder.

"Do you need change, sir?"

Mitch answered without moving his gaze off Jenny. "No, keep the change. It was an excellent meal." The waiter nodded and, recognizing the couple's need for privacy, removed himself.

Jenny stood, signaling her desire to leave. "Let's go. I'll meet you outside. I'm headed for the ladies'." Mitch followed her out of the dining room, following close behind her and gently guiding her through the tables by holding his hand at the small of her back. Jenny relished his closeness for an instant, but she knew it would lead to trouble. For the sake of the operation, they needed to create more distance, not close it.

She washed her hands and splashed some cold water on her face, attempting to cool the blush in her cheeks. Staring at herself in the mirror, she thought, *I must be crazy. I should be avoiding Mitch like the plague, not going out to dinner with him.* She'd known from the first time she'd seen him that he was trouble for her. How could she not be attracted to him? He was sexy as hell, and an FBI agent, besides having enough "redneck" in him to drive her crazy. The fact that he was also tall, dark, beefy, handsome, and a bad boy—the stuff women's dreams were made of, didn't help one bit. Now here she was flirting with him, spending time alone with him, and allowing their attraction to build. There were so many reasons that she should stop herself, she couldn't even count them. Resolutely wiping the water off her face, thankful that she'd not worn any makeup tonight, so there was nothing to fix, she fluffed her hair, straightened the hem of her skirt, and strode out the door of the ladies room.

Mitch, dang him, was patiently waiting for her just across the entryway. Solicitously he asked, "All ready to go?" She nodded the affirmative, and they left the restaurant for the coolness of the starry night.

Millions of stars punctuated the dark blue sky overhead. Once they reached the Suburban, Jenny headed automatically to the passenger side to wait for Mitch to unlock the doors, but this was not to be. Instead of going to the driver's side of the truck, Mitch followed Jenny and came to stand directly behind her. Jenny tensed. She could feel him behind her, the warmth from his body emanating forward to warm her in the cool breeze. She lowered her head and tried to slow her pounding heart and catch her breath.

Mitch leaned forward to breathe in her perfume and whisper in her ear, "Turn around, honey." *Of course he has to do this to me,* Jenny thought as she turned from the truck door to look at Mitch. *Of course he's standing as close as possible, and damn him, but he looks fine.* Once again, Jenny's thoughts were swirling in her brain. Instinctively, she knew she was going to be kissed. Mitch practically emanated male interest and dominance. She was no biochemist, but she now firmly believed in human pheromones; the man was practically engulfing her with his intent—she felt physical waves of "Mitch" almost like breath or the wind. He was going to sweep her away with him.

She stood looking up at him, breathless and half scared as she stared up into eyes that were wide, dark, and deep. They were parked facing away from the restaurant, and the Suburban blocked the light from the streetlights behind her, allowing starlight alone to bathe them. He moved forward and leaned into her and pushed her back against the Suburban. Looking into her eyes, he reached down and clasped her left hand. Pulling it up and draping it across his neck he smiled as he did the same with her right hand. She stood stiffly, uncomfortable with the unfamiliar feel of his purposeful closeness, but unwilling to do anything to stop it. Smiling, Mitch reached down to hold her around her waist. He pulled her even closer as he whispered, "Relax." If anything, his command made Jenny even more tense. Unsure of what to do now, she looked up at him and was saved from having to do anything when his lips reached hers.

Sometime later, Jenny didn't know how long, Mitch pulled his face away from hers. Even in the semi-darkness, she could see his lips, the outline of his strong jaw—the bristles she'd felt on her face. However, the moon was now higher in the sky, signaling the lateness of the hour. It was time to go. She paused for a moment, struggling to catch her breath. Slowly, Mitch pulled her hands down from around his neck and held them in his as he watched her recover.

After a while, Jenny came into herself. "Wow" was replaced by "shit" in her thoughts as the enormity of her actions came to her. *Shit, but that man can kiss,* seemed to play in her head on a repeating loop. He was just standing there looking at her. Now what? Deciding that it was time for this thing to stop once and for all, and secretly unnerved by her first real, deep kiss, Jenny moved, startling Mitch as she yanked her hands out of his. "What the heck are you doing?" she asked. "That was the most irresponsible, unethical, inappropriate action!" Mitch's eyes widened. She continued to rant at him. "You're the damn team leader. You have no right to get 'involved' with one of your team members!" Near sobs, she recanted, "Not that I even tried to stop you, hell, I wanted you to."

Mitch's own temper seemed to flare at her unfair accusations. "Number one, the team's official action hasn't officially started yet, and two, you were acting like a 'consenting adult' here!"

Jenny knew somewhere within herself that her illogical fit of temper was due to her raging hormones, not to any inappropriate action on Mitch's part, but she couldn't very well do what her body was screaming for. Sex with Mitch was out of the question, for many reasons; not the least of these was her belief in chastity before marriage. *It's bad enough I swear all the time when I shouldn't, I can't fall any further.*

Although many considered the Christian belief in chastity to be extremely old-fashioned, Jenny didn't. It was a fundamental belief in her Mormon faith, and to Jenny, extremely well founded. Sex messed things up, disrupting the normal relations between people deciding on lifetime commitments, and it was transitory. There had to be a strong foundation in the relationship besides it, or the pairing would not last. Of course it was easy for her to decide such things having never had sex, but since meeting Mitch it was sometimes real hard to live them. In her past, the biggest "commandements" Jenny had a hard time with were her nasty swearing habit and not shopping or "recreating" on Sundays. Too many of her Christian friends who were not LDS couldn't seem to understand what they considered Jenny's fascination with these little things lately. *I am entirely too neurotic to worry about such frivolous stuff,* Jenny thought to herself as she felt herself physically respond to Mitch's very presence.

In a few frantic, pounding heartbeats her thoughts had flown along, slowing down some until they started to make sense. She silently spoke to herself. *Take me and Mitch. We hardly have had the chance to get to know each other well enough to know if we suit as marital partners, which was is the only way I can ever consider getting that close with a man. Hell, men are messy, animals.* Wrinkling her forehead, she shook her head. There was no way that she was going to risk her heart or risk getting pregnant and having kids with someone unless they were well committed to her and a life together—marriage. In the next breath, she thought, *I may have grown up with this idea, but I have tested it for myself. Too many of my friends have done it the other way and gotten burned.*

As a young adult, Jenny had questioned the idea of chaste living, not drinking, and all the other tenants in the religion of her youth and her faith in the Supreme Being, her Heavenly Father, in her search for her own individual identity. She'd half expected to find that it was really too strict like some of her friends thought, but she'd found instead that she believed in her religion and in Christ with her whole soul and felt that it was the right path for her. She began "fixing" things in her life. She was naturally an honest person, but still had problems with profane language and swore a lot, along with having a nasty temper that was difficult to curb. She'd managed to be a better friend and to be kinder to people and began to read the scriptures daily. She also had resolved to hold off on sex until she'd found "Mr. Right" and marriage—marriage first, sex later. She'd never had to really test her resolve until now.

No one she knew was like Mitch or affected her like he had. Her cousin Megan called what Jenny and Mitch were experiencing "testosterone poisoning" and would often declare that the only cure or antidote was a good, healthy exercise of testosterone—either sex or a killer fight. Jenny now consciously decided that since she was *not* going to use sex to cool down, and since it seemed to be the lesser of two evils, she'd choose a good fight, and let loose her hold on her passion in order to let it ignite her temper. A niggling thought lingered. *Maybe this is a bad idea...* Jenny ignored it.

Jenny hadn't really thought her actions through, as she forgot that Mitch had a temper to match hers, or she wouldn't have continued to argue with him. But it was too late; her temper was well and truly pricked.

"*Consenting adult*, my ass. You were acting like a horny teenager and yanked me along."

Mitch glowered. "Don't give me that shit, sister. You were right there with me, and you enjoyed it just as much. Don't deny it and get on your high horse now!"

"Who followed me to the car, when I was staying the hell away from you? You should have kept control of yourself. I was doing my damnedest to stay out of your reach."

"And looking at me the whole time with that 'come hither' look like Mae West. Hell, you should have left me alone and gone with the others to their freedom-from-Mitch party! You had me so fooled with your Miss Priss, perfect

Mormon act, when deep down you were as hot for it as I was."

Jenny, who really needed no more fuel for her own temper fit, lost what restraint she'd had as Mitch's baiting stung her deep down. "You're a dirty, low-down bastard!" she said vehemently. The next thing she knew, she'd slapped Mitch as hard as she could across the face.

Mitch recoiled, the shock seeming to effectively douse his anger. For a moment he just stood there and watched as Jenny zipped up her jacket, then spun away from him. She stomped through the parking lot and out to the street—away from him as fast as she could go.

Jenny had never hit a guy, ever. The last time she'd slapped anyone, she had been a grade-schooler riding home on the school bus, and that time she'd hit a girl her own age—who'd deserved it, by the way. But now, she smiled in satisfaction. She knew that she'd left a mark on Mitch's face. She better have, considering the way her right hand stung and throbbed. The pain and satisfaction nearly cooled her temper, but in its place she began to feel a bit chagrined. *Stop it!* she commanded herself as her conscience, which had previously been overwhelmed, started screaming for her attention. She started to feel shame over her behavior. Tears came unbidden and unwanted to her eyes. As she brushed them away, she reached the sidewalk and automatically slowed her pace. She couldn't decide whether the anger or her shame was a worse or better way to feel.

Latter Day Saints, most commonly called Mormons after one of their ancient prophets, referred to the quiet influences of the Holy Spirit as the Holy Ghost or Still Small Voice and He was trying to get Jenny's attention in earnest. As a devout Mormon, Jenny knew she could have the help of the Holy Ghost to help her throughout this life when she was living worthy of such heavenly guidance. Lately, she'd been thinking too many carnal thoughts, but she had been striving to live a better, good life. Before this adventure, she had had a much easier time being righteous during her "trials," though that term now seemed trivial. She had felt and knew when the divine was guiding her. As a daughter of God, she knew how to listen for His influence. But tonight she'd severed the connections with God. She'd been "on one" and let her pride get the best of her all day and for weeks. Jenny felt guilty; she'd been "hard hearted" as her Mom would say. *Of course, I've gone off the path, right when I really need His help.* Jenny put one foot in front of the other, thinking about God and not wanting to, then going back to those thoughts, trying desperately to get her spiritual self back in charge.

She'd left the compound thinking that she had a sound and logical plan for tonight. However, she'd ignored the promptings sent by the Holy Ghost as He'd tried to help her do the right thing all night.

As she walked down the street and began listening to that inner voice in her heart for the first time since breakfast, she knew she should turn back and go with Mitch, but now she didn't want to face him. "Why don't I ever listen when I should?" Jenny asked herself.

As she did so, she knew that to keep walking away was a bad idea. She felt the Spirit of the Lord leaving as she continued. That was not good. Down deep inside she began feeling like she was in the "wrong place" doing the "wrong thing."

Taking a deep breath, she turned back—and turned smack into a large male body. For an instant, she panicked. It was dark, and she was in a strange city. What if this was a stranger attacking her? In an instant those thoughts vanished as she recognized Mitch as the one holding her.

Mitch stared down at her as she shivered and began to sob in his arms. She cried quietly, but actively. It was as if her whole body expressed her grief. Mitch tightened his arms around her. Gently he turned with Jenny and walked her back to the Suburban. She stopped crying when they got to the vehicle, but she remained silent.

She stood while Mitch opened her door and only climbed up onto the seat when he nudged her arm. Woodenly she pulled the seat belt across her body and sat there staring straight ahead or away from him out the window to her right.

From the corner of her eye, Jenny saw Mitch look over at her as he pulled out onto the highway, but she just sat there, staring out the window, ignoring him. They drove back to the compound in silence.

"Jenny…"

Jenny shook her head, then continued to stare into nothing in a vain attempt to feel nothing. She was back in the car, which was where she was supposed to be, but she needed to now apologize for her atrocious behavior. Too bad she didn't know how. Worse, her pride wasn't letting her. She knew her silence wasn't helping.

Before she could gather enough courage to clear the air, they reached the gate to the compound. The stony silence continued and got rockier by the minute.

Mitch parked the car and turned off the ignition, but continued to sit and rested his wrists over the steering wheel, obviously waiting for Jenny to say something. Jenny glanced over at him. Mitch met her gaze. He seemed calmer than before, no blazing hatred in his eyes; they were merely impassive. She took a deep breath. *Hey, you can handle him cool and controlled. He's like that all the time,* she reminded herself in an effort to bolster her courage.

"Mitch, I'm sorry about tonight. I just wanted to help you have a good night after the rest of the team ditched you." Jenny stared down at her hands in her lap after her apology.

Mitch reached over and grasped her left hand. "I'm sorry too. I shouldn't have said those things. I lost my temper, when I should have held it."

Surprisingly, their short, joint apologies seemed to cut through some of the tension. Jenny spoke next. "I should say more, but I don't know what to say. There are a few things you need to know...do we have time right now?"

Mitch pushed the button on the stereo to check the time. "It's ten thirty. The meeting's at eight thirty tomorrow morning. I can stay up a bit later."

Jenny took a deep breath. "Okay. Well, really there's only one thing we need to clear up, the attraction between us." She didn't know whether she wanted Mitch to be attracted to her or not. She did know it hurt her to stop this. If Jenny took the time to think about it, she knew she'd find that she really cared for this guy who was technically her boss.

Mitch sighed. "I know," he finally said, finishing the last thought for both of them. "Okay, I agree to halt things until the mission's over. Can you handle that?"

Jenny gave the only answer that she could. "I can."

"Good, then we're agreed. No more... For the foreseeable future."

"Fine." She hoped the resolution would stick.

Chapter Thirty-eight

Through the last week of May, the task force continued the rigorous training of their newbies, getting them ready to hunt down a madman. Everyone was back from their regular assignments and the permanent team assignments had been made. Time was running short, but Homer's plans were coming together, partly due to Memorial Day becoming a working holiday.

Too bad Mitch was being a grouch. The team members believed he and Jenny had reached some sort of agreement, which lessened the tension, but as a team leader he was relentless. Those who had never worked for him before believed that it was all Jenny's fault—including Jenny—but the seasoned agents seemed to know better; they knew this was his way. Mitch expected everyone to live up to his expectations, and since he expected nothing short of perfection from himself, everyone else had to give a hundred and ten percent too. In any case, Jenny received no special treatment, for which she was grateful. The tiredness helped her ignore any romantic feelings she still had.

Just before sunset on May 25, Jenny ran the obstacle course one last time. In the three months since she had been recruited, she'd experienced too many changes for her psyche to cope, or so she felt, and she needed the physical release of running. Lately anywhere was fine, but tonight she also needed a big boost of privacy. Helping the other agents and trainees handle the news of the latest bombing and the reality of that attack had only increased her stress level.

A Marine's training facility in Arizona had been bombed in what the media reported as a terrorist attack. Hand-carried missile launchers had blown up a bunker in the middle of the night at a desert camp a hundred miles from Phoenix. Only the task force knew that Gooding was behind it, thanks to a couple of gruesome photographs he mailed to Albert in a jar of bloody sand. For now, local law enforcement was accepting the FBI's story of a yet-unidentified terrorist. How Gooding was able to take a trip from London to Mexico City without them finding out was amazing in itself. That he was able to sneak across the Mexican border into Arizona was astounding. He'd left the launcher and the jeep he'd used near the base. They had no fingerprints or actual proof, but the sand-encrusted photograph showed Gooding near the bunker. When the agents tested the blood in the sand, they found it contained anti-coagulant agents and traced it to a local Red Cross donation center where the Marines had held a blood drive a few days before. Gooding, or someone helping him, had used his credit card to make a donation to the Red Cross the day of the blood drive. He was now back in Scotland, and the information had been verified by both the CIA operatives there and the British undercover agents. In a freak blessing, the troops that should have been asleep in that bunker were actually sleeping outside in tents after their air-conditioning system died. The fact that the cooler had died was suspicious, but there were some inconsistencies with this attack and its timing. Homer and Stan were beginning to hope that either Gooding was finding some uncharacteristic mercy or somebody was betraying their boss.

However, Jenny wasn't in Phoenix or Denver, or Salt Lake for that matter. She was back in Georgia for the last time and hoped that after tomorrow, when the mission officially began, she could begin to actively attack the source of her stress, Gooding.

Tomorrow she was headed for Washington DC and her latest briefing with Stan. He required at least one last interview with her before she headed to England.

Jumping a half-rotten log in her path, Jenny began to feel the slight ascent in the trail. She felt the stretch in the back of her legs, but she was also feeling the endorphins pumping through her system after twenty minutes of running the trail. She'd checked with Reva and the undercover dudes watching the trail and had been assured that the net was still in place—the last training group to train here before the Memorial Day holiday was slotted for their run tomorrow. Thankfully it was also a full moon tonight, so if she got entangled and had to make her way back, she would be able to see. Not that Mitch and Bill wouldn't track her down before too long. She scowled with frustration over that thought.

How she wished that she didn't feel any attraction for Mitch anymore. As if she needed any more stress in her life. She wished she could just turn it off like a faucet, but no such luck. Worse, since he'd kissed her that night last week, she now knew that he was supremely conscious of her as well. They'd done so well keeping it professional, other than the crevasse incident. Then he'd lost it or something. Of all the rotten luck, to have found out that her heart wasn't dead, just dormant—it had just been waiting, apparently for the most inopportune time. She *would* have to finally find someone to make her system go haywire right when she couldn't do anything about it. Not only was an attraction incredibly inappropriate professionally on this team, but Mitch was also team leader, so she couldn't ignore him in order to keep a safe distance from her raging hormones.

Turning northward toward the gully, she continued to fume. *Speaking of hormones, someone has a little too much testosterone in his system, the big control freak!*

Mitch, besides being a perfectionist and conscientious leader, was worried about Jenny to the point of freaking out. He had started giving her daily lectures. Reva said he couldn't bear the thought of her getting hurt.

So he was doing everything he could to prepare her for their mission. This included riding her harder than the other team members and pushing her to her very outermost limits. He was absolutely merciless.

Jenny was grateful for Reva and Millie. They would back her up when they could and help her vent when they couldn't. Actually, Reva had confided that she was glad of the distraction of helping Jenny; otherwise she wouldn't have been able to handle the stress. Doing things like ordering pizza for the girls only and running the obstacle course at night were great pressure valves for the female agents.

Just ahead the trees opened up. Jenny could see the gray cliffs of the gully that were still tinged pink by the fading sunset. Aiming for the markers where the ropes hung listlessly, she steered herself to the left. She spotted Cooper, the head undercover officer, who'd been waiting for her and waved as she leaped into thin air. She'd made a habit of leaping into the gorge whenever she came to this spot. It was an unconscious acting out of how she felt about her life. Jenny was well and truly out of her comfort zone, but the net always caught her. Deep down she knew that it was her way of expressing her frustration over her lack of control over her emotions and the situation the mission placed her in, but it still felt good to just let go for a minute.

***

Bill swallowed and breathed a sigh of relief. Turning back from the monitor, he remarked as casually as he could, "She's landed in the net. Cooper will bring her back on the ATV in a half hour." He watched Mitch for any reaction. Mitch kept his attention focused on the documents in his hands, but nodded to show Bill that he'd heard him. Then Mitch's shoulders relaxed a little and he took a deep breath and turned to face Bill. Acting nonchalant, as if he didn't find his way up to the security desk every night as Jenny made her run, he rolled his shoulders and swung his head sideways to stretch the tensed muscles in his neck and bundled those same papers.

"Well, I guess I'll head down to dinner. Are you coming?"

Bill shook his head. "No, I think I'll watch and meet them at the tower. Save a spot for us." Mitch nodded and left. The security officer sighed, drawing Bill's attention,

"I'll be glad when you guys ship out. I don't think I can handle much more of his worrying."

Bill clasped his shoulder and sat down to wait and watch Jenny finish her run. "Me neither."

***

The night sky was glorious overhead. What had been pink was now purple and lavender, swirled with fiery pink bits of clouds. After the long run and another muggy day, Jenny relished the cool breeze coming up from the water underneath her. She lay spread eagle on the gently swaying net, enjoying the adrenaline rush. She wiggled her fingers and her toes and stretched and flexed her muscles. It felt so good to lay here, no cares, no worries, and pretend she didn't have to go back, ever.

Too soon, Cooper popped his head over the side of the cliff. A southern boy, born and bred, he called all the lady recruits "miss" as often as possible, something Jenny was still getting used to. "Miss Jenny, it's been fifteen minutes. We need to get moving." He seemed to hesitate a moment before he added, "Bill radioed in. He's waiting by the tower, and said that Mitch is holding dinner for you, we only have twenty minutes to get back."

"Fine, drop the line and we're gone," Jenny called up to him. Normally, she'd finish the course at a fast run to build up her endurance. Cooper would probably use the four-wheeler tonight instead. Her best time in from this point was twenty-three minutes, but she didn't think Mitch would wait tonight.

The other nice thing that Jenny and Reva had learned from the nighttime runs was that the undercover guys usually kept a skeleton force out and about all night, so that there was help if needed. They seemed to enjoy the distraction of having something besides potential threats to worry about in these woods. Besides, a few of them simply enjoyed having girls around on the trails—it gave them something pretty to look at during boring shifts. They all appreciated that those same guys had ATV-type vehicles stashed at various points in the woods to facilitate the movement of personnel in emergencies. Cooper led Jenny to one of these and proceeded to speed her down the mountain to the trail tower.

"Thanks for the ride, Coop. Have a good night tonight." Jenny patted Cooper's shoulder as she swung off the souped-up four-wheeler.

Flirting, as was his custom, he replied, "I will have the memory of your latest flight to keep me company tonight, Miss Jenny!" He laughed and turned back, revving the engine as he disappeared into the now dark woods.

Jenny walked up to Bill. "Thanks for waiting for me. How's the fire-breathing dragon now?"

Bill smiled at her continuing angst at Mitch. "At a low smoke tonight, missy. He hates it when you go take fool chances like doing the night run without night-vision goggles or the lights on."

Bill looked at Jenny and seemed almost hesitant for a moment. She could guess why. She had yelled at Mitch this morning, and although she'd done it in the privacy of the conference room, Reva and a few other agents had walked in at the end of the tirade and had shared the news of the incident far and wide. Mitch had even made amends to Jenny by addressing the issue in front of everybody. He'd apologized when he'd addressed the team during their lunchtime meeting when he'd explained that he and Jenny had had a loud discussion that morning because he, Mitch, had been remiss in explaining a few issues to Jenny. Mitch then had shared some key information with the team, enabling those who'd been resenting his closed-mouthed attitude to relax. Mitch seemed to know that to help the team cope with the stress, they needed some information about their situation in order to handle the fact that they had no control over that situation. But clearly he had also wanted to spare them from the awful reality. However, with this team, they seemed to have too much imagination, and it was actually better to level with them to let them know just how bad it was. Jenny had listened as Mitch explained this needed change in his leadership style and had been glad to know that Mitch had finally clued in. *Maybe I should yell at him more often.* Tilting her head to one side, she regarded Bill's frowning face and decided that he, too, needed to tell her what was happening. "Bill?" she asked, raising a brow.

"He hates to see you risk your neck, you know." Jenny took a deep breath, startled that Bill would say it out loud. "Yes. He can't watch you fling yourself into space. Hell, I've had to help Coop check the net every day to make sure that it's sound, and we can't hardly stand to see you do that. I also have to pass on this data to you-know-who so he won't pester Cooper about it after."

Jenny went absolutely still and continued to look at him expectantly. After a moment, Bill plunged into what she really needed know. "Okay. Now this may seem like it's none of my business, but he's my partner, and I have to take care of him. You need to know something, but before I tell you, you have to promise to not pounce on Mitch. He's under more stress than we are right now."

When Jenny saw that Bill wasn't going to continue without her response, she replied, "Of course, I won't pounce on Mitch. After this morning, do you honestly think I would lay into him again?"

Bill shrugged. "Jenny, I've never seen Mitch act like this. He's always overprotective of his teams, but he's gone overboard with his actions toward you. I don't think he can help it." He paused for breath. "I think he cares for you, and the *only* way he can handle the fact that you are going to be bait for Gooding is to make damn sure you have every weapon available. So, I am asking you, as a friend, as a team member, and as an experienced field agent to please try to endure Mitch's unreasonable attitude toward you. I know it's unfair, but when he can mother hen you, it makes life bearable for the rest of us. And, finally, before you think I am asking you to be a martyr for us, I need to say that since this morning, I think Mitch has realized how hard he's been on you in particular and that I think he will try to lay off you. But if not, I think Stan will compensate you for being his pressure valve, if only you can keep going. So, can you keep up with this?"

Jenny looked at Bill, then turned her face upward. "I don't know. I'll try."

"I know he kissed you," he said gently. Jenny started. Bill reached over and put a hand on her arm to steady her. "Hey, I am the only one who knows. No one else saw you. I left the group dinner early that night and went to the restaurant. I was looking for him about a last-minute detail and saw y'all there in the parking lot. I waited to see what Mitch would do after you ran off, and when he went after you, I knew I needed to catch him at another time. You're not a casual fling for him. I know this is not the best time to discuss this, but you are very important to him, please remember that."

Jenny's thoughts were spinning round and round in her head. She looked up at Bill's earnest face. *I can't believe he's telling me this. What do I do now? Can this be true?* She knew Bill. He might be a flirt and tease her like crazy, but he would never lie to her, and although she'd only known these guys a few months, she knew Bill was right to tell her the truth and she trusted his motives. He was only trying to help. And Mitch was his best friend as well as partner. Mitch would never admit if he had feelings for her, not during the mission, and maybe not after, so she'd have to act to protect him and herself from their chemistry. *What fun,* she thought sarcastically. Still, she was glad Bill had warned her. Vibes and woman's intuition had told her that Mitch had been pushing her harder than any normal FBI recruit out of concern, not vindictiveness, but now she had acid proof. *What a mess.* Bill clasped her hand in a restraining gesture. Jenny half shrugged away, but stayed. "Fine, I will. Let's go back." And the two of them went in for dinner with the crew.

Chapter Thirty-nine

The waves melted smoothly under the prow of the yacht. Some vague part of Mitch could hardly believe he was four days into the seven-day journey across the Atlantic to Ole Britannia. The past two and a half months had zipped by in a blur of last minute and top secret activities. He dragged slowly on his cigarette, glad for once that he still smoked now and again. He was often surprised at his ability to leave the habit for weeks at a time, but on nights when he couldn't sleep, the nicotine seemed to lull him to rest.

Of course, he always smoked on dangerous missions. The stress seemed to call for it. Non-smokers seemed to be inured, almost immune, to those moving smoking instances in the movies. But smokers felt the poetry in those scenes. Some stress could only be relieved by a deep drag off a sweet cancer stick.

The moon was full overhead. Mitch couldn't help but picture the moonlit nights shown on the *Love Boat*. There'd been a dance or something and the guests that week would somehow end up on deck and the camera would catch them in front of the silvery moonlight glimmering on the waves on the TV show. This night seemed to be just like that—and that thought was too poetic for him, a sure sign that he was not resting. He had tons of reasons for not sleeping tonight. The moonlight was part of it. He could sleep in the midst of a traffic jam, with neon lights glaring around his bedroom blinds, but the cool bright moonlight of a full moon always harked him back to the long, summer nights in Montana, when he and his cousins would play "no bears are out tonight" or "kick the can" in the dark. He could never seem to sleep in that bright light. Mitch always thought of the oft-quoted poem, the "Night Before Christmas." The phrase that came to mind was: *The moon shone down on the snow like the sun at noon,* or something like that. Of course tonight he was worried about some half-crazed genius trying to destroy the US government, and a certain honey-haired girl who'd bewitched him. Mitch could admit the last part to himself, only, and only rarely. Personal feelings like that had no place while on assignment.

Tonight, he'd been musing on Jenny's uncommon knack for shooting. For someone who had never really shot a handgun before, or even owned a firearm, she was a great shot. He couldn't credit Jonesey's story that she'd only shot an old revolver before. She'd quickly mastered the kickback on the .44 mm automatic that seemed to suit her, and shocked the socks off all witnesses when she produced an antique 1927 Winchester 30/30 rifle and begged Bill to rate her skill with it. Bill, who loved guns, especially ones with a history, had been ecstatic to get his hands on this one, and took it as a point of pride that Jenny had become a crack shot at it.

The gun was her legacy from her maternal great-grandpa, who'd used it to kill the coyotes who ate his sheep after they were caught in traps from his saddle. Also according to Jenny, her mom, who'd been the one herding sheep with Great-Grandpa, had bought her first .22 pistol when it became her turn to kill the coyotes, and had used it in response to the fur explosions that the 30/30 created. Her mom said that "a .22 will kill as easily as a bigger caliber; it just makes a smaller hole." Mitch had gone with the bunch as they went down to the special range, the one that handled long-range shots. Mitch and Bill were the only ones who knew Ms. Jenny was only half kidding when she mentioned that the rifle would serve as better protection, saying, "Better to get them hundreds of yards away than let any bad guy get within range of my pistol." Bill and Jenny had spent hours calculating the damage her old rifle could do to a car a mile away. Mitch shook his head. He knew

Jenny would much rather have trained with the CIA snipers than have to take on Gooding face to face. Mitch sighed, thinking of how much both Jenny and Bill enjoyed that gun. Bill had been unable to contain his excitement, because he was a huge Browning fan. He'd remarked, "Dang Mitch, she gets to drive past the old Browning ranch every day."

Of course, these musings didn't lessen Mitch's lustful thoughts. He felt his attraction to Jenny was just another hazard of the job, just something caused in him when he watched a gorgeous lady handle a gun like that. All the penile comparisons between guns and that favorite piece of male anatomy may have explained the virile connections, but Mitch couldn't deny the stirrings caused by a female who expertly handled guns—especially that particular female.

Mitch wished Jonesey was here. Not only would Amy probably figure out Mitch's growing fixation with Jenny, she'd tell her husband, and Jonesey was pragmatic enough and honest enough that he would help make him aware of the problem and help him get perspective or fix it. Then again, Jonesey was only human when his wife was around, and he was known to have a deep and wide romantic streak hidden away. Mitch was now glad Jonesey was far away tonight.

With effort, Mitch returned his focus on the mission at hand. Jenny's cherished rifle was safe at home in her parents' gun safe, and Bill himself was keeping her .44 until the rendezvous. Everyone hoped she'd not need it. As the waves continued underneath and behind him, Mitch finished his cigarette and fervently prayed Jenny—and the rest of the team—would remain safe. She ought to be in London by now. Mitch stubbed his cigarette out in the nearby ashtray (no sense poisoning dolphins) and lightly fingered the golden cross on the chain around his neck. Always a Christian, but not usually obvious, Mitch sent a fervent prayer upward as he retired on what he knew to be one of the last peaceful nights ahead.

Chapter Forty

The London dining room was opulent. Gooding and Alicia had arrived at the posh restaurant via his grandfather's limousine in order to treat Alicia to the night on the town she'd required as part of her payment for her participation in the Summer Plan.

Alicia was keenly aware of and excited by Gooding's status as a member of the British aristocracy. While Gooding knew that if Alicia were not so ignorant, she would understand his true unimportance and low standing. His grandfather was a minor lord who bore only a minor title that included few holdings, and that had a relatively small fortune when compared to the true aristocracy, until his financial success after World War II. They were barely upper class in most circles. But, to Alicia, a crass American who had no true understanding of England's still existent class system, Gooding's family titles made him seem to be a true prince of the realm. And his status clearly added to the thrill she derived from aiding him in his designs. Gooding, knowing that the shimmer and shine Alicia saw in his social standing allowed him to buy her services more cheaply than expected, saw the parading of her and himself as a small price to pay to keep her content and out of his hair when he was busy with the actual important events for his plan.

He smiled with true amusement as he kept from being bored during the first course by remembering Alicia's delight when he'd produced "Granny's jewels" for her inspection. In a manner calculated to use her own greed to blind her to the fact that he, Gooding, was beginning to despise her company, he handed Alicia a box crammed full of glittering, false, gem-encrusted jewelry with the instructions that she must choose the perfect ones to grace her beauty for dinner that very evening. He smiled, knowing his mother would go ballistic when she found her gems were missing, replaced by paste versions. The real ones were on the freighter "just in case." Mortimer would take them back later this week. The act of getting and giving the jewelry had also given Gooding the time he needed to coordinate the last-minute details for the Air Force attack tomorrow. Alicia had whiled away the afternoon far away from him, presumably trying on various gowns and gems and alternating her selections until she was sure that she presented the most alluring picture possible. He watched her eat and was glad that his anticipation about tomorrow kept her slight lack of manners from ruining his appetite.

After enjoying the delicious meal and even the opera, Gooding took Alicia back to the London flat and left her for Scotland around dawn.

"Good night, Gooding! What is all this crap?" Mortimer stood in the doorway to what Gooding and he referred to as "the lair."

"For being a master criminal, you sure know how to take a breather."

Gooding glanced up from his puzzle and looked at Mortimer expectantly. "Did you need something?"

"Not really. I just came in to pass a message. 'Licia triggered the device just like you wanted, but she's staying a few extra nights in London. She said something about needing some clubbing and 'like she's gonna stagnate in BFE Scotland.'"

Gooding stood for a moment, stretched, then sat down with his back to the door and Mortimer. "I expected no less from Alicia." Dismissing Mortimer, Gooding focused on the 5,000-piece, Renaissance puzzle.

"Sir, I've secured the perimeter and will lock down the radio and computer network on my way to the freighter." After making his usual evening announcement, Mortimer turned and left for Aberdeen.

Gooding had let himself in through the security gates and rested all day, waiting for the reports. Later that night he headed up to the castle walls to meditate on his final bombs. The night was beautifully clear and he could see the sky across the entire valley. His final decisions made, Gooding had descended to his workroom off the kitchen in the castle to while away the hours until morning.

Gooding continued quietly fitting pieces together. Sometimes putting a puzzle together suited his meticulous nature and rested his eyes from straining in the darkroom. This particular puzzle was extremely restful for him. His grandfather had owned the painting featured in the puzzle. One of Gooding's mother's escapades last year had cost his grandfather the painting. He had thoroughly enjoyed his grandfather's reaction when his mother had announced she had taken the painting from the castle and sold it to a chintzy gallery in Brighton, who'd immediately marketed it on coffee mugs, calendars, and this puzzle. Grandfather really hated the idea of commoners enjoying a priceless painting brought to the family in the sixteenth century from Italy.

Soon the assembly of his final bombs would be complete with the components he'd gathered on the last few trips. The San Diego blasts and the final bombing of Washington DC were finally possible. Tomorrow he'd leave Scotland for the freighter to stay indefinitely or maybe even permanently. But first, he needed to check on his expositions and watch for that art student from the States who Mortimer had spotted going through his exhibits over and over and hitting each museum in turn. He looked past the puzzle to the grainy shots from the surveillance cameras. Tall, leggy, young and blonde, Mortimer had seen her on three different occasions, spending hours amongst Gooding's photographs and collages. "Just as instructed, he may have found just the replacement for Alicia's mouth." Gooding smiled. Things were just fine.

Chapter Forty-one

Jenny had had a busy day. After wasting all morning in the gallery, spending her lunchtime with a nice professor she'd met a few hours before in the bowels of the same gallery, spending the afternoon and early evening with her school group and taking in a late task force meeting that night, she was tired.

Jenny tried to remain alert and actually listen to the questions lobbed at her. "So, what kinds of pictures were in the back?" Anthony asked her.

"Like I told you, they were similar to the ones in the exhibit, lots of dead bodies and war-time stuff, only set in park-type areas. No burned out buildings or roads, just things like lawns or in the shade of trees."

Bill, taking notes, asked for clarification. "What do you mean by park-like?"

Jenny, really tired of reiterating her impressions yet again, tried to be clear. "Like Hyde Park. You know, green grass, flowers—the kind of place you'd want to picnic in."

Mitch frowned. "Why did you say Hyde Park? Why not Central Park or just any park as you've seen them?"

Jenny, realizing that he'd picked up on a clue she'd missed, thought about it and answered, "Oh, that's right. It was the grass." She bent down and held her hand about nine inches off the floor to demonstrate as she continued, "The grass was too tall—not a few inches like mowed grass, but tall and meadow-like. In all the pictures, the grass was lush, green, and tall—knee high."

Anthony, seeming satisfied with the report so far, asked, "So, these pictures were in color, dead bodies, but no apparent focus on race or ethnicity, taken in park-like places, that appeared to be British to you, right?"

Jenny looked up from where she'd been resting her head on her knees and nodded. "Yup. I'm sorry, that's as much as I can recall right now. Let me stew over it, and I'll tell you if I have any more."

Anthony came over to stand next to her. "That's fine, Jenny. You need to get some rest. Are you guys off to Glasgow tomorrow?"

"Yup, bright and early. Good thing Dianna's driving first, I need to sleep," Jenny said. The rest of the team looked at Jenny for a moment. Mitch looked at Bill with a question in his eyes. Bill looked at Anthony and the CIA and British guys who'd tailed the professor out of the gallery. Everyone nodded back to him. He turned and nodded to Mitch. As group leader, Mitch reported directly to Stan, consulted with Albert and other FBI officials. The other agencies involved saw him as the task force leader, though from what Jenny could see, the CIA and British agents sometimes balked at deferring to him.

Regardless of the tensions involved, Mitch was also personally responsible for the team's physical safety and psychological welfare. Jenny slumped in her chair and sighed as she took in the looks the men exchanged, the way Mitch squared his shoulders and faced her fully. It was clear he had something to tell her before she would be given a break and the opportunity to rest.

Motioning the others to back away and give them some privacy, Mitch walked over to Jenny and crouched down in front of her. He breathed deeply for just a minute, then plunged ahead. "Jenny, after you called in to let us know that you were exploring Gooding's photographs again with that professor, we sent a couple of the UK guys in to tail you, just in case. When you left the main gallery floor to go to lunch, the guys came back here, and we've spent all day fixing an ID on the guy."

Jenny looked up at him, worried. She knew she didn't have enough experience in undercover work to spot another agent, and her anxiety colored her question. "Do you think he's somehow messed up in this?"

"Well..." Mitch glanced down before raising his eyes to hers again. "Did you happen to see his shoes?"

"What about them?" Jenny was starting to get a bad feeling about this. She looked around and noticed that the others were trying to be busy elsewhere. Mitch turned her face back to his.

"They were platforms. They made the professor appear at least two inches taller. And the undercover guys found some sunless tanning lotion and a fake beard in the men's washroom after tailing him from there. They checked the fingerprints." He paused for a deep breath. "It was Gooding."

Jenny felt sick. "You mean I spent all afternoon with the man you are trying to catch?" Her temper exploded. "Did I have a gun? Did I have a wire? Were any agents near me to help? *No!* Holy crap!" She put her face back in her lap and tried to slow her breathing.

"We don't think he knew you were an agent. He appeared to be interested in you like we'd hoped," Mitch continued, his jaw clenching as his whole body seemed to tense. "He was trying to pick you up."

"Of *course* he was trying to pick me up," Jenny interrupted. "You people put me in these slutty clothes, highlighted my hair, and left me there to be pawed by anyone who can get close enough. Duh!"

Mitch's expression darkened. "What do you mean 'pawed'?"

Very sarcastically, Jenny told him, "Oh, like you don't know, being a guy. Like bumping into me, and reaching across to get a paper, just happening to brush my boobs in the process, acting all klutzy and half tripping with him ending up against me, pinning me to the wall or a door. Ick." Disgusted, Jenny stood and turned away. When she spun back around to face Mitch, a muscle in his jaw ticked dangerously, but otherwise he remained still and silent.

Jenny, wide awake now, asked, "So, what, is my cover blown, do I have to do any more of these assignments?"

"No, your cover's intact from what we can tell and you need to keep going. We really think Gooding was just into you. It's a good sign, his scoping you out personally. You did mention that you were on a school trip and were actually studying Gooding's work, right?"

On the chance that the guy happened to be a friend of Gooding—not Gooding, himself!—Jenny had explained in detail her itinerary, including the galleries she was going to be visiting to see Gooding's work. "Yes, as instructed, I did." With sarcasm bordering on insubordination, she added, "That's all part of the trap, right, let Gooding know where he can find the cheese—me, in these cheesy outfits, the bait for a rat."

Mitch remained cool in the face of her sarcasm. "You knew that this was the plan. You need to accept it and get over it." His voice became hard as he said, "You are going to continue the remaining visits on your itinerary, wear the skimpy outfits, and hope that Gooding takes the bait." Jenny went to interrupt, but he held up his hand. "And, you are going to wear a wire and your knife and gun and will have the full support of Bill and I as well as two two-agent teams undercover with you in the gallery. Also, the retired army captain and his wife and various other moles will be around to help you. Got that?"

Boy, did she get it. Now, she was embarrassed on top of being tired. She must have really pissed Mitch off to make him lay into her like that. It hurt. Jenny realized she was taking this a bit personal, but she couldn't help it. *It's midnight, I'm still half jet-lagged, and now he yells at me. I just want to go home.* She knew the thoughts were irrational, but she was at her limit.

Mitch frowned when Jenny started crying. "You'll be all right, hush," he told her.

"Oh, stop it, leave me alone!" Jenny yelled back at him. Noticing that the rest of the crew had given up their pretense of ignoring them, Jenny addressed the room. "I get it. I will be the tougher, skanky bait you all want. I'll wear the wire and the clothes and my weapons, but in the meantime, the minute I get to Scotland, I want you people off my back." She addressed Mitch as group leader. "You got me? I am taking the next four days off. I don't want to hear any more from you people until Aberdeen." She stood and, ignoring the overtures made to help her, stomped out of the room.

Reva and Carl, on night shift as usual, followed Jenny downstairs and out through the pub. Reva came up beside her and nudged her as she walked. "Better now?"

Glad to have a good friend near, Jenny hugged her and replied, "Yes. Thank you. It feels good to vent every so often."

"You're right. I wish I could have seen Mitch's face, though. He is so funny about you. I swear he doesn't know what to think."

At that, Carl piped up, "Now girls, remember you have an audience. Please do not talk about boys in front of me, okay?"

Reva turned back to him. "Sorry, sir. Won't happen again."

Jenny made it to her school group in one piece and departed for Western Scotland the next day.

Chapter Forty-two

On the edge of the Sound, people sluggishly milled about. The ocean water below was an impossible shade of dark, Prussian blue, matched only in intensity by the green, grass-clad hills and islands across the way and the dark gloomy gray of the sky overhead.

It was misting. Being from the desert of Northern Utah, Jenny had never experienced "misting" before she arrived in Britain. Today, on this pier, the novelty of the experience only enhanced the feeling of fantasy. She was in Scotland, for cripe's sake. On the western coast of Scotland, to be particular, and would have been on her way to the Isle of Skye had Gooding not detonated another bomb specifically targeted at the task force, unlike his other bombs that seemed to fit into a larger, grander scheme somehow. Jenny had only found out about the two agents that would be traveling on her ferry after she received the last briefing before she departed for the "school-only," four days in Scotland portion of her trip.

She'd met Bill and Mitch at the hostel in London after she arrived in England. She had experienced one of her two weeks of a fun school trip before the first gallery showing and she became active in the task force team. Until then she was just a student on a trip who happened to be carrying a .44 handgun in her gear.

How did Gooding find out about the FBI/CIA task force? Had he found out about Jenny too? Only last week the entire FBI/CIA team was in London after Alicia's bombing practice at a bus stop. Jenny didn't think any of the team had realized that Gooding hadn't been in England at the time. No, he'd been holed away somewhere in the wilds of Scotland, but that news had only broken yesterday. No one yet knew where Gooding was, but Alicia had been tracked to Edinburgh. Too bad Gooding's network was even more shifty and loyal above Hadrian's Wall.

The task force was praying for a break. So far, they had nothing to go on until this explosion. Now, it appeared that Gooding had sniffed out one of the teams heading out into the Hebrides to look for him. Unfortunately for them, they had been on time for the ferry. Fortunately for Jenny and her school group, they'd been late—delayed by a flat on their seventeen-passenger van. Of course it had been one of the rear dual wheels, and had been the inside tire, or rather "tyre," as shown on the card given to them by the man who'd been summoned to help them fix the tire, and had taken a horribly long time to fix.

Jenny, as one of the few "over twenty-five" aged students on the trip, was one of the "drivers" in the bunch. To keep the school's costs down, they hadn't hired any drivers, and depended on the professors and older students to drive the vans. She'd been driving the other van behind the bus as it lost the tire. They had been traveling south along the coast to Stornaway to catch the ferry. Looking at the chaos on the dock, including bodies covered by blankets, Jenny was grateful that they'd had a flat tire out in the countryside and had been late. She still felt tense and stressed out from driving, and the ferry explosion just seemed to be the icing on the cake, a metaphor for her rotten day.

She was not used to the roads in the UK, let alone driving down and sitting on the wrong side of the road. The "normal" roads were narrower and skinnier than even the secondary or dirt roads back home. Even the motorways seemed smaller than the grand stretches of freeway Jenny knew in the Western US. To make matters worse, in what must be called towns, parishes, or villages, the narrow roads were hazardous and made Jenny extremely nervous because of the heavy traffic. The first hedgerows she'd driven were bad enough, worse than any mountain trails she'd driven through. But when Jenny had to slide the van down the side of a brick-walled bridge to let a truck pass by and her professor said it was okay, the university's rental insurance would cover it, she was shocked and unnerved. She'd made more dents and deep scratches in this van in two days than she'd put on any of her family vehicles in the ten years she'd been driving.

Jenny was grateful she was driving the smaller of the group's two vans, what back home was a minivan, a Kia Sedona. However, in Britain, it was a monster. Even the larger seventeen-passenger bus was narrower and shorter than most of the trucks back home. She was grateful that she didn't have to drive her own GMC truck through the lanes. Even on the motorway, she felt squished. Out in the country between parishes, there was less traffic, and no houses near the roads so, although they weren't able to pull very far off the road, there was little enough traffic to bother them. Especially considering the seventy-five-mile trek down to Brighton from London was considered an "all-day venture" to the locals. Their weekday travels on the country lanes of Northern England and Scotland were uncommon and subsequently taken alone.

Jenny looked over to the edge of the pier. Even the emergency vehicles were different. Fluorescent yellow-and-blue flashers on white vehicles with blue slashing stripes surrounded the pier. Like the candy cane stripes on the caution tape out on the trails that warned walkers to beware lest they bring back "mad cow disease" on their sneakers, when black and yellow signaled caution to her American mind, the blue-and-yellow emergency lights were foreign to Jenny. As Americans, the students were much more familiar with the flashing red-and-blue lights and massive red fire engines, not the greenish-yellow vans used by the UK emergency personnel.

Their student vans were still up on the edge of the pier where they'd stopped as they watched the ferry pulling out of the harbor. The emergency personnel and police had yet to clear them away. The policemen were still busy helping survivors. Mary and Debbie, as the leaders of the school expedition, were still in the ferry headquarters with the head of the investigation as they tried to clear the group so that they could leave. Many of Jenny's fellow students were sitting as she was, in clusters and groups along the benches in the village before the pier. The hardier ones had ventured into the village to get sustenance like fish and chips once they'd been questioned by officials. Jenny watched one of the mothers in the group bring her son the newspaper-wrapped, salt-and-vinegar sprinkled chips. As she watched him began to eat, Jenny checked herself mentally, looking for nervous tension in her stomach, but felt herself nearly calm. It was refreshing to be a victim, not an official in this bombing.

How many times in the last few months had she felt responsible or a responsibility to fix the crime or clean up the aftermath? After all, she was part of the FBI/CIA task force to handle Gooding, but today she was just a student who'd nearly been a casualty. She knew, however, that this restful feeling could only be temporary. The officer assigned to watch them stood only a few feet away and was staring at her with a queer look on his face. Jenny felt a blush coming on and tried to duck and surreptitiously hide it. The police had been alerted to Gooding's plan and had been informed to look for him. Jenny couldn't help but hear his name when it had been uttered near her; she'd picked up on the word "bomb" also. She'd glanced up quickly, trying to learn all she could about what the police knew about Gooding, before she'd remembered that in this instance, she was just a tourist, a student, not a half-initiated FBI agent. A couple of the officers had, of course, noticed her attention. She hoped she would act more innocent than she felt. *Dang their suspicious natures and training,* Jenny thought irrationally, looking at the policeman standing nearby. She really wanted Gooding caught, but she was tired of being around law enforcement. The suspicion, cynicism, and bleak outlook she'd been encountering were wearing on her naturally optimistic, upbeat personality.

There, the young officer was staring at her again. Jenny tried to remember her training in Georgia. That class she'd attended by Reva, how to blend into the background. Jenny was never able to recede enough; she couldn't really grasp the concept of being in the background, like wallpaper or scenery. She wished she could now.

"Focus, Johnson. Just breathe." Jenny spoke quietly to herself. She glanced over to where her friends sat a few yards away. Regret washed over her. Nine months ago, she had planned this trip as reward for herself—a celebration of her schooling nearly being over. A trip wherein she could commune with fellow students, have fun, and hopefully make some new friends. Now, thanks to her extracurricular nighttime activities this past week, she'd been away from the group more than she'd been a part of it. The budding friendships she'd formed before the trip had not had the chance to grow, and more than likely, now, never would. Since she'd been gone last week, she'd missed enough fun moments that the other girls on the trip felt like strangers to her, but were friends to each other. Jenny glanced up at the young officer; no change there. He still watched her like a hawk. The girls across the way were still talking together, but a laugh could be heard now and again. They at least appeared to be recovering.

Humming to gather her scattered thoughts, Jenny concentrated on her breathing, Reva's relaxation tip #1— breathe. She forced her breath in, out, keeping it deep and constant. A feeling of peace enveloped her. Things were going to be okay. Thankfully the breathing worked. Her panic ebbed. Next week would be a mess. Who knew if she would even survive until tomorrow, but for now things would be okay, doable even.

Having closed her eyes to quiet herself, Jenny didn't see the man approach. A large hand clamped down on her shoulder. "Come with us, miss," said a burly voice as Jenny jumped, having been jolted from her relaxed state.

The large hand not-so-gently pulled her up by her arm as Jenny grabbed her shoulder pack with her free hand. Just behind the Scottish police officer, she could see Mary gathering the rest of the school group as Debbie stood nearby. In her usual calm way, Debbie explained, "Jenny, these officers just need to ask you a few questions. We're going into the village to have dinner while we wait for the vans to be released. We'll save you a spot."

Jenny looked at Debbie's concerned face and was comforted by her smile. "Thanks." Debbie turned away to join the group from Weber State. *I guess it won't matter if the group has more stories to tell about me,* Jenny thought. *Whatever my school group thinks, it won't be that I am some international agent working for the FBI and CIA.*

Jenny followed the officer to the makeshift headquarters. She noticed that the other young officer who'd been sent to watch her dutifully followed behind them. Jenny tugged the handle to her bag higher on her shoulder, amazed that her fingers didn't shake and betray her apprehension. She glanced back to Debbie's receding figure. Debbie was nearly psychic in Jenny's estimation—she had a way of understanding a situation and knowing just how to handle it. Plus, she was English and Irish and had lived in Scotland for years and was the force behind this school group. She kept everyone enjoying themselves while they absorbed the culture around them. If she could leave Jenny with these officers, everything would be okay. With that thought followed by others like, *Yeah, and she has twenty other kids to worry about, you may be the sacrificial lamb,* and *Whatever you do, don't give up your passport,* running through her head, Jenny obediently continued into the brightly lit building as the sun set over her right shoulder.

"Sit here, miss. We'd like to ask you a few questions," the officer in charge said as Jenny was settled in a chair against the wall. But he didn't have a chance to get any answers or say anything else, because at that moment, the door opened. Bill and Jonesey stepped in. *Thank you, Jesus!* Jenny had never been so grateful to see any two people in her life. Gratefully she took Jonesey's hand as he helped her out of the chair and took her outside. "Just let Bill take care of things. We've found Gooding's hideout, but I can't tell you anything more at this time. Go with your group. Someone will meet you tonight." With that and a gentle push, Jonesey steered her toward the village and dinner with her college group. With relief and shock, Jenny went to dinner, the mental picture of Bill pulling out his badge and speaking to the British police officers still fresh and a scripture fragment "...even the sparrows that fall..." in her head.

Chapter Forty-three

That night the castle looked massive, but warm and inviting when the group arrived well after dark. It had been converted into a hostel, but only after tasteful spotlights had been installed in the greenery. Gothic revival arches created out of sandy tan stones encased each window and door opening. Jenny marveled again at how even neo-Gothic castles 200 years old were still considered new. The oldest buildings in her town were just houses and they were only barely a century old. The oldest structures she'd seen in Salt Lake City dated only to the 1850's. After seeing 400-year-old houses in York, and buildings that had stood in Stratford-on-Avon before Shakespeare's time, Jenny had ceased to date things as being "old" in the same way. However, as she steered the van along the crunchy gravel drive, she felt relief at being able to stop for the night and rest.

They should have been sleeping in stone cottages called "black houses," so called not because of the color, but for the dark interiors caused by a lack of windows, on the Isle of Lewis in the Scots Hebrides, but for the ferry explosion. Mary had been ecstatic to hear that the hostel here near Loch Lomond had enough openings to accommodate the students two days earlier than expected.

As Jenny tiredly swung heavy suitcases out of the back of the smaller van and stacked them, a wave of exhaustion nearly toppled her and the pile of cases. The other two drivers, Charles and Yoshi, came to her aid after parking the larger van. After the other students had collected their bags, the three drivers hefted the last of the bags, their own, and headed in to sleep.

Jenny was the last in the large sleeping room. Six institution-style bunk beds greeted her view, and of course as the last girl to arrive, she was allocated the bottom bunk of the bed nearest the door, which suited her fine. On her many adventures this year, she had learned to appreciate a dark room and a safe bed as good enablers of sleep, regardless of location or noise. Close proximity to the door was also good for quick escapes.

Most of the group had gone downstairs for the day's recap. Thankfully tonight's meeting would be short, but lively. Mary and Debbie had recovered from their ferry explosion ordeal and were looking forward to the discussion, which would focus on the group's interaction with British law enforcement and compare/contrast with their American experience. *Only professors could take enjoyment of the group's experience by having them write a paper about it.*

As Jenny plunked her cases on the bed and tried to determine whether it would be better to make the bed now or later, her head began to pound and she sneezed violently. "Shit. I hope I'm not getting sick," she muttered to herself.

A voice echoed behind her, "You really need to stop talking to yourself. It doesn't reflect well on the Agency." Jenny looked up to see Mitch lounging in the doorway and noted distractedly that she wasn't surprised to see him.

"Good thing I'm not really an agent, then," she commented as she decided that now was a good time to make her bed. Making a show of scooting her cases onto the floor and pushing them under the bed, she walked out from between the bunks to pick up the folded bedding left on the shelf at the foot of the bed. Not bothering to look at Mitch, she turned back and began unfolding the mattress and covering it with the sheet and comforter.

***

Mitch watched her work. Warmth seeped into his heart as he stood there. Jenny was okay. He'd known that all day, but some part of him still appreciated seeing her in order to make it a reality. The first reports of the day had come in minutes after the ferry explosion. It was so quick, because the British team members took pride in keeping excellent track of all of the operatives in their territories. Their connections with the local law enforcement served the team well. Those first reports also included information about the student group who'd arrived too late to catch the ferry, but just in time to witness the explosion and subsequent sinking of the vessel. Although it was only for those few moments when her fate was unknown, Mitch had experienced absolute terror as he imagined Jenny being one of the victims of the explosion. The experience had only cemented the knowledge that he wasn't going to get "over" Ms. Jenny Johnson anytime soon, if ever.

With a flourish, Jenny dropped the comforter on the bed and sacked up the pillow in the pillowcase. She turned to Mitch when she had arranged the bed to her satisfaction. "Okay, what?"

"We can't really talk here. Walls have ears, you know," Mitch said in his typically sarcastic manner. He reached out and took Jenny's hand, his gentlemanly behavior belied by his gruff voice. "Let's talk outside."

Jenny pulled back. "Hey, I have a class meeting that I'm already late for. Can't this wait until tomorrow?" Then she froze. "Oh no, my cover's blown, isn't it?" she asked, looking horrified.

Mitch hurried to reassure her. "No, no, we don't think so. I just need to update your orders. Bill gave your professors some story…don't worry, they won't expect you downstairs."

They headed out into the hall and down the back stairs. At the bottom of the castle's stairwell, Mitch eased the door open. Kitty-corner to their left, the lounge door was open. Mitch slid out to the left, out the door, taking care to stick close to the wall and tugged Jenny out of the stairwell, past the kitchen, and outside. "This must have been the servant's entrance," Jenny said awkwardly as they passed the plain moldings and doorways in the hall. They emerged on the back of the castle. There were no spotlights back here, just a rusty-looking porch light over the door.

Mitch continued to lead Jenny, enjoying the feel of her hand in his. They crunched through the gravel, past the dumpster, beyond the back wall, all the way to the gate in the pasture where the sheep grazed during the day. Behind them, Bill moved into sight across the back of the castle by the parked vehicles. Mitch noticed him when he looked back at the castle to see if anyone followed them. He also saw his two-way radio when he waved it to them. From Mitch's pocket came the muffled comment, "Okay, buddy, you have ten minutes. Then we need to get back on the road." Mitch waved back to Bill as he switched off the power to his radio and leaned back against the gatepost, leaving Jenny no choice but to follow as he did not release her hand. "Business before pleasure, honey," Mitch said, starting into her orders. Jenny tugged her hand free and raised a brow at him, but otherwise remained silent.

"At this time, we don't think your cover was compromised, but are looking into it, and since we've changed the itinerary enough to give us a couple more days we have some extra time to find out for sure before you have to meet Gooding again and interact."

"But I'm supposed to meet Gooding in Glasgow as the student the day after tomorrow," Jenny interrupted, crossing her arms over her chest.

"Not anymore. It's too risky. We've analyzed Gooding's clues and it seems certain that he's planning to unveil things in Aberdeen in a week. We've found a shipping connection that's headquartered in Aberdeen, and figure one of the fuel freighters will be his escape plan." Mitch pulled Jenny into himself, tired of holding her at arm's length for now. "So, you're not to worry about your task force duties for five more days until you arrive in Aberdeen. We'll connect with you then. We've just found the true freighter connection after piles of paper trails and dummy corporations. Homer and Stan think that's how he was able to escape from the Coast Guard and get out to Mexico City and Iceland so easy."

Jenny frowned but didn't pull away from him. "So, I report to you after we arrive on Queens Street at the hostel."

"Yup. Jonesey will find you," Mitch answered as he pulled her close and rubbed the top of her head with his chin.

Jenny sighed. "I'll be so glad when you're no longer my supervisor. I am tired of being professional around you."

Mitch's mouth curved up into a smile. He loved it when Jenny went all soft and sentimental, when she spoke from her heart, especially when she was too tired to be evasive and responded to him. "Baby, I'm off the clock now," he murmured.

Jenny looked up at him, and Mitch met her gaze. He wasn't about to wait until she'd remembered where they were and pulled away from him. He bent down and kissed her for all he was worth. All day he'd been worried for her, ever since he'd heard that her ferry was gone. As he stared at her and she stared back, a strong devotion came out between them all of a sudden. She seemed to lose herself in their embrace for a while, but regained control with a vengeance. Mitch felt her start to struggle against him and let go of her. Shaky, but still upright, Jenny backed away. For a moment she looked up at him. Huffing, she turned away and stalked back to the castle, muttering as she went. "Dammit. I said hands-off until the mission's over, and still he paws me. Damn man." She waved Bill off as she disappeared into the castle.

Bill moved more fully into the light by the back door where Mitch could see him, then gestured to his wrist and pointed at the watch. Mitch pushed off from the fence and headed to the car for the beginning of another long night of reconnaissance.

Chapter Forty-four

Sure enough, the next morning dawned a bright sunny day, but Jenny was miserable and hated to see it. She *had* caught a nasty head cold. After helping to change the tire on the van the day before, spending all afternoon at the dock where the ferry went down, and the late-night meeting with Mitch outside the castle, she was worn out. She supposed the stress of the situation and the rainy chill yesterday—besides a country full of new germs—had combined to give her a massive head cold.

She was miserable, her head hurt so bad she could barely see, and none of the British cold remedies produced by helpful trip mates or for sale in the pharmacies looked remotely familiar. Had she remembered to bring her preferred cold medicine with her, she would have been more able to cope. Jenny had forgotten that even doses of familiar medicines were different here in Britain than they were in the States. Cursing herself for not following her professors' advice to bring medicine with her, Jenny stood staring at the cold medicines in the pharmacy. "What I wouldn't do for some pseudoephedrine and guaifenesin combined with Tylenol right now."

"Are you finding anything?" a cute blonde gal asked as she came to stand next to Jenny. This was Devon, one of Jenny's fellow students on the trip, who'd became a friend on their journey. As a staff member of Weber State's school newspaper, Devon was smart, funny, and had a great eye for detail. She also was a caring person and had taken some time out of their day exploring the village to help Jenny find some relief.

"I guess this will have to do." Jenny paused to sneeze. "But my throat hurts. Do you think we could find some lemon juice for a hot lemon drink?" The girls continued to look through the pharmacy, but found no lemon juice.

"Here, Jenny, get some of these tissues," offered their professor Debbie. "I call them manly tissues, because they're twice the size of your American variety."

Jenny and Devon stared at her as if she was kidding. The box of tissues was longer than and nearly twice as wide as a standard American box, but it was much shallower. Jenny sneezed again. "I'll take your word for it."

Debbie shepherded the girls to the checkout, approving their selection and promising to pick up some lemon juice for Jenny when she got provisions for dinner at the grocery. She then steered Jenny back to the castle where they were staying, admonishing her to get some rest. "As one of our drivers, you need to get your strength back so we can depart in a few days."

Devon and Debbie waved goodbye to Jenny as they headed toward the parish church down the street. Jenny was bone-tired. She had two days left here, two days in Glasgow, then a day's travel to Aberdeen, and the fifth day was the Gooding day. She just had to get over this cold. Debbie was sure she contracted it as a reaction to a combination of new germs in the new country and a lack of sleep caused by the jet-lag, time change, and Jenny's shift of schedule from night shift to daylight.

Miserable, Jenny clutched her bag of meager remedies and headed up the hill to the castle. The group had originally planned to stay two days and nights on the Isle of Lewis in the Hebrides Islands, but when the ferry sank, they opted to stay on the mainland. Luckily, the castle had enough open rooms for the group to check in early and would serve as base while they were turned loose upon the countryside to "soak up some local color" after their stressful interrogations by the police yesterday as expressed by Mary, the other professor. Jenny was just glad the hostel was nearly empty so that she could have some privacy while she hopefully recovered.

It was actually an opportune time for Jenny to get sick. She had a week-long break from schoolwork, of which four days remained from her undercover, task force assignments, and her professors assured her that her grade wouldn't suffer if she missed "soaking in some color." She just hoped she could get some rest in the uncomfortable bunk bed in her communal bedroom at the castle.

A handful of foreign cold pills and half a box of man-sized tissues later, Jenny was ensconced in the sunny, deserted, dorm-room style bedroom. The rest of her group as well as most of the other people staying at the hostel had split and vacated the building. Part of the group stayed in the village to watch a local dance group practice their steps and the rest venturing into Glasgow to do some sightseeing. Tensions were still a little high around Jenny. Some of the girls in the group were jealous that she'd found some cute guy to go sneaking off with, because one of them had spotted her with Mitch, while others just seemed to enjoy clashing with her, and found it easy, as she was still a stranger to them. It was amazing how stress caused by a long trip could express itself in resentment toward others. Jenny felt it herself, and though she was ashamed of her child-like behavior, found it hard to resist. *A little snapping and backbiting can be satisfying when you've had a long day of driving,* Jenny thought, trying to justify her own waspishness by deciding that it was acceptable to be a snot. "Especially when your target is insecure enough to act snotty at all opportunities and has the bad form to be younger and cuter than you," she muttered.

Jenny had mostly ignored the tension so far, even if she couldn't stop herself from making it worse sometimes through her bad tempers. She attempted to try to accept that strong personalities were destined to clash. But, boy, it felt good to just rest and be by herself today, even while being miserably sick. No one was around to pester her, and no one would ask her about her destinations or choices. She didn't have to be polite or professional or think at all. Then the recriminations ate at her. She would have to try to apologize tomorrow and be nicer to her whole group as well as those she seemed to irritate by just breathing. Having made her resolution, she became worry free and settled deeper into the covers, hoping for sleep.

Jenny had just started to fall asleep when she heard the voices. Her eyes popped open but she remained still as Mitch and Bill came into the room.

"I should have known that any woman of yours could be found in bed on her day off," Bill whispered as he and Mitch stealthily crept into the room. Jenny stiffened but didn't move. Clearly, they didn't know she was awake.

Mitch responded angrily, but quietly. "She is *not* my woman."

"Yeah, right," Bill said, seemingly unconcerned by the heat in Mitch's voice. Turning, she sat up and fixed both men with a glare, then ruined the effect by sneezing loudly.

Bill chuckled. "Sorry, gal, didn't mean to wake you."

Miffed, Jenny whined, "Can't you people leave a girl alone on her day off? Dammit, I'm sick!" She sniffled, sneezed again, and blew her nose. Moaning, she lay back down. Not bothering to sit up or attempt another glare at the two agents, she angrily demanded, "What the heck do you want now?"

Bill moved in closer and scrunched down to sit on the bottom bunk of the bed next to Jenny as Mitch followed and leaned against the footboard. "Well we knew you would be available after we watched the rest of your group head into Glasgow after some went into the village and you came back here alone. And, sorry to talk task force stuff to you on your day off, especially after we talked to you yesterday, but there's been a development. Gooding has succeeded in three more bombs."

Jenny sat up then. "What bombs? I thought you guys had found his headquarters last night during the ferry investigation and were blocking his transmissions?"

Mitch squeezed the bridge of his nose between his thumb and forefinger and answered her question. "Well, seems Gooding was on to us. The castle at his grandfather's estate, which served as his headquarters, was destroyed this morning—apparent sabotage. The blast was felt across the loch by a fisherman who called the police. An hour later, Gooding bombed a second Coast Guard vessel in Florida, another marine training facility, this one in El Paso, Texas, and one of our Air Force bases in Essex, England, simultaneously."

During the pause, Bill continued for Mitch, "We were jamming all the signals at Gooding's headquarters, but we only had time to get a pair of officers physically out there. They were still busy watching the castle and trying to pinpoint any communications when the explosion hit. And they didn't get a chance to locate Gooding. They didn't see him leave, or verify that he'd actually been there, and they hadn't noticed that the staff had been dismissed last night. However, after talking to the local people, they were able to piece this much together…"

Jenny held up her hand, stopping him. "Wait. Before you finish, I need to get a drink and wake up first." Without waiting for a response, Jenny threw off her covers and swung her feet out of bed.

Jenny hurried downstairs, grabbed a cold bottle of water from the fridge, and returned a few moments later. Holding the bottle to her warm forehead, she glanced down. Suddenly remembering that she not only wasn't wearing her nightwear, but she had taken her bra off to sleep, her face heated as she asked, "Can you guys please wait for me in the lounge downstairs? I need to get dressed."

Putting on a show as if he were a charming host, Bill bowed. "Of course, Miss Johnson. We await your shining presence directly." He curved off the bed and headed out of the room, sliding past Mitch, who continued to stand by the bed. Jenny stood there expectantly looking at him.

With a nod, Mitch turned and left. Jenny sighed and began to drag her suitcase up on the bed so she could dress.

A sick Jenny and a tired-looking Bill took an obviously vexed Mitch on a long drive out into the countryside. They reached the blackened hill that had been Gooding's family estate. Millie and the CIA guys were there going over the wreckage. As they headed down to help investigate, Jenny thought about how they would all meet Gooding next week in Aberdeen.

Chapter Forty-five

Gooding was practically jumping up and down with excitement. Oh, you couldn't tell it by looking at him. The one aspect of aristocracy he'd been able to reproduce exceptionally was a cool demeanor. It was the one trait his grandfather hadn't had to drum into him by force; he'd had it naturally.

Then there was his equally natural flair for the dramatic that came from his superior, dramatic mother— practically theatrical. This exposition was possibly the best example of his expertise with drama. The gallery holding his photographs had blocked off an entire wing for weeks while he'd prepared. What objects d'art he'd allowed to remain in the gallery had been swathed with black fabric while he completed setting up. It was going to be a great day.

From an access hallway across the room, Gooding took note of Jenny's position in his exposition. After making her acquaintance in the London gallery, his attention could always be found on her when she was present. He was particularly pleased to see her in the little gallery in Glasgow. He knew that he'd frightened her when he'd surprised her unexpectedly the last time they'd met. If she hadn't have gone into the ladies and the cleaning lady interrupted him, she would have been his days ago. However, she was making out to be a fine diversion for him while he completed his Summer Plan. Gooding always enjoyed a new conquest and Jenny was turning out to be a bit of a tough egg for him to crack. For one, she was an innocent and was very skittish around him. Also, whenever something sexual came up she became very uncomfortable. He'd just bet she was a virgin. How fun. Also, she knew her art. She challenged him slightly, even as a student artist.

Gooding had never dallied with any women who shared his artistic talents. He enjoyed wooing the "A," left-brained, obsessive compulsive women. The women he enjoyed couldn't understand his personality or his art and were fascinated by him. The lack of complete understanding caused friction sometimes, but that only added sparks to the game as far as Gooding cared. But, this one knew the language and had no idea the kind of sparks she could set. This was getting fun. He knew when she was around just by keeping a few of his assistants in the museums. They enjoyed her long legs in the short skirts she favored and now watched for her. Any heterosexual men in the gallery were drawn to her like needles in a giant compass.

Gooding smiled as he watched Jenny adjust the strap on her camera. She did it instinctively, without slowing her step or changing her rhythm. She was a bone-deep photographer and he decided that he really liked that. Maybe it was time to find someone to share his vision for a while. He remembered following her in the London gallery when he'd first noticed her to see which objects of art caught her attention. She could tell the good ones in an instant and her whole being focused on it intensely. More than once he'd seen her get totally distracted by a particularly stunning piece. She appreciated all types of art as well, and when she'd paused at one of his favorite sculptures he'd grudgingly admitted that she had a good eye for art.

Gooding thought of his mother suddenly—Jenny carried her camera almost as if it were another appendage, like another limb—just like his mother carried her purse. Gooding laughed inside; just like his mother carried her bag when shopping, Jenny carried her camera while looking at life. It was an extension of herself, and kept ready for that shot that needed to be captured at a moment's notice.

Only another photographer could recognize that need. Gooding had seen Jenny use her old-fashioned, heavy, sleek-looking SLR single lens reflex camera. She preferred a fast, manual Nikon. Recognizing the skill she employed using the beastly thing and knowing the prints she probably gained from it earned his respect. He thought of how Alicia couldn't even get a Polaroid® to work and cringed.

Just watching her handle the thing and slip through F-stops and focus so fast incited Gooding's lust like no other woman had in a long time. Then, the fact that she was totally off-limits and apparently oblivious to him made her irresistible. He just had to try to disarm her. He truly felt like a cat getting ready to pounce on a fat, juicy mouse.

Of course the whole FBI thing was a great turn-on as well. She'd caught his interest in London, but catching her with Harper and his partner in Scotland, well, that just meant she'd be the cherry on top his celebratory sundae when his Summer Plan was over. The FBI had actually gotten a mole this close to him. He was proud of their ingenuity. The more tricks in the game, the better. That's why he'd set up a special "artists only" pre-show of his exhibition. He'd opened up his wing of the gallery two days before the presentation this evening to his fellow artists and students—knowing Jenny and her FBI cohorts wouldn't be able to resist analyzing his creations. The fact that Jenny didn't make it until today just made the game more fun after a day and a half of anticipation. He felt an extensive burst of pleasure knowing that the FBI probably handpicked her just for him. He imagined what the profilers imagined for him, knew that they purposely wanted to work his libido, and that he was really going to enjoy this tasty treat they'd given him.

He also used the time to make sure that all was ready for the last set of bombs.

***

"Would you look at that?" The statement was made in a funny, curious tone. Jonesey, who'd been half listening to Jenny while she wandered the rooms and hallways of the Aberdeen gallery, picked up his attention from his FBI surveillance post. Jenny was well known among the surveillance crew for being a "talker." She was always talking. In fact, she kept a running commentary going and talking quietly to herself nearly all the time she was "wired." Carl, having spent a day with Reva in the surveillance room, had commented, "At least she turns the mike off in the bathroom so we can have a minute of peace and quiet now and then."

Reva had jabbed him. "You know we can't encourage that. For her own good, Jenny needs to keep the mike on all the time since we caught Gooding following her to the bathroom and loitering outside in Glasgow. If the cleaning lady hadn't been waiting for the restroom to clear, you know Gooding would have followed Jenny inside." Luckily for the ones stuck listening for something important, Jenny was a facile speaker and quite entertaining, and she knew when to emphasize something. Her instincts were as good as ever. Millie swore that she could feel when something was important or going to happen. All the surveillance guys could tell by her body language and the tone of her voice when Jenny spotted something significant. Bill even remarked that she even had created a special, different, "FBI voice" she used when she picked up something they needed to hear. That voice was what caught Jonesey's attention.

Jenny continued talking to herself. "That's just like the one in New York—the Washington Monument again, only…is it backward, or part of the puzzle?"

Needing to see what had caught Jenny's eye, Jonesey flipped on to the view of her via the gallery's security system. Jenny had paused before the two largest images in Gooding's exposition. As Jonesey watched

Jenny, he'd learned that she was unaware of how easily she caught on when Gooding slipped and spoke in artistic terms. As an artist she just knew the lingo and as she was also a photographer, she always had her camera with her. Homer had warned her that these qualities were the main reason she was their mole, and that she just had to be herself to entice him. All the guys watching knew she was self-conscious, but because her artistic nature was part of who she was, even fidgety she turned Gooding on.

***

Both Jenny and her surveillance team were unaware of Gooding's attention when Jenny stopped her circuit of the room and stared fixedly at the image before her. Something about Gooding's so-called Summer Plan clicked in her head. Jenny was thinking, *The Washington Monument...Gooding shows it over and over. Is his big bomb centered there? Let's see, how many times did he show it? Three or four? But why did he show it in so many different ways and angles?* Jenny said out loud, "It's close. I feel like I almost got it. The Washington Monument stands for something and the number of times he repeats it..."

***

When her mike went to static and the gallery surveillance video went black for thirty seconds, Jonesey was on the mike, hailing Jenny, "Jenny, are you there. Answer me, dammit, Jenny..." as he signaled for backup and stared at the empty space where Jenny had been on his video feed. A few minutes later the FBI/CIA video feed went dead. At the same time, the static suddenly cleared and Jenny's voice sounded in Jonesey's earpiece, "Uh, Jonesey, I think I need some help..." and changed drastically into a panicked shriek "Jonesey!" before going silent.

Chapter Forty-six

"Why ten bombs?" Jenny asked Gooding, shifting around as much as she could with her hands bound behind her and her ankles tied. She was probably trying to get to her cell phone in her jacket pocket. Gooding smirked and ignored her prattling questions.

Jenny didn't know that, having finished his final preparation for the Summer Plan last night, Gooding was done and ready to start. Today, after the exposition, Gooding planned to forward a copy of his demands to the UK task force's leaders in London. He was sure that after the explosion of the pub below the task force's headquarters, the inquiry would include a thorough search of the rubble, so he would include clues about his plan there as well.

As Gooding worked in the basement, gathering equipment, he looked at Jenny wriggling against her bonds and smiled. He really was enjoying the chase and thrill of playing his game with those FBI guys here enough that he wouldn't try to kill all of the operatives, just a lot of them. *Boom, boom, boom!* he thought. *Fun.*

Gooding ignored Jenny on most levels as he effortlessly worked to subdue her. He was thrilled to have caught her. Those agents were just full of surprises; imagine sending this innocent to spy on him. She really was handpicked just for him. He knew now that Jenny was truly a naive farm girl for all her maturity and artistic sense. Initially, he'd been caught totally off guard after expecting them to plant a smooth seductress in his path. He never expected that they'd go for the innocent ingénue.

Just yesterday he'd found some irregular payments and transfers in his financial scanning of the FBI & CIA payroll system. He hadn't even suspected that they'd find another way to plant some bait. He never expected that the

CIA and FBI would reroute their payroll through the US government's main payroll office, OPM, the Office of Personnel Management. He'd done some final research and found the student. He'd found the Jenny Johnson who worked for the IRS that was receiving FBI payments. When he discovered that, the pieces fell together. It was the proof that she had been planted. Gooding had recognized Jenny in the student group at the ferry. He'd had to double-check to be sure, but Mortimer had confirmed it with more photographs. He'd tracked them to the castle hostel, wondering whether he could grab Jenny there, when he'd seen the FBI agents arrive. He'd known that it was too much of a coincidence for Harper to be kissing the same American student he himself had met in London. They had planted a mole to follow him down his path to glory. He chuckled at their audacity. This was going to be a special treat. He had figured her out finally and he was going to enjoy this, especially if one of the FBI guys got personally shafted in the process.

Gooding had been deciding on when to grab Jenny in the gallery when she'd stopped at his largest photographic collage. She kept coming back to the Washington Monument photograph. He'd figured she'd stop there, because it was the biggest, but he'd watched her stand there for too long. When he saw her starting to count one, two, three on her fingers he knew she was too close. He'd figured the FBI would think he'd expect him *not* to put the most important collage in the center and make it the biggest, but he had just to be perverse. Jenny looked confused, but the counting meant she was getting closer to solving the puzzle. When Jenny started to talk into her mike, he acted. It was time to get her out of the gallery. He'd signaled Mortimer to clear the surveillance cameras as planned, and grabbed his chance to teach Jenny a lesson about meddling in other people's affairs.

***

As she watched Gooding working, Jenny tried not to think about the pending explosions. Gooding had told her all about his Summer Plan as he tied her up and gathered his extra bomb equipment. There were bigger and more explosions coming. But he didn't elaborate. It was like he skirted all around the whos, wheres, and whens. *If I wasn't scared out of my mind, I'd be frustrated,* she thought. He'd been storing some of his supplies with his exposition equipment here in the museum. She hadn't known that Gooding had spotted her staring at his largest photo and decided to grab her and drag her down here. He told her that yesterday he'd finally deduced the reason behind their recent meetings that he'd taken as coincidence originally. Jenny hadn't figured out that she'd messed up something until Gooding grabbed her and manhandled her out of the gallery into the basement. She hadn't known that he'd seen her at the pier by the ferry or followed her group to the Scotland hostel. He told her that he just recognized her as the woman photographed in the group of students that just missed his ferry bomb, that he'd seen her kissing "that FBI agent, Mitch Harper," and he'd proven her connection to the task force yesterday through her payroll. She was deeply afraid. She'd thought Gooding didn't know about her. She was wrong. Today, Gooding had been waiting for her and she hadn't even known it.

Jenny worried about the wire on her body and thought of the task force. They had heard Gooding talk to her at the exposition at the earlier exhibits. The tapes of the conversation earlier today between her and Gooding were the first concrete proof of his masterminding the bombs in Iceland and New York. The profiles of the person who'd placed the most believable statements declaring responsibility for the bombs so far matched Gooding perfectly, but the team still had to prove that it was Gooding who was guilty. Jenny had been trained enough and knew that she would have to wear a wire to capture

Gooding, but the experience had still been terrifying. Tonight marked the fourth time she had been sent, wired, to talk to Gooding in her guise as a student touring England and Scotland. As she listened to Gooding, she thought of the past few weeks and prayed that Jonesey was listening and that the FBI was recording all this.

Irony hit Jenny hard. All this time she thought she was safe. After the ferry bomb, when Mitch had confirmed to Jenny that her cover was *not* blown, because the team had found out in their investigation that Jenny had not been the actual target, she'd relaxed a little. The two CIA agents on the ferry as part of their assignment watching out for Jenny while her school group toured the Hebrides had been the real targets of Gooding's latest bomb. Gooding had found the agents on the Isle of Skye, and intersected their ferry just as it left Skye for mainland Scotland. To be sneaky, and to ensure that the two were actually agents, his henchman had watched the agents to make sure that they stayed on the ferry rather than heading to England. To camouflage his targeting of the CIA agents, he waited until the ferry was departing back to Skye before detonating the bomb. Gooding hadn't known or worried about the group of students. He was unaware that the group of students from Weber State was supposed to be on the ferry, nor did he connect Jenny's group with the task force. At that time he hadn't known this school group was Jenny's. He had fallen for the story fed to him in the gallery, that Jenny's group was studying art and heading to the Continent. There had been no reason to believe they were heading out to the Hebrides. Bad luck had caused Gooding to capture Jenny in some of his ferry photographs. Worse luck, he recognized her from the London gallery and followed her group to the hostel where he saw Bill and Mitch. He knew who they were, and now he knew her involvement in the plan.

***

Gooding had targeted the ferry after intercepting the communications and orders redirecting the CIA agents from the Isle of Skye to Lewis. He figured that the agents were tracking him through Scotland. He'd found Alicia shopping in some of the little villages in Western Scotland on her way to his grandfather's castle. She'd even taken the ferry to Skye, just so she could brag that she'd been there. Angry and stunned at her lack of caution, Gooding had just barely sent Alicia back to London after she'd arrived back on the main island when he'd spotted the agents in an inn on the road on their way to catch the same ferry.

Concerned that the task force may have gotten too close to his Western headquarters, Gooding delayed the planned bombing of the task force headquarters that he'd planned to coincide with an attack at lunchtime the next day. He decided that since he would no longer be at the castle, it may be handy to have the task force out in Western Scotland, looking for him while he made sure Alicia was disposed of permanently before she left London.

He dispatched a smaller bomb from the castle to the ferry. It would be a good diversion, and while only two agents killed was rather a small payoff, he loved the efficiency of catching the Americans off guard while protecting his escape route at the same time.

Only a couple of hours after the ferry bomb, Gooding had driven past the port to personally see the aftermath of this bomb. He knew by then that the task force thought he was in a big city in the UK somewhere, so for once it was safer to be at the bombsite.

At the ferry scene the dead were gone, the emergency personnel having had enough time to remove the worst wounded and the clearly dead. The living were wandering around aimlessly. The Stornaway port was too small to hold them, as it was late afternoon and the daytime businesses were shutting down. He had been careful to avoid law enforcement as he took pictures while he and Mortimer drove in.

"Ten is just a rather even number, don't you agree, Ms. Johnson? There will be ten big bombs plus as many little bombs as I deem necessary." Gooding wondered whether the FBI had cracked his use of the number ten as the "key" number in his exhibits. Gooding spoke to Jenny conversationally as he fiddled with a black box with wires protruding from the bottom. He turned back to Jenny, set the box down just out of reach, and smiled as he approached.

Jenny didn't seem to have anything to say. Gooding could tell she was worried as he stood over her. He could see her pulse hammering in her neck. "If I cared about your personal welfare or was a better host, I'd apologize for the cold stone floor you are laying on. However, in a few minutes you won't notice it anymore once the numbness sets in," he remarked as he bent down and neatly retrieved the tiny phone from Jenny's side pocket of her jacket. "Having observed you using this little goody in the gallery this afternoon, I toyed with the idea of letting you sit on your jacket to keep your bottom warm, but decided that you would try to reach the buttons with your tied fingers. You're stretching to the side trying to accomplish the same thing by pressing your phone toward your hipbone has been much more entertaining. The wiggling opening your jacket and allowing me to observe your luscious breasts jutting forward has been quite entertaining."

Gently, he reached over with his free hand and hefted her right breast in his palm through her shirt. "Nice size and shape, and oh-so-soft." With a firm kneading, he enjoyed watching Jenny's face flush and her eyes flare as he intentionally violated her by rubbing her soft chest through her T-shirt. He really enjoyed ruffling her feathers this way. Not just because she was such a tempting morsel, but because she clearly hated this violation so much more.

Gooding knew that this was an invasion Jenny would take personally. It was also his only chance to taste her. She was just too dangerous to take with him. The task force would take her kidnapping personally and he'd never be free of them. He shouldn't kill her for the same reason.

Tucking her phone in his pocket, Gooding forcefully held Jenny's mouth and jaw with his left hand as he moved closer to speak to her. "Just think of what I could do to you if I were inclined to rape or maim you." He gestured across the indentation between her breasts. A knife slit right here and your shirt and bra would be out of the way, allowing me to do all sorts of interesting things to you. I wonder. Are your nipples pink and lush like your lips, or as soft?" Gooding smiled and squeezed harder, causing Jenny to choke on a contained sob as the pain brought tears to her eyes.

He watched Jenny squeeze her eyes tightly shut. He bet she was praying for a miracle.

Gooding squeezed her chin again, which caused Jenny to open her eyes and look at him. "I could do anything I wanted to you, but too bad for you that I am not that kind of person. Your charms will be wasted for now. Maybe I should change my mind. Maybe I should take you with me. But that would give them a reason to chase me, and they need to stay here." He grinned, and Jenny closed her eyes. "Don't worry, my dear, if I were to use you as you deserve, I would provide a blindfold and gag to keep you silently feeling the sensations you earned without having any visual stimulation to numb the pain." Releasing her jaw and breast, he was hardly able to contain how much he enjoyed her terror, especially as he had no intention of using her. He was not a rapist, nor ever would be, but he absolutely loved terrorizing people who deserved it. Jenny deserved the terror, where tormenting Alicia would be a waste of time and energy—she was too dense and greedy to appreciate it.

Back to business, Gooding chopped Jenny on the temple with the handle of a large knife he produced from his leg holster, knocking her out before she could respond. He then reached down to Jenny's unconscious form and pulled her feet forward until she was lying flat on her back with her arms and hands wedged underneath herself. He then casually used the serrated hunting knife to slit her shirt from neck to hem. Laying the sides of the shirt open to reveal her lacy bra and the wires taped to her stomach, he retrieved the recorder from the special pocket inside her waistband.

He pulled the wires off her skin and meticulously curled them around the recorder, leaving the microphone end trailing. The device he placed on her exposed abdomen, taking care to curl the tail just so. When he was finished, the recorder was positioned as if it were a newborn baby laid on its mother's stomach before the umbilical cord was removed. He then took the knife and brought it down, pantomiming a stabbing blow and inserting it, pointing down toward her belly button, blade facing up in Jenny's cleavage under her bra, the handle lying between her collarbones. Leaving her thusly revealed, exposed and implying both his threat to her and his gracious mercy, Gooding picked up the black box he'd retrieved and crossed the cold storage room. As he walked, he flipped on Jenny's cell phone, and cleared the numerous voice mail notifications, then scanned her scant speed dial list until he saw "M&B." Pressing the send button, he hoped to get one of her FBI contacts. He was thrilled when he recognized the voice as one of the FBI agents tailing him. Gooding heard the man answer, "Thank God! Jenny, what happened? Are you okay?"

Gooding answered, "Hello, Mr. FBI Agent. Please inform your superiors that Ms. Johnson is currently indisposed behind some crates in the Aberdeen Museum." Glancing at his timepiece, Gooding continued conversationally, "It's rather cold and if someone doesn't retrieve her in say, twenty minutes, she may suffer from shock or hypothermia...in addition to other things. With the cold weather today she shouldn't be running around half clothed."

Gooding lowered the phone from his ear and left it with the connection still open on the floor near the door as he turned to exit the building. The agent could be heard yelling on the other end of the phone, "Dammit, trace the line quick! Anthony, get Mitch now, and get those CIA boys in there."

Gooding closed the portal and continued down the alley into the back streets of the city.

Chapter Forty-seven

By the time the CIA agents were able to find Jenny in the labyrinth of storerooms and warehouses behind and below the gallery, Gooding was long gone. A few minutes later, Mitch and Bill and the FBI team got to the museum's storeroom, having followed the signal from Jenny's cell phone connection. One of the CIA guys was checking Jenny's pulse as the other temporarily covered her with his coat—she remained unconscious. Mitch held the other agents at the alley way as he scanned the storeroom.

The bays for trucks were all empty as was the room. Bill motioned for two pairs of FBI agents to take two of the three Scottish agents and look for Gooding nearby, as Mitch pushed past Bill to Jenny, asking the agent nearest Jenny, "What happened?"

The agent glanced up. "Well, she has a nasty bump on her left temple, bad bruising along her jaw, and has been trussed up, but her pulse is strong and her body temperature is only slightly cold. We hated to leave her like this, but wanted you to see Gooding's message, and she's still out." The agent motioned Mitch closer, then pulled down the coat to display Jenny's torso with the knife and wire.

Mitch's jaw tightened and, lips pursed, he yelled, "Bill, get Anthony over here with his camera so we can get her the hell out of here." As the photographer worked, Mitch worried that Gooding may have left one of his surprise bombs on Jenny or somewhere in the room, and the rest of the team quickly went over the storeroom, looking for suspicious items.

After the initial search turned up nothing, and when Anthony and the CIA agents finished photographing Jenny and the immediate vicinity around her, Mitch reached under the jacket covering and pulled out the knife and recorder and handed them to Bill for processing. He sighed.

There's little hope of finding proof that Gooding did this. He probably wore gloves the whole time. Then he lifted Jenny to a sitting position and broke a smelling salts packet under her nose to revive her.

Jenny snorted and started, sneezing as Mitch waved the acrid-smelling packet beneath her nose. She immediately thrashed, trying to free her arms. Mitch and Anthony held her still as she began to shiver uncontrollably. "Are you okay, Jenny?" Mitch asked her, concerned. She opened her eyes and blinked rapidly. After several seconds, she seemed to wake up a bit more. She jerked away from his hands and squealed. "Hold on, honey, you're safe," Mitch said as he pulled her forward to investigate her hands tied behind her. "Anthony, can you take some pictures of these knots before I cut them off. I'll try to save evidence as much as I can."

Anthony came closer and obediently documented Gooding's rope-tying ability. Mitch reached behind her and used his own blade to slice open the ropes, then reached down and cut the bonds on her ankles. "Wiggle your feet and toes as much as you can with the pins and needles," he instructed as he swiped the latex gloves from his hands and pulled Jenny's loosened hands forward to her lap where he began briskly rubbing her wrists, desperately biting back a white-hot anger.

Watching the tears flow down her cheeks from between her closed lashes, he asked, "Can you stand yet? We need to get you out of here."

Jenny shook her head and answered so quietly that he barely caught it. "Not yet, give me a minute, please." He stared at the clear finger marks along her jaw as he continued stroking her red and wrinkled wrists.

Bill came over and retrieved the remaining pieces of Jenny's wire.

"I wonder if any of the tape was saved. I can't tell what exactly Gooding did to the recorder. It looks okay, but it clearly stopped before she left the gallery," Bill remarked and reached over to touch Jenny's shoulder. "You did a great job, kid. We heard most of it while you were in the gallery. But when Gooding dragged you down here, we couldn't get a fix on you through the masonry. Then he took you out of range."

Jenny looked up at him and said vehemently, "I hope that's the *last* time I wear a wire for you, Bill Thomas!"

Bill laughed. "You're correct, Ms. Johnson. Let's get you back."

Jenny jolted again as a sudden realization struck her. "I can't go back! We need to warn or move the Weber State group. Gooding knows my job and my connection. My cover is blown!" She was beginning to panic.

Mitch shushed her as he glared up at Bill. "Shshsh, you'll be okay. We'll take care of your friends, but first we need to get you and the evidence back to HQ." Mitch looked at her and hoped they wouldn't need the rape kit, but he'd leave that up to the female British agents waiting for them outside.

***

When Jenny had recovered enough to realize that Mitch was holding her hands and warmly looking at her, she jerked her hands out of his and tried to gain some distance. She'd had a hell of a day. Even if all she wanted to do was sob on this man's shoulder, she couldn't. She had to maintain her composure—remain professional. More importantly, she needed to get somewhere safe and private before she lost it completely. Shivering less now, she asked, "Can we find me a shirt before I have to go out in public?" She was humiliated by the memory of Gooding manhandling her and very aware of her cut shirt hanging open. She wanted some kind of warm drink, a hot shower, and privacy, with a comfy bed where she could hide under the covers for the rest of her days and forget today had happened. First, she'd experienced becoming Gooding's prisoner, hearing him elaborate his plan, and finally her rescue. She hoped the rest of her day went better.

Mortified at that moment, her burst of strength deserted her and she sat on the floor, head bowed, no energy left to fight. Mitch stood and looked down at her. With a big, dramatic sigh, he took off his coat and pulled off his sweatshirt. He put his coat back on over his white crew neck T-shirt. Reaching down, he pulled Jenny to her feet, letting the overlaid jacket hit the floor. "You guys turn your backs," he ordered the agents nearby. Without letting her protest, he slid Jenny's jacket off her shoulders and down her arms, whisked her torn T-shirt off, raised her arms, and pulled his sweatshirt down her arms and over her head. She continued to stand there almost obediently as he scooped her jacket off the floor and pulled her arms through it. Anthony came over and retrieved the other jacket. Mitch stood for a moment, as if waiting for her to make some move or take some action to show she was feeling better. When she continued to stand there mutely, he reached for her nape and pulled her hair out of the back of the sweatshirt and out of her jacket. She looked up at him and blinked back the tears, wondering if he could see the uncertainty, sorrow, and humiliation in her eyes. He sighed again even bigger, and folded her into his arms. She sobbed against his chest for a few seconds. Mitch just held her close and let her cry, seeming to know she needed a release.

Bill stepped in after a few moments. "If you're through being a long-suffering supervisor, Mitch, it's time to get moving." To Jenny, he said, "The car's here. We need to leave you with the British team for an hour or so, but we'll be back to pick you up and take you back to HQ. We're going to stop at the hostel, get your gear, and talk to your professors. We'll work on getting your school group moved to a more secure location. Okay?"

Jenny nodded and stepped back from Mitch, wiping the tears from her cheeks. "I'm ready."

Jenny was grateful to the British agents for their efficiency. They had camped out with the CIA monitoring team, including Millie, but had called in two female agents when the CIA called in Jenny's location. The questions were humiliating, but Jenny was grateful that she could answer "no" to most. She was sure that Gooding had only touched her chest and face, but the agents had to be sure, and everyone was relieved when the rape test was not needed. Even better, the British gals had secured a change of clothes for Jenny so she could turn in her FBI outfit for evidence. The slacks and British sweater or jumper were wooly and warm and very comforting. Jenny wore Mitch's sweatshirt over the top and felt much better. Soon enough, Mitch and Bill were back to get her. They had her gear in the boot, but were willing to take her to the new location to say goodbye to her school group.

The short ride to the hostel was uneventful, compared to the rest of the afternoon. The driver and agents scanned the route for any danger and crisscrossed and backtracked to make sure no one could trail them. They'd left most of the team members around the museum to see if Gooding was still around.

They made a quick side trip to the new hostel for the school group. The prior meeting where Mitch and Bill flashed their FBI badges and identification and explained Jenny's mission to her professors was surprisingly short and anticlimactic. The professors were glad to know that Jenny had a reason for her late-night disappearances and apologized for their lectures. They gave Jenny her final school assignments and told her she was free to go. They'd catch up with her once she was back in the States.

Her friend Devon had been dispatched to gather her belongings from their room. She had lingered until Jenny came back. Jenny hugged her teachers and the fellow students, saying her goodbyes. Reaching Devon lastly, Jenny hugged her. "Thanks for taking such good care of me."

Devon hugged her back. "Thanks, yourself. See you back in the States in a few weeks."

Jenny broke the hug and waved to her friends as Mitch and Bill escorted her out the door. "Be safe, you guys," Jenny said in farewell. She was now a full-fledged task force member—no longer undercover. Also, as one of the few members who had spoken to Gooding directly, her input would be needed as they tried to stop him from doing more damage. She would only see her school group at special times over the next few days if at all.

She blocked all bad thoughts, including the forbidding knowledge that Jonesey and the CIA guys were going to pump her for details about Gooding, and Homer's team would drag everything else they could from her head. At least the Brits could start filling them in first. She tried to focus on the trip as they headed to the pub that served as the combined task force's headquarters. She wouldn't think about Gooding again today, and she refused to think about how her enjoyment of the trip was at its end. No more playful school time, back to work, full time. *What a depressing thought.*

She wondered idly if she was still jet-lagged. It had been nearly four weeks since she'd arrived in the UK, but the seven-hour time change wasn't as hard as trying to learn to get up in the mornings and stay up all day and night. How Jenny wished she was home in her cool bed, sleeping the day away. She really missed her swing-shift schedule and the freedom to just take a nap in the afternoon. "Too bad Gooding didn't put his plan into motion in Spain—at least they do siestas," Jenny mused.

They had just turned onto the street where the pub housing headquarters was located when an explosion shot across the road. There were no parking zones in this area.

Everyone had to be dropped off, then walk in. Mitch and Bill had paused behind Jenny to talk to a pair of British undercover guards lounging at the pharmacy just a few doors down from HQ. Jenny had moved ahead, anxious to drop off her bags and coerce Reva and Carl into getting some fish and chips with her.

The explosion blew Jenny off her feet. Dazed, she realized she was on her back on the paved sidewalk. For a moment she panicked as she frantically tried to breathe. The wind had been knocked out of her. As she finally felt air in her lungs, she lay still for a moment. Jenny was too shocked for a moment to feel any pain and did a quick inventory. All her body parts were accounted for, even if she couldn't isolate any particular pains—she felt hurt all over. A smoke and dust cloud blew out from the pub into the street. Jenny struggled to sit up, staying down on the sidewalk, with her bags strewn out beside her along with a few other pedestrians. Some, she noted, were laying down where they were thrown and a couple others were sitting up and looking around. She watched as Bill began running toward the building, with Mitch and the other two agents following him out into the chaos.

Bill and Mitch reached Jenny at the same time as the other agents ran to the hole where the doorway to the pub used to be.

What had been an innocuous-looking pub and inn now appeared to be a pile of rubble and a gaping hole between two buildings on the left side of the street.

Bill motioned Mitch to take care of Jenny as he followed the British agents. Jenny couldn't see anything in the rubbish due to the smoke and dust in the air for a moment. Mitch knelt beside her as Bill and the other agents turned around and appeared to take stock of the wounded on the street. Mitch also began to glance around. "He could still be hanging around, watching," he explained tersely at

Jenny's furrowed brow. A chill crept up her spine and she, too, scanned the area, but no one looked suspicious.

Luckily most of the passersby didn't appear very hurt. Most were cognizant, and those who were up and about were assisting those who weren't.

A few paces into the street brought them to the nearest group of people. As they lent assistance, sirens could be heard coming closer. Bill and the other two agents stood up and moved away from the wounded for a moment. They spoke for a moment and quickly made an agreement. One of the Brits would wait for the emergency workers. Bill and the other Brit would cover their nose and mouth with handkerchiefs and cut through the jewelry shop to the south of the pub. They would go to the alley behind the pub and use the inn's rear stairway to look for survivors and be there to watch for sensitive items in the rubble when the emergency workers arrived.

Structurally, the building that had housed the task force was reduced to a three-walled shell. The front of the pub and the bar area had been blown away.

Jenny tried to get up and winced when her left hand scraped the pavement next to her. She held it up to her face and saw a long gash across her palm. Thankfully it wasn't very deep, but it stung like crazy. Her eyes focused on Mitch as he leaned closer to her. "Are you okay?" he asked.

Jenny started to shake with laughter. "Sure, I'm fine, just a little hysterical. Can you help me up, there's a rock or something digging me in the backside?" Jenny asked, her voice going shrill as she noticed her overwhelmed state.

"Lay back down and wait a minute while I check you for broken bones."

Mitch gently put his emergency training to good use as he efficiently handled Jenny, to make sure she wasn't hurt. Jenny closed her eyes and concentrated on breathing while she endured Mitch's poking and prodding of her as he felt and quickly manipulated each part of her body, from her neck to her ankles. When done, Mitch stated, "No broken bones or sprains from what I can tell. The blast knocked you off your feet, but you're only bruised and a bit scratched up. You'll really feel it tomorrow." He helped her sit. "Do you think you can stand up?" he asked.

"I think so, if you can steady me a bit," Jenny responded.

They stood for a moment, watching the ambulances and fire trucks arrive and begin to spew emergency workers all around. "Shouldn't you, as task force leader, go try to find Bill and check out the headquarters?" Jenny quietly asked.

Mitch shook his head. "No. Bill will do that for me. You and I need to hang out here and start gathering our people as they arrive and watch for those who were hurt. Per the plan, I am in charge of the head count." Mitch was somber, and Jenny bit her lip as she stared at the chaos around them. She couldn't see anyone coming out of the rubble of their own volition. Motioning Jenny to pick up her bags, Mitch pulled out his note pad and nudged her toward the emergency vehicle as they began the task of accounting for the team. Jenny walked beside Mitch as they began identifying the wounded, dead, and living.

Of the Americans stationed at headquarters, Jenny knew most had been off-site at the time, except for Reva and Carl. Reva had been seriously hurt. She and Carl had been taking the night shift and had only arrived back at HQ for some much-earned rest—they had been asleep upstairs along with the other night-shifters.

After the personnel and emergency crews went through the rubble, they were able to account for everyone. Fourteen people were hurt, and of the fifty stationed there, three were dead.

Her injury meant that Reva would be out of the field for a while now as her left arm healed. It had been broken in one place and sliced nearly to the bone near her shoulder. Anthony was grim as he gave the details to Jenny. A beam from the roof had landed on Reva's bed as she slept, crashing down on her left side, injuring her arm and breaking her left leg in the process. Unfortunately, Carl and two of the British agents next door had not survived the destructive rubble in the next room when the roof crashed in on them. The huge timber had protected Reva from worse damage, but she would never be the same, physically or mentally, after having lost her partner. For some freak reason, the CIA guys in the back room were all injured, but none were dead. Other casualties included local Brits hanging out at their favorite pub.

An hour later, the recovery crew found a box like an airplane's flight recorder with the promised plans/package from Gooding hidden in the wreckage. The whole group was now focused on decoding Gooding's plan. The news was not good. The targets listed so far included the president of the United States, but Gooding's logic was so twisted, the task force had yet to figure out when, why, where, or how he would explain this, or the next attack. They only knew that the next target involved the Secret Service, who they had just warned, while they frantically searched for answers.

At that moment, Gooding would have been angry if he had known that he would have totally crippled the task force had he not captured Jenny earlier that day, because his taking of their mole mobilized the task force. Because of his act, relatively few agents were left at headquarters when the explosion hit, due to their tracking down Jenny after she went missing. Gooding didn't know that Jonesey had alerted the team to a problem the instant her radio went silent. Gooding also didn't know that he'd made his last mistake. He was on his way to the freighter with the bombs needed for the official finale of the Summer Plan.

Chapter Forty-eight

Mitch ran his fingers again through the staticky hair at his hairline. Once again he was suffering extreme frustration. He was tired of this operation and tired of Gooding. He glanced sideways to Bill, who had laid his head on the borrowed desk. This posture and his slumped shoulders heralded Bill's own negative state.

The death of Carl was the last straw. Of course the loss of the other agents in the bombing was heart wrenching, but Carl had been with he and Bill at the academy. Due to their differing assignments, Mitch and Bill usually didn't get to work with Carl and Reva. Reva and Carl specialized in deep undercover operations, while Mitch and Bill handled mainly terrorist threats. From day one, Mitch had experienced an uncomfortable mix of excitement and dread when he'd learned that Carl and Reva would be part of the task force looking for Gooding. They were the best undercover combination, and to require their skill meant that the operation would be of the highest priority, and also "most covert" or, as Stan liked to joke, "sneaky," but Mitch had been uneasy.

He sat down and tried to handle the bad news, image after image bombarding him. Jenny had recognized Reva's hair when the ambulance team had brought her out on a stretcher. Bill had left the building soon after. Mitch figured that Bill was remembering. He was sure that Bill's thoughts mirrored his own, that he was also remembering that day back in New York when they'd stalked around the cabin. They hadn't had the joy of working with Carl on an assignment in four years. Mitch thought about how it'd felt good to crunch through the snow with Carl, just like they had in Colorado during their first year as agents. They'd attended a winter training exercise that served as their graduation when they became greenhorns. Missing Carl, he felt like a hole had been ripped out of his heart. It just felt like one wound too many.

***

Across Aberdeen, Jenny was spending her time with Reva at an FBI apartment, helping her recover from her injuries. She hoped and prayed for guidance on how to handle everything as she folded Reva's now clean laundry.

Her school group had all left for their last trip through Aberdeen on which they planned to tour the town, do some of their own laundry, and finish the night with a festive, group dinner at a fancy restaurant courtesy of Weber State. They were reveling in their final days in the UK. They would be heading back to Glasgow in a few days and flying back to the States from there. Jenny had spent the dinner with them last night, but she had left early, pleading illness.

She needed to spend some time with Reva before her final task force assignment. Frustration ran through her. She needed the credits from her school trip so she could graduate in the fall, but the task force absences had added up. In a few weeks, when she was home, she promised to meet with her professors and they'd decide how many credits she'd earned. Flinging the wet laundry into the tiny dryer in the kitchen that was next to the just as tiny washer and dishwasher, she wished her professors knew how much she was learning about the UK from the British officers on the task force and how much time she spent living in British apartments and houses while on task force duties. "As if any of the Americans I know wash and dry their clothes in a kitchen," Jenny said to herself. Now that she was no longer undercover, she actually belonged to the task force, and it hurt to leave her school group early. Stan had granted her some freedom since she had accomplished her part of the mission by drawing Gooding out. Right now, she was the only one who could be spared to stay with Reva, which was convenient for both her and Reva, since neither of them wanted it any other way. Reva had lost control and slapped Anthony for suggesting that she stay in safe hospital under psychiatric care for a while. Jenny had pulled her back as Bill moved Anthony out of the way. So, Jenny would stay here for a day or so, but she soon would need to report to Stan and do her time with the task force until Gooding was captured. By then, Reva was determined to fly home. The doctors reluctantly agreed. If Reva's stitches did not become infected, neither her arm nor leg casts required hospitalization. Reva had promised to take it easy and head straight to the hospital when she reached DC. Stan had condoned the plan and arranged for a nurse escort to take Reva through the airport and on to DC.

Jenny said a prayer for help to have this trip be successful both in terms of her school as well as catching Gooding. Then she added some gratitude for her life being spared and asked for some comfort for Reva and for Carl's family. The thought of the two ten-page papers she would be writing on the plays she'd be seeing in Utah on top of the six other regular papers required by the trip to get credit was a daunting thought that could wait until they'd captured Gooding. Working undercover and doing her school trip under false pretenses was certainly a draining way to live. Now she understood better why Amy hated Jonesey's job so much.

She glanced over to the couch across the room. Thankfully, Reva had fallen asleep. Not that Jenny usually condoned the use of sleeping aids, but this was an emergency. She had been genuinely shocked when Stan had buzzed her on her FBI beeper during breakfast. She desperately needed a break from the task force to deal with the incident with Gooding yesterday, the bombing and to make up with her professors. She would have dearly loved to have been left alone. Concern replaced her shock when she met Stan standing with Reva at the kitchen entrance of the hostel a few minutes later. Having shared her grief over her cousin's death those months ago, Reva had requested that she be allowed to talk to Jenny instead of another agent before speaking to the grief counselor helping the task force cope with the latest attack that caused Carl's death. It was bad enough that Reva had flatly refused to stay in a hospital. With her arm stitched and in a half-cast in a sling, her leg having not been "that damaged" and in a walking cast, she'd left the hospital as soon as she was conscious with a bag of pills "for emergencies."

Stan matter-of-factly handed Jenny another bottle of sleeping pills and motioned her to follow another agent through the kitchen of the hostel and up the service stairs. They had installed Reva in the hostel manager's apartment for secrecy. Luckily he and his wife were visiting relatives and had no problem with the British task force's use of the suite. Hefting part of Reva's baggage after the two-man escort had checked the room for any uninvited guests and carried in the rest, Jenny followed Stan and Reva into the apartment. Even in the dim light caused by the drawn drapes, Jenny could see the ashen paleness of Reva's face. The woman needed to be in bed. Stan had said, "Watch out for her and talk to her over the next two days until her flight home. Albert and his staff will take over her care once she's back in DC."

Jenny realized that Reva also needed her companionship. On the plane ride from Denver to Georgia, the women had discovered that they shared a similar, strong faith in God. Reva often found comfort in her Jewish faith, while Jenny couldn't imagine living her life without her Mormon-ness and the spiritual living as a follower of Christ.

They'd discussed death and life and how families dealt with the tragic loss of a loved one. Jenny remembered a conversation she'd had early in the spring, when Carl had told her that Reva hadn't opened up to anyone about Jordan's death besides herself and her mother and that he was grateful that Jenny had been there for Reva. Carl understood that sometimes a woman could only share some things with another female.

Now, Reva had to deal with the loss of her closest, dearest friend and partner. Jenny had watched Reva deal with Jordan's death by helping Millie handle it, but she had no idea how she could help Reva now.

A knock sounded on the door, jolting Jenny from her stupor. Nervously, she felt for her tiny spare pistol in the holster at her side. Palming it, she endured memories from the last few weeks that combined with her training from the last few months to guide her quickly and stealthily to rest beside the kitchen door. Holding the gun with both hands elevated in front of her, she waited and concentrated on any noises or movement through the door. The knock came again, but this time with a whispered voice. "Jenny, are you in there? Are you okay? We brought the rest of your and Reva's laundry." She heard a soft sound like a bundle being dropped and the clear sound of a snap being opened. She pictured Mitch on one side of the portal and Bill on the other as they prepared to storm into the apartment. Quickly, she reached across the door and opened it toward her as she held her pistol ready just in case it wasn't Bill's voice she'd heard. Adrenaline flowed as she tried to decide how to diffuse the situation.

"It's okay, you guys. I just wasn't expecting company," she said in relief as Bill poked his head around the door and his eyes found her. He relaxed and restored his pistol to the snapped compartment at his side. Reaching out to hold the door open, he maneuvered into the room and eased nearer to Jenny to let Mitch in behind him.

"Nice technique. I must say, I didn't expect to see you behind the door, holding a gun at my head. Remind me never to date you, okay? I'd be killed just trying to pick you up," Bill joked as Jenny clicked the safety and tucked her own pistol away. "That holster looks sexy on you, by the way. What do your professors think of that particular accessory?" Bill asked.

Mitch turned to glare at Bill. Bill winked at him, peeked out the door, and nodded to the guard sitting in the hallway. He closed the door and locked it and glanced at Jenny.

Jenny just shook her head at him. "On another day, I'm sure that your cracks will entertain me, but for now, knock it off. I've had a bad couple of days."

Bill smiled. "That's why I love you, darlin'. Not many people are immune to my many manly charms." They sat down for a long afternoon of card playing, waiting for Reva to wake up and rejoin the living.

Chapter Forty-nine

Alicia smiled gleefully. She was riding high on the rush she'd gained from blowing up the pub. She'd spotted the agents leaving the rear of the club and head up the back stairs and knew that she'd understood Gooding correctly. As instructed, she'd waited until the back door closed and the agents were inside before pushing the "call" button on her cell phone to trigger the explosion.

She'd chosen to take a few extra days in London. She hated the chilly castle Gooding had chosen to drag her to when they first arrived in the UK. The cold wind in Scotland went right through her, and to be stuck in some "compound" of Gooding's with no TV or shopping or anything grated on her. If she wanted to stay cooped up somewhere, she'd have stayed in the US.

Alicia bent over and picked up a heavier set of hand-weights. She continued a few reps designed to make her upper arms look like Madonna's. Ever since she'd spent those few days recovering on Gooding's ship from the plastic surgery he'd required, she found it impossible to sit still for any length of time. And, since she couldn't go shopping all the time without Gooding's money and was not much of a sightseer, she spent her free time in the various spas and gyms she encountered. She hated the new hair color Gooding chose for her last night; the mousy brown was nothing like her natural blonde. But the exercise had certainly improved her figure. Her arms were toned and slender, while her middle was once again flat and rippled like it had been as a teenager when she was still a dancer.

Her bobbed hair was itching the back of her neck and she couldn't wear the colored contacts often as they irritated her eyes. But Gooding had insisted, and after watching how he treated his helpers who didn't cooperate, Alicia was not willing to disobey him lightly. She had wheedled this extra time in London out of him, but knew he'd granted it as a reward for her blowing up the pub as requested. She had also promised to get used to her new identity, so that she would no longer be a liability to the Summer Plan. Mortimer had told her the truth yesterday. He'd told her about how her fit at the airport had drawn the FBI operatives to her. It was her own damn fault that she had to radically alter her appearance again. Mortimer had provided the words for Gooding's anger that day. "Your mouth nearly blew our cover."

Soon Gooding would be done. Then he'd promised to take her to Rome or back to the Riviera for a while. She'd find a better man there and ditch Gooding once and for all. She would finally be able to have some fun.

That was her last thought. The London flat owned by Gooding blew up a few minutes later. The police suspected a gas leak, until they received a fax from Gooding's grandfather's phone, which told them where to find the bomb. Gooding was done with the UK and Scotland for a while. Aberdeen was his last stop to pick up Mortimer, then on to DC.

Chapter Fifty

Jonesey grabbed his ringing cell phone and saw that it was his friend from the Secret Service calling. "My boss is calling Stan right now. Jonesey, we got the tape and cracked the code with the pictures you sent us from Gooding. It's not the Secret Service that's the target. It's the president. Gooding's coming to DC. He's coming here to blow up the White House!" Jonesey quickly jotted down the details while motioning to Mitch. He'd only arrived at Reva's apartment a few minutes before getting the call on his cell phone. He checked his watch and told his friend that he had to go.

"Did Bill get the details on Gooding's freighter from the CIA yet?" Jonesey asked Mitch.

Mitch shook his head. "No, not yet. They have a list of the family's ships, and they're doing cross-checks to see if any are coming in to dock anytime soon here in Aberdeen. Why?" Jonesey explained what he'd heard as Bill and Jenny came over to listen.

Bill added, "The CIA guys were working with the British authorities to determine when the ship is docking. Both the Brits and the CIA guys are working feverishly to find out when and where, but they don't have any definite details at this time." They all felt the urgency.

"We've got to find that freighter and get Gooding before he leaves Scotland," Mitch said, stating the obvious.

"How did the Secret Service guys crack this?" Bill asked.

"They got a fax of the first ten collages from the New York exhibit and there was a problem with the transmission, so one of the technicians e-mailed a collage of the collages." Jonesey paused for breath. "Well, the scanned images weren't of the best quality, so the technician converted the files into grayscale printing and didn't properly name the files. When they showed up in DC, the Secret Service guys thought that the ten images were actually part of one larger image and printed them out and then sat and put them together like a puzzle. When they got the picture together it looked like the back porch of the White House."

Jenny interrupted. "That's why I saw the Washington Monument in part of collage number three, and Gooding kept repeating that image, isn't it?"

Jonesey nodded. "Yup. Because they are trained to spot direct threats to the president, the Secret Service spotted the presidential hints immediately. Gooding showed the Washington Monument four times, and each time placed it in the image as if it were the president. The Secret Service guys recognized the presidential surroundings. They figured four times was the date and think Gooding's planning on blowing up the president in the White House in three days on July Fourth."

Chapter Fifty-one

"Boss, the freighter is ready. The Iceland devices have been jettisoned and the crew has finished the loading of the helicopter and your remaining personal effects," Mortimer reported upon Gooding's questioning look.

"Good. With Alicia taken care of, we can leave Scotland at last. Is the boat ready?"

"Yes. Petrol level full and your last case is aboard."

"Excellent. To the docks, then."

Manuel was waiting at the corner as Mortimer pulled into the alleyway at the front of the building. With its brick walls and barred windows, the Thornton Industries warehouse was foreboding, as planned. It had been part of Gooding's family holdings since the late eighteenth century, when a great-great-grandfather had first started his shipping business in Aberdeen. Strongly constructed, it had remained stubbornly guarding its access to the North Sea as the more modern and less seedy warehouse district grew up around it.

As the car approached, Manuel rushed to open the large door used by lorries. He waited just inside the building until the rear boot cleared the entrance, then quickly lowered the door and locked it. Gooding exited the rear door and headed up the stairs to the main office to finish the tasks necessary to facilitate his vacating the UK for some years. In his wake, Mortimer and Manuel hurried to clear the car of all forensic evidence of Gooding's presence. While Mortimer used an industrial vacuum to clear all fibers, Manuel pulled on latex gloves and began wiping down the car's interior. For some time Gooding had controlled where authorities could find his fingerprints in key places thanks to the work of his employees.

Above the noise of the vacuum, the warehouse's AP system chimed, indicating a call was coming in. Gooding answered the phone. "What time does the manifest say we are cleared for departure?" He paused, listening to his freighter's captain. "No, five this evening is fine. We will be along shortly. Call in the crew, have the cook get the final provisions, and prepare for the Southern Africa route to the Indies."

Gooding hung up the phone and powered down his laptop. Making a note in his planner, he picked up his cell phone and dialed his grandfather's office. "Yes, Jasmine, it's I. Will you tell Grandfather that I will be unable to attend the gala tonight." He examined his nails as she gave him the standard lecture. Mortimer entered the office as Gooding said, "No. I cannot. Pressing business matters. Yes. The China shipment is experiencing some difficulty. We're shipping off tonight in a few hours—at eight tonight. Yes. I'll be at the warehouse if he has the time. Certainly I can meet him at six. I will wait for him. Yes. Please tell him to bring the papers if he so chooses. Yes, I will have a light meal ready. No, Alicia is not going with me. She's staying in London. Yes, I will tell Grandfather." Gooding ended the call. His grandfather's secretary was predictable as always.

Noticing Mortimer, he asked, "Is the car clean?"

"Yes, Manuel is dusting it as we speak. It will look as if it hasn't moved in months by the time your grandfather arrives."

"Good. Get the boat ready as I gather the last items. I'll meet you downstairs in ten minutes." Mortimer nodded.

***

Manuel finished spraying a light coat of dust on the car and put the special can away. "I'll meet you in South Carolina in two days," he stated.

"Yes. We should be at the rendezvous point at four, local time. Your leathers are with the bike in the north room," Mortimer responded. He handed Manuel a packet with airplane tickets, money, and new identification. "The flight is tonight on a charter. If you have problems, go to George. We'll find the Maryann if we have problems." As the two clasped hands in farewell, Manuel said, "Thank you. I will be out of the city within an hour." Even in the buildings under Gooding's control, these two long-term comrades were wary of Grandfather Thornton's spy equipment and spoke in implied sentences.

***

Soon after, a black bullet-bike sped out the alley as Manuel left Aberdeen. Gooding watched him leave from the office window. Nodding, he locked the desk, pocketed the key, and went downstairs. He inspected his grandfather's Rolls Royce. "Good work, Mortimer." The two reached the rear of the warehouse to the waiting speedboat. Mortimer started the engine and they too left Aberdeen.

Chapter Fifty-two

Mitch grabbed the railing and held on with both hands to keep the momentum that had built up as he'd ran down the beach from carrying him head over rail and into the sea. Bill and Jonesey had been closing in on Mitch's left. He could see Jonesey's head hanging down as he ran behind him, holding his side, and tried to catch his breath. They all stood looking out into the North Sea, watching the speedboat arc out to the waiting freighter just beyond the breakers. The British agents and some of the CIA guys joined them on the dock, watching the sea to the east.

While the computer geeks had been deciphering Gooding's plan back at the base thanks to the help from DC and the Secret Service, Jonesey had looked at the black box. "It doesn't look like an aircraft box. See the waterproofing seals and this busted link here?" Jonesey had remarked to Mitch.

Bill came over and glanced at it. "Yeah, doesn't it feel too light, like it should be heavier?" They called over the British specialist who confirmed that the black box was of marine origin. Near the base of it, they found a partial serial number that someone had tried to file away. Tracing the number and maker, they found that the box was registered to an oil freighter registered out of Scotland to Gooding's grandfather.

"You guys knew that Gooding had a boat, right?" Stan asked the team. Bill explained that they'd only recently identified the correct freighters owned by Gooding's family.

"It took us too long to find the right freighters in the Thornton Industries paper mess, boss, I don't know how we could have missed that this was a boat box," Mitch stated. Some quick work by the British team found the freighter had already arrived in Scotland and was currently docked out in the North Sea off Aberdeen, presumably loading oil for transport.

"Where was her last port of call?" Bill asked. "Looks she arrived here from Iceland about ten days ago. Says here, they docked there for some repairs to their navigating equipment and sent a boat ashore to get some parts," remarked Stan, checking the report. Just ten days ago, the US Army's winter training group was bombed while on a training exercise in Iceland.

In a few minutes, the task force mobilized and headed down to the docks in an attempt to catch Gooding before he left the UK on his way back to the US.

***

Jenny, having met Millie the minute she arrived in the team's new headquarters, had pulled her with as she escorted Reva to her flight. Reva was accompanying Carl and another deceased US agent who had succumbed to his injuries back to DC, stating that she was done with this operation. Jenny and Millie hugged Reva as they put her on the plane home. Stan had agreed and stated that her part in this mission was over until she healed.

The girls took their time walking back to the car waiting to take them back to headquarters. Millie confessed to being full of excitement now that her first trip overseas was ending and was full of plans for her return to the States. Her job was over now that Jenny was no longer bait. Millie had been in a CIA safe house, far away from the pub explosion, and for this, Jenny was grateful. She thought again of Reva—and Carl—who hadn't been so lucky.

As they and their escort left the personnel-only part of the airport, a movement caught Jenny's gaze. She spotted a bright yellow sea chest being carted out to a commercial vehicle just down from where their car waited. The insignia on the van caught her attention. The white lorry had a black pyramid shape with a yellow "T" logo in the center. An image flashed in her mind's eye. While

Gooding had leaned over to tie her ankles, his jacket had come open and she'd seen a similar logo on a small notebook. She'd forgotten until this moment what the logo said. A clear image of it popped into her head. "Thorne Shipping." The name clicked in her brain. Thornton Michael Gooding had gone as Thorne as a student.

"Hey, Jenny. Jen!" Millie tugged on her arm. "Hey, Jen, what are you talking about—what's Thorne Shipping?"

Jenny hadn't realized she'd spoken aloud. She grabbed Millie at once and started to run to the car, yelling to their escorts, "That's Gooding's van, we have to follow them!"

Jenny and Millie, along with Anthony, as their official CIA escort, made it to the car just as the van pulled past them. Their driver was startled when Anthony yelled at him to follow the van.

In a panic, Jenny called Jonesey, because she knew he was meeting with Stan this morning, and he was likely to be in the new FBI HQ with Bill and Mitch.

***

"Mitch, there's a call for you." Jonesey handed him his cell phone. Mitch took it, wondering who would call for him on Jonesey's phone.

"Mitch, it's Jenny. We need to get down to the docks, that's how he's leaving."

Mitch nearly dropped the phone as he answered and, meeting Jonesey's and Bill's questioning looks, nodded to them. "Yeah, we know, we're on the way down there now. Where are you?" He hung up the phone and handed it back to Jonesey. Mitch looked to Stan for approval. "We need to go now. I'll explain in the car."

Stan answered, "God speed. I'll call the Brits."

Chapter Fifty-three

They were too late. Minutes after Jenny had called, Anthony radioed to tell them they had just finished scoping out the Thorne Industries building. Gooding was on his way to the ship. The warehouse was empty and, worse, when Anthony had returned to the car, he'd found that they girls were missing. Mitch was frantic.

Jonesey had motioned the driver of the car carrying him, Bill, and Mitch to drive directly down to the sea from where they were. "We're calling for the British port authority to send a helicopter besides the frigate that's on the way." Jonesey spoke matter-of-factly as he checked the clip in his gun. "You boys ready?" he asked as the car slid to a stop at the edge of the pier.

Gooding's speedboat was just clearing the warehouses heading northeast to the open sea where the freighter could be seen anchored past the shallows. The group ran down to the beach where the cement walls and railings buffered the beach from the frigid North Sea.

From the railing above the beach they could see Gooding's two boats. The first small craft had reached the freighter and was unloading, but Gooding's speedboat was much closer to them. Too far for a clean shot. Not for Gooding, though. He stood up in the back of the boat and shot at them with a high-powered rifle. The agents ducked for cover behind the sea wall, but Jonesey caught a ricochet in his shoulder.

Mitch stood frantically stiff with frustration, his hands clenching and unclenching as he watched Gooding escape before his eyes. He looked straight ahead, compelled to stare at the speedboat, watching the freighter as well. For an instant, he felt all hope slip away in its wake. *I wish the CIA snipers were here. Maybe the helicopter?* Then he chanced to see a golden glint coming up the cabin hatch in the speedboat. It kept low behind the aft seats; a brunette head followed and hunched beyond the right-hand rear seat.

***

Gooding sat back down in the copilot's seat and stowed the rifle, satisfied that he'd saved them from pursuit as Mortimer drove the boat closer to the freighter and freedom. He could just see his dock crew unloading the other boat and the final supplies and gear being pulled up the side of his freighter. A deep satisfaction and excitement filled him. Success. Soon he'd be on his way to the culmination of his plan.

***

Unbelievable, the British guys had missed the speedboat, thought Jenny. She and Millie had spotted them going into the warehouse after Anthony had left them with instructions to stay put. Then they'd seen Gooding's crony, Mortimer, go in a neighboring door. Gooding had a second warehouse down here. The girls had followed Mortimer into the warehouse and watched as Gooding gave directions to two others who immediately left in a speedboat. They paused for a minute, but neither the British agents nor Anthony had shown up yet.

"We're gonna miss him!" whispered Millie.

"Yeah. Wait, I have an idea," Jenny said as she pointed to a second speedboat nearby.

While Gooding gave Mortimer some last minute instructions, Jenny and Millie had found the getaway craft and hitched a ride below decks.

***

From the pier, the FBI guys watched Gooding's speedboat. Before Jonesey, Mitch, Bill, or any of the other agents on the dock could think to worry, they watched Millie's arm come up and fire a gun. The report of her weapon was lost to the wind, but they saw Gooding fall sideways as he stood up in the boat, then hunched over grabbing his side.

As Gooding shook himself and started after Millie, he pulled a pistol from his pocket. Jenny leaped forward and cold-cocked the driver of the boat with the fire extinguisher she must have found in the hold as Millie dove down the hatch at the rear of the seats. Gooding had been able to take a few steps and nearly got Millie, but was thrown off balance when Jenny swung the fire extinguisher again and knocked him into the North Sea. She then started pulling the unconscious driver out of the seat.

Even wounded, Gooding was a powerful swimmer and began cutting out across the water toward the freighter. Mitch could see the freighter lowering another boat as Bill frantically called dispatch to check on the British shore authority dock craft's status. Before dispatch answered, they saw it was already in the water, speeding toward the speedboat.

Jenny yelled that Gooding had gone overboard, and Millie came forward and grabbed the steering wheel while Jenny stuffed the driver face down in the passenger seat. The agents saw Jenny bend to do something to the downed driver. "Maybe she's securing him, like he's not dead," Bill speculated. Millie had taken over the speedboat's controls which had turned the boat away from the freighter when Jenny cold-cocked the driver. The wind whipped her hair about her head, but the agents saw her note the oncoming crafts, one coming back from the freighter and the British patrol craft farther away following behind. She yelled to Jenny, "Ring that guy's neck with the preserver!" and gunned the boat back toward Gooding and the freighter.

Jenny nodded and grabbed a spare lifesaving ring, then made her way awkwardly to the rear of the moving craft. Jonesey asked, "Do you think they can grab Gooding from the water? That's crazy. God, I hope they can."

In a great show of marine driving, Millie rammed the throttle and turned to jump the boat over the waves and wakes, crazy-fast after Gooding to block his escape, then accelerated even more and spun it around in front of him.

Mitch and Bill watched as Millie maneuvered the speedboat between Gooding's swimming form and the skiff from the freighter. Jonesey, still panting, commented, "They're not going to get to him in time."

Gooding, breathing heavily, wasted precious seconds to look up to the craft coming at him. Taking a deep lungful of air, he prepared to dive, but Jenny's rope flew through the sky and neatly ringed his left wrist. Rather than trying to loop the life preserver over his neck and chancing that Gooding would wiggle out of it, in a crazy stunt Jenny had dropped the life ring and used the loose end of the rope to lasso him instead.

"Holy shit, go girl!" echoed from more than one watcher standing on the wharf. Mitch grinned as he saw Jenny send the loop flying over the water. She'd admitted to doing FFA classes in high school and practicing calf roping against her rodeo fanatic cousins just for fun. He looked over to Jonesey, Bill, and the rest of the guys. Their jaws were hanging down as they stared. Mitch remarked, "In a million years, no one is going to believe us when we put that in the report."

Chapter Fifty-four

Gooding frantically tried to loosen the lasso off his wrist to no avail. His frenzied jerking and the cold water served to screw the loop tighter to his wrist. He fought and fought and became cognizant of the irresistible pull toward the boat. Using the last of his strength, he started kicking away, and felt the rope go taut. He could feel Jenny pulling on the rope and began dragging the rope away from her as he remembered his knife in his ankle holster. He ceased kicking and redoubled his struggles to get his knife from the ankle sheath tightly strapped there. His only thought repeated in his head as he struggled. *Damn that bitch. I will get free. No FBI twit will get me. I will get free, damn her I will get away...*

***

Jenny's face was flushed with exertion and the cold bite of the wind. When Gooding stopped working the rope, she got worried. She could only think of the old adage, "a tiger by the tail..." She looked over her shoulder and saw Millie turning the boat back to shore, and could see the freighter's craft getting closer. Jenny knew they had to hurry. They might be able to outrun the other boat, but they had to have a head start. *Come on, girl, he's like a stubborn heifer, rein him in! Keep going, Millie. We only need to get the Brit boat between us and the freighter crew,* she told herself.

Jenny pulled with all her might and shortly Gooding was about six feet off the side of the boat. Just then she heard shots fire around her, getting closer each second. Jenny hunched down and tried to pull Gooding closer. In response, Millie cut the throttle and fired a few shots back at the freighter boat. The oncoming crew dove down for protection after she winged the driver. Before Jenny had realized her intent, she saw Millie reach down in the bottom of the boat, grab a spar in her hands, and smack Gooding straight on the head. Gooding's struggles had moved him a few feet from the boat, but his movements ceased as he went unconscious with the blow. Millie then dove out of the boat and swan to catch Gooding. Meanwhile, Jenny yanked on his rope and pulled him closer. Millie reached him just as Gooding was going under.

Millie grabbed Gooding's torso before he could sink further and yelled to Jenny, "Get us the hell outta here!" Jenny turned back to the controls, ducking bullets from the less scared freighter skiff and opened the throttle back up while wrapping her end of the rope around and around the gearshift, the only vertical object to hand. She was able to force the speedboat into a neat 180-degree turnabout. *Please help me get Millie and Gooding out of here,* she prayed.

Millie held on to the rope and Gooding, and kept them in tow. In a few moments, the bullets stopped when the British patrol boats passed them on their way to the Gooding craft. Millie held tightly in their wake. Millie seemed to split her attention between keeping her breath and her hold on Gooding. Jenny watched the Brits travel en route to the freighter's boat, whose crew realized the futility of continuing the pursuit and were half turned and halfway back to the freighter with another patrol boat closing quickly on their heels. Just then the two military helicopters landed on the deck of the freighter. The freighter's crew in the boat reached the ship in time to watch their fellow crewmen leap off the deck and hit the water. Before the smaller craft could dash out to sea, the patrol boat reached them, removing all chances of escape.

***

Millie felt more than heard the speedboat slow. With the water in her ears and the rough ride, she felt like she'd been dragged down a dirt road, not a choppy sea. In her waterlogged state she barely felt the drag as Jenny swiftly pulled her in. Before long, she was helping to hoist the unconscious Gooding up the side of the hull from the water. Jenny pulled hard and landed on her butt, with Gooding's form facedown at her feet after Millie used the last bit of strength to muscle the rest of him in and over the side of the boat. Jenny grabbed the rope and tied Gooding's free hand to the bluish left one, then grabbed Millie and hauled the rest of her in too. As Millie caught a few dry breaths, Jenny lightly steered the boat back to shore. Within a couple of minutes—that felt like a couple of years—they were at the edge of the beach down from the dock, staring at their companions on the seawall.

Jonesey was the first to reach them. He jumped down into the boat with his knife and sliced the bonds off Gooding. Mitch followed, grabbed Gooding's wrists, and slapped the cuffs on. Mitch rolled Gooding over and Jonesey confirmed that he was still alive. After all the mayhem it seemed unjust somehow. "Too bad he's just unconscious unfortunately." Jonesey's comment echoed Millie's thoughts.

With a clinical detachment, Mitch used the towel Millie had found in the hold and silently handed him to staunch the blood slowly oozing from the gun wound in Gooding's side. He remarked, "Hell of a goose egg on his head. We can take comfort that he'll have a headache for days." He then grabbed a second towel from Millie and gave it to Jonesey. "Your shot looks worse than Gooding."

The British ambulance crew and the rest of the task force team members arrived soon after. Gooding was strapped to a backboard and onto a gurney, then loaded in the ambulance van prepared to transport him to the waiting, secure, military hospital. Mitch, Bill, and Jonesey nodded to Stan who had arrived with his British counterpart to accompany him. On the way, Stan stopped and clasped both Jenny and Millie on their shoulders and congratulated them on a job well done.

Mitch and Bill finally had a chance to examine Jonesey's wound and held him up as a second set of medical personnel arrived to look over him and the wounded members of Gooding's crew. His bleeding had stopped, but he'd need a few stitches from the bullet ricochet. Meanwhile, other medical personnel looked over Millie and Jenny. Millie's hands were scraped raw and Jenny had wrenched her shoulder somehow on the boat. Anthony came over and offered to drive them to the hospital, and Jonesey joined them for the comfort of the black cab the CIA had acquired. The rest of the task force piled into the waiting FBI van that would take most of the team back to HQ, but would go to the hospital after.

Chapter Fifty-five

The British military hospital was dark and eerily silent. After all the excitement earlier that afternoon, everything had really quieted down around the task force. Gooding had been booked into CIA/FBI custody about two hours before. Bill had gone with Jonesey and Anthony accompanied by Stan and Homer, who would personally escort Gooding home on the USS Sandpiper. "What a misnamed destroyer," Homer had remarked as he disembarked in Liverpool. Bill was to be the escort for Homer to the ship and would deliver their initial final report on the way. The rest of the report was to be officially completed stateside. Once the ship was on its way, Bill, Jonesey, and Anthony with the other CIA guys were going to cash in the Brits' bet.

The British officers who'd stood by Bill on the pier had bet a night on the town that the Yanks would lose Gooding. Then they'd doubled the bet by adding that Jenny would miss her target when she'd lassoed Gooding. The discussion then centered on how Millie, a girl from the land-locked, desert state of Arizona, and a cowgirl who couldn't possibly swim, could drive a marine watercraft, since they'd probably never even seen a boat, let alone maneuvered it in the choppy waves to grasp Gooding. In fascination they'd all watched as Millie held the boat steady and Jenny's aim was true. Even the quiet British boys had been impressed when Jenny snagged Gooding's wrist. To hear Jenny tell the story, she was adamant that it was all luck, that she'd been really scared she'd get his neck and suffocate him.

Millie and Jenny both tried to explain their actions so the guys would quit picking on them. The unending teasing was loud and was drawing a crowd. Jenny laughed after Millie had addressed the group of CIA guys seeing the

Sandpiper off. "Knock it off, you assholes. Like any of you could have caught them."

Millie avoided approaching them. Jenny nudged Millie. "Mill, they are just teasing you, they are proud of you. You should go off with them. Anthony is holding a drink for you, girl. You'd better head over."

Millie looked over at Anthony, and a slow smile spread across her face. She looked back and smiled as she walked away. "Yeah, you just want me gone so you can go bear hunting." Jenny grinned, seemingly unconcerned that Millie referred to Mitch as the bear.

Now that Millie was taken care of, Jenny was headed back to the hostel. The Weber State crew had left for Glasgow. With them gone and Gooding caught, Bill figured she could finally relax for the first time in weeks. She looked drained after the rush and stress of the last few months Bill watched as Mitch trotted over to her as she waved the CIA guys off to their partying. "As team leader, I'm here telling you to head back to the hostel and get some shut-eye, shorty," Mitch said conversationally as he looked down on Jenny. She nodded, and didn't seem to mind Mitch's hand on the small of her back. Bill stood back and watched Mitch farm Jenny over to one of the cars waiting to take the task force team members back to their various lodgings. Lowly he said, "Good for them. It's been a long summer."

Now that Mitch and Jenny were taken care of, Bill was free to wait here for Anthony to return to pick him up. The CIA guys were grabbing some of the Brits, and a big group was going partying tonight to celebrate their victory. Watching Jenny, he figured Mitch would probably be heading back to the hostel for some much-earned rest. Mitch, as team leader, had spent a great deal of his time yesterday worrying about the head count of the FBI staff after the bombing. He had also volunteered earlier for the duty to be the one who'd called Carl's wife and told her the news.

Watching Mitch coming over to see him, Bill decided to steer Mitch in the right direction. So it was with fond thoughts that he said, "Go on, dude. You don't want to go out with us. We'll be drinking all night... You need to tuck little Jenny in." Mitch raised one eyebrow, so Bill continued, "Hey man, seriously, after all that paperwork, you ought to go on back to the hostel and get some rest." Bill pushed Mitch toward the cars. When Mitch protested, he kept pushing him. "Nah, you'll hate it, warm beer and stale smoke—go on back to the hostel. The boys owe me and Jonesey a round or three."

"At least Jonesey's tab will be light, soda pop can't cost that much. I could help you guys run up a deep tab. I could use a shot or five of some fifty-year-old Scotch," Mitch responded. Bill flipped him off and stepped off the curb into the car that had pulled up as they were talking. It was Jonesey and Anthony to pick up Bill.

Jonesey yelled from the other side of the car, "Even I ain't cheap in the UK. Pop is a novelty here, so I may as well be drinking the beer. Besides, the night on the town includes a steak dinner, mad cow disease or not, and I am not wasting a steak on you!" The group departed, but waved goodbye to Mitch.

***

Mitch went over to the last FBI car that would take him back to the hostel. Just then, an official motorcade car pulled up and Stan rolled down the window in the limousine.

Mitch had been planning on calling to check in with Stan later tonight and determine their plans for the team to leave for the States once Gooding was transported, but Stan and Homer had changed plans. On the way back to the hostel, Stan explained, "I am staying here for a day or so while Homer escorts Gooding to the US tonight. It will take a few days for Albert to coordinate the flights home, but starting tomorrow, I can clear small groups of agents to return to DC. If you want, you and Bill can take the last flight and stay in the UK for a while—like a mini-vacation. I know neither of you have really taken any time off since Christmas and know how much you, Bill, and Jonesey would enjoy some tourist time here."

Mitch agreed. "Thanks, boss. That is a good idea."

The car reached the back door to the hostel. Before exiting, Mitch shook Stan's hand. "Call me tomorrow if you have an update."

"Will do."

Mitch had to swing by the British team's office for a while, so that the Brits could leave the next day. *I'll stop off at the Brits', check on Jenny, and then crash,* Mitch thought as he entered the hostel through the kitchen's back entrance.

For the first time in nearly a year, Mitch was looking forward to crashing in his hotel room. He was tired of being in charge, of being the only worrier around. The British bed was about a foot too narrow and two feet too long, but he was gonna enjoy the crash tonight. He intended to pretend he was home in DC, tucked into his California king-sized waterbed.

Thinking of the big bed the staff had found for him had Mitch smiling and thinking of his partner. Bill had spent the last three long shifts on stakeout teasing Mitch about the king-sized bed he'd requested special from the hostelry. He'd claimed that the staff wouldn't be able to find a bed big enough for him in the entire country. He'd been so obnoxious about it with some of the hostel's staff that they'd razzed Bill back, then called his bluff; the bed they found barely fit in the room, and couldn't make it in the front door let alone up the stairs. Bill had laughed until he bawled when he finally saw the "double" they scrounged up. It had to be brought down the skylight and wheeled down the hall from the top floor of the hostel. They even reassigned Mitch to a new room upstairs as they couldn't get the bed down the stairs any more than they could get it up them.

Mitch didn't care at this point. The hostel staff had been nice to him about it and gave him a pleasant, if small, room. He could stretch out and lay down without his feet hanging off the bed. Maybe with this bed he could enjoy some peace and sleep well until they left. He'd lost too many good friends and good nights of sleep to Gooding. Tonight he was gonna sleep like a newborn baby.

His meeting with the Brits' leader was quick. Mitch waved him goodbye. "Have a great time tonight. You guys saved our bacon, man!"

Mitch made it to his room, finally. He dropped his gun and holster into the safe the hostel had provided, and mentally checked his list of "to do" items: First, he needed to be a good team leader and make sure everyone was okay for the night. "Reva is home by now, I know where Bill and Jonesey are, and they have the other five guys with them. That leaves..." He paused at the last name. He only needed to check on Jenny. She was the only one here at the hostel right now besides him. He wondered if she'd really came back here as planned.

Mitch smiled. He was proud of Jenny. This whole time she'd handled everything that hit her like a trooper—never flinching or losing courage or her grip. He headed down to her room and stopped. He knew that Bill had sent him here hoping for them to make a connection and he refused to be manipulated by one of his partner's wild schemes. Bill's motives aside, Mitch wondered if Jenny needed him tonight. Her college pals had left and with Reva gone and Millie with the CIA guys, she might be lonely.

At least that's what he told himself to justify going to see her. He and Jenny had talked back in Georgia about how she really appreciated her civilian friends—they helped her feel grounded during stressful times at work. She'd appreciated Reva in the same way. Mitch knew that Jenny would be missing her female companionship, and he told himself that although he was a poor second, he could give her a measure of comfort. "Like hell," Mitch muttered to himself. He could tell himself that his motives were pure, that he was being altruistic, but some small part of him knew the truth. He just wanted to be with Jenny as a woman, finally.

The thought put a spring in his step as he realized that for the first time in six months, he would be all alone for more than a brief minute with the woman who'd affected him more strongly than anyone else had in years. And for the first time in months he didn't have to worry that his world would probably end tomorrow because of what Gooding had planned. Their task was completed and the team could stand down and enjoy some plain old camaraderie. He was now free. *Finally, I am no longer her boss!*

As he climbed down to the seventh level, he enjoyed the new-felt pleasure at the knowledge that as soon as he "tucked" Jenny in if she didn't invite him to stay, he could head back to his own room and go to bed. Tomorrow would start another day and maybe he could try again. Another part of him was looking forward to the "mop-up" to close the mission. It would take at least a week to get most of the staff home to DC. Then it could take six more weeks to finish the reports. In the meantime, they could all enjoy some recreation after work. Maybe Jenny could even stay in DC to finish. In fact, tonight would be the first time Jenny would be staying in the same place as he and Bill. There was even a chance that they could keep working with Jenny permanently. Both Homer and Stan wanted to keep her on. The future looked open and welcoming to him.

Some nights he'd endured torturous waits at whatever hostel Jenny's college group would be spending the night, while worrying that one of Gooding's goons had spotted them. Then, after the tricky process of briefing Jenny for the next day's events, he and Bill would have to make their way back to their own hotel or hostel without blowing their cover. Twice, the nice boys from the CIA had scared the living be-jeepers out of them before escorting them home, just to be funny. Thankfully the group rivalry seemed to have finally ended when Millie and Jenny had captured Gooding together after stowing away on his boat, proving the FBI and CIA guys could cooperate. Since both groups shared the win 50/50, they had been more willing to act like comrades and brothers, even if it had been the "sisters" who'd won the day.

Mitch knew that the Brits were planning a week's worth of celebration, including dancing and partying all night long. He himself hated clubbing, but he might change his mind if Jenny could be included. He thought of dancing with Jenny, of pulling her close. Then he thought of her soft lips and nearly bounded the last few steps to her room. *I can have her all to myself tonight. Maybe I should take her clubbing just to spend some more time with her.* He was sure the farm-girl lifestyle she enjoyed at home didn't include hot clubs and long parties. It may be fun.

Chapter Fifty-six

Mitch gathered his courage to knock on Jenny's door.

Bill had quit commenting every time Mitch's gaze would stray to Jenny's eyes, chest, hips or legs. He'd only mentioned Mitch's lustful stares at her mouth once in the past week, although his eyebrows seemed to lift all the time now. Mitch just knew Bill had made that crack about "tucking in" Jenny just to put one more screw in his hide. Bill had noticed the dirty look Mitch had shot back at him and remarked in his usual smart-aleck way. *Bill is probably right, but I don't have to admit it.*

Another small part of him knew that although it wasn't professional, he at least wanted to tell her goodbye. Mitch needed and wanted some contact now that the job was nearly done. He ached to share a small slice of normality with Jenny. Her flight was leaving tomorrow afternoon. Stan and Jonesey were taking her to brunch, and she was heading to the airport to check in by noon. That CIA guy, Anthony, and Jonesey would be on the same flight since it was heading on to Denver, then Salt Lake City, and finally Portland. Jonesey's folks now lived in Oregon, so he would stay with Jenny all the way back to SLC, where he'd then head to Portland to burn his six-week sabbatical time. Anthony would leave them when they switched planes at Denver.

Jenny had stated that she would be packing and finishing her school journal tonight, so Mitch figured she'd grabbed some snacks when she'd retired to her room, as was her habit. *Jonesey, Bill, the CIA guys, and the British Intelligence dudes should be well started on their first night of well-deserved clubbing by now. At least Bill isn't here to razz me over what I'm about to do.*

That's where his logic had left his motives as he raised his hand to knock. He took a last look around and noticed from the bare hallway and quiet tone of the rooms that all the tired folks were in bed already, and the clubbers wouldn't be back for hours. He and Jenny were the only people awake around here. Those thoughts coupled with the warm feeling coursing through him. She opened the door before he could knock. *How does she do that?* He looked down at her, absorbing the vision. Jenny seemed to always know when he was near. Mitch's tight rein on himself dissolved as her lovely hand, attached to her lovely arm, pulled the door inward.

"I thought that was you," she remarked as she stepped back. He found himself rushing into her room like a wave to the shore. She was dressed for bed. Her hair was newly washed and only half dry, which made the wavy curls float all around her head as well as down her back.

She was wearing the softest flannel pajama bottoms he'd ever seen, and he knew if she knew how well they showed off every luscious curve of her rear and legs, that she'd never wear them again. Then, worse, his eyes drank in her curvy waist and chest. *She isn't wearing a bra!* The statement exploded in his head and loins as he looked past her packed suitcases blocking the door and spotted her bed right there and realized she had her room to herself tonight. Here she was, all packed and ready to leave his life.

Quickly, panicked thoughts ran through his brain. The paperwork that could be done here was mostly complete. Had Al had already contacted her boss and arranged for her return to regular duty and for her final hazard pay and bonus to be put in her account? As a temporarily assigned agent, she'd done her job by helping capture Gooding in the UK. Although Stan had offered a position, she hadn't tendered her final answer. Would she follow the rest of the team to DC? She could finish her paperwork out of the Salt Lake City FBI office. *Maybe she's planning on that already, excited to go home to the States and be done with this. Maybe she's decided to stay in Utah. Maybe she's decided to leave me.* Jenny could be flying out of his life forever tomorrow.

As these thoughts stole the power from Mitch's frontal lobe, and his animal brain tried to take over, he fought to remain a gentleman. He clamped down and remembered Bill had thoughtfully sent a huge take-out dinner to Mitch's room so "he could stay in—*wink, wink.* With an extra set of silverware, just in case." Mitch hadn't even wondered why two sets of silverware until his invitation popped out of his mouth, "Bill sent us some dinner. Are ya hungry?" His brilliant smile must have disarmed her, because she smiled back and said yes, and he really noticed her plump lips. He could only watch her turn to grab her room key and step out in front of him. He walked behind her, speechless and nervous.

As she locked her door, Mitch appreciated the view down the back of Jenny's neck where her T-shirt gapped away from her back. He looked at that bare skin until she scooted forward under his arm, leaning on the wall above her head, and looked up at him. "Lead on, I'm starving."

For the first time in a while, Mitch was starving too, for her. He could drown in the scent of her shampoo. As his eyes followed her graceful movements down the hall and up the stairs, his palms felt swollen and itchy. He looked down and saw that he was unconsciously flexing his fingers as he imagined touching her skin—any part of her skin. He was really going downhill fast.

He reached over her shoulder and, with a flick of the wrist, opened the door to his room for them both. He gently pushed her in, but she hesitated on the threshold. The double bed left a scant six-inch gap for the door to open and close—all the room was to the side of the bed. He scooted Jenny forward past the bed and closed the gap between her back and his chest, then closed the door behind them without backing away from her.

She stood there laughing at the bed. "Bill told me the staff calls you the porn king 'cause of the size of your..." She turned to look at him to finish the jab and stopped with her head halfcocked, looking back at him. Her face heated and she leaned back a bit, as if just now realizing how close Mitch was. Mitch had trapped her between his massive frame and the huge bed. The frontal contact of their bodies absorbed his attention. The food on the table near the wall was forgotten.

The heat that flared in Jenny's gaze set off a panicked rhythm in Mitch's heart. For twelve weeks, he had fantasized and lusted after this woman almost constantly. He'd fought battles with her, swapped jokes with her, at times had teased her unmercifully, and had been losing the battle to keep his heart free of her. She stared back at him in silence, her eyes reflecting what Mitch was feeling as she leaned toward him. Up until now, she'd tried to keep her feelings from showing, Mitch knew, but now it was too late. She had no barriers to protect her from him any longer.

Mitch lost control staring at her wide eyes and the pink cheeks and lips and her face. He moved in even closer to her, and felt his heart thump harder at her sharp intake of breath. He glanced down at her and nearly groaned. Her nipples were hard and pebbled, as if straining for his touch. Mitch's hands framed her face and pulled her to him for their first real kiss in weeks.

That kiss turned their mutual blazes into a raging inferno, which ended in the inevitable conclusion predicted by many. Mitch felt Jenny surrender totally. She acted lost to the feelings and emotions of the moment, just like him. And for the first time in a long time, he was glad to have someone share his room for the night.

Chapter Fifty-seven

The next morning, in the gray dusky light of 5:00 a.m., Jenny's face kept a perpetual blush as she frantically, quietly tried to find that damn, tight T-shirt that must be hiding on Mitch's side of the bed. "Actually, the whole damn bed is his," she muttered as she tried not to notice his naked body spread-eagle beside her as she reached as far back to the headboard as she could get. "No good, but he's not sleeping on it. Dammit, where is it?"

As she rummaged on her hands and knees, the crouching position on the floor made it perfectly clear how much damage her night of fun had done to some never-before-used areas. *Oh my heavens,* she thought as tears of mortification joined her blush. "Of course, I should have told him I was a virgin a little quicker, but damn, how does one bring that up when one is *not* supposed to be interested in a guy, and has to be *professional* all the time." *Shit, shit, shit, shit, shit,* she thought over and over. She squelched the thought that followed the cussing, *At least he made it all feel better...more than once!* Grasping a short sleeve, she pulled her T-shirt from between the bed and the wall. "Thank heavens!" The comment was audible, but only to dogs and small children. Not to the massive, very satisfied, sleeping giant on the bed. "At least he was ecstatic when he felt the obvious evidence. Too bad I didn't know all that crap about 'bursting the cherry' was true." As she pulled the T-shirt down into place and bumped a love bite, she muttered, "Ouch, I wish I'd known what *keeping going* and *repeating as necessary* would feel like in the morning."

Mitch shifted on the bed, and Jenny froze, embarrassed as she remembered the night before. Mitch had paused at that key moment early in the night, shocked. Then she'd seen him get all possessive and things just kept getting better and better. Of course, they'd both slept like the dead after. She looked over at Mitch, admiring the view for a second. *Thank heavens. He's just rolled over.* Her conscience didn't get her attention until it roared at her when it returned with a vengeance this morning. Guilty thoughts woke her up. She felt the tears coming. "Damn it, I should have never left my room. Damn." Jenny grabbed her socks and slippers. *I have to leave now. Go, woman. Get the heck out of here now!*

True tears of sadness crept down her cheeks as she fumbled with the key to her room. Her stomach growled to let her know that she hadn't eaten enough last night, then clenched with the anxiety overwhelming her. She rushed inside, took a super-fast shower, got dressed, and after a quick call to Jonesey—who was thankfully up, having turned in early rather than party all night last night in preparation for their trip home—made it down to the lobby with all her gear in twenty minutes flat. Jenny had just plunked her carry-on on top of her huge suitcase, and was turning back from grabbing the jacket she'd dropped, when she smacked into a Bill, who was coming in from the night of partying. Bill was the second-to-last person she'd wanted to meet, but Jenny was glad it was him so she could tell him goodbye.

Jenny quickly hugged him and gave a hasty farewell and mumbled explanation. "I'll miss you awful, we gotta go, plane leaves in forty-five minutes. I'll call you when I hit the States." While Jenny was talking to Bill, Jonesey moved past them to where Anthony was getting ready to park and stopped him. With the hostel door open, Jenny could just hear Jonesey talking to Anthony as he threw her bags in the boot. "No. Dammit, we're leaving now. Here's my stuff and part of Jenny's. I'll get the rest of hers and finish checking out as she's talking to Bill. If you want to go with us, you have three minutes to get your bags that I packed, but left upstairs, and get your CIA ass back down here. Here's a note from your boss."

***

Bill's instincts were screaming at him. Something was terribly, terribly wrong, but rather than stop to tell him what had happened exactly, Jenny had grabbed him for a hug and a quick peck on the cheek before she rushed out of the hotel. He had just enough time to get on his way toward the door to chase her down, when Anthony rushed past him on his way to meet Jonesey and Jenny in the waiting car, saying, "Bill, buddy, I'll explain later. Just let her go, and take care of Mitch. I don't know what's gone sour, but the shit's hit the fan, and Stan wants her gone now."

Bill embraced him. "Thanks for all your help. Send me an e-mail when you can. I'm gonna go find out what the mess is."

They both turned to go their separate ways, but Anthony dropped his bag and grabbed him. "No wait, man, you gotta give us an hour. Jenny pleaded with Stan to let her get off the ground before Mitch gets up. I think they had a huge fight or something, but you know how the kid got to Stan. She's like the daughter he never had. She called him before she woke us. He wants her on the early CIA flight this morning. He went so far as to pull me and Jonesey to go with her instead of leaving this afternoon. And if Mitch stops us, we're all dead. Please, just one hour. I'll call you when you hit DC." Jonesey honked the car horn again. Anthony grabbed his bag and was out the door, launching down the steps, across the sidewalk, and into the car.

Bill made his way up the stairs, cautiously, wishing he'd had some sleep before fixing messes. Despite his hangover receding somewhat, the headache made it hard going. The nasty vibe in his gut was a good indication of how much he would not like what he found in Mitch's room. Good thing he could pick the lock half drunk, because he wasn't sure he could have kept his nerve longer than the thirty seconds it took to break into Mitch's room.

One look at the satisfied smile on Mitch's sleeping face, and seeing his obviously naked body, and Bill's heart sank. He saw the disarray of the bedding, the uneaten food on the shelf, and turned to leave Mitch sleeping for the remainder of his golden hour. He then noticed the reddish stain on the sheet, peeking from under Mitch's side. *Damn it! Double damn! Holy shit, no wonder the shit's hit the fan,* he thought as he left the room and altered his course, heading down the hall rather than down two flights of stairs to his own room. Seeing the stain, he could now almost understand Jenny's state and Stan's temper. *That girl had been a virgin. This whole thing has probably freaked her out.*

Stan, like all FBI chiefs, disapproved of his agents getting personally involved, and had been worried about Mitch and Jenny throughout this whole assignment. Now, Bill would have to intercept his sorry cuss of a partner when he woke up, before Mitch realized Jenny was gone and all hell broke loose. And, since he wasn't about to stay in the porn king's room, Bill headed for the first place Mitch would look for Jenny—her room. He'd sack out on Jenny's bed until Mitch got there. Mitch would find Jenny before he'd go tearing into anyone else. Bill muttered as he picked Jenny's lock, "Porn king, indeed. Defiling virgins now. Holy shit. What a mess!" If there was one thing to ensure that Mitch would stop the fling from being a one-night-stand, a cherry was it. Besides, Bill knew Mitch well enough to know that Jenny was no one-night-only to Mitch; he loved her. *Not that that bastard will admit it, especially now,* he thought as he shut Jenny's door behind him.

Bill knew Mitch would go ape-shit when he found Jenny gone. He'd go first to her room, then back to Kansas, Dorothy. He'd have to catch Mitch here, so he could keep him out of Stan's path as long as he could. He tried to remember what Jenny and Anthony said. If Stan knew what Mitch had done, then Mitch was probably in double deep shit, hence Jonesey and Anthony escorting Jenny home post haste. Bill wondered if Stan put Jenny in his spot. If so, then Stan would still be in London. His foggy brain had it figured out. *If Stan put Jenny on the plane, she'll be safe back home. Meantime, Anthony said to keep Mitch on ice for an hour, which probably means Stan's pissed, and needs time to cool off before reprimanding Mitch. Also, that's enough time for Mitch to cool down so he doesn't tell our boss to go to hell.* Having satisfied his brain, Bill drifted off to sleep. Stan had taken to Jenny more strongly than Homer, once he'd gotten to know her. If Jenny was "compromised," Stan would probably shoot the guy who'd touched her, due to some misplaced papa bear feelings. *The man should never have had five daughters.*

The thought, *Damn, it's a good thing those British dudes know how to party, 'cause that's the last fun night I'm gonna have until this thing blows over,* danced out of Bill's head as sleep won.

Chapter Fifty-eight

Two hours after Jenny left, Mitch had a good long stretch and smiled, working the sleep out of his eyes and smiling some more when he noticed the sheet with its telltale stain, got up, and laughed himself into the loo. Then he ducked back into the room to examine the sheet again. "Holy crap, I didn't imagine it." He felt a swelling in his heart, and knew then, for sure, that he loved that girl. "Twenty-five, she'd said, and that she was glad it was me and now, that it was getting embarrassing contemplating *the* conversation when she'd have to explain that. God love her." He smiled, then something in his brain clicked.

Something was wrong. *Hey. Where's Jenny?* The last thing he remembered was being ensconced with her oh-so-soft body in a lovely comforter on his huge bed and falling asleep. Now she was gone. He jerked on his watch, thinking, "Good, only eight in the morning." Still four hours to go. She'd probably gone to get a shower and get dressed. He had time before he'd crash her brunch with Jonesey. First he'd head out to make sure she was okay. He cleaned up a bit and got dressed, then quickly dashed down the hall to find her.

Mitch hummed a small tune as he trotted the few steps down the stairs and down the hall to her room. The first thing he noticed was the "maid service requested" sign on her door, the second thing was that the door was ajar, and thirdly—as he rushed in—that it was Bill snoring on the bed.

The maid came in behind him. "Sir, do you know that man? I need to get this room clean. It should have been cleaned two hours ago after the lady left."

"*Left!*" Mitch's heart stopped. Then great bursts of tension, fear, and adrenaline flushed his system. He grabbed Bill, shoved him off the bed, and began dragging him out of the room. "Where *is she?*"

***

Bill came awake amazingly fast when the maid came into the room the first time. He'd actually been waiting for Mitch. Then he heard him come in. He stayed slumped for a moment as he planted his feet while Mitch's hands ripped his collar, pulling him upright. Just as Mitch opened his mouth to shout again, Bill brought his right foot down hard on Mitch's instep and, as Mitch was leaning off-kilter, followed the stomp by a nasty chop to the jaw. Mitch went down in a slump.

After some phone calls and some help from the Brits—who were in almost as bad a shape as Bill when woken up, but were more than happy to vent their angst on an ornery FBI agent—a trussed up, out-cold Mitch was carted into Stan's borrowed quarters at a nearby hotel. Michael, one of the Brits, remarked as they left, "Good thing you made friends with the hotel nurse, so she'd loan you the gurney, man. Good luck."

A thoroughly irritated Stan asked a just as thoroughly irritated Bill, "You'd think that Mitchell would remember that she was still in FBI custody and that the CIA guys would be interested in knowing where she spent the night, and collecting the evidence thereof. Take this and use it as needed when you think best. I'm leaving now. I am not going to personally castigate Mitch right now." To punctuate the statement, Stan chucked the sheet at Bill's chest and continued on his way out the door, "At least the CIA guys waited until you'd both left the room before sneaking in to snatch the sheet, but I could've gone without seeing *evidence!*" He paused for breath, and his shouting became more controlled as he snarled, "Wait, I've changed my mind. I won't wait to talk to him. If he's sensible by noon, bring him to me. I'm taking Jenny's place on the four o'clock flight." Stan turned to head out the door, ordering behind him, "If he's not ready to talk by then, you get him out on the seven o'clock tonight, and we'll talk first thing Monday, *at headquarters!*"

Bill mock saluted as his boss left them in his rapidly emptying hotel suite. A few minutes later, the assistant hotel manager let in the busboy carrying Mitch's and Bill's luggage into the suite and waited for it to be deposited on the suitcase rack before accompanying the busboy out. Bill waved goodbye to the hotel staff, muttering, "At least those CIA guys can pack."

As the door opened, Bill saluted the CIA guys outside the door. "No more sightseeing. Eh, guys?" He smiled as the taller one shot a nasty grin at him.

"I think you two FBI guys have seen enough sights for this week, Bill. Oh, by the way, do you have any kids?"

Bill responded smartly; he was in no mood for tricks. "Of course not, Harry. Get to the point."

The CIA guys laughed. "Well, Bill, I have two lovely daughters, ten and fourteen, and let me tell you, if any guy boinked one of them on a job, he'd be dead or I'd know why." Deadly smiles were shared all around.

"I hear ya, man." Bill was seriously out of patience now. He couldn't stand any more ribbing. *He* wanted to pound Mitch himself. Bill sighed. The irony of all this was the fact that if Jenny had stayed with Mitch and they'd quietly gone home as a couple, no one would have cared— they were consenting adults after all, and the task force was basically over. *Oh well. Jenny must have panicked and set this roller coaster off.*

Mitch was lying comatose on the suite's couch. Bill looked back at him now and then and strove to make sense of the situation and his emotions amidst the headache pounding his cranium. Did he need to knock some sense into Mitch for compromising Jenny, or for taking forever to do something about her? He was tired, but knowing that

Mitch should have either moved in faster, or waited to start loving Jenny later, he knew that it was time to be serious.

Bill spoke up to the CIA guy guarding them in the room. "Would it help to know that I think he loves her?"

Harry's countenance, too, turned serious. "Bill, you and I both know this thing is no big deal. But, consider Stan. I know we play rough, but I'd have a hard time hearing some dude explain how he compromised my daughter before marriage and commitment. Even if the guy told me he loved her enough for marriage, which your guy has yet to explain. Even though my wife and I couldn't wait until the wedding day, and I know my father-in-law only suspects that's the case, watching Stan look at Mitch I can finally understand why my wife's father hates me. Look, I need to step out. I'll be back." On that sad note, he left, leaving Bill to his thoughts and a silent watch over his buddy.

Twenty minutes later, just as Bill was debating just where on Mitch's body to put out the cigarette he'd just finished, the bastard groaned, then twitched. "About bloody time, ya reprobate," he remarked to his good buddy.

"Why the hell did you conk me, and why the hell am I tied up?" Mitch gritted out amidst his struggles.

Bill leisurely rose out of the chair and, with a flick of the wrist, stubbed out his cigarette in the waiting ashtray. He ignored the twitches in his hands telling him to flick it at Mitch, thinking better of it, and slit the cords binding his friend's hands behind his back. Mitch rolled off his stomach and sat up only to fall back on his side on the gurney. Rubbing his jaw, he said conversationally, "Thanks to that boxing-champ love tap you gave me, I'll bet my headache rivals your hangover."

"Not anymore, Mr. Romance. You jerk! I was gonna enjoy a day of sleep today before partying my way through our last days in London, only to stumble into the holy hurricane you created by defiling Homer and Stan's little star princess!" He continued, surprised at his own heated tone. "I'd just stumbled into the hostel, aiming for my bed, when Miss Jenny nearly knocked me over on her haste to get outta there. My hangover practically disappeared in the same instant as our Miss Jenny rushed through her goodbye—with tears all over her face, mind— and then desperately demanded that I keep, you, the bear, sleeping for at least an hour so she could get an ocean away from you. Of course a newer, better headache came on and intensified ten minutes later after Stan took his anger at you out on me and the boys. Not to mention the lovely reception I received carrying you in here when the CIA guys arrived for guard duty. They're waiting for us just outside this door to escort us to a plane, if needed, and they know very well where Miss Jenny spent the night. So, I damn well hope your headache rivals mine, especially as mine no longer stems from the fantastic fun I had last night." With a good imitation of the mean nastiness Stan had bestowed on everyone that morning, Bill continued. "So, buddy, how was your night, really? I've only heard bits and pieces and saw one hell of a hickey on a certain blonde," he said as he held up the bloody sheet from Mitch's bed.

***

Mitch sat up for a minute, then thought better of it and slumped down on the couch. *What happened to me?* he thought. The last twenty-four hours seemed more than surreal. Yesterday, he'd been contemplating a simple, quiet ten-hour nap when he'd been broadsided by his lustful attack on Jenny. After he'd finally acted on their feelings and felt the full fireworks for the first time, he'd been looking forward to a lovely brunch today, some more, quieter fireworks, and anticipating a well-earned, month-long vacation in the Rocky Mountains with his grandpa and coincidentally nearer to the sweet woman who should now be his. How, in the last hour, had it all changed? He'd not only made his boss so mad that Stan had ordered Bill to cold-cock him and hog-tie him, but somehow he'd lost Jenny. He felt confused, upset, tired, and lost. Meanwhile, a whole maelstrom of feelings regarding that sweet golden-haired beauty he'd spent the night with were pushing their way to center-front of his consciousness.

Mitch groaned. "Man, I wanna die."

Bill lit another cigarette. "I am glad that the gravity of your situation has finally struck you."

Mitch looked up and asked the first question. "How pissed off is Stan?"

Bill seemed to consider his response. "Well, it was noisy and crazy earlier, but you have a reprieve while Stan heads back to DC." This startled Mitch, and Bill went back to looking pissed off. "Come on, Mitch, for all the fireworks this morning, you know he'll blow over it in a few days. And you had to know that he'd be more worried about Jenny than you. After all, you're a horse's ass around women all the time—we're all used to it." Then, with a sideways tilt of his head and a wink, he added, "But, I'd stay out of sight for at least a week once we get home, if I were you."

Mitch closed his eyes, not knowing what to think as he mentally calculated how much trouble he was in and how long Stan's rarely shown, hot-burning temper would last. "Well, at least the CIA guys are in the dark about the messy details." Mitch opened his mouth to continue, only to be stopped by Bill's uproarious laughter.

"Jeez, Mitch, just *who* do you think filled Stan in on the details? You must have truly left your brain in your other pants. The round-the-clock surveillance doesn't stop until all of us FBI staff ship out. While Anthony and I were out partying with the Brits, trying to get some fun out of this whole blasted trip, we figured that no one else would be around the hostel, and you and Jenny could finally get it together. I figured you'd remember that the CIA team leader was keeping a skeleton crew on the lookout just in case and take yourselves out somewhere to party. Hell, the CIA guys knew what you were doing before you did. I just happened to walk in this morning as Miss Jenny and Jonesey were leaving. By the way, I heard that Jenny called Stan before she woke up Jonesey."

Mitch groaned again in real agony this time. "Shit, you'd think we were just a couple consenting adults."

"Not when the other half of this improbable scenario panics and calls Stan and wakes him up at dawn, then proceeds to convince him to trade her plane tickets with the control-freak CIA twins Cassie and Charles' ones on the earlier flight. Then Stan, being instantly reminded of his daughter's fiasco in Atlanta last year, orders Anthony and Jonesey to accompany Jenny home. Meanwhile, thanks to Harry and the surveillance guys, who caught her entrance to and exit from your room on tape, we *all* know that she hustled out of your room at five in the morning and was on a plane and on her way out of the UK by six. She must have really upset Stan, who gave me orders that you not leave the hotel until noon."

"Hell." Mitch shoved a hand through his hair.

"By the time we finally carted your sorry ass up here to his suite, he was too pissed to yell at you, so he left for home a day early, but he is willing to 'talk' if you're feeling 'responsible' by noon. By the way, partner, I wouldn't bother him until tomorrow if you're smart. But there's the phone. You can call him if you like, just don't blame me if he tells you what an ass you've been. You'll note that Stan picked *Anthony* to go with Jonesey and Jenny. Stan had enough CIA phone calls about this same subject, that it had to be a joint team to take her home."

Bill had been pacing around the room as he ranted, but now that his tirade was over he sat on the couch across from Mitch and concentrated on making smoke rings. Mitch's system was trying to recover from this latest shock, in order to get a better grip. "Okay, so what am I supposed to do now?" he asked. "Are we still leaving Friday night?"

Bill answered with a markedly long, drawn out sigh. "Nope, tonight, but we are free to keep the hell out of the CIA guys' sight until check-in tonight for the seven o'clock flight. Then, first thing Monday morning, you and I are to present ourselves to Stan and Homer for the recap and your lecture. After which, I am going home to Georgia until September, and you will have the time you need to do something to fix your life with the six weeks of forced vacation we've been granted."

Mitch looked up as Bill stood as if to leave, and the words fell from his lips, uncontrolled. "Bill, I think I understand what's going on. I mean I think I know what's happening, but I don't know why she left. I didn't even know I wanted her to stay until I woke up and found her gone. I don't know what to do. How can I talk to her after she ran out on me?"

"It must be hell admitting for the first time in your life that you're not a coldhearted SOB made of stone."

Mitch narrowed his eyes. "Funny, Bill."

Bill sighed. "Well, buddy, I think that she was just overworked, stressed, and overwhelmed. Try to reach her when we're back in the States. I doubt she'll be receptive before she's had a week to get over the jet-lag. But she's usually reasonable and may listen after she cools off. Heck, if I were you, I'd drive down to Utah from Montana while you're out there. Jenny's folks live, what, an eighteen-hour drive from the Harper homestead?"

The room became silent. Bill seemed to sense that Mitch needed some alone time and left, purportedly to find a needed jolt of caffeine. Mitch stared dejectedly at the floor. He had a feeling that neither of them would meet the noon deadline.

Chapter Fifty-nine

Jenny didn't just feel numb, she *was* numb, all over. Thank goodness she had made friends on this assignment and she had the two best agents taking her home. Jonesey and Anthony weren't giving her condescending or dirty leers like the CIA dudes around Stan's suite had done. Instead they seemed quietly respectful, even understanding. She shouldn't have been surprised by how the task force onlookers had treated her. She should have remembered the rivalry between the FBI Denver Bunch and Anthony's CIA cronies. She ought to have realized that until the final UK work was done, and they were all called back to the States, that the CIA guys would consider the mission still going.

Anthony had been especially nice when he'd escorted her in and out of Stan's suite. The other CIA guy, Harry, had been there waiting for her to arrive, and had probably filled Stan in on all the gory details long before she'd 'fessed up. Millie also had heard about things and had called her. Jenny was really grateful for this support as well as Bill's, Jonesey's, and Anthony's. She felt bad about her early morning panic. She'd succeeded in ruining their morning naps after all the partying last night. Only Jonesey had turned in early. *I wish I were smarter like Jonesey.*

Worse, Jenny knew her theatrics had made it all worse, though the whole group could use a good laugh after their ordeals in the past five months. They were already eating up the story. Even though she wished she could stop acting immature, she couldn't help it. She wasn't a suave, sophisticated femme fatale that chewed through men. She was an uncomplicated, silly, naive country girl who'd made a fool of herself. She refused to let her thoughts dwell on Mitch, preferring to think that he'd gotten what he'd wanted. She resolved to leave the whole thing filed away in her life under the heading "one-night stand." However, as the customs agent handed her her passport and frowned at her emotional appearance (she should remember she was in Britain, and it was never good to make a scene), she resolved to leave it all here and now. The past started now, the present moved onward to the future.

Jonesey was honest with her as always, but understanding. "Hey, I get it. I understand. Go home and figure some things out." Jonesey had looked at her and it was clear he debated whether to say anything further.

Jenny urged him on. "I know you don't want to say it, but I need to hear what you have to say." Jenny looked over at Anthony on her other side. She trusted both these guys. They would keep her confidences, and only Jonesey would level with her.

"Fine. If you're ever in this kind of situation again, consider this. Everyone saw the chemistry between you two. Had you picked up with him later today and were say, holding hands, over brunch, even with a big hickey, and the CIA guys having the sheet, no one would have said a word."

Jenny nodded, feeling blame land on her shoulders. "Jonesey, you are so right. I screwed up horribly."

He nodded. "Don't stress more than you need to. Remember, all the fruit from my loins is female, so I get you and understand Stan's position. You can't change what you did, you *can* learn from it. But it's been a long day and long few months. Sleep on it for a couple of days and then formulate your next steps." He handed her his cell phone. "Amy got a new number. Write it down and call her after I've had a couple of days with my girls."

***

Stan fumed. He'd lost control for a second. Now, on his way over Greenland, he was angrier with himself then at Jenny and Mitch. *Hell, liaisons happened all time on assignment,* he thought to himself. In fact, it had been a complicating aspect of all missions that had ever involved both the sexes—or interested parties of the same sex, for that matter. He'd overreacted because he'd tried to personally protect Jenny. He'd known all along that she was too kindhearted and good-natured to handle the job—the psych tests proved that. It was just that they needed her other strengths desperately. He and Homer had argued over this point endlessly, with Homer prevailing. Homer and the profilers had pushed her to the top of the mole list. And it had worked. They had Gooding, and when they had them in their sights, all the CIA and FBI pros had failed and stood helplessly watching him escape. But Jenny and Millie, the greenest, most irregular members of this team, had followed their instincts and did what they needed to in order to capture a killer. They'd known and partially exploited the strength in Jenny's character, but even Homer, who was a whiz at accurately predicting agents' behavior, had not predicted her ability to rebound from the darkest moments of terror like she had—her natural resilience amazed everyone.

Confidentially, the FBI psychologists had advised Stan and Homer that they should exploit the more vulnerable aspects of Jenny's personality. They felt that Gooding would not be able to resist her innocent charm. Gooding had a particular weakness for the right type of female. Stan and Homer agreed on the fact that Jenny was the perfect bait, and did everything they could to make her irresistible to Gooding, all the while promising Jenny's father that they would watch out for her. They had mostly succeeded. Thankfully that moment in the gallery had ended well, but now what? *How would her father accept Jenny's current state?* Stan couldn't help but think of his own daughter. He'd forcibly separated her from that kid in Atlanta, but the resulting rift between he and his daughter had not healed and felt as if it never would. To this day his daughter rarely spoke directly to him, and then only in stilted terms. *At least she still talks to her mother, who will pass on the info,* Stan thought to himself.

He continued to stare out over the North Atlantic. He had been a supervisor in the FBI for years. He knew how to get the most from his people. He went out of his way to keep his people from forming unhealthy relationships. Fraternizing agents were always separated, and even if they married at a later point, they never worked together again. But, perversely, part of him had been glad when the mutual attraction between Mitch and Jenny had started to flare. Heaven knew that Mitch could use some lighthearted goodness in his life, but he'd also watched Mitch convince himself that Jenny was tougher than she appeared. Stan had let that go, as he knew that Mitch wouldn't be as effective a team lead if he had to worry about one of the team being so vulnerable to attack. Meanwhile, he'd secretly spoken to both Jonesey and Reva and told them to keep an eye out for Jenny. Bill was too smart and already knew what was happening and continued to protect Jenny and Mitch in his own way all summer long.

Stan replayed the events of the last months to himself. Jenny had succeeded far beyond all expectations. She openly accepted that the world was a nasty place, but her kind nature had hidden a natural skepticism and suspiciousness well suited to solving crimes.

Jenny had helped them capture Gooding, but her competency had also convinced Mitch that she was just like all the other lady agents he knew. She was so competent and skillful during the investigation that even Stan found himself forgetting her inexperience. Her skills made her even more attractive to Mitch and had further blinded him to her vulnerability. Stan felt his burdens grow lighter for a blessed moment. He was a God-fearing man and prayed every day for the safety of those he cared for. He knew that Jenny was also a deeply spiritual person. Through his anger he'd attempted to calm her and help her past last night. But, he'd sensed that her sorrow came from her actions, which pained her heart, on a deeply spiritual level. She had wounded herself by disobeying the rules of her life and faith, and Stan knew that Mitch could not understand this type of pain right now.

Stan's regret began to creep back in. *I probably made it worse by lashing out at Mitch this morning.* After all, Mitch was just a red-blooded male who'd spent the past six months tormented by a man who had no problem blowing up innocent civilians, and flirting with a beautiful woman who was off-limits in all senses of the phrase. Mitch and Jenny had been through a lot in the last few weeks. *How can I blame Mitch for cracking under the pressure as it kept building and he and Jenny began to care for each other? Maybe I could have calmed Jenny down. She was clearly running away. I think I blew it.* Now, besides enduring the personal pain of being left, how could Mitch ever forgive Jenny after she ran from him, and his boss chastised him for being with her? As his boss, why did he care anyway? He needed to think about it long and hard before Mitch got back to the office. *I missed my chance with Jenny. She's going to have to calm down before I can talk to her again, but Mitch needs a good talking-to, ASAP. And I think I have a handle on it now.*

Chapter Sixty

George sat floating on a small raft in the water, anchored to the Maryann by a thin line. The barrier island off the coast sheltered him from the worst waves coming from the Atlantic. He stuck a waterproof radio in his pocket as he enjoyed the sunshine on the breezy summer day. The water here was gray and cloudy, but watching the seagulls coast in the breeze with their wings fluttering made for pleasant viewing anyway. He thought of the clear blue waters of his home and missed his daughter Arianna. Since he and Maria had married and Arianna had been born, he'd sunk himself deeply into his home life and being a proud papa. Meeting Manuel, Gooding, and Mortimer for the last trip would be his final official duty. Soon his only work assignment was to provide a safe house whenever, if ever, Gooding would need a refuge. But that was after they helped with this last bomb.

He lay with his feet in the water as he thought about Gooding's plan. All he knew was that he and Manuel would be delivering Gooding to the final bomb's destination. That was all they were allowed to know per their contract. Gooding purposely kept his staff from knowing the full details of any operation to protect both them and himself. This way if anyone were caught they could safely and honestly tell the authorities all that they knew and not be implicated. He smiled. He could guess where they were going but didn't know for sure. After all, here he was in South Carolina, waiting for his brother and boss with an unregistered, unmarked black yacht so they could head north in the next forty-eight hours. Relaxing and trying to nap, he thought to himself, *No, Officer, I had no idea that Gooding was having me take him to Washington DC. No idea at all.*

A jarring, vibrating ring woke George up. The radio blared, "Hey, bro, where are you? I am at the dock. Will you get here already? There's been a big change of plans. It's just me and you, bro, and we need to stop at the Charleston warehouse before heading up." Sighing, George shut off the radio and pulled himself back to the yacht. Soon enough he was over the side, anchoring the raft to the deck and hauling anchor to the shore.

***

"Stan, sir, you need to take this." Stan scowled at his secretary Denise as she reached across the desk to hand him a cell phone. "It's Jonesey. He called Albert when you didn't answer the phone." She glanced over to her boss' cell phone, which was switched off. "He wants a secure line."

Stan shook his head, peeved. "Why the hell does he want a secure line? Oh never mind. Give me that." He turned from Denise as he picked up the phone she'd offered. "What?"

"Sorry, boss, but we just touched down and I don't have much time between flights."

"Well, what is it? You are taking Jenny home, right?"

"Oh yes, sir. It's just news from my Secret Service bud. I can't say, but you need to call over there. Something big just went down." Jonesey's voice cut out, then came back. "Sorry boss, gotta go, just call over there. Forget that secure line. I'll call back in a few hours. Just call over there." *Click.*

Stan sighed and rolled his eyes. "Damn those agents of mine." He called out to the outer office, "Denise, do you have Stimpson's number over at the White House?"

"Yes, sir, do you want me to call her?"

"Yes, please. Thank you." Stan breathed deeply, trying to not be sarcastic to his best secretary. He thought about how long a day he was having, but he knew that

Jonesey, of all his agents, wouldn't have interrupted a long day of meetings for nothing.

A few minutes later, Stan was more relaxed than he'd been in days. They had foiled a terrorist plot after all. He sat down and called Homer down from his office. When he arrived, Stan recounted his ten-minute conversation with his Secret Service liaison.

Homer called Denise in to take notes for their report as Stan repeated the information once again. It was a lot to take in as he made the report again for Denise's benefit.

"The Secret Service got a tip from someone in South Carolina that two men on a black yacht were heading north to DC. They found the craft on radar and satellite and monitored it until it arrived in the waters off DC. They were waiting as the craft laid anchor and captured their activities on video. Sure enough, they spotted the surface-to-air missile launcher and went in. A fire-fight ensued and somehow in the melee the craft exploded, destroying much of the evidence. In this confusion, one of the perpetrators was knocked unconscious, but they were able to fish him out of the bay and keep him in custody. The other, I am sad to say, got away somehow. They saw him clearly on video before the explosion, but they don't know what happened to him after. They found no body, but they found some survival gear missing from the wreck. They continue to search the area, but expect him to show up in Jamaica if he gets the chance. Both men were identified as known associates of Gooding and were on Thornton Industries' payroll."

The big bosses were relieved and excited at the news. Stan opened his desk drawer and pulled out two cups and a bottle. "To another job well done," he and Homer toasted. Not only had they captured Gooding, but they'd caught one of his helpers and while they lost the other, they had a positive identification on him. Even better, they had irrefutable proof that the two were preparing to send a bomb into the White House with a laser-guided missile. The Summer Plan was done and finished, unsuccessfully. Finally, no more people would die because of Gooding.

Chapter Sixty-one

Bill sat at his desk, typing as quickly as possible. In a few hours he would have his paperwork finished so he could finally start his much-deserved and twice-earned vacation. He couldn't wait to head out to Georgia tomorrow. He and Mitch had made it back to the States yesterday, while Jonesey had been back for a day already after dropping Jenny off in Salt Lake City. He looked up to see Jonesey standing there looking at him with a worried expression. It wasn't like Jonesey to not say what was on his mind. Curious at his silence and figuring what it was about, Bill asked, "So, did Jenny come back to DC with you and Anthony this trip?"

Jonesey glanced over at Mitch's empty desk nearby before answering. "No, Amy tried to convince her to come with us, even offered to join along to give her support, but she balked." Jonesey paused for a moment. "Bill, I gotta level with you. I don't know what's going on. But, it's a real mess."

Everyone in the office spoke to Mitch and related to him in the same way they always had, but there was a hardness in Mitch and an unforgiving manner in him that had not existed before this summer. In the short time since he and Mitch had arrived from the UK, the whole office had felt the heat of Mitch's anger more than once. Stan hadn't counseled Mitch about his attitude, yet, because he was giving him time to calm down.

Jonesey adjusted his hat. "Jenny called Stan yesterday and said she'd finish her part of the reports in the Salt Lake City or Denver office and fax it in sometime next week."

Bill's face fell. He'd been hoping like the rest of the team that Jenny would finally show up and clear the air between her and Mitch. "Did Stan accept those terms?"

"Yeah," Jonesey answered. "Jenny told Amy that she and Stan had a long talk about things and that she didn't want to come out to DC. Amy thinks Stan is giving Jenny space for now. But I don't know what I'd do in either of their situations, honestly. The only time Amy could get Jenny to come back to DC is if Reva decides to go live with her parents in Tel Aviv. She said she may come out to tell her goodbye, but only then." He paused and ran his fingers through his hair before continuing. "There's other talk that she'll come out at Christmas and stay with Albert and Jessica, but that's all up in the air right now. Stan isn't pressuring her to come out permanently any more, even after she graduates in December."

Bill opened his mouth, but Jonesey interrupted him. "Look, man, I don't know what the problem is. But don't expect her in DC anytime soon." Both men were silent, and Bill once again felt a foreboding deep in his bones. Mitch was mad now, but Bill had never seen him this tied up over a woman. Bill didn't know if he'd cool off and go looking for Jenny, or whether he'd turn bitter and try to forget the whole thing.

Jonesey spoke, and echoed Bill's worries. "I sure hope he cools off and takes himself out to Utah and shakes some sense into her."

"Me too."

Jonesey shook his head. "I know if it were me, I'd fight for my woman, make her tell me to my face, but I don't know what Mitch will do, and frankly I'm worried about them both. I screwed up in London. I should have called Stan back and marched her back upstairs to Mitch. What a damn mess."

Bill sighed in agreement. "Me too. Damn."

Chapter Sixty-two

It was a sunny fall day. Jenny stared at the bright yellow leaves starting to fall from the cottonwood tree shading the lawn of her parents' house. The winter semester had finally started. She could hardly wait to finish her last school term. After seven years she'd finally complete her degree. All the years of working full time, buying her truck, paying for school, and putting as much as possible away for her own house would finally pay off.

This morning was certainly a test, though. Jenny rushed out of her parents' house and flew down the porch steps, narrowly avoiding one of the barn cats yowling for breakfast in her mad dash to her truck. She'd gotten to sleep late that morning after her nightly shift, and even though it was a Tuesday, one of her lighter days in school, she'd overslept. She couldn't miss today's lecture in Professional and Technical Writing. They were finishing their section on writing for the Web, and Jenny had finally figured out how to compose information in HTML so she could do graphic design work after college. Part of her wished she were a more diligent student. If she hadn't already skipped two lectures this term, she could have missed class today so that she would be ready for her doctor's appointment later this afternoon. However, the excitement of making and posting her first real web page helped her be happy regardless of her late start.

She practically leapt onto her bench in her truck, simultaneously turning the key in the ignition as she slammed the door shut and reached for her seat belt. Again, as usual, she cursed GM's safety device as she put her foot more firmly on the brake so the transmission would shift out of park. Spewing gravel in her wake, she roared down her parents' driveway, checked for oncoming traffic, then zoomed out onto the highway. "Five after seven, crap! I *so* did not want to be late today." She should have been on the road by 6:35 a.m. Jenny's outburst intensified the churning in her stomach. Consciously, she forced herself to calm down. There were times she could wish for a less high-strung personality. After about ten minutes, she left the highway and entered the freeway southbound for Ogden.

After reaching her comfortable traveling pace set at an "affordable ticket" and a "let's hope we make it to class on time" speed of eighty-two miles per hour, Jenny began her usual routine of thinking her way through her commute. She made the doctor's appointment for today because she only had two classes on Tuesdays, so she had more time between school and work. As it was, she would have to rush after her 9:00 a.m. class to get to the doctor on time, and she may even miss her 8:00 a.m. class if she couldn't be on time. Jenny began hustling south to get to Weber State in time to park and book it to class on time, by 8:05 at the latest. She'd started out twenty minutes late today. "Oh well, I can pay a dollar per hour and park in the visitor's parking today to save the long walk from student parking. Good thing I work full time and have plenty of money," she joked to herself. Jenny's experiences as an adult (even her summertime work) didn't curb her need to talk to herself. Her job with its night-shift work schedule intensified this need. Not many people were awake at one in the morning. It was easier to talk to herself when no one else was around, especially during long, quiet, dark, night drives.

Thinking about work opened the floodgates in her mind, and Jenny began to mutter to herself about her real problem. "Yeah, the other good reason I work full time is health insurance, for things like strep throat and female exams, and prenatal care. Not that I *need* that yet, I hope." Jenny swallowed hard and forced her innards to calm once again.

It had been two months since what she termed "the incident." Two months since she had ran out of the UK and back to own usual boring life. She'd left Mitch and the UK and her summer-long liaison as an FBI agent behind. She prayed that her life now could stay a little more normal and to schedule, but she was worried. Jonesey had been right; she could learn from her mistakes, but Jenny was fairly sure there was a permanent consequence to having sex with Mitch.

Jenny had missed two periods and found for the first time in her life that she really needed a doctor's appointment. She could picture her maternal grandmother saying "monthly courses" in a prim, Victorian fashion while speaking to one of her aunts who thought she was pregnant. That memory came from a childhood of sunshine on a day like today, but today Jenny was sure, based on gut reaction, instinct, and her own experience with her own bad luck, that she was indeed pregnant with Mitchell Harper's child.

"Shit, shit, shit..." She found that when she talked to herself about this particular issue, the litany of "shits" helped her immensely. Almost like a pressure valve, these little expletives helped to remove excess heat from her brain and allowed her to concentrate on real thoughts and plans. Reva's relaxation techniques couldn't begin to calm this stress. She couldn't even feel very guilty over that night. It had been wonderful mostly, and she knew damn well that pregnancy was a natural result of sex. She just had been too caught up in the moment to care very much at the time. She cared now.

This morning would reveal the truth. Although Jenny had experienced no "morning" sickness, she was queasy all night. Nausea started for her during her second work break, about 11:00 p.m., until she could fall asleep at anywhere between 1:30 a.m. and 4:00 a.m. Her normally iron stomach had disappeared. She also felt sleepy all the time. Although her frantic school and work schedule made very little room for sleep, Jenny could now sleep anytime, anywhere, a real variance from her typical patterns. Usually, no matter how little sleep she'd gotten that day, she was wired and frisky at 4:00 p.m. through 8:00 p.m. and again for a few hours at midnight, but no longer.

Her breasts felt funny too, not that she could really explain that. She'd been called too irresponsible about her body and her sexual health for too long by some good-meaning ladies at work. Also, to meet the requirements of her faith and abstain from sexual thoughts, she'd ignored all sexual parts of herself. She ignored lustful thoughts and pretended that "womanly" parts of her body simply didn't exist when her longings got too bad. That is, she had ignored her sexual side until she'd met Mitch. Before, she consciously focused on not being a sexual creature. *That's a successful strategy, right. Mitch blew that all to hell.* Mitch's looks, smell, sweetness, smartness, even his bossiness, had gotten to her on every level, including the physical.

Now, after nine weeks, she could almost squelch what she couldn't help but think of as "dirty" and "nasty" thoughts about Mitch when she tried very hard. However, Mitch had become so ingrained in her thought processes that she was repressing many other thoughts that just might remind her of Mitch. Suppressing her thoughts suppressed her talking, and now her mother was starting to question her abnormal behavior—Jenny was never this quiet. Her parents knew of course that she'd been masquerading as a big, bad FBI agent all summer, but she didn't know how she'd explain that their "perfect," responsible daughter had most likely gotten herself pregnant. These were just more of those many thoughts she'd been ignoring.

Her life was now even worse, because she knew what she was missing in the sex department. Her tingling breasts and the hormone changes she experienced convinced her that she needed to change things. *Sex with the right person is dynamite. I really screwed up.* It was time to face reality. She couldn't ignore her body any longer. It wanted Mitch, sex, and sleep, but she could no longer tell what need was greater or more urgent. Her heart, on the other hand, was turned off. She refused to think about the love she'd grasped, then dropped.

Jenny had lost count of the number of times that she'd awoke with those newly experienced sexual tremors running through her body just like that morning in July. She was now firmly convinced that that was why a good Christian should have no sex before marriage and commitment. "Once experienced, how do you *not* do something that fantastic?" Jenny queried out loud. She could remember friends as teenagers who'd slept around, then tried to live better lives when they found they really believed in Christ or God or a higher power and tried to live their lives accordingly. All those who'd "done it" constantly complained about how hard it was to live without "doing it."

Then, just last week, Amy Jones had called and urged her (again) to call Mitch. Jenny wondered if she'd ever have the strength to do so, especially if she was pregnant.

Jenny remembered her junior year of high school. Her best girlfriend had admitted that she'd fallen off the wagon, so to speak, when she'd met her husband in college after having become sexually active at sixteen with her first boyfriend and trying to fix the problem at seventeen. She'd told Jenny frankly in one of their deep heart-to-heart conversations about how hard it was to not have sex when you didn't have your virginity or ignorance to protect yourself anymore. Jenny believed her, and now after experiencing sex for herself knew her best friend had been right. She *had* been better able to live a clean life because she hadn't known what she was missing—ignorance *was* bliss.

Luckily, the cold chills she experienced thinking that she was probably pregnant and the guilt she felt over her incorrect behavior usually quelled the warm, gushy, physical feelings. In the cold light of day, she had facts to face and plans to make. Hopefully, lucidity and rational thoughts and behaviors would return to her life.

Full of resolve, she said aloud, "It's better to think about the pregnancy, as the cold chills quell the juices like nothing else." Jenny began going over her plan again, to pass the rest of her drive. Her plan calmed her because it gave her a road map on how to handle "the rest of her life."

As plans go, hers was simple, practical, and doable for an overworked student: take the money and bonuses from the "Gooding exploits" and pay off her truck, then use part of the remainder as a down payment on that house she'd had her eye on. Health insurance was covered by work, and as a single mother she could get a more flexible work schedule if things got too rough. As for school, she would, in fact, graduate this December, thanks to the credits she'd earned for school in Britain. Come next March, she would still have enough money in her savings account to work less hours and swap babysitting with her cousin Megan for room and board for a few months until the baby was older. Jenny experienced another chill and had to add mentally, "If I'm actually pregnant." She was apparently still in denial.

Practicality took over as she got her thoughts back in-line. Besides, she was already working swing shift and made a good hourly wage, so she could watch the baby during the day while Megan stayed with him or her at night. Also, with her sister and brother living in the Ogden area, Jenny knew she could trade babysitting with them. After all, she was already the weekend babysitter for most of the Johnson grandkids in three counties in Northern Utah.

Jenny refused to think about the other big, spiritual truth niggling in the back of her mind. She knew that no matter how much she tried and planned or plotted, she needed to cleanse herself. She had sinned, grievously, and when she thought about the damage she had done to her spiritual self, the ache in her heart hurt as bad as missing Mitch. In fact, when Jenny thought about it, the hurts were equally bad. She was convinced that she had been feeling hell on earth. No Mitch; no God, either. She had distanced herself from God and the comfort that only He could give her. Damned indeed, she felt the true definition of that type of separation. It made it triply harder to fix her life, as for the first time, she was out of her own choice, on her own. Holy thoughts, Christian thoughts, brought her to the biggest thing she needed to do. She had been wrong to run from Mitch. She needed to call him and tell him the truth of things. Would she ever find a way? *Yeah, going to the doctor could provide the perfect excuse to call him,* she thought.

Jenny pictured the conversation in her head. "Hey, Mitch, it's Jenny. I was wrong. I think I love you and also, I'm pregnant. It's yours, due in March." Those thoughts filled her with such dread she instantly began to close them off, or else she'd drive off the road. Pulling herself back to reality, she banished all thoughts of Mitch from her head. The last one that left her brain lingered. "Funny thing is, in May I thought he was a gift from God, just for me."

Finally, mostly awake and able to almost enjoy the sunny morning after tuning out the reality of her situation, adrenaline pumping through her body and making her wide awake (all the better to go work and to school), Jenny turned on the radio as she entered Weber County and passed Smith & Edwards. A bit of rock-n-roll and smart-aleck comments were called for instead of worry and anxiety. She found her favorite station's morning show. However, instead of hearing "Mick and Allen on Rock 99," she heard Peter Jennings talking. He was saying something about New York City and the Twin Towers at the World Trade Center. *What's happening?*

Jenny had heard only a little bit about some airplanes this morning as she got ready for school, thanks to her mother's habit of watching CNN Headline News each morning, but hadn't had time to worry about it or really listen in her rush to get to school. Now, she listened as ABC News reported on the smoking buildings and explained about the jets colliding with the buildings at the World Trade Center. The report was continuing in the manner of all breaking news stories, with speculation and expert commentary. Jenny's daily routine changed drastically as she heard and experienced as all the Americans who listened with her and watched and shared that morning, the shock in Peter Jennings' voice as the first tower fell. By then, she was crossing into Ogden proper and continued to listen to the escalating reports in her own deepening state of shock and unreality.

Calmly driving, but churning inside, she pulled into the school's visitor parking lot while grabbing her ticket in an automatic fashion. Jenny then hustled into her English class, determined to find out more about what was happening.

Few students were outside the buildings or loitering today. Most were in the student center and in various classrooms, watching the news. The important lecture in her class was canceled that day, as the students and professor sat as if in a stupor, watching the TV monitor.

Jenny sat down in her customary spot in the back of the classroom and listened with growing horror as one of her "more mature" classmates rushed in to notify the teacher that he'd been called to duty at the air base where he was stationed. Hill Air Force base, just south of Ogden, was under lockdown, and all necessary personnel were being recalled. The guy in class was in the class to beef up for his computer work writing SGML code. He left as quickly as he'd come, having received the call on his cell phone from the commander. Their professor followed him out on her way to the main office to determine if Weber State was taking any precautions. She came back a few minutes later, announcing that school was commencing as always until they heard more, and sat down to watch the TV with her students.

The class sat together for the rest of the hour and listened as the news reported that all commercial and private planes were being grounded and that some commercial flights were still missing. *How can you lose a 747?* wondered Jenny.

Air Force jets like F-16s were being called into service patrolling US skies. A feeling of horror descended on the campus. Through tears, Jenny watched the replaying news clips of the plane hitting the Twin Tower and its subsequent demise. Then the second tower fell as she watched it on the TV.

The surreal day continued. During her second and last class of the day, they continued to watch the news. Jenny thought of the last time she'd watched history at school. She'd been in grade school as NASA's Space Shuttle Challenger blew up in the sky with that nice teacher lady on board. She felt the same lack of reality as she drove across the street to the McKay Dee hospital professional building for her appointment with her new ob-gyn. Her stupor continued and deepened as she sat in the office after the examination, waiting for the preliminary results from her pregnancy test. The TVs in the waiting room were tuned to the news like the TVs at school.

Scenes from just a few months earlier ran through her head. She'd spent the early part of this year and all summer fighting to capture a terrorist who was intent on bringing the US to its knees for his own wild purposes, only to find that somebody else's plans came through and accomplished worse acts than she'd imagined and had been working to prevent. Gooding's threat had been real. They'd found a huge amount of explosives and missiles on Gooding's freighter, enough to bankrupt a small country, in Stan's estimation. Jenny couldn't even imagine the compound where Gooding was imprisoned while the UK and US decided who would be in charge of the trial. These Twin Towers guys didn't even use bombs.

"Damn," Jenny said quietly as she thought of Mitch, Bill, Jonesey, and the rest. Worry engulfed her. She knew exactly what they'd be doing and knew that they would be in greater danger than ever. It was their job, they were the FBI. "Please, dear God, keep them safe," she prayed quietly, knowing that of all prayers uttered right then, she was probably the most unworthy asker. "Please protect them, even though I, as such a sinner, ask." The tears came to her eyes but wouldn't fall, not yet. She resolved to call Amy as soon as she was out of the office. Jenny shook her head, thinking a mundane thought on this awful day. *I hope my cell phone is charged, since I left it in the truck last night.*

The doctor's office was quieter than could be expected. Many patients had canceled their appointments and, from where she sat, Jenny could hear the office personnel speaking excitedly but quietly in the back behind the receptionist's counter. She watched two gals in scrubs hurriedly leave the office on their way home to their families, calling on their cell phones as they went. In fact, Jenny and the person who had an appointment directly after her were the only patients that showed up that morning. The afternoon appointments had already been canceled.

Worried about the fact that she felt like crying, but couldn't, Jenny wondered about her state of mind. *Shouldn't I be more upset? How can I be calm at a time like this? Is this the start of World War three, or the end of the world? Why am I not panicking? I must be in shock.*

Where are Mitch and Bill? Isn't this just what they were trying to prevent? I hope everyone is okay. That thought was followed by something much deeper, uglier, and absolutely terrifying for Jenny. "If it is the Second Coming, I am dead, burned to a crisp in my sins." That thought was stopped almost as soon as it entered her mind. This was not the end of the world, but something big happening. Jenny said a quick prayer of thanks for that small comfort from above. Even in her weakened spiritual state, God was still watching out for her. *I have to remember that we reach out to Him. He's waiting for us to reach.* But she still had such a long way to go spiritually to heal herself and to find happiness again.

A spasm hit Jenny at that moment—she felt light-headed and nearly passed out for a minute. Her thoughts went to her belly and she knew, absolutely, that she was pregnant. Wishing she could crawl into a hole and die, or that she could make herself dig her set of scriptures out of her bag and read them, she began to cry in earnest, but silently, as she lowered her head between her knees. Her last coherent thought reverberated in her head, *welcome to the sorrows of sin.* As she prayed, she consciously made herself relax and breathe more calmly.

Thankfully, the doctor and staff were sufficiently rattled and distracted to not remark on Jenny's upset state. It helped that they were upset themselves. Someone had changed the waiting room televisions to CNN, and she could hear the reports from her examination room. After a few minutes of holding her middle, Jenny felt a little better. The doctor came out to where she sat, all business, brisk and efficient. He asked her to come back to his office. There he gave her the report. Everything had gone okay with the exam itself. This surprised Jenny for a minute, especially considering Jenny hated "female" exams and had only had one once before. She was also grateful that

Jonesey's wife Amy had friends in Ogden and was able to recommend a good doctor.

When the doctor confirmed her pregnancy and gave her her projected due date of March 31, Jenny was more than ready to go home. Dr. Murphy was a sympathetic soul. He knew her dad's family and had understood her unease at having him know her status and the reason for her visit. He had also been an LDS bishop and strongly urged Jenny to talk to her own bishop for a big dose of spiritual advisement. He handed her some tissues and gave her a small smile. "You know that the Lord only lets us experience what we can handle." He held her hand for a moment, then followed her to the front desk to pay her copay as he finished his preparations to finish his last appointment and close the office.

Jenny knew she was in shock like everyone else over the state of the United States in the face of this attack, but she felt that it would be best to get on with her day as best she could. Maybe she should go to work now, so that she could go home early and maybe get some rest that night. "Oh yeah, and meditate on the fact that I'm pregnant with Mitch Harper's child, who I haven't spoken to for months." Sarcasm, it seemed, was her only ally at this moment. "Maybe I should call the office and leave him a message." Her voice changed pitch into a sing-song, sickly kind of tone as she repeated the phrases she'd been thinking about for weeks and added a little twist in honor of today's events. "Hey, Mitchell, it's Jenny. You know that night a few months ago, well, I'm well and truly pregnant and I love you anyway. Just thought you needed to know. Hope you have fun finding the hijackers. Bye-bye."

When she got to her truck, she saw two missed calls on her cell phone, grabbed it, and dialed her voice mail service. She listened as she headed to her work across Ogden city to find the day shift boss who was in charge of her when she worked early. Her mother's voice on the message told her that her boss had called home telling her not to report to work that night. The next message, also from her mom, explained that the service center was closed and locked down; all employees had been sent home. Apparently, all government installations were on high alert after the attack on the Pentagon.

Jenny finished listening to the second message as she was driving past the IRS' service center. Eerily she looked closely at it as she drove past. The gates were closed and there were no cars in the parking lot. In the four years she'd worked there, Jenny had never seen the parking lot empty, even at 3:00 a.m. But no cars were there, and the only movement that could be seen in the compound was the high number of security guards and vehicles patrolling the parking lots and exterior of the buildings. She had never seen so much security at her job, ever.

The sense of unreality settled deeper on Jenny as she continued past work and out onto the freeway. *I might as well go home. Both work and school are shot today.* The news station on her radio declared that all non-military government installations were locked down, and the military ones elevated to active duty. The United States was in a state of war, she was pregnant, and the one she'd loved was out there. She had screwed up her life royally, and may not have time to fix it. A new, horrible fear overtook her. What about her baby? He or she was now her responsibility to protect and care for. "*Shit.*"

The news people and analysts figured that someone had attacked the United States in a terrorist attack like the attack when terrorists had bombed the Twin Towers nearly ten years before—this was just on a much larger scale. Jenny listened to the news all the way home and finally heard about the plane crash in Pennsylvania and the plane that hit the Pentagon. Eventually, listening to the news programs overwhelmed her, so she turned the radio off and continued her drive in silence.

At home she stepped out of her truck, bent over and threw up, immediately, right there in the gravel driveway. *Thankfully, I haven't eaten much today. Just another thing I'll have to get better at, eating properly.* She finished as the heaving stopped. She kicked some dirt and gravel over the mess and headed inside to get a drink of water to rinse her mouth.

Just as she cleared the gravel at the edge of the cement sidewalk, she looked up and saw that her mother, always a patriotic soul who flew their US flag often from two hooks on the porch, had hung the flag today. On the way home, Jenny had noticed a lot of businesses and private homes displaying the flag, and had been touched by the ones who hung it at half-staff. It was still a bright, sunny day. No clouds in the sky. The last of her mom's annuals were blooming in the flowerbed below the porch, and the black "Halloween" cat that lived in the barn was resting in the shadow under the flag. The bright colors and contrasting values struck Jenny as suddenly beautiful. She felt the warmth that signaled inspiration coming to her wash through her. The thought came into her mind that God was watching over her and the United States, sheltering her, just as the flag sheltered the cat from the intense afternoon sun. All of a sudden she felt better.

Once inside the house, she hugged her mom in the kitchen, petted the indoor cats, and went upstairs to call Amy and brush her teeth, while she tried to get the shaking and shivering shock reaction under control. Her mom had looked at her funny, clearly having noticed Jenny's pale face and teary eyes, but seemed to accept the tears as a natural reaction to the news today. "Damn, piss, crap, and *shit!*" She was so having an awful day.

Chapter Sixty-three

Jenny sat in the kitchen, trying to think of something to cook. In the two days since September 11, she'd had a hard time doing much of anything. Yesterday they'd reopened the Ogden IRS service center after President Bush urged US workers to go back to work to show that acts of terror didn't terrorize them. He placed special emphasis on his request to all federal employees—requesting that they lead the way back to normalcy in this new age of terror. Jenny hadn't gone to work yesterday, not because she was overwrought about the crashes, but because they'd offered liberal leave—so she hadn't had to work and was able to crash. As a student, she'd spent the full day yesterday catching up on her schoolwork—mostly weaving to finish her latest art project. The repetitive clacking of the loom and the shuttle sliding back and forth soothed Jenny and she found great satisfaction in finishing next week's project early. Today, having finished all her homework, she was planning on working tonight. She was pregnant—that fact wasn't going away. Since she'd avoided admitting the truth for weeks now, the previously suppressed thoughts overwhelmed her. She was certainly living in a new world and she needed to adjust, fast.

Just then the phone rang. Thankfully, her mother hadn't been home to get this phone call. Stan and Homer had met with her parents as part of her "pre-mole" testing in April, and her parents and her temporary bosses had really hit it off. Mom would have recognized Stan's East Coast voice immediately. But she would have wondered about Jenny's reaction today. Jenny had called Amy and was able to talk to both her and Jonesey. She'd gone so far as to leave messages for Millie and Reva, but told Jonesey to have Stan call her if he needed her. She didn't want to distract anybody right now that they were busy.

Jenny was also glad her mom hadn't overheard this particular conversation or the lecture that she was treated to either. Stan's request and the resulting conversation reduced Jenny to tears. Stan had called to activate her as an FBI support agent for a few weeks. Not field work, as he knew that she couldn't handle that much stress, but for her experience to back up the office. All the team's active personnel were busy to the maximum level, and Jenny was one of their back-up contacts. Stan's tone had gone from disappointed to shocked, to disapproving and back to disappointed, as she'd declined his offer and stated the reasons for her denial. She'd really wanted to help, but couldn't uproot her life now that she needed her entire support group around.

Stan, of course, pressed for the real reason, and said she'd better have a "damn better excuse than that" when she'd started to put him off because of school. When she'd then told him that she was pregnant with Mitch's baby, Stan exploded. He had been really angry at both of them after the incident in July and had lectured both her and Mitch. He'd forgiven Mitch, because of his contriteness in the face of Jenny's refusal to reconcile, but was still angry with Jenny for not patching things up or at least talking to Mitch.

Jenny knew Stan cared for his team like they were his kids and had adopted her into his personal bunch of agents. He told her about how Mitch, even after spending six weeks in Montana with his grandfather once he got home, was still withdrawn, and although his work was acceptable, his personal life was in shambles. "Thanks to you, missy," Stan had told her. "Call him." Eventually Stan's voice had changed from an order to pleading. "Would you please call him? Just call him. Just try to find out if you two can work something, anything out."

Jenny's voice failed her, and she held the phone in silence, trying to speak up. Stan quietly continued. "You two were happy together. Are you really going to abandon him? He has a right to know what really happened, especially now with the baby!"

Jenny sobbed, "I can't. I just can't... Not now."

Stan sighed. "Well, I've done my best, but I have to get more bodies in the office. I'll let you off the hook for now, but if you ever change your mind, there's a place in DC, and you know Jessica would be more than willing to look after your little one. I won't lay a guilt trip on you any more than this: You ought to at least tell him about the baby, but you're the one who has to live with the consequences. You are *not* the only one you're affecting with this decision. Also, I repeat my offer. You will have a safe place to work out here if you will just come to DC. We can really use your help."

Jenny nodded, then realized Stan couldn't see her. "I will consider it. Okay?" She wished him and the team luck and told him how she would continue praying for them. Stan wished her well and disconnected.

Amy Jones had called Jenny back yesterday and Jenny, needing someone to lean on, had told her the whole situation. Now only her bishop, her cousin Megan, Amy, and Stan knew about her pregnancy. Telling each person in turn had helped her deal with the ramifications of her situation and the different aspects of what she'd have to deal with. Everyone had told her to talk to Mitch, her bishop for honesty's sake and the sake of her soul, while Megan, Amy, and Stan worried about Mitch's feelings and a final closure to the situation for both of them. Her romantic friends, they just knew Mitch was the one for her and wanted her to work something out with him.

Three phone conversations—one to Megan and two to Amy—and three guilt trips later, and Jenny felt better, even though Amy had told her that marrying an agent wasn't as bad as she feared. "Besides, it's Mitch," she'd said. Jenny put the idea of confronting Mitch or working for Stan out of her mind. In the meantime, while she pondered, she could go forward with her original plans. She had paid off her truck today after a trip to the bank. She had an appointment with her Realtor® next week to make an offer on the house she wanted in Ogden. If the offer went through, she could move next week, and Megan had agreed to be her live-in babysitter in exchange for rent, so the baby thing would be okay where she wouldn't be living alone.

Jenny refused to think about telling Mitch. She'd made her decision the night before and refused to even imagine living with him. She was the one who'd lost control in July. She was the one who'd run away. Mitch had yet to contact her. For all that Stan and Amy talked about him moping around, he hadn't called her himself. Montana wasn't that far. *Heck I could've made the trip and back over a weekend. You knew he was coming out here. He may not have come down, but you didn't go up either.*

Jenny's reasons for *not* contacting Mitch solidified. She wasn't going to trap Mitch into anything. She'd gotten pregnant; she'd deal with the situation herself. At twenty-five years old, she was no green teenager. She had a good job and would soon have her degree and her own house. Her family and friends were close and they'd help her out.

Shrugging, Jenny mentally shook off the doubtful thoughts that skulked around in the back of her mind. She refused to think about the lectures she'd received, especially the conversation with Megan. Snippets of Megan's statements echoed in her head. "How do you expect me to keep seeing Bill when he's out here, when you're in this predicament? Bill's gonna notice your belly soon enough. Do you honestly expect me to keep this pregnancy secret from the daddy? Are you insane?" Eventually Megan, like the others, had capitulated to Jenny's will, but it wasn't sitting well. Jenny refused to reconsider her choice. Mitch would have to call her. It was his job to let her know he cared. If he never did, then that was fine, she told herself. She was determined to be on her own. She ignored Megan's voice saying, "Dang, stubborn Johnson. Jenny, you are so bullheaded!"

Chapter Sixty-four

It was an overcast and cold November day. Jenny's new house was an old one in the federal, four-square style. Tall, pretty in brown-red brick, the two-story house was full of grace and charm. The house sat in the middle of a tree-lined block in an older section of Ogden city on the gentle slope that used to be foothills leading to the mountains nearby and faced the open valley to the Great Salt Lake. Normally, late afternoon sunshine from the west would overflow the front room, but a fall storm was brewing. Megan parked her car on the curb and ran through the cool breeze to the porch.

Megan entered the house, calling for Jenny. "Hey, woman! How are you? What did you need?" Her cheeks were pink from the cold and the combined excitement of an imminent party and a long weekend off from school. Megan nudged the door shut behind her with her hip and shrugged off her winter parka as she headed into the kitchen. She asked as she went, "Do you need help taking the salad and relish tray out to Grandma's?" She continued her merry way through Jenny's new home. "Ooh, I like the violet you chose for the front room," she said, headed up the weakly sunny stairwell when she heard Jenny's muffled response.

"Wow, Jenny, it's so bright up here, what did you do?" Megan remarked as she reached the second-floor landing. Jenny stepped out of the bathroom, still toweling her hair dry.

"I painted the walls white and yanked down those hideous yellow velour curtains in the stairwell. Do you like the new sheers I hung?"

Megan turned and looked behind herself appreciatively. "You know I adore your taste. Do I get to pick my own bedroom?"

Jenny smiled at her cousin's enthusiasm. Megan planned to move in after Jenny's graduation, during their Christmas break. "After I pick the nursery." Megan smiled some more as she followed Jenny into her new bedroom. Of all Jenny's family, so far only her cousin Megan, and her eldest brother Brett, knew about the pregnancy.

Jenny thought about the family dinner planned for today. At least Brett knew about the pregnancy; he'd caught her packing prenatal vitamins when he'd helped move her stuff out of Mom and Dad's a few weeks ago. At his questioning look, she'd told him, "Not now. I'll explain on the way down to Ogden." Through the hour-long ride, Jenny confided the truth of her situation to her oldest and closest sibling. Brett had not judged her, had accepted her decision, and had done what he could to support her, although he, too, disagreed with her decision not to tell Mitch.

"Are you planning to tell them today?" Megan asked, pulling Jenny into the present.

"Actually, I was, but I can't find anything to wear. I had to go buy some maternity jeans, 'cause my tummy's too big for my 501s, but I can't find a shirt that fits both my tummy and these." Jenny emphasized her tender breasts.

"How many cup sizes have you grown, then?"

"Technically, only one and a half, but I went from a barely there B to a full D. I can't wait until I start breastfeeding to see how monstrous they're gonna be." They laughed. Jenny, being the older of the cousins, had always been the one to help Megan with the "girly" stuff she hadn't wanted to share with her mom. She thought about all those times they'd gone underwear shopping together and had teased about how nasty two single girls' underwear should be, especially if they were going to stay pure and chaste.

After an exhausting search through still packed boxes and the closet, Megan found one of Jenny's oversized, heavyweight, manly sweaters. "Good thing you hate clingy knits, this should do the trick." Megan handed the sweater to Jenny.

"Too bad this thing is so hot. I am going to cook today, even with the cold snap," Jenny answered, grasping the bundle.

"Is the pregnancy still causing you to overheat?"

"Yup, in every sense of the word." Jenny smiled. She was so glad to have Megan around. They may be cousins and a couple years apart in age, but they were best friends.

"Jenny, are you saying you still feel like a sex monster?" Jenny just smiled bigger and nodded. "Hormones, you know."

Megan shot back a matching grin. "Makes me wish Bill came out here more often myself."

Jenny chuckled slightly. "What a wicked pair we make."

"Yup." Both girls laughed at their own joking, especially since they were just joking. Both were determined to remain sexually abstinent until they got married. This way of life had intrigued Mitch last summer, and was currently driving Bill crazy and Jenny too, a lot of the time.

Megan moved behind Jenny to sit on the edge of the bed. "So why did you call me over here? You didn't really need wardrobe help, did you?" Megan began plaiting Jenny's hair for a braid.

"I need to tell Mitch." Jenny spoke and stiffened her spine, waiting for the "I told you so" as she remembered her promise to Albert almost two months before.

A week after Stan had called, Albert had called her on a Sunday afternoon, "just to talk." His office was as busy as ever, but now things had settled down after September 11, and he'd taken the time to call her. They had a good conversation and she'd had a good cry. He thanked her for taking his mind off "September 11" stuff for a while. Then he, too, urged her to tell Mitch. Unlike Stan, Albert had had a little time to observe Mitch in the office and he elaborated on the behavior he'd seen, but Jessica had told him that her "FBI boys" had been complaining about Mitch's orneriness.

Jenny had finally considered the possibility of telling Mitch. Al worried about her waiting until it was too late, and forced her to commit to telling him by Christmas, if not sooner.

Megan paused and held the hair in her hands. Jenny tentatively continued her speech, having made it that far without being yelled at. "I've been thinking and thinking about what you said last time we discussed it after you talked to Bill at Halloween. I even dreamed about Mitch last night. Now that things have quieted down a little after September 11, I need to tell him."

"So, are you going to call him now, today, or when?"

"Well, I want to after dinner, but I need to tell Mom and Dad first."

Megan was silent for a moment, then asked, "Do you think telling them at the family party is wise? I mean all we usually do at the Johnson family parties, especially Thanksgiving after the meal, is argue about religion and politics. The last thing I want to hear about today is a religious discussion about sex, and you know as well as I do how the crew will pounce on your news. I can just hear Angela being snide and spouting, 'little Molly Mormon Jenny went out and got herself knocked up.'"

Jenny grimaced at Megan's immensely accurate imitation of their older cousin. "I know, but with Emily and Steve moving back in with Mom and Dad, I think I have a better chance catching my parents alone at Grandma's. Plus, I don't have to worry about the kids overhearing and shouting it through the house, because they'll be too busy riding Grandpa's horses and having a killer time chasing each other through the barn to worry about what the 'adults' are discussing."

Megan seemed thoughtful for a moment. "Can you believe we're now 'adults' at dinner? No more kiddie table for us."

"Nope. Just a second, I need to shift places," Jenny answered as she rearranged herself and settled back down. Megan held the partially braided hair up as she waited. "It feels like only last summer, we were snaking in and out of the house at dinner time, running like, as Grandma Jean would say, 'wild Indians,' through the place, and now we actually have dinner assignments and food to bring."

Megan tsked. "Makes you feel almost responsible, doesn't it?"

Jenny looked down to the bulge of her belly and her thick waist. "Yeah, sure."

"You know, I need you to know that I told Bill you're pregnant."

At that news Jenny's head jerked up, ruining the mostly complete braid. She'd been afraid that Megan or Amy Jones would tell Bill. Bill finding out started most of her worst nightmare scenarios. She knew that Megan and Bill had really hit it off and spoke regularly and dated when he was out here with the Denver Bunch. She should have known this would happen, but couldn't hold back the flow of words. "What! Why did you do that?"

Megan held Jenny's shoulders down and picked up the loose ends to start the braid again. "Calm down. I had to tell him. When we talked during his break, he started pestering me. He wouldn't let up about you. He's really concerned about Mitch. You know that Bill works on me because he can't work on you, since you won't talk to him. We are talking about FBI agents here. They have their ways of getting folks to talk, you know."

Megan tugged on Jenny's hair. "Now before I get into it, you need to be appreciative of what I learned, and be glad that I handled things so well. All he got out of me is that you're pregnant, and were planning on telling Mitch ASAP. Bill, being the big softie he is around me, needed to unload. He admitted he felt better knowing that I'd pass his worry on to you. He thinks that *you* should be the one to babysit Mitch as he says that you're cause of Mitch's snits."

"What do you mean?" Jenny asked, trying to maintain her composure and unable to keep from being morbidly curious about Mitch's behavior, but unwilling to admit her interest.

"Well, Bill asked me to tell you, to get to you, to let you know about Mitch, because he's too chicken to call you at your mom's—he didn't know that you'd moved out already. Anyway, he and Mitch have been busy, as we all know, with their terrorist task force, but before September 11, ever since Mitch came back from his Montana vacation this summer, he's been moody and unresponsive to everyone, including Bill."

"Like usual?" Jenny quipped sarcastically.

Megan yanked her hair again. "Yes, like a certain pregnant cousin of mine, positively hard to live with."

Jenny slapped Megan's hand for the snide remark. "Thanks."

"So, to paraphrase Bill: Since the report on this summer's activities was finished in the end of August, Mitch's attitude has gone downhill. Reportedly, he's been as ornery and gruff as a grizzly bear with a sore paw, and less talkative than usual. Stan even called him in for a heart to heart, but that made things worse, as Stan let him know that *he* knew that you were okay as he and Jonesey had talked to you. Mitch didn't take that news well, and stomped out of the office early. Bill said that he thinks Mitch was pissed that you'd speak to them and not him.

Not that Mitch actually opened up and admitted that. Anyway, that next day, the towers fell, and he and Bill got distracted by the terrorists."

"So why didn't Bill call Jonesey, or Amy or you, right then to get me? Why weeks later?" Jenny asked, her irritation rising.

"Well, to hear him tell it, he was trying to give Mitch time to get over you."

"Oh." Jenny's response sounded hurt and small, even to herself.

"Hey, can you blame the guy? You said yourself you ran out on him, severing all ties."

Really upset now, Jenny responded loudly, and a touch out of control. "I know, but it was a mistake. I didn't know how to fix it, and I still don't." They were having the same argument that they'd had all summer and fall. The same argument Jenny had had with Jonesey on the very first day. Megan and Jenny both sighed, then laughed at their sighing in unison.

Megan finally finished the braid with a flourish. "You know there are no hard feelings on Bill's end. He saw it coming, the fireworks between you two, I mean, and he's forgiven your part in things after he understood your take on the situation, after we talked about it a bit, but he also saw Mitch's part. He told me about how bad you pissed Mitch off. Mitch was red-hot angry at first. Bill said Mitch was even angrier than Stan that morning after he came to. Bill has been trying to help Mitch rejoin the living ever since. Although he said that he'd actually been trying to get Mitch to act as a civilized human being and not a caveman." Megan let the long, thick braid fall, and Jenny leaned forward to rest her face on her hands.

"Hey that reminds me of that old song, something about 'Johnny get angry, Johnny get mad.' Maybe you'd be happier with Mitch, the caveman. Or maybe you need the balls to take some action. That's it, you take the song yourself. That's what you need, a lecture!" They laughed, then were serious again.

Megan continued conversationally, "Bill wanted to know if you care for Mitch or not, because he thinks Mitch's not over you, and he was scared that maybe Mitch can't get over you without you speaking to him. Bill told me that without talking to you or seeing you again, he's concerned Mitch can't get closure. And besides, the guy knew you had feelings for Mitch and so part of his concern is for you. I think his ulterior motive was to let you know that if you care for Mitch, you need to reach out to him. He's turning out to be closet romantic. I think he wants to see you two get together, patch it up."

Finally admitting the truth in what Megan said and what she'd been trying to convince herself all along, Jenny acquiesced. "Okay. I'll call Mitch tonight after the party."

Chapter Sixty-five

Later that same night, after a satisfying Thanksgiving meal with all the trimmings (at least the ones Jenny could get down anyway), a very tired Jenny and Megan went back to Jenny's house.

"Your mom took things rather well, I thought," remarked Megan as Jenny shivered and focused her shaking fingers on unlocking the kitchen door.

"Yeah, well, she knew something was up when I wouldn't talk to her about England. Even after years of living with Dad's talking about military secrecy, she knew something wasn't right about my behavior."

"Yeah, well, at least she didn't scream 'Oh my God!' and fall to the floor."

Jenny gave Megan a nasty look and replied, "As if saying 'I see,' and pursing her lips in a disapproving way as she went for a long car ride with Dad was comforting."

"I am sorry for you, Miss Jenny," Megan said sarcastically and kept laughing. Pausing for a breath, she continued, "I just sat at dinner waiting for you to announce it like Molly Ringwald did in *For Keeps*. 'Pass the potatoes, I'm pregnant.' You missed a fantastic opportunity, you know."

Jenny shot her an ugly glare. "Oh, shut up. Leave me be."

Megan brushed past Jenny and settled herself in the rocking chair in the living room. "I'll leave after you've called him," she said smugly.

"Fine, but if you're gonna eavesdrop, you have to stay close for moral support," Jenny threatened from the kitchen archway, waving the telephone headset in a menacing manner.

Megan just laughed it off, saying, "Sure, I even know where we can find some Ben and Jerry's ice cream this time of night on a holiday." Jenny turned away and stood near the wall-mounted phone, bracing herself. She looked at her kitchen clock and saw that it was just about 8:00 p.m., and as Mitch rarely turned in before 11:00, she knew it was okay to call this late as she quickly calculated the time change. She also knew Mitch wasn't going to Montana this Thanksgiving, thanks to information from the Joneses. Steeling her nerves, she dialed the phone and heard a familiar voice message. It was gruff, no identification, just a command to leave a message or leave off. Jenny wondered if she should tell Megan that she'd called Mitch a few times, but never dared leave a message. She almost hoped he had caller ID, but knew better. Mitch thought people who just called and set off the caller ID instead of leaving a message were lazy. So, he purposely didn't carry caller ID, just to be irritating. He also hated crank calls at midnight. Even knowing Mitch may not be home yet, Jenny felt the familiar butterflies of worry in her stomach. While waiting to leave her message, she muttered, "Shit, but this is important, and no government employee likes to work the Friday after Thanksgiving. He could be out late to celebrate." Jenny also knew from talking to Jonesey that Stan had let the whole crew have Friday as an extra holiday as it was their first break since the planes hit the towers.

***

Mitch lay sprawled out across his monstrous bed. Mercilessly, he forced any thoughts about life out of his head. It was hard after having today off and not having to work tomorrow and not having enough days to do a full week's workload. Albert and Jessica had invited him for Thanksgiving dinner at their place, but he'd refused. Hell, even Reva had offered to drag him with her over to Carl's family's feast. But Mitch had refused all offers. He didn't want to be around anyone right now, not anymore. For what seemed like the hundredth night in a row, he grumped and stewed at night instead of sleeping. Today's second pack of smokes lay by his head on the dresser, the last one smoking itself away in the ashtray. He could hardly finish it. Bill had told him day before yesterday that he looked like hell, and if he didn't do something about it this weekend, he, Bill, was going to snag one of the undercover agent's tranquilizer guns and put him under for at least seventy-two hours. Albert just shook his head, and Stan, well Stan just lectured him whenever the mood struck and forced him to take time off like this weekend.

Mitch lay stiffly on his bed. He didn't like the idea of sleeping for thirty-six hours straight, but that was the only way he figured he could make it until Monday with his sanity intact. Although he supposed his body needed the rest. Since that day in July, he always woke up dreaming about Jenny every morning and sometimes in the middle of the night. On the bad nights, bleary morning sunlight would awaken him in the middle of a nightmare about her. He would see her lying in a pool of blood on that basement floor back in Aberdeen. At other times he would see divers pulling her bloated and drowned body out of the ocean, sometimes off the Florida Keys and sometimes out of the cold North Sea.

How could he possibly explain to Bill that he wasn't even angry at her anymore, that he was done with her or at least he wished he was? Mitch laughed at that thought, then started hacking with the unexpected movement the laughter caused in his diaphragm. "Hell, of course I don't think about her. I don't have to. I breathe her, I feel her, and I'm haunted by her, so I dream of her instead." Having expelled those words in anger at his ceiling, he flopped over on his stomach and proceeded to pretend to sleep, praying that for once he could find his way to Morpheus' domain.

Not five minutes later, he heard the phone ring. Lately he'd heard it ring with no answer a few times in the early evenings. Somebody was consistently calling him, then hanging up at his message. "Damn stalker." But he nearly answered it tonight—just to tell them to lay off calling him. Having lain in bed for what seemed like hours, Mitch figured it was midnight. "Damn them, if they can call in the middle of the night, I should yell at them for sure." He looked at the clock and saw it was only 10:00 p.m. "Still too damn late to call." For a moment, he took inventory of his body aches and pounding headache and thought better of answering it. "Come Monday, I'll get a tracer installed from work." This time, though, there was a message. He heard the machine start to record and light up. "Damn, must be important, hope everyone's okay." He dove off the bed and grabbed the headset across the room, thinking worriedly of his elderly grandfather in Montana.

Mitch cursed, "Shit too late," as he heard the dial tone. Owing to his general hatred of new technology most of the time and his lack of creature comforts in his apartment, his answering machine was a dinosaur, which he resolved to replace first thing tomorrow as he rewound the machine's tiny tape and hit play.

All he heard was a woman's voice. "Mitch, I really need to talk…" as the machine ate the tape.

"Shit!" He ripped out the tape, but it was too late. Not only had the tape in the cassette been twisted and ripped, but the machine must have shorted out, because it had melted the tape. No way would he be able to preserve the message. No caller ID, no idea who that was, although, there were very few women who'd call him at all, especially this late. Immediately he thought of Jenny. His machine was so old it distorted voices beyond recognition, so he couldn't be sure.

The demon in his head had an idea though. Compulsively he calculated the time zones. "Let's see, it's nine fifty-two here, that would be seven fifty-two in Utah. Jenny is a typical government desk jockey and adores four-day weekends. I bet she's taken tomorrow off. She could have called me finally." Mad at himself, he refused to consider the thought that it may have been Jenny. "Yeah, here you are waiting by the phone like an old maid. There's no way that she would call after all this time, you're foolin' yourself, man." Slamming the defective answering machine down on the table, he stomped into his bathroom. "That is the last effin' time I am going to think about her. Dammit!" The cold shower helped cool his temper and his body. By the time he heard the kitchen clock quietly chime the midnight hour, he was ready to fall into bed at last, having resolved to *not* have the office crew trace the call. If it was Jenny, let her call him back, and if it was some other ghost from his past, he'd keep on ignoring them. He didn't care to dig up any more skeletons, ever. Just because he woke up every morning with the feel of her cuddled up to his side and the mother of all hard-ons, remembering something that had only happened during a single night in reality, he'd be damned before he let her ruin any more of his nights.

Resolved to stick to his plan, blessedly Mitch slept through the night for once and decided in the morning that he would never really believe Jenny had called him or would, especially after so many weeks since they last spoke and the way she ran out on him. He told himself that he was finally done with her, at last. The night before seemed like a sign from heaven that he'd made the right choice and that eventually peace would come back into his life.

The next week, he upgraded his phone and answering machine and changed his phone number. Around the office, his coworkers stopped razzing him for his grumpiness. Mitch stopped being touchy. He became quiet, cold, calculating, and hard, and dug himself so deeply into the September 11 task force that Bill and Stan stopped trying to reach him on any level other than a professional one after failing to get a deeper response from him. Albert was the only one who persisted by swinging by to visit

Mitch every few days or so, but when Mitch told him to leave off for the sixth time in a row, Albert did. Clearly, he could tell a lost cause when he saw one.

***

Jenny never realized what Mitch was doing or feeling. After that night's aborted message, she never tried to call Mitch again. She felt guilty over it, but she felt so stupid for the way she'd handled things and silly for having blurted into his machine that she was wrong, sorry, and in deep trouble, the nine-month kind, and never got a response. Her guilty conscience was only too easily appeased when she convinced herself that she had done her duty. Mitch could call or he could not; the ball was in his court. She had told him straight out she was pregnant, so if he wouldn't or couldn't stand up for her, she was done with him. And after a few weeks, when he still hadn't called her back, she felt relieved and decided to give up on speaking to him again, ever.

Chapter Sixty-six

At Christmastime, Jenny was twenty-six weeks pregnant. Her belly was obvious now. Her parents had told everyone in the family weeks before, but most of her aunts, uncles, and cousins hadn't actually seen her until the extended family Christmas party on Christmas Eve at Grandma and Grandpa Johnson's.

Comments were made and teasing occurred, but Jenny survived it, even had a good time with her loved ones. Blessedly, the Johnsons were a close-knit family and everyone loved Jenny, so it wasn't as bad as it could have been, even considering the family's LDS faith. They actually acted Christian to her and forgave her for her mistake. Then the aunts cooked up a baby shower. Jenny absolutely refused to accept it. Her guilty conscience could not let her celebrate her pregnancy, though she did celebrate the fact that she carried another life in her body. But she wasn't going to pretend that it was a joyous occasion for her to be pregnant. The aunts decided to ambush her with secret baby gifts for Christmas instead. And Jenny was very grateful for the lack of fanfare. She felt bad enough for the whole situation and relished forgetting her troubles for as long as possible, especially now that she had graduated and things were calmer in her life.

Also, thanks to her mom, everyone knew that Jenny and "the daddy" had had a bit of a falling out, so everyone was almost tactful. She'd not told the family at large about her stint as an FBI agent, and no one knew she'd been on a special assignment at all. Those that knew that she'd been away were only told that she'd been called to travel for work. Besides, the family was somewhat mollified by Jenny's behavior over the past couple of months. Most of them could appreciate that she was living her own life and appeared to be successful, even as a single-mom-to-be. She had changed her life, so there was no need to call her to repentance collectively even among the more judgmental aunts, when she was correcting the problem already. The youngest may not have gotten married, but from all appearances she'd gotten close.

Chapter Sixty-seven

"The whole world for America changed September 11, 2001." Jenny listened to the local radio program's announcer continue a panel discussion about the sociological effects of 9/11 on Americans and Utahans. She felt the truth of this statement within her as she absorbed the words. Personally, September 11 had marked her, because she risked losing many of her good friends in Washington DC as they fought the "War on Terror." However, Utah was a long way from DC or Afghanistan and felt far distanced from the war. Here in Salt Lake City at the International Airport, the signs were stronger than anywhere else in Utah.

Having been driving along her old early morning commute, Jenny had had her typical morning music and deep thoughts interrupted by the news reports of the towers falling, but since she'd also found out that her suspicions were correct and that she was pregnant that day, September 11 had scarred her on a deeper personal level. Now, in late January, she felt some distance from the tragedies.

To entertain herself on the freeway, Jenny began to count the cars that had flag decals on their bumpers and back windows. After realizing that more than half the cars on the road had these markers of patriotism, Jenny felt better about her own decision to slap one on the back window of her truck. One day in late September, she'd picked up a free US flag sticker at the gas station. She'd admired all the flags she'd seen and felt proud to display it on her truck. Since then, she'd noticed less people doing this, but she accepted the fact that time does heal wounds of the spirit, even if you don't want the healing to happen. At times she was amazed at the transformation in herself. Megan told her she was nesting and preparing for the baby, but Jenny wasn't sure. She did feel extremely introspective and seemed to be ruled by her body's needs, but she felt more at peace today than she had for a long time.

The airport, of course, still reflected a strong remembrance of the terrorist attacks. Jenny had to present her special FBI credentials before the Utah National Guard officers would let her park in the right area of the terminal. This didn't surprise her with the 2002 Winter Olympic Games starting in a matter of days. Salt Lake City along with the rest of Utah had been gearing up for the games for years. All law enforcement agencies had been preparing for the security nightmare of the international events ever since the international committee chose Salt Lake City for the 2002 games. Then September 11, 2001 changed the scene. Extra security measures were taken at all airports, especially those with international routes. Salt Lake's was no exception, but they had ramped things up in light of the upcoming events. Jenny was used to seeing happy families greeting loved ones in the relaxed atmosphere of the airport's open doors. Instead she was greeted by armed personnel in fatigues and Army Humvees.

The spirit of terror was alive and well today. As Jenny maneuvered her new bulk down out of the Suburban she had borrowed for this trip, she remembered back to that day. On September 11, she'd sat in the doctor's office, half listening to the continuing news reports as her doctor finished the tests. Sure enough, pregnant. Now there were armed guards all over the airport. She'd even been told to use her passport along with her driver's license and her FBI papers to get into the secure area due to the new security measures.

Five months had passed since that day, and things were really different. Jenny felt tired, worn out. Not only had she acquired a pregnancy last summer, in the last six months she'd bought a house, got a new job at the IRS, and graduated from Weber State University, cum laude, and had loved and lost a handsome man.

How the world had changed, she thought as she went through the second x-ray machine, holding her hand protectively over her belly. She thought of Michael Gooding, who'd wanted the attention of "Americans." His plan had been thwarted, but she knew he was probably in some maximum security federal prison, blissfully watching Osama bin Laden and applauding that man's success in terrorizing the entire United States.

The security at the airport was beefier than Jenny remembered. As she stood patiently near an "employees only," nondescript door waiting for a scary-looking lady to go through her purse with minute detail, she reminisced on how the world right here in Utah had changed since September 11. Six months ago, anyone could walk down the airport corridors, loiter by the gates, and wander practically right up to the plane after passing through an x-ray, no tickets, no ID, no one would even glance your way.

Utah, being the homeland of the Mormons, had a lot of Mormon missionaries being sent all over the world to preach the church's message. Consequently many missionary moms and dads and families made every trip to Salt Lake International Airport for a missionary send-off a sight to behold. Amateurs used balloons and posters, experts at the tradition of greeting your loved one with as much fanfare as possible met their sons and daughters after two years or eighteen months with camcorders, confetti, balloons and hordes of happy people and lots of hugs. Today, three weeks out from the 2002 Winter Olympics in the age of terrorism, Jenny could just barely see the concourse from the gallery where non-ticketed persons were corralled, not due to crowds of people, but due to barricades and armed guards.

To her left, Jenny could make out the luggage carousels and about a dozen national guardsmen. She saw about double that many TSA personnel in their white or blue shirts and dark ties. Jenny had never realized how much things had changed due to the new security measures. She couldn't even see the huge map of the world in the floor tiles as it was covered by stacks of suitcases waiting to be examined before they could be taken back to the planes. The airport had not been designed to hold people outside the gates, but within them. All the room was on the other side of that barricade. To her, Salt Lake City, Utah didn't feel like much of a target, but it was an international airport, thus a possible security threat. Of course, no one could forget the terrorist actions that had taken place at previous Olympics. The 1972 games came to Jenny's mind and she shuddered to think of how the Israelis had reacted.

Jenny didn't know whether to be grateful or not for her newly acquired and obviously pregnant mass as the cute, blond guardsmen who rechecked her ID escorted her to a soft seat near the restrooms on the upper level outside the actual terminal itself. Hell, she couldn't even flirt, not that that was a good idea this pregnant, but she entertained herself by imagining that some of these newly activated guardsmen possibly left very pregnant wives at home. She was not aware of how fetching she looked today. Her normally slender build had carried the bulging belly well and with more grace than she felt. The hormones put rosy apples in her cheeks and brightened her blue eyes to give her face an exceptionally pretty flushed beauty.

Bill would be arriving from DC in about forty minutes. Jenny didn't know if Jonesey was coming from Denver or if he'd been in DC preparing with Stan and Homer. She wondered how he and Bill had been able to convince Stan to let Bill come out to Utah to help him on the FBI's security detail for the games. She'd worried about speaking to Bill in person for the first time in a long time. He knew she was pregnant, but she worried about what he'd think of her new figure.

Jenny fidgeted as she waited. Her watch showed that she was late, as usual. Normally she'd have to wait an hour for the passengers to disembark. Today she only had about twenty minutes to spare if the plane was on time.

This morning's delay was caused by an issue with her expanded waistline and her modest pregnancy wardrobe that offered few options for a first-timer pregnant woman with a tight budget. She would have felt worse about her late arrival, but the new, extra security meant that she had an even shorter wait today. There were a lot of other people waiting just like she was. This airport was not designed to hold this many bodies outside the concourses. There weren't enough chairs and Jenny could see frayed tempers and people standing all over the relatively small area by the baggage claims. Family and friends picking up family and friends, i.e. "people without boarding passes" couldn't get down the terminals to watch the planes land or get anywhere near the disembarking passengers, so there was no point in arriving early to the airport anymore. "Rides" like Jenny—everyone not flying themselves, now had to wait for the passengers to reach the baggage claim area. She'd watched the waiting groups compress to get out of the way of the passengers, then re-expand when that flight had cleaned out their luggage. Most of the people without chairs were actually sitting on the edges of the luggage carousel and would hurriedly jump up when it started to rotate.

Jenny suppressed a shudder and sent another prayer to her Maker, thanking Him for Bill, Jonesey, and Mitch's continued health as she thought of the threats that the US was under and for the seat she had to rest herself. She'd had contact from Bill off and on through her cousin Megan. Stan had also sent him out as an envoy to convince her to go work for the FBI in DC when he'd sent Bill to meet Jonesey in Salt Lake City for a security task force meeting in August with the Denver Bunch. The day Bill had come to see her, Jenny had introduced him to Megan. They'd hit it off and began a romance of sorts; Bill and Megan would double with the bombshell Nelson, from Denver, was dating when the boys would go out. Bill and Megan didn't mention the specifics of these dates to Jenny out of sensitivity to her single state, which only served to make Jenny more sensitive. Now, she felt slightly more realistic. She claimed full responsibility for the mess. She'd sabotaged the budding love between her and Mitch, not Mitch.

Thinking of Megan made Jenny smile. Megan was a big help to Jenny and was a lot of fun to have around since she'd moved in during Christmas break. Because Megan had told him about the pregnancy, it was no problem for Jenny to pick Bill up at the airport today since Megan had to work. Jenny's family and friends knew she was pregnant, but she was still uncomfortable thinking about Mitch not knowing, or knowing and not caring. Because Bill knew already, she could relax and not guard herself as much as she did around Nelson, who was clueless still. She could trust Bill and Stan to honor her wish to speak to Mitch herself—not his answering machine—if she ever reached that point. Jenny wasn't stupid, she knew she had some explaining to do, especially after her aborted attempts to contact Mitch, but it was much easier to just grow a baby, work and be a homebody, and pretend that her life was peachy.

The Denver Bunch and Bill, along with a couple of the CIA guys from the task force who'd captured Gooding, had been selected to help the Olympic task force help with the security at the Olympics. Over the last few months prior to this January, the winter task force had been meeting in Salt Lake City every few weeks, helping Nelson's and Bill's love lives to flourish. However, since Megan would drive down to Salt Lake to visit Bill after work, Jenny had yet to see him in person since last August.

Bill had called Jenny last week to finalize their itinerary. It was good to speak to him and be on good terms again. It seemed that over the last few weeks he'd almost forgiven her for messing up Mitch's life. Bill would stay with her and Megan in Ogden while the task force checked out the Olympic venues in, north of, and around Salt Lake City. With all the travelers for the events, hotel space was at a premium.

Megan was thrilled; she was sure Jenny would be a great chaperone and school would be out during the Winter Olympics, so she could hang out with Bill at the venues. Like other Utah schools, Weber State University had canceled all classes for the two weeks during the games. Megan would be volunteering near Bill, and they were absolutely silly over the prospect of having nearly a month to be together.

After a while, the latest plane's passengers left the carousels, and Jenny saw the baggage carousel begin to turn yet again. Red lights showed Delta flight 1434 from Denver was arriving. People began trickling down from the security gates. Of course at that moment, little feet decided to jump up and down on her bladder. She propelled herself vertical with great effort and waddled into the restroom downstairs. After exiting the restroom, she decided to walk a bit to get some air into lungs and stretch her aching back. Jenny spoke aloud as she stepped onto the escalator. "Well since I'm no good at hauling luggage in this shape, I'll hang out upstairs where I was to wait and watch."

The flight was full. *There must be over three hundred people,* Jenny thought. She stood at the second floor railing near six guardsmen who also had nodded to her, with a couple of smiles even in their serious attitude, as they watched her laborious approach. The airport was a great place to people-watch. She watched an older lady point out her bag to a younger man who appeared to be related, and watched another young man in a suit who must have just returned from an LDS mission being thronged by a "Mormon mob." That family was squished in the narrow aisle between the carousels and the vending machines. She noted a lack of the usual pomp, but thought that the smiles and joy seemed as bright as usual as the family looked to the returning missionary; their shouts of joy and laughter echoed up to her. The dad showed him a bouquet of balloons that he couldn't reach in the crush, then people grabbed his luggage and they hustled the entire crew out into the daylight along the lane that separate the airport terminals from the parking garage. Looking out the windows behind her, Jenny watched the family group pause on the sidewalk next to the waiting vehicles and group together for some quick photos where they had more room to stand together. The whole group then melted into a dozen vehicles, parked in a row, and took off in a caravan.

Looking back into the terminal, off to her right, she saw a successful-looking couple claiming their off-size luggage—skis. They carried designer luggage and matching ski bags. Jenny was used to the sight of skis on planes. She'd flown down the perfect powdered snow of Utahan ski resorts all over the state. As she watched the couple maneuver through the crowd, her gaze skimmed past an unassuming door just down from the off-size claiming desk. It opened before her eyes. She saw Bill in profile as he exited from what appeared to be a long hallway and went into another door a few feet down the wall. She blessed Bill for his bright red hair. Tall, sexy redheads were easy to spot in a crowd. He was carrying a smallish black case, which she recognized as his gun case. "He must have had to follow some weird security procedure in order to bring his gun along, even as an FBI agent. I'm frankly surprised they let him with the expanded security since September eleventh." She still kept her habit of talking to herself, even now when she had a roommate, because she and Megan weren't together most of the time since they still worked opposite shifts.

Out of the corner of her eye, Jenny noticed that the cute blond guardsman was smiling and staring at her again. *Oops. I wonder if he heard that.* He seemed to be preparing to approach her. *Oh no, I hope he doesn't think I was talking to him.* She turned away and proceeded to stare intently at the unassuming door by the rear wall of the area. She saw the baggage carousel finally start to turn across her line of sight. Its marquee lit up with the Denver flight's information. *Finally,* Jenny thought, stretching in preparation to hike down to greet the group. She watched for Bill to catch his attention when he came to collect the rest of his bags.

Covertly Jenny saw the blond guardsman settle down and breathed a sigh of relief. She really hated flirting in her pregnant state. She couldn't tell if the guys were just curious about her belly or if they were thinking of a wife or girlfriend in a similar state, or if they had some weird hang-ups about pregnant woman. She didn't believe that crap about how beautiful pregnant women were reported to be. In her experience that was a story made up to protect unwitting spouses from getting killed by a hormonally challenged female when they told their pregnant wives they were fat. The door had opened when she looked back. *Here comes Bill,* she thought, moving to stand at the rail on the upper level. Right behind Bill came Nelson, Jonesey, and Smith (she could never remember his first name), along with some other official/FBI/TSA-looking guys, but behind the group walked Mitch.

Chapter Sixty-eight

Jenny had spent the last few weeks since she'd learned that Bill and Jonesey would be in Salt Lake City covering the Olympics hoping and planning (she now realized in vain) that she would never have to face Mitch again. After failing to get a response after leaving him that voice mail and eventually giving up on calling him, she realized that she should have made sure he knew she was pregnant and didn't want her or contact with the baby months ago. She should have made sure. It hit her, hard. Stan and Albert and all her friends and family were right. She should have stayed with him; she should have talked with him. She should never have ran out that day. *Sure I'd be in DC working for the FBI, but shoot.* If not today, she fully expected to see Mitch when/if Megan and Bill married. She'd quieted her conscience with that voice mail message, because it was easier than dealing with Mitch angry in person. *Woulda, coulda, shoulda, dammit shit!* played on a loop in Jenny's brain. She felt as if the earth had shifted under her feet, and her knees nearly gave out.

Mitch hadn't seen her yet. He appeared to be arguing with the security officer who was escorting their group. *That would explain why he's in the back, Mr. Take Charge,* Jenny managed to think through her shock. She took in the fact that all of the agents save Mitch were carrying their own gun cases. Mitch was gesturing animatedly to the security officer who kept shaking his head back at him.

Her attention were drawn away from Mitch, when, just then, Bill spotted her and waved. Jenny could also see Jonesey's expression from where she stood, forty feet away and fifteen feet higher. The corners of his mouth turned downward. He looked back at Mitch and glanced at Bill questioningly. Bill gave a small nod of affirmation and handed Jonesey his case and what must have been their baggage tags. Jonesey worked hard to steer the rest of the group toward the carousel as Bill strode purposely toward the stairs below Jenny.

She stood transfixed, gripping the railing. Her fingers began to ache and she glanced down, noticing that her knuckles were white as she forced herself to relax. "Be calm, you have to do this. You can do this." She bolstered her courage and prepared herself to meet her match. "Use Bill to warm up your story, girl. Maybe Mitch can take a cab. Maybe Smith and Nelson will take him," she said to herself illogically.

Mitch was going to be so pissed off at her. Funny, until that moment, Jenny hadn't wanted to remember that Mitch was her match in temper. Only now did she think, *how do you tell someone that you were wrong after nearly eight months or even two months or even a few days or weeks, hours or minutes?* She realized belatedly that this had been her problem. How do you explain to someone that you pray for them each day and your love for them will kill you if you think about the mistake you made? Jenny didn't know how, but she realized she'd better figure it out and damn soon.

In the same breath, Jenny learned that the psychic connection between her and Mitch still existed. It flared instantly between them, causing him to pause his tirade with the TSA officer. Jenny could tell he'd confused the officer. Just like those cold nights in Georgia and Aberdeen, she could feel his presence in her bones today. And she stood still, witnessing the fact that he knew when she was near as well.

***

Mitch stopped talking to the security officer mid-word. His infamous internal radar was screaming at him. He felt invisible antennae draw his attention to the upper level balcony. He turned away from the incompetent security idiot who'd seemed to have lost his gun, and looked past the baggage claim and up and saw her. He saw just a female form for a moment, as his brain told him from analyzing the back of that red head, that that was Bill climbing the stairs toward her. Mitch's brain forced his conscious brain to recognize what the animal part of his brain already knew, to see her again, this time not as a woman but as Jenny. Realization dawned. "Holy hell!"

Mitch's head was spinning. *There she was!* He'd suffered months without a peep from her. In that time he'd endured months of Bill and Al and Stan not meeting his eyes and cold lectures from Jonesey. Months and weeks of hiding her picture deep in his desk drawer as he pretended she never existed, but there she was. *She's here. She's real and goddammit, what's that belly? What, no, she...she's pregnant!* With that thought, his brain no longer functioned in words; the chemicals took over.

A primal, possessive urge exploded in Mitch, the knowledge that here was his woman and she carried his baby. He absolutely knew it. He began to move toward her. After looking at her pregnant belly, he caught her gaze before she turned and ran. She actually ran from him. His woman was running away. All caveman now, Mitch ran to chase her down.

Mitch bounded to the stairs and saw Bill reach the upper level and start running after Jenny. Mitch took off after them. *She must be parked on the upper level*, he thought. He reached the second level at the same time that Bill reached the outer doors and ran through them. He burst through them as the automatic doors tried to close on him. Icy wind blasted him as he spotted Bill chasing Jenny to the right. He chased after them.

***

Jenny knew then she was crazy, and worse, panicked. What was she doing running like a fool? Her stomach and back were killing her. She ran on, holding her belly awkwardly with one hand. She had to stop. Her lungs squished by Baby Harper couldn't take this abuse. She panted, trying to get enough oxygen. She heard Bill yell at her, but she was almost to her dad's Suburban. A few more feet and she'd make it, but Bill made up the distance and grabbed her arm, forcing her to sop. Jenny looked at him, her mouth open and gasping for breath. Bill had just enough time to say, "You need to talk to him," before Mitch arrived and jerked him away from her.

Jenny had no breath to speak, and hated the panting puffs of breath her body required. Before she could to respond to Bill, her brain processed that he had been dragged away and she was confronted by the angriest man she had ever seen. Mitch had caught up with her.

Chapter Sixty-nine

"Get your hands off her!" Mitch yelled irrationally at Bill. He was utterly, completely angry. All the built-up anger he'd felt and had to suppress that morning in July and ever since washed over him. He'd reached the SUV and his objective, Jenny. She had the gall to just stand there looking at him. He stared back at her, his level gaze burning a hole into her. Jenny began backing up to the Suburban behind her as her chest continued heaving and she stared back at him. His eyes never lost contact with her. Mitch advanced. He saw a sudden hurt in her eyes, and realized she was afraid of him. His anger began to cool at that thought.

Mitch had seen Jenny panicked before as a result of her intensive FBI training. If it was very bad, Jenny usually hyperventilated when upset, but this time he wasn't sure of her problem. His concern for her had overrode his anger, and it was killing him to see her discomfort, to know that he'd caused it, made it worse. On another level he felt like strangling her or shaking some sense into her for all that she'd done to him. He didn't know enough about pregnant women to understand how Jenny's lungs were compromised. Jenny stopped her retreat when her back collided with the rear door of the large SUV. Mitch closed the remaining distance and stood toe-to-toe with her. As he began to stare her down, Mitch felt the sharp pain of a gun barrel poke him in his back.

***

Jenny stared at Mitch. He gave her little choice. Until this moment, she'd only imagined his reaction. Nothing she'd imagined could compare to the actual reality of him. His presence awoke her senses. She needed this man. She'd last seen him in the pre-dawn dusk of a hotel room months ago. The details of that day in July were hazy to her, because of her severe panic that day. Stan refused to mention any details about the last day in Scotland. Amy, Jonesey's wife, had told her only the little bits she had gleaned from the Denver Bunch. She knew, for instance, that Bill had had to cold-cock Mitch, and that Stan had ordered him restrained. But she was shocked at what she saw: hot, pure fury in his eyes. But he seemed a little calmer with each breath he took. As she looked harder into his handsome eyes, she saw beneath his fury that there appeared to be a pain buried deep. She had hurt him. This shocked her. He was always so tough and gruff around her. Sorrow struck her. She hadn't meant to hurt him. Even as she'd regretted running out on him, she hadn't considered that she may have hurt him. All fear left her. Her hand began to lift, aiming to hold his cheek, as Jenny mouth opened to say "I'm sorry."

That was the last coherent thought Jenny had for him. Just then, the blond national guardsman reached them. Jenny watched, as if in slow motion, as the blond jabbed Mitch in the back with the barrel of his gun and when Mitch didn't turn toward him, flicked his rifle around and put Mitch on the ground. Other guardsmen soon followed and two guarded her as she stared, horrified, at Mitch being handcuffed on the pavement at her feet. When Mitch was secured, a pair of soldiers forced her away from her vehicle and directed her attention to a small, squat, hard-looking woman who appeared to be in charge and standing a few feet away with Bill, who was also handcuffed, hands behind his back.

The woman looked her up and down with and aura of no-nonsense authority and frisked her. She then motioned the guards to watch her. She didn't handcuff her, but her grip on Jenny's wrist didn't encourage resistance. The woman called over her shoulder to a handful of guards standing nearby to surround Mitch where he lay face down on the cement. Jenny wanted to rush forward to his side, but stopped the impulse. She didn't know where she stood with Mitch, and he had been angrier than she'd ever seen him just a few minutes before, but every part of her wanted to push those soldiers away from him and help him up, the woman who had a hold of her be damned.

The commander must have sensed Jenny's growing discontent, because she changed her grip on Jenny's arm and propelled her backward away from Mitch and closer to Bill. "Look, missy, I have no idea what's going on here, but if you don't stay back, you'll find yourself in the same position as your friend here, pregnant or not!" The harridan then turned away from Jenny to survey the scene around Mitch. Threat or not, Jenny wasn't about to push her way through the circle of soldiers surrounding Mitch just now. Even if she didn't have a huge pregnant belly in her way, she knew when not to tangle with soldiers doing their duty. However, she didn't like the look of this woman, who was wearing a suit but had yet to identify herself. Jenny was about to break the woman's grip when Jonesey came behind her and held her still with a gentle pressure on her shoulders as he began speaking to the woman in charge. He motioned Bill forward, and by the flashing of his and the other agents' FBI badges, the soldiers backed away from Mitch and Bill and stood near the woman who appeared to be their commander.

The soldiers left Mitch where he lay, and one of the FBI agents Jenny couldn't recognize helped him to his feet. Jenny noted that Bill and Mitch were left in cuffs for the moment.

***

Mitch was very aware on the fact that he was face down on the freezing concrete with his hands cuffed behind his back. Jenny was nowhere to be seen, so he tried to focus on the cement to calm down. Not that he could have seen much of her above her ankles had she been near. He lay there and felt a building despair as he listened to the ranting going on somewhere above and beyond him. He realized clinically that for the first time in his life his temper had nearly got the best of him, and if Jonesey hadn't arrived to give the reserve guys the idea that they were legitimately FBI, he would have had hypothermia by the time they released him. Surprised, Mitch also realized the cold pavement was doing wonders to cool off his temper. He decided to let Jonesey and Bill handle things a moment while he attempted to make sense of the bizarre events in his life and tried to deal with the fact that Jenny was here and she was pregnant. *My God, Jenny is having a baby...my baby.* That thought drowned out all the others.

Finally, Mitch heard the CO respond to Jonesey's entreaties. "The girl knew these guys, then. But, why run—especially when she's pregnant? I'm confused here." Like a shot, the CO changed her tack. "It's damn cold. Your badges look genuine, and this girl is supposedly an innocent civilian. But I don't like this. You're coming with me."

Mitch was pulled to his feet. His cheek was numb where it had rested against the cold concrete, but his capture had cooled his head.

Janice, the CO, spoke. "There should be just enough room in my office and it will be warmer than out here." She led the group to an inconspicuous door across the parking lot and drive lane. "Best to handle this indoors," she announced to the group. She led the way, tugging Jenny with her as she motioned Jonesey and the Denver Bunch to shepherd Mitch and Bill through the door held open by another officer. The required national guardsmen returned to their posts, guarding the airport entrances as the rest followed Janice and the group inside. Two soldiers remained outside the office door, standing guard.

Chapter Seventy

In the office, Janice motioned for everyone to be seated, then removed Mitch's cuffs and set them in plain sight at the desk next to Jenny's arm, with a significant look. Jenny moved her arm off the lady's desk, sat quietly, and stared straight ahead. Mitch produced his own badge as requested and stood obediently in front of the desk while Janice sat checking his credentials in her computer.

He surreptitiously watched Jenny to his left across Janice's desk while he attempted to pretend Jenny wasn't in the room. She looked all rosy and pretty as she sat there. Her beauty still had the power to strike him, but she sat there looking great and calm and happy, which made him feel angry and frustrated all over again. Hell, here he was, still freezing from the concrete outside as Genghis Khan ran his information on her computer. Only pure stubbornness was keeping him from shivering violently. He reached into his breast pocket and retrieved his other IDs to add to the pile produced by Jonesey for the dragon lady when called for. Janice smiled when she saw his driver's license was issued from Washington DC, and said just low enough for them to hear, "Good riddance. Let his superiors handle this mess." Mitch jerked. He'd seen Janice see him watching Jenny. *Oh great*, he thought, *now I have some National Guard CO worrying about my love life. I am sure this will give them a good laugh two weeks from the Olympics.* Janice looked away as she continued checking their backgrounds.

After a few phone calls, their ID's being legitimate, and Jenny's own furnishment of her driver's license and IRS identification badge and FBI vouchers, they were cleared to go. Bill and Jonesey, being the most discreet, especially in this incident, agreed that Jenny and Mitch had some talking to do, and took themselves off to get the luggage. Nelson and Smith had left to track down Mitch's still missing gun. Janice graciously turned over her office and phone to Mitch and Jenny. But first she'd called Stan, chatted with him for a few minutes, then handed the phone to Jenny, stating, "He wants to talk to you first, missy. I'll leave you to it. Shut off the space heater when you're done in here." With that, Janice left.

In the phone conversations, Stan had asked for Bill, Jonesey, and lastly Mitch by turns. He wanted to check with Jenny first to ensure she was okay. He knew he could get his agents off, but didn't want to leave Jenny hanging. Stan then let his agents have it. He was not happy to be pulled from an important Olympic security meeting because his agents couldn't even get out of the Salt Lake City airport without incident. Heck, they were in Utah, for Pete's sake. The risks should have been few. Then Homer got on the phone.

Mitch's temper had improved, but deteriorated after speaking to Homer. Homer had urged Stan to put a report in Mitch's employee file. Not that Mitch had done anything wrong, but Homer asked him just what he thought about being so emotionally unstable as to chase the mother of his child across an icy parking lot. After the lecture, however, Homer left off any more chastisement. Mitch knew exactly what Homer was getting at. Even though they were on their own time, the team still had to maintain the dignity of the Agency. They were always agents of the FBI. Homer would get even, though. Mitch didn't know how bad it would be, but he could just imagine the jokes in the office. "Yeah, Mitch can't even catch a pregnant gal in a sprint." In a self-righteous moment he considered being miffed at the whole lecture.

Mitch let Bill and Jonesey and the boys go get his gear when they retrieved theirs. The statement Homer had made kept rolling through his brain. "The mother of your child." Neither Stan nor Homer had questioned the fact that

Jenny was pregnant, or that Mitch was the father. Stan hadn't even remarked on her pregnant state. That meant those bastards knew she was pregnant and kept it from him for at least some time. Mitch wasn't usually slow, but when he finally realized this, it shook him. Had he been such a pain in the butt since July that his bosses chose to not speak to him about a pregnancy he caused to protect the mother?

Mitch knew better than anyone that Jenny couldn't have been pregnant before him, before he "defiled" her, and she wasn't the kind of girl to let someone else get her that way after him. The old resentment he'd felt at her mistreatment of his person back in July came back to him. Who knew who she'd slept with once she'd gotten back to the States? As soon as Mitch had that thought, he ignored it. He may not have known Jenny her whole life, but he knew her and her beliefs. He also knew that her feelings for him had been real. At least in July he'd known that her feelings had been real and truly, deeply, for him alone. He was sure she hadn't slept with anyone else, but dammit, he wanted her to admit it. He wanted her to admit it now, to admit that she still cared. Admit she was pregnant with his kid, that she'd been wrong to leave him in England, that she'd been wrong to not speak to him since. When he realized that he wanted her to admit she loved him, he faltered for a moment.

He'd spent these past months, since they'd caught Gooding, pretending Jenny didn't exist. No one had even dared mention her name in his presence after that first week. He'd known both Jonesey and Bill had spoken to her lately, but whenever they were speaking of her and he'd come into the room, they fell silent. Bill had even found that picture of Jenny that they had recovered from Gooding's stash and after clearing it as evidence had given Mitch the copy he'd since kept stashed in his desk. Gooding had kept that photograph with his other pictures that proved Jenny's status as an FBI mole. Its retrieval along with other photographs of the bomb makings and targets in Gooding's personal papers on the freighter had helped prove Gooding's guilt.

Mitch told himself that he'd kept a copy of the print because it was a beautiful shot. In the end Gooding, was still a gifted photographer. Mitch kept the copy of the image under some folders, locked in his desk drawer. He hadn't been able to bring himself to let go of the picture. It was just another thing that Mitch needed to deal with in his own way, as he'd continued his attempt to live in a Jenny-free world.

Then September 11 had happened, confirming everyone's fears that Gooding was just one of a trend of terrorists out to prove something to the US. In the days that followed, it had been easier to pretend Jenny didn't exist. Mitch had bigger problems on his mind.

Bill and Jonesey came in with their luggage and Jenny moved quickly, clearly ready to leave. Mitch blocked her path and stopped her when they neared the outer door and grabbed Jenny's chin to force her to look at him. Jenny stared up at him, seemingly probing his gaze for something. After a moment, she sighed. When she went to pull away from him, Mitch tightened his hold on her, refusing to be put off. Jenny's eyes narrowed a second before she stomped on his foot, elbowed and shrugged out of his grasp and maneuvered around him, then strode from the building and out to her dad's Suburban.

Mitch followed, not even limping. He noticed she wasn't giving him the cold-shoulder treatment. She just wanted privacy. He could tell that Jenny wasn't *really* angry with him. She didn't hurt folks when she got angry. When she was really angry you didn't see her and she wouldn't acknowledge your existence.

***

Jenny waddled painfully across the driving lanes and parking stalls. Dang, her whole body ached from the sprint, and her lungs hurt. She could feel Mitch's gaze burning into her, but couldn't care about that now. She knew that once she broke down the dam keeping her emotions in check, she'd lose total control, and she wouldn't be able to drive these guys around. Right now, her back was hurting and her hands ached from being clenched. She had to make it at least an hour more. Once everyone had been dropped off, she could retreat to her very own home. Part of her wanted to blame Bill for this mess. He'd kept Mitch's appearance a secret. It was no use, though, because she was to blame. She decided that she would shoulder the blame, gladly, but later today, and in private with Mitch, if he would grant her that.

She reached the truck and realized she had to pee. "Damn pregnancy," she muttered as she turned to head back inside.

***

Mitch approached Jenny as she reached her dad's SUV. Silently, Mitch felt himself calm down. He didn't think he could forgive her, at least not yet, but the white-hot madness which had claimed him earlier was gone. He felt full of ashes. Not even smoldering, but burned out. Maybe he had been smoldering all along the summer and fall and the anger was blown into life by the sight of her. She moved in pain. He could count as well as the next man, and figured she had what, six weeks of pregnancy left? Thinking of his sister's pregnancy, he calculated. Thirty-four weeks, she should be. She could almost be full term in a couple of weeks. He felt a twinge of guilt at causing a pregnant woman, especially this one, any pain, but this one had angered him. As she reached the car and unlocked the door, then turned back, he saw the look of annoyance on her face and knew she was okay. She seemed to appear happiest when she was pissed off.

Mitch reached her side. "Are you gonna get in?" he asked her to make conversation.

"No, I've gotta go to the bathroom." She made to hand him the keys and sidle around him to go back into the airport, but Mitch was faster. He stopped her, then swooped her into his arms before she could protest. Jenny started breathing deep. Then she tucked her head against his neck and muttered something about trying not to throw up.

Mitch enjoyed the pounding of her pulse under her skin and smelling the perfume of her hair as he waited for her to regain her composure. He really enjoyed feeling her soft face against his neck. "Are you ready for travel?"

She poked her head up and gave him a dirty look. "Put me down, now!"

"No way, missy. I saw how you're not walking so good. You'll just have to direct me to the nearest ladies room."

After a moment, she awkwardly crossed her arms and sighed. "Fine. It's just past the door where you guys came out to the baggage claim."

Mitch smiled and headed back into the terminal. Jenny turned her face into his neck again and Mitch went back to enjoying her warm breath on his pulse and how good she felt in his arms. She didn't even feel that much heavier to him—maybe only thirty pounds. But after six months, who could tell.

Mitch decided as they felt the warm blast of air inside the airport, that he liked the feel of her in his arms. It was time to accept defeat and love her for the rest of his life, but first, she was going to admit she loved him back. He decided that she may not have to pay him back for the past few months of torture she'd caused him, after all, if he could spend more time with her in his arms.

He stood nervously outside the women's restroom. Jenny was taking forever. Over the usual airport noises, he half listened to make sure she was okay. He heard the flush and the water from the sink, but when they stopped, there was no sign of Jenny. He gave her a minute. He knew from experience that a girl sometimes just needed some time to gussy up. He started getting impatient. Just then, he heard a sob. *Dammit, now she's crying.* He looked around. No one was watching. No one else had gone into the restroom. Deciding Jenny was worth another explanation to airport security, he went into the restroom.

Mitch found Jenny bent over the sink, sobbing. "Hey, hey, what's wrong, baby?" He grasped her shoulders and pulled her around to face him.

Jenny hiccupped. "I am so sorry I didn't tell you about the baby. I am sorry that I left you in London. I can never make it up to you. You should hate me."

Mitch sighed and held her to him. "Hey, just you let me worry about that. I don't hate you. Give me a chance to get used to the idea of being your man for real and being a dad, okay?" He grabbed a paper towel and gently tried to wipe her tears away. "Just don't cry, okay?"

Jenny took the scratchy paper towel from him and wiped her tears away as she nodded mutely and they left the restroom.

Chapter Seventy-one

Jenny's patience was at its end. She was tired, upset, and drained. After ceremoniously losing it in the restroom, she'd barely regained equilibrium enough to want to lash out at Mitch for coming into the restroom to get her. Before she got the chance, however, his attention was turned elsewhere. He looked away from her to glare at the cute guardsman who'd spotted them leaving the lavatory. Mitch seemed to want to goad the man into challenging him for entering the ladies restroom. Jenny watched the dueling male protectiveness looks they were shooting at each other and disgustedly turned away and went back into the restroom to wash her face. Of course by the time she reemerged, Mitch stood waiting expectantly, and the soldier was nowhere to be seen. Thankful that her anger had cooled her upset, Jenny stayed back away from Mitch this time. She was not about to be carried again.

Then Bill came over announcing, "Are you guys ready? Ride's here." The blond guardsman drove up to them on one of those golf-cart-like people-movers, ready to take her out to her car. Only too grateful to be away from Mitch for a moment, Jenny hopped up front and motioned for Bill and Mitch to ride in the back. They reached the 'Burb, where Jenny shook the guardsman's hand and thanked him for his help. Mitch shared a parting glare with the soldier, then obeyed Jenny as she half turned and motioned him to get in the Suburban.

Bill started loading luggage as Jonesey and the Denver Bunch arrived. Mitch sat shotgun as Jenny reached into the truck and started the engine and jacked up the heater.

"You sure you don't want me to drive?" he asked and cringed at the look she glared back.

"No. Pregnancy makes me car sick. I am never car sick, but your kid won't let me just ride. I have to drive, to have the control, in order to not throw up. Live with it." Mitch just stared at her. He probably wondered if he could keep up with her hormonal moods for six more weeks. Jenny then closed the door and walked to the back of the 'Burb to retrieve a huge, fluffy quilt from behind the rear bench where she'd stashed it when they loaded the luggage in the third row. Walking up to the front passenger door, she opened it and handed him the quilt. She looked Mitch in the eye for a moment, then left him to thaw after her icy stare and her statement, "Front heater vent's busted. Only the back gets any heat."

***

Mitch wanted to die right then, in happiness, exhaustion, or confusion, he didn't know. She was speaking to him at least. The shock of the morning—the day wasn't half over yet—overcame him. He sat with the heater blowing cold air, wrapped in a quilt that he knew Jenny had made, and let the shivers fully overtake him. He surrendered to his body's needs while he meditated on how to handle the delicate woman next to him. Only peripherally was he aware of Jenny and the others getting in the car, stashing bags, and picking seats then their driving from the airport into downtown Salt Lake City.

The ride into Salt Lake City proper was uneventful. Everyone but Jenny and Mitch talked a little, making small talk, letting the excitement of the morning and a new assignment wear down. They dropped off Jonesey and the Bunch downtown to stay at their rental condo, which would serve as living quarters during the games. Mitch tried hard not to hate Jonesey as Jenny had hugged him goodbye in front of the hotel. Jenny then drove Bill up to the U of U campus where Megan was waiting to meet him after attending an Olympic volunteer's meeting. Again, Mitch watched his partner hug Jenny goodbye and tried not to hate him. By some sort of unspoken agreement, Mitch was heading to Ogden with Jenny. It was Monday morning, Martin Luther King, JR Day, human rights day. Jenny had it off, and the boys needed to report in on Wednesday, so they had a day and a half to settle in.

Bill claimed that Megan would take care of him and get him to her parents' home where they'd be staying that night. He would stay in SLC to make sure the Bunch was fine with their condo and to help Jonesey pick up their vehicles. In that way the group gently kept Mitch where he was—with Jenny by tacit agreement. Mitch had caught Jonesey talking to everyone before they'd got in the rig down at the airport. He felt sure that Jonesey had instructed everyone to give he and Jenny some time. Bill promised Mitch he'd come get him early on Wednesday. He and Megan might be up Tuesday night for dinner, depending on the weather and how they were able to get everyone settled.

After leaving the U of U's campus and hugging Megan goodbye for a few days, Jenny looked like she was ready for bed. She looked done in, and it was only 5:00 p.m. Mitch was with her and would remain so for days. What a strange concept. She had been avoiding him for months. Even now, she'd just spent the better part of an hour with him up front in the Suburban with her, but hadn't spoken to him. If anything, she looked increasingly uncomfortable with every passing mile.

Mitch enjoyed watching her discomfiture, especially the scrunched up lines between her eyebrows. His love was miffed for sure, and she wanted to drive, so he got to spend all the time he wanted watching her. Her thoughts were running across her face and she kept shrugging at some tightness in her shoulders and neck as she drove. Not that she could hide what she was thinking from him at this moment anyway. He felt like she was almost talking to him directly, as hard as she was thinking on him. He decided to be merciful to her. He knew she was tired, but was too good a hostess to leave him at loose ends.

Mitch reached over to Jenny and took her purse from her side. Reaching in, he asked, "Do you mind if I use this thing? I'll pay any extra charges," as he grabbed her cell phone.

"Yes, of course, why?"

He ignored her question as he dialed 411 and asked for the Pizza Hut in downtown Ogden. Before she could protest, he'd ordered two large pepperoni pizzas and some breadsticks. After disconnecting, he replaced her cell phone and looked at her. "Okay, now that you don't have to feed me, are you ready to take me home?"

"Pizza gives me killer heartburn."

"I wasn't planning on sharing," he remarked as he smiled back at her. Levity shared, the ride was much better on the way home. Mitch allowed Jenny time to gather her thoughts for a moment. After five minutes of waiting with no response, he dropped the bomb in her lap. "I figure after dinner you can tell me just what the hell is going on. I'm hungry and we're both tired, so let's just not worry about it for another couple of hours, okay?" Jenny nodded. Maybe they could work this out.

Chapter Seventy-two

A few forlorn slices of cold pizza sat on the table, empty Subway sandwich wrappings lay nearby, and empty glasses sat across the table. Jenny and Mitch sat in her freshly painted, classy, bright dining room.

She'd pained the walls a deep Prussian blue and found a mahogany-colored table for a cheap price at a yard sale and was able to repair its finish. Colorful and bright paintings painted by Jenny hung with others donated by Megan and were artfully arranged on the walls, and copper-colored fixtures graced the ceiling and walls as a sparkling chandelier and wall sconces.

Mitch felt much refreshed in her house. It was roomy yet cozy at the same time, and he really liked the colors Jenny used. He could see her artistic bent from her front door. Feeling comfortably full after eating an entire pizza on his own, he realized that it had been a long day and the meal helped him feel better. Of course, he felt alive just being near Jenny. He had only barely realized how lonely his life was before he'd met her early last year. No one had ever touched the places in his heart that Jenny seemed to reach into with no effort. He looked at her now, watching her rest, nearly asleep, and pictured another woman, the woman who'd obsessed him since seeing long legs pacing last March, nearly a year ago. Thinking of that previous Jenny, he thought of the lives we lead and the people we choose to share them with. His thoughts turned to another woman, a young widow he'd met a few months back who, at the time, had reminded him of Jenny.

In mid-October, Mitch had been assigned to one of the many FBI teams attempting to figure out the causes of September 11 and trying to capture all the conspirators and organizations, like the rest of the FBI, CIA, and every other government agency. Homer's group and hence, Stan's

Terrorist Crew, as they were known, were focused on the attacks on the Pentagon and the aborted attack on DC whose brave passengers had forced the plan to ground prematurely.

One of the people Mitch and Bill had interviewed in their investigations was a young widow whose husband had been on the flight that crashed in Pennsylvania. The husband had called her in those moments early on September 11, when the government was still trying to find all the missing commercial flights, to tell her how much he loved her. Mitch and Bill had gone to see her on a quiet Friday afternoon last fall to see if her husband's call could give rise to any new leads in their investigation.

The widow's mother had met them at the door and ushered them through the house into the kitchen. The lady sat there waiting for them at the kitchen table. The mother had apologized for having them meet in the kitchen by explaining, "Since Jack died, Emily hasn't been able to rest comfortably in the front room, too many memories." At which point, Emily herself jumped in with, "It's not the memories, but the quality of the memories. See, Jack, and I worked separate shifts. I worked during the day and he worked the night shift as a supervisor. Our best times were during breakfast, when we would sit and eat here and talk after he got home and before I left for work."

Emily smiled sadly. "The last time I saw him he was sitting right here grinning at me as we shared our breakfast." She had been four months pregnant on September 11 and to quote her husband, a "bit moody" that morning; he'd been teasing her in an effort to help her feel better before work. She was just noticeably pregnant, but not huge when Mitch and Bill interviewed her. Her pregnancy was what caused Jack to be on that plane. He'd had a job interview in San Francisco with another firm. Her parents lived out in California and they would be able to help with the new baby, while Jack's parents lived in

Seattle, and would be able to visit them more often. The four of them had sat around the table for a while until Emily's mom urged her to talk for her as the memories were too hard right then.

After the interview, as Mitch and Bill were leaving, Emily's mom stopped them in the living room and showed the agents the family portraits hung together and covering one wall. These pictures kept Emily from entering this room. Jack had been a smiling redhead like Bill. The mother thanked them for getting Emily to talk. She had not spoken of Jack very much since September 11, and her doctor was worried about the baby with Emily being so stressed.

Mitch remembered the look of peace on Emily's face as he and Bill left. Sharing the burden had eased her. Emily had stood to say goodbye and had impulsively hugged Bill (the likeness between Bill and the now-gone but not forgotten Jack was uncanny) close for a moment. Bill had held her tight for a moment, then they'd left.

Mitch looked at Jenny sitting across from him in her living room in her old battered rocking chair. There were other haunted images in his head. He remembered Reva's cousin Jordan and how he'd lost him down off the cliff. He saw the haunted looks of the FBI agents back in New York and the faces of those ferry passengers in Scotland. The few Army, Navy, and other personnel he'd interviewed had looked less lost, due to their training, but they too were shell-shocked as they did everything they could to help Mitch and Bill close up the Gooding case. The faces blurred to him into a mix of all the other "victims" he'd ever seen, helped, interviewed, or accosted in his efforts to do his job.

Jenny looked overwhelmed, tired and care-worn, just like all those folks. There were dark circles under her eyes and she had moved more sluggishly since they'd gotten home to her place. She'd stubbornly stopped at a

Subway sandwich store near her home to get a couple of sandwiches, since she refused to eat his pizza due to her constant pregnancy heartburn, but that previous energy was gone.

Standing up from the table, Mitch approached Jenny where she sat rocking. She looked up at him. He pulled her up gently by her hands and guided her to the nearby sofa. He settled her on the couch facing the softly lit dining room. After turning her so she sat sideways on the couch, he nestled a pillow behind her back and another under her feet and headed back to the dining room, saying, "Rest for a minute, I'll just put the food away."

***

Jenny laid back and felt her back and stomach muscles twitch and spasm as she relaxed. Mitch had left the living room light off, so the only light shone on her from the dining room through the alcove across from her. She could see Mitch cross the lighted opening and disappear again as he cleared the table's contents into the kitchen. After a moment and some banging around, she heard him start the dishwasher.

That was just what she really needed at this moment, a man to load her dishwasher. Just the thought of bending down to load the thing caused her back to twitch. Lately she'd rather get a backache from standing at the sink than bend down to get into the dishwasher. As Mitch continued to putter around, she remembered his luggage sitting by the back door in the kitchen. Soon, she'd have to get him and it upstairs. He should go in the guest room, but that thought fell together with the knot of thoughts in her head titled: "What is Mitch's status in your life." So she let it be for a moment. She couldn't admit that she wanted him in her bed, to hold her, and to rock her to sleep. It was hard being without him.

***

Mitch stood in the arch between the living and dining rooms, watching Jenny. She wasn't asleep yet, but her eyes were closed and she had settled deeper into the couch. He took one last swig of his drink and went back into the kitchen to set the empty glass on the counter. When he returned to the arch he debated for a moment, then decided to leave the lights in the kitchen on. Jenny might be more comfortable and therefore better able to speak to him in the dark, but she seemed jumpy and probably needed some light to see by. He glanced down at the dining chairs next to him. Jenny had bought this house with her bonus from last summer, but apparently hadn't had enough money for extra furniture yet. Besides the dining room set, there was no place to sit downstairs besides the couch and rocking chair in the living room. The only other furniture in that room was Jenny's TV, VCR, and secondhand entertainment center.

Making his decision, Mitch approached the couch, lifted Jenny gently, and replaced her on his lap as he sat back down. She looked up to him, all attempts to sleep forgotten, even though she still looked tired. They stared at each other for a moment in the half light from the dining room chandelier. Then Jenny sighed and laid her head against Mitch's neck and chest and he felt peace for the first time in nearly a year. He belonged here with this woman. This truth was forever.

Chapter Seventy-three

"Hey do you think they're still awake?" Bill asked Megan as they approached the front door to Jenny's house.

"I have no idea. Would you be after a day like today?" she answered.

Bill looked down on her cold and rosy cheeks and noticed how her smooth black hair shone in the light from the porch, and made a decision. "Okay, then. Let's go check just in case, and if they're still up, rather than staying the night I'll take you to your mom's and we can crash there instead."

"Sounds good, cutie, you lead. You're the big, mean FBI agent here. I'll be your backup." Megan smiled back at him as she pretended to hold a gun in her gloved hands.

Hand in hand they crept up to the porch. Bill slid sideways past the front door and peered into the living room through the wide picture window. He saw Jenny and Mitch on the couch just below him. "Yup. They're up and sitting on the couch," he whispered behind him.

"Okay. Now we know. Let's go, it's freezing out here," answered Megan.

Back down the walk they strolled to Megan's car, Bill resting his arm around Megan's shoulders as she clasped his waist. They walked to the passenger side of the car. Bill reached around Megan, opened the door for her, and gave her a hand down into the seat. When she was comfortable, he took over the driver's seat and they headed back to Salt Lake City.

In the warm quiet of the car, Megan asked, "Do you think they'll make it?"

Bill was quiet for a minute before he answered as he considered the situation between Mitch and Jenny. "I've wondered that for nearly a year now and I thought about it all day today. I don't know. Jonesey seems to think they will once they get past how they left things, but I don't really know. I do know he loves her, but is that enough?" He turned to Megan and met her eyes.

She reached over and grabbed his free hand as she answered, "It should be. It is for me."

Chapter Seventy-four

As the clock ticked quietly in the background, Mitch broke the silence between he and Jenny as they sat on the couch in her living room. "Are you ready to 'fess up and admit you love me, my dear?"

Jenny was speechless, but had been feeling quiet all evening, so it didn't bother her for once. She figured that waiting a few minutes to answer him wouldn't matter. This evening, this past day, was not what she imagined. She'd done so much wrong to him. Mitch sat the waiting expectantly. She was surprised that he wasn't madder at her.

"How much do you want to hear?" Jenny finally asked him, tentatively, unsure of how to proceed. Mitch wiggled a bit and settled down on the couch. "Me, I want to hear it *all*. I have all night, but get moving, I've waited nearly nine months, missy."

Short, sweet, to-the-point speech finished, Mitch waited to hear what she had to say.

Bracing herself, Jenny started her confession. "I found out I was pregnant for sure on September eleventh. The whole time the doctor's office was processing the blood test, me, the other patient, and the office staff were sitting behind the medical desk, watching the TV and the news." Mitch tightened his hold on her slightly, but he didn't interrupt.

"When I got home to Utah, I figured I was unlucky enough to have gotten pregnant after my first time. After Stan lecturing me in London, Al laying in to me by phone in DC until Stan got home and could lecture me again, and Jonesey entertaining himself on the plane ride home by doing the same—and the general disbelief on behalf of the rest of the team in the scene I caused—when I got to Mom's I could take no more. It had been forty-eight eventful hours, and I fell asleep. After a couple of hours I woke up and decided I was probably pregnant, because, one, I have positively shitty bad luck and. two, the timing was about right. And since I wasn't…well, uh…we…well, I hadn't planned on having sex, and—"

Mitch jumped in, taking pity on her flustered state. "Neither did I, but I should have had a condom on me. I would say I'm sorry, but having this little critter kick me in the ribs has messed up all my logic just now."

That statement made Jenny pause. For the first time, Mr. Harper and his baby were getting acquainted. Charmed, she smiled in the half light at Mitch and continued, "Well, too late for that now, and besides only the shittiest of bad luck people get pregnant their first time. Here's proof positive that I do have crappy luck. Anyway, I woke up realizing that I needed to get to the hospital ASAP. It was Saturday by then, and my doctor wouldn't be in the office, and they don't sell the morning-after pill over the counter in Utah, and, well the only way to get one was to get one from the hospital or your doctor in like a rape kit."

Jenny was silent for a moment. She had figured that once started, her confession would flow uninterrupted at the speed of light. She didn't know how to handle this choppy set of statements, and now she was so tired she nearly didn't care to keep going.

Mitch asked in the silence, "Couldn't you have taken two birth control pills or something?"

Jenny gulped, embarrassed more, but tired enough to not care too much. "I've never been on birth control." Before she figured Mitch would have the time to be shocked at her naiveté, she plunged onward. "It's not like I was sexually active or anything, and my periods were perfectly regular, so I have, I mean, I had no reason to be on birth control. Also, any of my friends and family would have known what I'd done had I asked them for their pills.

So, I wasn't about to go to the doctor for something like that and when I'd found the courage to do it anyway, I realized that it was probably too late, and I didn't know how to go about getting the pill, so I gave up. I'm pregnant 'cuz I was too terrified to ask for help." Jenny finished her confession with a gulped sob.

***

Mitch smiled, at peace for the first time in months. *Like Jenny asked anyone for help, ever,* he thought. He'd never known anyone so independent, except maybe Reva. *That's probably why those two get along so well—kindred spirits*, he mused. As Jenny explained her reasoning to him, he'd been reminded of her lifestyle and churchy upbringing. After all the women he'd known, Jenny continued to surprise him with her methods of dealing with "womanly issues." He'd never even considered that she wouldn't have ever taken birth control, because she wasn't having sex. In work, nothing missed his attention during a case, yet with his personal life, lately he'd been forgetting Jenny's background and how unsophisticated she really was. He'd listened to her explain her reasons for not terminating a possible pregnancy in the only way she'd even consider it. He was grateful she hadn't done so, even in her upset state of mind.

Mitch thought of other girlfriends he'd had and the one who'd called her unexpected pregnancy a "mistake" and ended it by abortion without consulting him or even telling him that she was pregnant before it was over. He hadn't expected the pain he'd felt about it at the time, never having even a near opportunity to be a father before. However, he'd been secretly grateful and guilty about how she'd handled the situation, not because of what she did, but her methods proved that she was not the type of woman he could have been with forever. He'd glossed over his relief when they'd broke up to her family and his friends.

They told everyone that they both realized they didn't want to get married.

That uncomfortable situation allowed him to ignore his feelings about the pregnancy, but it taught him a lot about himself. The idea of abortion offended his sense of fairness. For a time he had nightmares about the baby, dreams filled with fetuses and crying babies, but once he'd made his peace with what happened, the bad dreams went away and he could forgive himself his carelessness. Since then, he'd been fastidious about "mistakes" and had been practically compulsive about birth control, until that night with Jenny. A guilty pleasure stole over him. *My babies will be safe with Jenny.*

As Mitch sat there with Jenny sitting on his lap, all soft and warm with their baby kicking him in the ribs, he knew deep down that all this was meant to be. He would never have been able to really appreciate this woman without nearly losing her. He thought about how flippant and insensitive he had been to the other women who'd come before this one and felt peace at the gift and second chance he'd been given at happiness. He said, "No, you got pregnant 'cuz I love you, woman, and I couldn't resist your sexiness any longer, and I meant to keep you. I decided that I wanted you to be mine and only mine, and that night was part of that."

Jenny's head jerked up as she tried to probe Mitch's gaze in the low light through the tears in her eyes. "You still love me after all the messes I've dragged you through?"

Mitch hugged her closer glad he'd chosen to nestle with her on her comfy couch. "I'm not saying that I'm over the messes you put me through, but sitting here in the dark, holding you close, feeling you all soft and sweet and smelling so good, it does things to a man. How can I deny you anything of mine when you feel so good on the outside, and do so many good things to my insides, and are the mother of my child—especially when you have my love?" He choked up on that last word, but felt freer for having said it out loud. He guessed he'd been the one who needed to admit it all along.

"It's a boy," Jenny said.

Mitch held her tighter in his arms, taking her words as a gift into his heart. He had no words to contain his emotions at that statement and could only listen as Jenny continued, "I was going to name him Daniel Mitchell after you and your grandfather."

Warm feelings washed over Mitch as he absorbed her words. "Thank you," was all he could say. The feelings and thoughts were running around in his head too fast to capture them with his tongue. Somehow telling him these deep truths seemed to break the last of Jenny's barriers and she finished telling Mitch the things of her heart in a rush.

"Well, I bought this house with my bonus, and spent the few months I had left of school trying to not throw up every minute. I graduated in December with honors. Bill found out that I was pregnant in October, thanks to Megan when he met her that time when he flew out to meet Jonesey when they were revamping the Salt Lake Office. Amy helped me pick out the nursery furniture—all baby blue and cowboy in honor of your summers in Montana and my grandpa's ranch, and Megan helped me paint. I was gonna call you millions of times, but each time I couldn't make myself tell you. Also, you should know that Bill, Jonesey, Stan, Homer, and Albert have all lectured me about telling you. In fact, I'm surprised Al or Stan didn't tell you at Christmastime. Also, Jonesey lectured me on the plane as we left London on that day, that I should have stayed and had brunch with you. Maybe had I done that, we'd be better." Jenny paused for a small breath but continued before Mitch could interrupt her. "The only one who was okay with me not telling you about the baby was Reva, not that she agreed with me, but I think she stood by me as part of her whole reverse psychology plan to get us together once and for all."

Mitch sighed. "I honestly don't know what would have happened to us if you had stayed. Part of me hopes we'd be here in this same place, after months of happiness, but I don't know. Maybe I had to lose you to know I didn't want to lose you." Mitch changed his tone and asked, "So why didn't you tell me?"

Jenny sighed. "Albert is such a softie, such a good guy. You know how tenderhearted he is. Well, he's been watching you all along and after Thanksgiving, he noticed you got ornerier and ornerier so he was determined to shake you out of your blues by making you really, really mad at me." Jenny smiled and shook her head. "But, I was mostly scared."

They sat in comfortable silence for a while. After a bit, Jenny glanced up at him. "How can you forgive me for leaving and keeping this from you?" She gestured to her belly. "Heck, I heard that Stan had you hog-tied, which I know you must have hated. Why don't you hate me?" Then she had the audacity to yawn at him before Mitch could answer.

Mitch had pondered that question all day. *Why don't I hate her?* He looked at Jenny and assessed her need for rest and his own jet-lagged body's tiredness and couldn't be mad at her for being so sleepy. She was pregnant, after all. As for the rest… "I really don't know," he said. "I don't know if Bill would have told you this, but I've been pretending you didn't exist since that morning— just to survive in my dreary world without you. Yeah, I was royally pissed off that morning, but it's a long plane ride to the States, and Grandpa had asked me to visit him when I was done. So I spent six weeks in Montana, focusing on horses and hay. Then, when September eleventh happened, well, I guess you know how busy we've been, I threw myself into my work. In fact this Olympic detail has actually been a break for me, as it's a temporary, if intense assignment, and we have high hopes of no incidents. After this, it's back into September eleventh stuff. I don't know if we'll ever get to the bottom of the September eleventh attacks." Mitch took a deep breath and pressed on. "But...somewhere in the middle of one of my grandpa's hay fields, I realized I didn't want to be angry with you anymore. In fact, I realized I missed you more than was healthy and I gave you up to the sky. I imagined that you'd really flown away from me in Aberdeen, and I decided I had to let you go. I couldn't bring myself to call you. But I think I was still a bit miffed, so I refused to call you. I had no idea that the anger was still there until I saw you in the airport today. When I felt all those months of missing you come back, I just lost it. I have to admit, though, I was deeply unhappy, and not sleeping. I guess it really did turn me into a bear."

Jenny was silent. Mitch felt her tense up in his arms and spoke to calm her. "Things all changed after September eleventh. Life is too short to let the little things hold you back. I talked to too many people whose last connections with their loved ones were tiny moments of caring. I had felt that caring myself last summer when you harassed me all the time. I missed the caring when it was gone."

They just stared at each other for a minute. Mitch, feeling relaxed for the first time in a while, felt a warm feeling come over him. It started in his ribs and moved up his back and down to his toes. He felt something tell him that he should share something more with Jenny. Concerned, as he was never able to easily convey deep or spiritual thoughts even when he felt them, he didn't know how to talk to Jenny about this incident. He was grateful that Jenny was a deeply spiritual person who could and did talk about these things.

He remembered how Reva and Jenny had talked in Georgia, and how Jenny was the only person who could talk to Reva about Carl since his death. Mitch also knew that Carl had been LDS like Jenny was, a rarity in his experience, and that Reva's Jewish faith had enabled her and Carl and Jenny to talk about what Stan called "religious" things. Mitch didn't understand people who could talk about churchy stuff when not at church. It had taken him a long time to realize that some people lived a religion and mixed what he thought of as spiritual things into their everyday lives. He looked into Jenny's shadowed eyes there in the dark and realized that he trusted and loved this woman. He could tell her anything now, having admitted the big things to her already. And, in this, she of all the people he knew, at least, would understand and not judge him.

Mitch cleared his throat. "There is one thing I haven't told you. It's been on my mind and I knew I could talk about it with you. After September eleventh, when our nightmares came true, I was lost. I felt adrift in my world, and I kept thinking about Reva and you, and your prayer circles. And, of how I didn't feel connected to anything bigger than myself."

"Prayer circles?" Jenny asked, her brow furrowed.

Mitch struggled, not knowing how to put such difficult feelings into words for her. "You know, when things were a little scary and you and Reva and a couple of the others would pray together? Well, I saw Reva and Carl go to the back room and pray over one of the wounded recruits in New York. I watched as Reva closed the door, but it opened a crack. I saw Carl and Jacob, that South Carolina agent, put their hands on the wounded man's head, close their eyes, and move their mouths, whispering. Reva told me later, that they had given that man a blessing, what she called a "priesthood blessing." I knew that Carl and Jacob were *not* priests or chaplains, and my confusion must have shown, because Reva explained that they were Mormons, LDS, like you, and the Mormons do this, that worthy Mormon men are given the power or permission to help someone get well. She told me that Carl explained it to her like God sharing His power with those who tried to serve Him. I still don't understand it, and when Reva saw me still confused, she shooed me out of the room and told me to crack my Bible and ask God about it."

Mitch looked down, gauging Jenny's response. He couldn't handle her looking down on him. In his experience, big, tough macho men who worked for the FBI didn't talk about religion much, especially in front of a female, even if they believed in God and depended on Him daily.

***

Jenny was a little surprised, but not because Mitch brought up the topic of her religion. She just didn't like to make an issue of her faith. In fact, she didn't push religion on anyone, as she didn't want anyone pushing religion on her. She'd made it a point to *not* talk about being LDS or Mormon or start any inappropriate conversations while on assignment. As a government employee, Jenny was well aware that talking about religion could be considered offensive to some people, like sexual conversations. Any offensive matter in her workplace was frowned on. Because she and Reva had formed a kinship, they talked about faith and spirituality and God during their regular conversations. They were both deeply spiritual—the issue just happened to come up occasionally, as God was part of their lives. She had no idea Mitch or anyone else had noticed, and she hadn't known Carl was LDS until he was killed and Reva came to ask her about how LDS folks handled death. So, she really hadn't had an opportunity to observe any religious conversations with any of the team, and Mitch had never brought up the issue with her on a serious note like this.

Jenny put her hand over Mitch's to offer him the comfort he seemed to need. "Please go on." She nudged him verbally and physically, knowing that he wasn't done saying what he needed to say.

Mitch did as she asked. "On September twelfth, there were so many memorials around the city. Since it'd been so long since I had been in a church, I didn't know where to go to find God or comfort. I thought of you and Carl's faith and wondered what the Mormons were doing for comfort and how they found God. I didn't know where Reva was, or I would have found her. Bill had left to volunteer to watch the office. So, I found an LDS church house in DC. When I arrived at the chapel, I talked to a person leaving the building who happened to be the bishop. He told me that they weren't having a memorial, but he was going to one of the member's houses to offer them comfort as the woman's husband had been lost in the Pentagon plane." Mitch paused, and Jenny nodded encouragement.

"The bishop invited me to go with him. He said that God, who he called Heavenly Father, sent me to him, that he felt, that he *knew*, that I was needed to accompany him that day. I asked him how he knew this. He answered that some people would call this meeting between us chance or fate, but he knew that he was sent to the church house that day to find me. He'd left to go see the widow that morning, but realized he had left something locked in his office at the church the night before. The bishop said he never left his scriptures at church but that day he had. He had just retrieved them and was locking up the building when I pulled up."

"So, what happened?" Jenny asked.

"Well, we drove to the widow's, actually he called it the sister's, house. The family, friends, and members of that ward met us at the door. It took me a while to figure out that you guys call your parishes, wards—some of the terms you use are weird, like the stake thing and how you call a priest a bishop, and that you also have priests but use the term for your young men who hold specific offices in the church. Anyway, the bishop sat me down after and explained some things, but I'm getting off track…"

***

Mitch tried to calm his panic. It was difficult talking about the deep changes that had come into his life in the past year. He took a breath and continued. "In the living room of the house sat the widow and her mother on the couch crying. It wasn't the first time or the last time I've encountered a grieving widow—you know about the interview with Emily, and Bill and I interviewed many, many people after September eleventh. This lady looked vaguely familiar, and I soon recognized her. Her husband Steven had gone to school with me in Montana, and we had been loose friends in college. I had been to their wedding, but had lost track of them in the years since. My friend had been an only child, and his parents had died just after he married, so I was the only other person in the room directly connected to him. I knew he'd moved to DC after he'd graduated with a degree in political science and landed a good job with a large lobbying firm.

"Shelia, Steven's wife, was worrying that she didn't know enough about Steven's earlier life to pass it on to their kids. He had boxed up all his parents' stuff and left it in the attic, but she didn't know if she could make sense of things. My presence as someone who knew him was a comfort to her, and she said it was an answer to her prayer. We still keep in contact and I was able to refer her to some of our other buddies and one of Steven's former teachers in our hometown." Mitch took a deep breath.

"Shelia also said she needed God to tell her that Steven had been meant to die. My finding her bishop was proof to her that Steven was in a better place and that she would be okay. She said that she knew God was listening to her and if he could send an answer to that question, then she'd get the other answers she needed in her life. Though when we last talked, she said she's still upset that Steven's left her to carry on, but things were a little better. As for myself, I couldn't believe the warm comfort in that home. It had the peace and comfort I had been looking for, and when the bishop said a prayer, the warmth intensified. I felt the warmth burn all the fear inside of me away."

Mitch felt that same warmth surround him now just in speaking and he'd always felt this peace around Jenny. Since the summer, Mitch was beginning to believe that peace meant God was near. "So, then in October, the bishop called me. He said that he knew I wasn't really investigating the church, but if I ever wanted to, I should tune into a local radio station and listen to the LDS general conference that Sunday. He said that at the conference, talks would be given by various LDS church leaders and that their prophet would speak. He was right. I wasn't even thinking of joining his church, but I did listen to the sessions of the conference on Sunday after my morning run. I heard your prophet speak, and I felt that warmth again. I kept listening and knew that what I was feeling, you call the Holy Ghost, and He testified that what I was hearing was true. When I heard Mr. Hinckley speak about the start of the war and how the US was sending troops to the Middle East, I felt power in his words. Of course this was a lot to take in, but over the next few months, whenever I had a particularly hard week, I would go to Shelia's church and listen. Then, when they gave me and Bill the Olympic assignment, I decided to go with him and 'investigate' the Mormons on their home turf. 'When in Rome…,' but Salt Lake City instead. I went so far as to call Jonesey, and got his aunt's address in Sandy, which I knew was part of the Salt Lake metro area, so that I could go with her to church and talk to the missionaries at her house."

"You mean the discussions? You're going to have the missionary discussions?" Jenny jerked upright.

Mitch answered Jenny with his own excitement and a little trepidation, "Well, you and Shelia seem so much happier and peaceful. And, well, Bill has told me about how Megan doesn't worry about half of the stuff he worries about. They've joked, and he calls it her 'eternal perspective.' I want to know what makes you guys happier. I need some perspective myself."

***

Jenny waited before answering him. She knew he used his belief in a higher power to get through his work stress. And if he found out more about God, then that was fantastic. However, her conscience and fair-minded personality really kicked in at that moment—in the form of some questions. Mitch needed to do what he needed to for himself—nobody else. The way he was looking at her showed her that he was serious about her, and they had finally admitted that they loved each other, but they hadn't discussed any "issues." Not kids, or money, or religion. Jenny started to panic even as she tried hard not to. Here was Mitch talking about religion with her, and she didn't even know what his intentions were. She was assuming that they were going to start a serious relationship. To be fair, religion needed to be a non-issue in their relationship. She wouldn't change her religion, so it would be unfair to ask him to change his. But if he wanted to check it out, that was dandy with her. And she was seriously jumping the gun here. He hadn't said anything about *them*. Jenny applied her mental brakes full force. She would be happy to help him find comfort in his life and answer any questions he still had about the LDS church, but she had no right to influence him in that choice or even try to coerce him into marrying her, no matter how much she wanted him to ask.

In her upset, Jenny was still able to hug Mitch tight and smile at him for an instant. Mitch smiled over her excited state, but was clearly surprised when she pushed away and got off him and the couch in a hurry.

"What's wrong, Jenny? Where are you going?" Mitch asked, utterly confused by the turnabout in her behavior. He stood up and made to follow her.

Jenny, trying to not think of them as a couple, started speaking, pacing around him as she spoke, struggling to not think of how awkward she looked in her very pregnant state. "Don't do this Mormon thing just to make me happy. Mitch, I'd take you pink, purple, Catholic, Buddhist, or Islamic. I just want *you*, but we haven't even talked about me having you."

***

Mitch smiled. Now he understood. She wanted to make sure he was sure about any decisions he made about faith separate from "them." He wondered if she realized she just told him that she loved him. He could tell that her only concern was for his happiness. Joy filled him, along with a feeling he could only describe as "rightness." This was the woman he was meant to be with. He felt the confirmation in his soul. She was a bit too upset right now for his peace of mind, and he noticed in her ramblings she seemed to be worried about offending him, so he decided to focus her attention on the real issue he figured was bothering her and said, "I thought you Mormons weren't supposed to marry non-Mormons."

That stopped her pacing. Jenny looked at him, visibly shocked by his statement. "Yeah, well, I know you'd let me keep my religion and we could be fair with the kids, but I'd take forty years of life here and now with you before I'd ever take the option of never having you at all!"

Mitch smiled even more, having finally heard what he'd been waiting for. Shelia, who expected Steven to meet her in Heaven after she died, had well acquainted him with the idea of "marriage for time and all eternity." He knew many people who thought of love as being eternal, but the Mormons not only thought of it as eternal but lived life as if love was eternal. When they spoke of their families, they spoke of them as being "forever" and they lived that way. All the people Mitch had asked about this idea explained that their religion was about Christ, but also about families. They strove to live in the right way so that they could take their families with them to heaven; which, without those they loved, would be no kind of heaven at all. He'd learned from the bishop in Shelia's ward back in DC that Mormons had no "until death do us part" phrase in their temple marriage ceremony. There would be no end to their kind of marriage. He thought of Shelia and Steve. Their house still felt like a complete home. Shelia believed Steve was still there in spirit, like he was there watching over them. Mitch intended to find out if these things were real. And, looking at the woman across the room from him in the semi-darkness, he was willing to bet his life on it that they were.

Chapter Seventy-five

All the snow was gone here in the valleys of the Wasatch Mountains. Mitch hadn't had to shovel the walks for nearly ten days. Weeks had passed since he'd come to Utah. The Olympics had come and gone and his life was completely different, but better than he'd ever imagined it could be.

Jenny sat nestled beside him on his massive leather sofa. She had only a few days left of pregnancy, hopefully, and her monstrous stomach had grown even more than he could believe. She couldn't do anything anymore. Her slender frame, especially her hips, could hardly bear the weight of this active boy. Jenny constantly griped that, "My feet are a distant dream, and I can hardly sit still during my aches and pains, especially while at work." So she'd started her maternity leave early. Her ankles, though unseen, swelled and ached and hurt intermittently. Mitch did all he could, but they both knew there was only one cure to this ailment.

***

Jenny sat thinking of Mitch—one of her favorite pastimes. Mitchell, the sweetheart he was, had some sort of flaw, which caused him to adore her feet. The by-product of this adoration was his heavenly foot massages. They could also be sinfully erotic, but even the idea of sex was impossible right now. After so many months, she thought of that night last July as a distant memory. So she settled for foot massages on the sofa for now and hoped that they would be able to someday do something "else" after they married and she lost her baby weight. Jenny heard from Megan that Mitch had spoken to her bishop. Afterward, Mitch shyly asked Jenny to go with him to be interviewed as an engaged couple. In that meeting a couple of Sundays ago, they sat holding hands and talking with the bishop across his desk. As the bishop spoke to them about the importance of being a family and loving each other, Mitch set up a time for the marriage ceremony. He'd taken the lecture about being a good husband and father well and they promised the bishop and God that they would keep their hands off each other until they were married.

Mitch seemed to take all the advice in stride. Jenny knew that his grandfather had given him a far worse lecture about the improper situation created by his staying with Jenny until they were man and wife. Jenny's father was as bad, but so far both the Harper and Johnson camps had relented, as nobody wanted Jenny home alone when she went into labor. Her mother had remarked, "Who better to get her to the hospital than Mitch, after all."

Mitch's long, black sofa and monstrous king-sized bed, with the other contents of his old DC apartment, had just arrived here in Utah yesterday. Mitch was now reassigned to the Salt Lake City FBI office, as was Bill. Their relocations included "moving expenses" and the two had enjoyed filling a huge semi with their stuff. Of course, Grandpa Harper had also filled a horse trailer and brought the rest of Mitch's possessions down from the ranch in Montana. Jenny had watched in awe as the men in her life unloaded the semi and the trailer and filled her house. Especially as every one of the "boys" refused to let a pregnant woman help in any way. Mitch even promised to let Jenny take him shopping for a new vehicle. He teased her, telling her that he was going to buy her a new mini-van and steal her truck. To which she responded by hitting him and getting angry. Jenny grinned. She strongly suspected that he teased her just to see her reaction.

Bill and Mitch spent too much time with the bombings, in Jonesey's estimation. He shared this observation with Stan. He convinced the boss that both of them needed a break. As a result, Stan agreed to reassign them to Jonesey. They were now part of the Denver Bunch.

Stan was okay with the transfer, as Jonesey traded him Nelson and Smith, transferring them to DC to fill Mitch and Bill's spots.

Smith and Nelson, each being in their late twenties and relatively green, were ecstatic to be reassigned to the DC office, while Mitch and Bill, in their thirties, were even happier to scale down a bit. Mitch, Jonesey, Jenny, and Stan also knew that Bill was pleased to be closer to Megan.

Jenny laughed, remembering all the times she'd told Megan, "I'll never have enough furniture for this house. It has four bedrooms, two and half baths, a kitchen, dining and living rooms, plus the den and large workroom in the basement." Megan had teased her back by saying, "As long as you're shopping, you don't need one bed, you need four, one for each room." Now, with Mitch's stuff, her old house felt full and complete—like her heart. They had a home to build together. Mitch had agreed, saying, "Not that a massive eight-foot, gunmetal gray, leather sofa makes a home, but it helps."

Jenny placed a hand over her swollen stomach. Daniel Mitchell seemed quieter now. After the blow-up between his mom and dad the weeks before and the hassle of having his dad moving in, besides the excitement in the air during the 2002 Winter Olympics, he'd been more and more active lately. Today, however, Jenny felt restful for the first time in months. She worried that she'd hurt her baby by being so worked up over Mitch. Her doctor and Mitch both reassured her as best they could, and all the tests showed the baby was fine.

She'd weathered her mom and Megan teasing her about "nesting." Her mom had even chided, "Quit complaining about moving. Two months ago, all you could do was lament your lack of furniture, and now you imported a guy and all his stuff into your nest, so let him feather it for you. You should just smile and say thank you for having your dad and I help Mitch unpack." Her mom was so cute when she was on a tirade. This time she was successful in refocusing Jenny's thoughts toward her good fortune.

As she laid full length on the couch, belly reaching to heaven, Jenny spotted her dad coming downstairs. A minute before, he'd been outside. "What are you up to, Dad?"

"I dare you to come see," he'd taunted. The whole family had heard Jenny crabbing about climbing her stairs. Mitch had told her, "Hey, I'm not the one that picked a two-story house so you could have upstairs bedrooms."

Not one to resist a dare, and being so pregnant that laying belly up was awful, Jenny tried to get up. Her dad, seeing her distress, helped her roll to the side, then lifted her to her feet. She was slow moving, but he continued helping her up the stairs and into the nursery. Jenny's jaw dropped. Where the crib she and Megan had so lovingly painted white had stood forlorn all alone, there was now a new, matching dresser and changing table. Her mom stepped into the room from behind her and gently turned her head to the new quilt and bumper pads in the crib, and the matching changing cloth on the table.

Her dad spoke for both he and her mom. "Just in case Daniel decides he can't wait until after the wedding, we wanted you to be ready." They left Jenny alone in the nursery to absorb it all for a minute. Her parents smiled on their way downstairs, pleased with themselves. Mitch too, had teared up when they'd shown him the "new" nursery earlier.

Jenny left the nursery to find her bed and lie down for a bit. She smiled as she passed Mitch's temporary quarters now that Megan had moved out.

***

Jenny's dad had made his feelings about her and Mitch's relationship perfectly clear when he'd moved in Mitch's bed. "There will be no cohabitation until the wedding, you hear?" her parents had announced when they'd shown Mitch and Jenny the master bedroom where they'd installed Mitch's bed.

The bed was bare of sheets and blankets and triple wrapped with industrial shrink-wrap (courtesy of Jenny's brother's warehouse night job). Police tape saying "Do Not Cross" was tied across the bed. Before he could say anything, Mitch was shown the new lock on the spare bedroom's door, where Jenny's queen bed had been moved. Her dad continued, "For the next two days, I hope you'll enjoy your stay at the Johnson Family hacienda." He handed Mitch a suitcase and told him to pack. Mitch took the hint as well as Jenny did, but later had a long talk with Mr. Johnson. They were both aware that those kinds of relations weren't really possible with a thirty-eight-week pregnant female. After their discussion, Mitch moved back into the house but kept to the twin bed in the smallest bedroom, vowing to sleep in his big bed only when Jenny could share it with him.

Jenny and Mitch also shared a secret that helped them cohabitate peacefully. They hadn't told anyone, but they were not only preparing for the wedding, but also for Mitch's upcoming baptism. Mitch just smiled and nodded an affirmative to Jenny's dad's lectures as he thought, *As if I am going to jump Jenny in her delicate condition. That man must think I am some sort of animal.* Jonesey had warned him about the uptight ideas in Mormon Utah, but he was taking the ribbing all in stride. Jenny obviously hadn't told her parents about what had happened the first week he was in Utah when he and Jenny had discussed religion for the first time.

After that first night in Utah, Mitch had decided that he better not stay with Jenny, after all, and he'd initially stayed with Jonesey in the second FBI condo in Park City, rented especially for their Winter Olympics assignment. Most nights there, he was unable to sleep, worrying about

Jenny. Jonesey said, when Mitch's insomnia woke him up, "Just go stay with her. You're driving me nuts. If not Jenny, then go find Bill. I think Megan's mom has plenty of room." After many sleepless nights, Jonesey was really disgusted, and he'd ranted at Mitch, "I hate listening to you prowling this place. If you're so worried, then go rescue her. Hell, I would if it was Amy. What's keeping you here?" Mitch smiled, remembering. Jones was such a good friend. Of all the guys in the team, Jonesey really knew what it was like to be separated from the woman you love.

The next morning, the last one of the games, Jonesey clasped Mitch's shoulder, looked him in the eye, and told him, "Go to her. You will get no peace unless you can know deep down that she'd okay. I understand. I've been there, man. Amy refuses to tell me when she's pregnant, until it's painfully obvious. She knows I worry about her non-stop at that time and in her words, I suffocate her. But you know why. We see so much evil in the world. We have to be with our family to *know* that they are okay. So go, man. As long as you are in location at the required moments later tonight, you know Stan won't care what you do before then. Go!" Jonesey had then put Mitch's bag in his hand and shoved him out the door.

From that time on, Mitch had been rooming with Jenny and Megan when his assignment didn't require him to stay with the US athletes in Salt Lake City. He enjoyed the sunny nursery that served as his spare bedroom and tried to be helpful around Jenny's house. He relished the idea that soon it would be their house. When the games were over, the three of them devised a routine. Megan kept to day shift working and going to school while Jenny worked her swing shift. Mitch split his time between the two shifts, going to work during the day and going to bed early, then getting up for a time when Jenny got off work at midnight. He couldn't sleep until he was sure Jenny was tucked in and the house was secure. Megan was an excellent chaperone for them when Bill wasn't around. Eventually, Jenny's dad accepted the situation. Mitch thought, *Hell, if I had a daughter, there's no way some guy would be staying with her either.*

Chapter Seventy-six

Jenny awoke on her bed and was shocked to see a dark sky out her window. *How long did I sleep?* The house was quiet for a Saturday night. She and the family had spent all day organizing and finishing the rest of the unpacking. The nursery was done and all Mitch's gear was inside. She knew the entire Johnson clan plus Bill and Mitch's grandfather were heading out to eat tonight. She wondered if they had already left or not. Jenny called out for Mitch, and a moment later she heard his footsteps downstairs, then he called out, "Hey up there, you okay?"

"Yeah. What time is it?"

"Six thirty. You ready for dinner?"

"Yes, I'm starved. I'll be down in a minute."

Later, when the family members were gone, Mitch announced to Jenny that it was time for some "Saturday night alone vegetation." They sacked out on the couch, watching TV. Mitch napped while Jenny ruminated on the recent events of her life. She was at the end of her latest journey. Next week marked a new beginning. She'd be married Tuesday night. Their baby would hopefully wait to come until his due date a few days later. And she could get a new start in her new home, living her new life with her men. Problems, probably, love for sure, and maybe some fun mixed in. Feelings of joy and happiness overwhelmed her. She'd waited so long to have a husband and a family. She was glad to have it now, even tinted as it was with the turbulent memories of the past year.

Jenny thought of the past summer spent fighting against a possible terrorist attack, risking the love of her life and her faith. Then she thought of the fall when another, unanticipated attack risked her world again. She wondered how she was able to deal with the reality of loving someone who fought terrorism for a living. Even though she'd risked her own life fighting one terrorist, others had succeeded with their own schemes. She remembered Stan saying, "We never get them all, just the ones we can. We just have to keep going and not lose heart."

For the first time, Jenny felt no stress or worry when she thought on these things. A warm feeling of peace came over her as she felt the truth of what had happened in her life. Gooding had set out to change the focus of his fellow citizens. In his misguided way, he had succeeded in highlighting a very vulnerable area to a small segment of people. However, he was stopped from spreading his message further. Horrifically, other terrorists succeeded where he had failed. They exploited the same weaknesses Gooding had aimed for. They'd felt that average folks wouldn't worry too much about other "average" folks, and reached their goal of destroying a symbol of the American way of life.

Did the terrorists succeed in destroying the United States? *No.* Jenny knew the answer by watching those around her and she realized that the 9/11 terrorists had only strengthened the US. In God We Trust, indeed. Americans had needed a wake-up call. Gooding had tried to provide it, and where he failed, September 11 provided it. Jenny had thought about it a lot as she worried about her friends. She remembered an old e-mail she'd received a few weeks before. It was about September 11 and talked about where was God in September 11. The message told stories about people who were supposedly late for work or called into work for some reason and weren't in the towers when they fell. Jenny felt warm about this idea and realized that God *was* in charge. He was taking care of America. She couldn't help but think that because of people like Gooding, the people who had to handle September 11 had been prepared.

Jenny was also comforted by another truth she found in the symbolism of September 11: even if Gooding had succeeded, the results of his attack would have been the same as September 11. Many would die, but many, many more would be stronger, better people for it. Those left would live on in honor of those who were gone. Those left would also take better care of the US and their fellow citizens. The honorable NYC policemen's actions colored her neighborhood's outlook on the Ogden city policemen on her block. Then Jenny remembered a comment she'd heard, that none of us are safe, ever. We just forget that fact and go on in our lives.

A talk she'd heard a few months earlier in the LDS church's general conference came back to Jenny. She remembered something her church's leader and prophet, President Hinckley, had said. "Peace is fragile." At any time, anyone could be in danger, or taking their last breath. What can we do about it? Pray. God is in charge *all* the time, in all things, in all places, watching over all people.

Jenny sent a fervent prayer to her Maker, in thanks for her many blessings, especially for the big bear currently snoring in her ear and, for the first time in a very long time, fell asleep fully at peace.

***

Jenny rolled over on the couch and blinked, trying to adjust her eyes to the mostly dark living room. She sat up and focused on the clock on the VCR. "Eleven thirty. Good, just enough time to get up and go to bed," she said to herself. She braced her hands at her sides and began to push herself up. A spasm caught her across her lower belly, stronger and more intense than the Braxton-Hicks contractions she'd felt on and off for the past few weeks. "I am not going into labor. I'm not!" she said to herself. She spoke a little louder than she intended, because Mitch snorted as he woke, then sat straight up, asking, "Did you say labor, honey?"

Jenny couldn't answer right then as the pain was finishing. Mitch came over to her and crouched down in front of her. When the pain had passed, she said, "Better get a clock and start timing these to be sure."

Pragmatic as always, Jenny's instincts were right on, even if she didn't want to face them. In an hour her contractions had sped up to every eight minutes and as she was standing up to get her coat, she felt the horrible gush as her water broke. "Damn, not on my good wood floor," she moaned. Refusing to go to the hospital in soiled panties, Jenny made Mitch get her some new underwear and pants when he went upstairs to get her overnight bag. He then helped her change as she stood in the hallway by the front door, and did what he could to mop up the mess.

McKay-Dee hospital was only about twenty-five blocks away, and they arrived in good time, just in time for the weekly Saturday night rush on the emergency room. Because Jenny's water had already broken and her contractions were speeding up, the staff pulled her directly up to the maternity ward, past the groups of people waiting in various states of distress. Mitch had never seen a human birth and Jenny figured he wasn't excited at the prospect of seeing her stretched like his grandpa's cows. Mitch scowled, clearly not thrilled to be rushed into a hospital gown and installed at his fiancée's side. Jenny refused to relinquish her grip on his knuckles through the worst pains. Jenny said very little, but moaned and screamed periodically when the pain got the best of her. Mostly she breathed and tried to not die as she felt ripped apart. Mitch had barely had time to call Megan on her cell as they left the house. But Megan and Bill arrived at the hospital about thirty minutes after they moved Jenny to a delivery room. When Jenny saw Megan and Bill, she smiled, then told them to "get the hell out" of the room with the next pain. Thankfully, Meagan called the family and they spread the news.

Jenny's parents received the same treatment as Bill and Megan an hour later and joined them in the waiting room. Jenny's dad sat holding his camcorder dejectedly, having been informed that to use it meant death by his sweet daughter. "At least it made Mitch laugh," he told Bill when he shared the story.

Although he took his time, Daniel Mitchell Harper was delivered in a no-complications manner a couple of hours later after five hours of labor. His mother survived her first delivery with only a little tearing, but otherwise both of them were fine. At eight pounds and twenty-one inches, he was a good size for being ten days early. Mitch was speechless for two hours as he alternated between holding his son and holding Jenny's hand as she rested. Black tufts of hair covered the baby's head, and he kept his bright pink color throughout the morning.

Later Sunday afternoon after all the family arrived, Daniel witnessed the marriage of his mother and father in the hospital's tiny chapel from the arms of his godmother and first-cousin-once-removed, Megan. His godfather, Bill, stood by her side as he and Jenny's dad were the witnesses to the ceremony. Jenny and Mitch's bishop came up that morning to visit them and see the baby and was roped into the quick ceremony to appease an impatient Mitch, who was determined to not leave the hospital until both his son and his woman carried his name. Jenny didn't even care that her wedding gown was a hospital one covering her pink pajamas and Mitch wore his jeans from the night before. She had her men and was happy.

Chapter Seventy-seven

Blue moonlight turned the gray cement that was usually an eerie, otherworldly green in the nighttime security lights into the neon blue color of ice deep in a glacial crevasse. Gooding sat on his bunk, meditating when he should have been asleep. Sleep was something he now partook of on his own terms, fitting it in between meditations, meals, and his one hour of release from this cell. He'd grown accustomed to the time he had and the limitations of maximum security federal prison in the United States. This night was graced by the moon shining through the six inch by eight inch security glass for the first time. Sometimes sun, usually sky, and rarely stars lit this space above his head. Even standing on the bunk, he was unable to see out the window, but he could see the light from outside and a small piece of sky. It calmed him. His transfer to this new facility had shown him enough to know that there wouldn't be a view outside the window anyway.

Tonight he was thankful for the color change. He could endure the green, but the blue helped him maintain a better focus for his mediation. He had scaled glaciers as a teen with world-renowned climbers. Once he'd taken a risky route down through a water tube near the base of the ice when the surface was too treacherous to pass. The clear water, the peace of the scenery and of that moment deep beneath the ice, surrounded him now. Breathing deeply, he imagined he was in that place, then mentally brought his problems out to sort.

The problems came into focus and Gooding began the most important internal discussion of his life. *George escaped. Mortimer is in custody as is Manuel and the entire freighter crew. However, if their training holds, everyone should be able to convince the authorities that they were only following orders—that I was the mastermind and they had no idea of the plan. The last communiqué from Mortimer confirmed that the Secret Service found the plans for the White House missile in the laptop with Manuel. After George escaped, the Secret Service found the computer fragments and saw that the ship had been pre-programmed with the White House coordinates.*

They have proof that Manuel did not know the details of what he was doing. They cannot prove he was going to bomb the White House. They can only prove that I sent him there, that I made the bomb and bought the launcher. Which is as it should be. These thoughts were the positive ones. Gooding forced himself to breathe deeply and continue through to the difficult truth of his present situation.

Senator Jackson owes me for the work I did for him, but he's the only one willing and able to step in. There is no way that he can get me out of custody at this time, even if Grandfather steps in with the necessary funds. But he should be able to secure the release of Manuel or Mortimer. Either way, either one could get the other out. So I need to have him just work on one. Mortimer's case seems shakier and thus it should be easier for him to walk. The authorities have no idea of his position in the organization. If Manuel's story holds, he will be a lowly deckhand on the freighter, or a driver, not my best man.

The freighter crew will have to stay incarcerated, but they should get minimal sentencing. Mortimer confirmed that the freighter's data also implicated only myself. Luckily he successfully contacted Jacques before our capture, and Jacques and the other lawyers are already working on securing the lower level employees' release. That leaves George as the only loose end. If Mortimer and Manuel roll over as instructed and give the Yanks the evidence they need against me, the lawyers should be able to keep George free and clear of any serious charges if he surrenders as well. This final thought brought Gooding to his first task.

In his mind Gooding pictured a mental "to do" list and made item number one: *Get George to Jacques and have him turn State's evidence like his brother. That should take care of him.*

Gooding's mental image changed and cleared. *With the personnel covered, that still leaves me in this prison. If I remain true to the premises of the Summer Plan, things will go the best for me. I will remain a nutcase bent on making a statement, but not a traitor to my sovereign. I will still be here for years, and possibly forever, even if they try me for death as a traitor.*

Gooding gulped and fought to remain calm. Here was the biggest problem. *No. I was not wrong!* This thought was the most difficult to voice, even internally. Knowing that he had to make peace with the truth of his situation, Gooding examined the last few months and the coming years with all his courage and determination. *I said what I needed to say. I made the right point. Even if the September eleventh event made the point more clearly and overshadowed my plan, the point was made. Americans are now more as they should be—more patriotic, more God-fearing, and more American than ever. Even if I did not achieve this result personally, it was done. I have nothing to be ashamed of. All of my attacks went off perfectly, even for their small scale.* He admitted the truth of these things only to himself, and for now he would accept them and move on.

I can do nothing to escape right now. Utter bitterness galled him. He'd been fighting a deep depression for weeks. Lately he'd been having nightmares about Steve McQueen. On the bad nights, he would wake in a cold sweat, tearing at his chest and fearing to see the purple butterfly from the movie *Papillion.* The nightmare was the same, with only small variations of scene. He was caught in the movie, trapped in the foreign French prison, but sometimes he was the rich character played by Dustin Hoffman and at other times he was Steve McQueen trying over and over to escape over the course of years. At the end of his dream he would be standing on the cliff's edge, having flung the coconut raft into the tide.

Each time, his dream self would jump off the rocks—aiming for the tiny raft—only to land on the cold cement floor in his cell. He would break bones on this floor in his dream and the pain of shattered limbs awoke him to see no butterfly tattoo, but the same tiny cell. Here he was completely confined—trapped for the full future he could conceive.

The mental Gooding was now lying in the fetal position on an icy glacier, freezing and shivering in an Arctic storm. Using all his mental strength, Gooding rearranged his inner environment. After a few minutes he pictured himself lying in an imaginary field of heather on a sunny summer day outside his grandfather's castle. Warmth came into his limbs; his breathing regulated. This had to be faced. He'd already wasted weeks in a numb state, automatically making what decisions he could and taking advantage of each tiny opportunity.

Mortimer knows the plan, as does Manuel. Jacques is ready. The crew will be okay. I cannot change my situation at this time, but there will be a day, a chance at some possible escape. For now I must wait and endure. The mental list appeared with item number two: *Endure, for now.*

With the most emotional topics cleared, Gooding moved on to his final item. Item number three had no list of things to do, as it was the most secret and most important of all Gooding's issues. So deep were his internal protections of this subject that internally he had to open the item before he could think about it. *Item number three: Caleb.*

What will happen to my son if I remain here? Grandfather still does not know of him, nor does Jacques. Only Mortimer and George know. With Vanessa dead this past decade, there is no one besides myself to bring the knowledge of the heir to Grandfather. An image of the blonde and beautiful Vanessa floated through his mind. For a time, they'd been happy during university. *She'd wanted to abort him, but I made her keep him. She never forgave me, and hated me for refusing to tell Grandfather. She would have married me for the castle and the titles and been just like Mother. She never understood me.*

He saw her in his mind. Her pale face in the casket floated into view. Her mother's maid found her body one day while her parents were on holiday. The authorities found a bottle of sleeping pills and the maid holding her screaming infant in the room. He heard her mother's words soon after the inquest. "We want no part of Vanessa's bastard without your name and funds." Gooding remembered being slightly shocked that she would come out and say it aloud. He'd taken the boy and made peace, of a sort, with the family.

Caleb was a problem. Only Mortimer knew his location and even if he could get a message to him, George would have no authority and no way to or knowledge of how to enter the British boarding school to get the boy. Thoughts that refused to be spoken came through his mind. For years he'd seen the boy taken care of in the best upper-crust ways. The excellent school, the nannies, the manservant were in all ways better than his own youthful experiences.

Caleb knows his grandmother and is aware of his mother's family, even if he doesn't live with them except during summer term. They have given him no stigma, per our arrangement, and he is their heir as well as mine. They forgave his mother her mistake, labeling it a "youthful tryst" and kept her suicide from him. They tolerate my interference because of Grandfather's position and my money, and they have kept the boy's birth secret from Grandfather, as contracted, or they lose my funding. What now? I have tied their hands with the damned contract. They cannot see to the boy properly without me. They lack the funds and they cannot take him to Grandfather. Their solicitors have the contract and will enforce it or be disbarred. Without me, the boy will be penniless like his mother. True regret engulfed him. *I made ample provisions for my employees, but made inadequate provision for my son.* Gooding sorrowed for a moment, all thoughts of himself forgotten for a time.

Reword item number three: Get message to Mortimer. Once he's out, he needs to take Caleb to Grandfather and help raise the boy. Once it was planned, Gooding knew he'd made the right choice. Even if it took him years to extricate himself from prison, he could still provide for his son now, immediately. *Mortimer and Grandfather will take care of him. I may be a disappointment to Grandfather, but he will be happy to use my millions to save my son, the true heir.*

A picture of his grandfather at his sternest came through Gooding's mind. *Having my son will make up for losing his castle,* he mused with a rare smile. *He'll probably make the boy help him rebuild it—in a true Scots style.* A rarer peace enveloped Gooding and he unwound his legs from their customary meditation position to lay down as a deep sleep found him for the first time in weeks. *Mortimer will save my son. He will get him. He will know what to do. Tell Mortimer to get my son. Tell him...*

About the Author:

Virginia Babcock grew up in Northern Utah where she now makes her home with her husband and cat.

Social Media Links:

Facebook:
https://www.facebook.com/pages/September-Summer/

Email: VirginiaBabcockBooks@gmail.com

www.ingramcontent.com/pod-product-compliance
Lightning Source LLC
Chambersburg PA
CBHW060803030726
47503CB00002B/319